No Ear for Music

For Peter Mayer,
all My Best wishes and
Happy Reding.
The author.
Julian fox. (June 2019)

Also by Julian Fox

Woody: Movies from Manhattan

Murder, Suicide and Other Bad Habits

No Ear for

Music

an alternative history

Julian Fox

First published in Great Britain in 2019 by
Cruachan Productions

This book is a work of fiction. Names, characters, businesses, organisations, places and events are either the product of the author's imagination or are used fictitiously. Any resemblance to actual living persons is entirely coincidental.

Edited, designed and produced by Tandem Publishing Limited

tandem-publishing.yolasite.com

ISBN: 978 1 5272 4151 0

10 9 8 7 6 5 4 3 2 1

A CIP catalogue record for this book is available from the British Library.

Printed and bound in Great Britain by CPI Group (UK) Ltd, Croydon CR0 4YY

For Annabel and Ňako

on the onset of their big adventure

'He [Vincent] constantly compared painting to music, and to gain a better understanding of the values and gradations of tones, he began to take piano lessons from an old music teacher, who was also the organist in Eindhoven. This did not last long, however, because during the lessons, Van Gogh was continually comparing the sounds made by the piano to Prussian blue, and dark green or dark ochre to bright cadmium, so that the good man thought he was confronted with a lunatic, and grew so afraid of him that he called a halt to the lessons.'

Anton Kerssemakers, 'Herinneringen aan Vincent Van Gogh' *De Amsterdammer 39* (1912)

I

Arles

'The Yellow House'

ONE

Paul was watching Vincent from the corner of his eye. Vincent, in his familiar granddad shirt and rolled-up trousers, was mixing colours on his palette, starting with various shades of yellow. Yellow like the cornfields, this house, that battered straw hat Vincent wore. As he proceeded to cover the canvas with a woven pattern of brush strokes, his gaunt, slant-eyed features bore a look of painful intensity, as if the work, itself, were torture. Paul moved closer.

'You're obsessed with yellow, methinks?'

'*Oui*. Yellow. Oh, how beautiful yellow is! And orange. Orange and yellow, the old colours of hope and friendship. For welcome, too. It's to welcome *you*, Paul – to this house.'

'Ah, right. Got it. That's why you painted my bedroom yellow and filled it with pictures of sunflowers. *Mon Dieu*, Vincent! No artist can be overjoyed to see his walls covered with another painter's work.'

'I meant it as a compliment. Sunflowers come from Peru, Paul, as you did. *Chrysanthemum Peruvianum*. So it seemed to me – ?'

'Was only there as a kid, Vincent, nothing more.'

'Well, I thought you'd be pleased?'

'More pleased when you moved them out.' Paul mopped his brow with a red spotted handkerchief. 'Whew! It's hot.' He scanned the walls around him. 'And now we've got them in here, almost as bad. Haven't we got enough sunflowers?' His eyes came to rest on a picture by the door. 'But what's this? Irises? Good. And oleander? Bravo! But look at it, *c'est mignon*. When did you do these?'

'Recently.'

'Good again, Vincent, splendid. They're so real, the scent is overpowering! Too much yellow in the background again, in among the green, but guess we're stuck with it?'

'Guess we are.' A grin. A pause. 'You don't think they're a bit *too* exact?'

'Not to worry, a little realism works wonders! The secret is not to be afraid of your paint.'

'I'm not, we're comfortable together.'

'Fine.'

Vincent gestured to the painting, 'And you really like it?'

'I said so, capital.' Paul raised an eyebrow. 'But your favourite plant – still sunflowers?'

'Ivy. It turns me on.'

'We'll let that pass. Reminds me of burials and old buildings.' Paul continued to look around. 'But I'm dizzy with yellow, there's too much yellow, altogether. Even the beds and chairs are yellow. It's unsettling, oppressive, like working in a sulphur mine. One day, if you have your way, we'll be painting a whole gallery yellow.'

'An encouraging shade, all the better to shift our unsold paintings!'

Vincent chuckled, scrabbling in a pocket for his pipe. He filled it, lit up and drew in slowly. A lot of smoke, then a lively glow followed. Paul wrinkled his nose and pulled a face. Vincent, meanwhile, fingered his tobacco pouch. Almost the last wad, he told himself, even this cheap stuff – he'd have to ration it. With a shrug, he returned to his work.

Paul continued to watch, as Vincent perfected the background blues, as many blues as there were adjectives to describe them. He glanced at the unfinished painting. This was distinctive, in complementary shades, marvellous passages of paint overflowing the richness of Vincent's palette in an expressive use of line and colour. The result seemed to transcend the everyday, the real presence of the subject. Paul, though, preferred more robust shades, with plenty of reds and greens: just little dabs and taking his time, but startling, vivid, a synthesis of form and texture.

The studio they were in was just as depicted in Vincent's paintings. Wedge-shaped, untidy, with empty frames stacked against the walls, it also had a fast-diminishing bolt of coarse jute for canvas in one corner and numerous paintings on the walls higher up. There was an old wood stove, presently unlit, along with easels, orange crates and an ageing upright piano, staggering on wobbly wheels and in serious need of tuning.

Pride of place went to a plain, white deal table, with simple fare – a bottle of cheap wine, bread, cheese, fruit and sausage already laid out. This stood, with two rickety rush-bottomed chairs, right in the centre of the room.

Outside, through the somewhat smeary windows, the friends could see the gardens of *La Place Lamartine*, as well as catching glimpses of the folks hereabouts. For their part, aware of the occupants' lifestyle and deeming them only minimally advantageous to the town's reputation, these worthies, stopping or simply passing by, would habitually peer into 'The Yellow House' with invasive, increasingly suspicious eyes.

Paul turned away, to get on with his own painting – the portrait of a naked Polynesian girl, just as he imagined her. She was also coming along nicely, dusky, voluptuous, full of dark promise. He glanced again at Vincent. From looking eager, intense, the man now seemed bored and listless, lacking inspiration. Paul couldn't bear to look at him.

Busying himself with the girl's breasts, he let out a sigh. It developed into a groan, followed by a deep grumble. At the same time, Vincent sank into a mournful reverie, as Paul now entertained himself flicking a spider off the table. Then something else caught his eye. '*Nom d'un chien*, Vincent! Bloody hell!'

'What is it, Paul? Can't you see I'm concentrating?'

'So am I – or trying to. But look at that.' Paul now was pointing to a large insect, running up the wall. 'Thought we'd got rid of those buggers, damn them!'

He stepped towards the wall and raised his foot. Squish! Crunch! He wiped the sole of his boot on a shred of matting.

Vincent shook his head. 'Did you have to do that? It's horrible. Just leave them, Paul, leave them. Cockroaches, spiders, they have as much right to be here as we do.'

'Who says?'

'I says – say. Besides, if, each time you see one of those little chaps and address your boot to it, this place won't be worth living in.'

'It isn't now. Why the Hell did I come here? It's like a fucking midden. It was supposed to be an artists' colony, that's what I was promised. But the others cried off and all I've got from this debacle is *you*. You, going mad on yellow and an invasion of bloody insects!'

'Spiders aren't insects.'

'The others are. Fleas, flies, beetles, cockroaches, they're all a bloody menace. Anyhow, I'd rather have them dead than alive. You don't mind them in your food or getting into bed with you, but I do.'

'You're always moaning, Paul, can't you calm down? We should be grateful to be on our own. The rest of the crowd would have distracted us. Carousing, chewing the fat, discussing this girl or that, pooling ideas, the latest movements in Art? An abomination, when would we ever work? Besides, I like it here. The light's great, I'm making progress. And the countryside, it's indescribable. Apart from our insect friends and those vicious gulls out there, what exactly's wrong with it?'

'It's Arles, Vincent, Arles! The whole fucking place! You sold me on a "Studio of the South", a Provençale Arcadia. Or, rather, your brother Theo did. Twisted my arm – Ha. Ha – with a promise to buy my work. But what do I get? Smudgy streets with smudgy houses. Doleful characters with doleful faces, and that includes the women. They turn even the shortest walk to the shops into a majestic funeral procession. As for that ludicrous dialect of theirs –'

'*Occitan.* It's *Occitan.*'

'Occi – what? Well, whatever it is, I can't make head or tail of it. They should learn to speak properly, be more like normal people. Less like foreigners in their own country.'

'Don't agree. Folk here are inspirational, a privilege to know them.'

'I'll leave you to it, then. To me Arles is stultifying.

Tawdry, dirty, it's always dirty, the dirtiest hole in the South! The pavements are dirty, the people are dirty. And it's dirty in here. Dust on every surface.'

'It's surely not that bad, Paul? Quite healthy, in fact, nothing extraneous. Someone I read recently said the dust we see is primarily composed of human skin.'

'That so? Ha. Ha. Then why don't you sweep *yourself* away?'

'You're getting too fussy, Paul. What else is wrong? We've a great ambience. *Oui?*'

'*Non.* Awful, no home comforts.'

'But I did give you the most comfortable chair – and the best bed. Mine's meant for a child.'

'Quite fitting, really. Sometimes you *are* a child. It's reflected in your painting. Child art. Ha. Ha. Ha.'

'I wouldn't say that. I –'

'But can't you see, Vincent? It was even dirty when I arrived – that day you forgot to meet me at the station. Your housekeeping's disorderly, it has no system, almost as bad as your cooking.'

'What's wrong with my cooking?'

'Put it this way. I'd rather eat a bowl of my own pubic hair than touch the stuff you make. I never know what I'll find in it!'

'What? What?'

'And you never mop the floor, when did you last wash the windows? If you're now going to paint in here so much, instead of down there on the *Alyscamps*, how d'you *see*? Look, cobwebs on the ceilings, a massive infestation in the kitchen. Those bastards I try to squash are just the thin end of the wedge. We've gnats, too, and snails. And there, there! Bread crumbs, wine stains, torn canvas and cat shit! I mean, look at it, look at it! A fucking rat's nest, a plague outbreak waiting to happen. Why don't you clear this junk away? Scrub the plates, for fuck's sake?'

'Why don't you?'

'And. Vincent, you stink, your hair and beard are maggoty, I've told you before. You fixed the pump, that, at least. We've no bath nor bog, so why don't you use it? It's all so fucking sordid.'

'Why don't *you* use the pump, Paul? No excuse.'

'Later, maybe, *ce soir*. Both of us. You scrub my back, I'll scrub yours.'

'*Et mon cul, j'espère?*'

'We'll see.' Paul grinned. 'But first, you filthy sod, you must promise me. Stop what you're fucking doing, clean the place up!'

'You sound like my mother.'

'God forbid.' A chuckle. Paul looked at Vincent, curiously. 'Did she really swear like that?'

'Not actually. Just kept telling me always to tidy my things. But the mess, the grime, Paul, it goes with the territory. It's the contrast I like, one reason I came here. Like the landscape – fiery and sun-drenched in summer, cool and sombre in autumn, with a magical light. Then there's the village, this house, the people, as you say, a little on the sleazy side. There's an underlying violence here, too, Paul. I love it, love it. 'Specially at the café up the road. A place where one can ruin oneself, run mad or commit a crime.'

'And you'll probably end up doing all three. Is that why you paint those types so well? All the drunks and whores in there, slumped around the bar – they're meat and potatoes to you, aren't they? Like those wretched miners in Belgium, the ones you tried to convert?'

'I didn't need to, just did my best for them.'

'Maybe, but there's a basic seaminess to your nature,

Vincent, first thing I noticed. It could only come from being the son of a priest, with a touch of madness in you! Gathering the unfortunates, the derelicts of society to your bosom, assuming the sins of the world, like some reborn Christ. Why don't you just paint them and be done with it. Don't suffer so. Fine, Vincent, fine, you like roughing it with the peasants, leading them towards God. But you don't have to *be* one.'

'Hah. You can talk. From what I've heard about you at *Pont-Aven*, communing with those Breton fishermen' – Vincent locked the fingers of both hands together and pulled hard – 'you were like … this.'

'No, I wasn't. They took against me. Ended by beating me up. Broke my ankle, in fact, it's still painful.'

'Why, what had you done?'

'Nothing much. Something to do with this young Javanese girl. Annette, or was it Anna? She wasn't too popular, either.'

'Young? How young?'

'Thirteen. The people complained. After that, from being a well-regarded interpreter of Christian mysticism, I was *persona non grata*!'

'Hah. Good. You deserved to be beaten.'

'Whatever I deserved, it didn't last. She skipped, with all my things.'

'All of them?'

'Mostly. Stripped the studio bare. Except for the paintings.'

'She knew what was worthless.'

Paul glanced at Vincent, to see if he were joking. Maybe, maybe not. He grinned and made a fist.

Vincent shook his head. 'And you sure had it coming, Paul. She was only a child.'

'Didn't seem like it. Anyhow, I like them young.'

'So do I, but not *that* young. It's not … right.'

Paul shrugged. 'Please yourself. But I still say you stink, I can't bear to sit at the same table with you. You can have a rub down, wash yourself once in a while?'

'I'll do it when I'm good and ready. Meanwhile, I'll follow my path.'

'Right. To the hock shop, the tavern and those tarts of yours. That's when you can get it up. Better to be out with the wind in your sails, painting in the fields or by the river, as you did at first. The river view is fabulous.'

'You know I'm not good at water, Paul. A tragedy, I try hard, but I just can't get it. Least, not as I'd like to. Transforming it into an image that lives and flows on the canvas, it's too complex, fluid, the reflection tricky, too many things to get right. Monet can do it – *mon Dieu* how I envy him! – he's brilliant. Manet called him the Raphael of water. Sisley, too, he can paint the sea. At times, one feels, he really *is* the sea…'

'That's 'cos he's wet, all that half-baked English reticence! But okay, Vincent, no water. You can at least paint the trees in the Gardens, you're a dab hand at those, instead of trying to see them through the window.'

'The Gardens are too public, I keep getting stared at. Or the kids shout "*fou roux!*" The red-haired loony – it puts me right off. Besides, the weather's changeable, I've got a cold, and there's plenty to paint around town. Factory chimneys, human flotsam, bars and backstreets. You name it.'

'Again, that's part of your problem. You think by going in search of the grimmer sensations, you'll be let off doing what you do best. Capturing nature in all its seasons. Summer and autumn, as you say, painting at all hours. If you want to depict the perfectly ordinary, use your imagination.'

Vincent sighed and shook his head, He picked up a rag and wiped his brush. 'It's all right for you Paul, you've got it down pat. You can work from memory. Or just like that native girl there, from your imagination, from something you haven't seen. Me, I need the stimulus of reality, a direct encounter with familiar persons and things.'

He moved to the table, sat and helped himself to the wine. 'A subject has to be there, before my eyes, Paul, else I can't interpret it. Even a life model or a group of farm hands, I need them as a *tableau vivant*. It's a nuisance, really is. But no matter how many sittings it takes, the subject has to be with me, perfectly in view. I was saying something like that to our neighbour, *Madame* Ginoux, only last week.'

'*Eh oui*, your latest portrait? *L'Arlésienne*, that odd bod who never smiles? Who stots about in funereal black with a face like a greyish-brown cantaloupe!'

'Eh? What? No, Paul. Her face is quite pink and rosy, with fine cheekbones.'

'Not in your painting, she doesn't – she looks green about the gills.'

'Appealing, too, *une belle paysanne*, if you look at her properly.'

'And you evidently weren't – looking at her properly! Any more than you did that big-bearded Roulin character, our friendly neighbourhood postman. You weren't looking at him, either.'

'Well, I think I was. Same way as I look at you.'

'Me? God help us.'

Paul gestured to a sketch on the table, he poked Vincent in the ribs. 'You couldn't have looked at me at all. What's *that* supposed to be?'

'You, Paul.'

'God's teeth, nothing like me.'

'It is. Exactly like you. You told me so – I thought you liked it?'

'I did. But you should do a proper painting, not some skimpy charcoal. Like the one I did of you.'

'Which one?'

'That one.' Paul pointed. 'You, painting sunflowers.'

'It's me all right, but me gone mad. *Très bien.*'

'*Merci.* You should return the compliment. Where's that *Man in a Red Beret* you promised? What's holding you back?'

'You're a difficult subject, Paul. Your dark complexion, the beaky nose. Besides, your forehead's too small, a sign of imbecility.'

'You looking for a punch in the eye?'

'And you always seem to pose, preen, rather. You're all vanity, *amour propre.* You remind me of what someone said to *Madame* Du Barry: "You can't seem to pass a mirror without seducing it."'

'That'll be *both* eyes.'

'Anyhow, I did do a painting of you, remember? Just the other day. Look, there it is.' Vincent pointed to a size 30 canvas, or rather sailcloth, daubed in thick *impasto.* It was leaning with others against the wall.

Paul exploded. 'That? That's my armchair, you arsehole! I wasn't sitting on it. The portrait of a subject *in absentia* doesn't count.'

'Does.'

'Doesn't.'

'Does.'

'Doesn't.'

11

'Does.'

Paul groaned and shook his head. 'Okay, Corporal, you're right. Vincent's latest masterpiece – *The Invisible Paul*.'

'But it did capture you, didn't it? Doesn't it? Your essence, your absent presence, couldn't you feel it?'

'No. How? I didn't see it then, I don't see it now. Like, what essence?'

'The way you are, the way you seem. There, Paul, there, the things that represent you? The paperback novels and the candle on the straw seat, suggesting your absorption with literature and a commitment to the intellectual life. It marks your personal aesthetic and everything about you.'

'And what's that, pray?'

'Um, well, it captures your – er, your overbearing aura, cold and haughty, a strange remoteness even, the feelings you bring out in others, your air of creative danger, your – your – what I'm trying to say, how can one put it? I can't seem to paint a direct likeness. I know you too well.'

'In my hole! You don't know me a-fucking-tall.'

'I do, with my painterly eye. You just won't admit it, that some subjects are difficult to capture. One needs a little distance.'

'Distance, as *well* as close to? Should be interesting. And in my own case – Ha. Ha – the further away the better. At least it'd relieve me of the smell! Or from being distorted, like that silly Ginoux woman's grey-brown face. She can't have been present then, either. She must have had you paint her from some far-off vantage point. Perpignan, *peut-être*? As if afraid, like most folk round here, that having one's likeness captured will attract "the evil eye!"'

'Pink, pink,' said Vincent, mildly, 'her face is pink. But

12

what I think I've caught with that chair of yours, if you'll forgive my presumption, is a sort of brooding, even sinister look, your latent cruelty and brutishness, as if the chair, itself – that's your essence, in other words … *you*, were taking possession of the canvas. As you, Paul, seem to do in real life. Of your own paintings, this room, the fields out there, the lives of other people?'

There was a brief pause. Then Paul, letting out a roar, rushed at Vincent. 'What? I what? What's this? What? You talkin' to me? You talkin' to *me*?'

'Why, who else is here? Who d'you think I'm talking to?'

'So? Eh? You speak of me like this? Like *this*? Ah, ah, fuck you, double fuck you!' Grabbing Vincent by the shoulders, Paul started to shake him. 'You know nothing about me! You don't! Not a jot, not a sot, not a fucking pot! "Overbearing"? "Sinister"? "Taking possession"? Bah. You carrot-headed little fart! Who are you to tell to me such things – things you know nothing about? You crazy, bright orange turd!'

Wriggling and kicking, Vincent broke free and dodged around the table. 'S – sorry, Paul, I think … I've upset you?'

He took a deep gulp of air, heart beating furiously, trying to regain his composure. Then, still behind the table, edging towards the door, he gazed nervously at Paul, ready if necessary to make a bolt for it. Happily, Paul had calmed down a bit and, likewise getting his breath back, slumped into the real-life equivalent of the chair in the picture. Sliding it as far away from Vincent as possible, Paul mopped his brow with that same spotted handkerchief, then filled a glass from the bottle. Grabbing a crust and a lump of cheese, he stuffed them in his mouth.

'Well, you (yerm) have. You (munch munch) have. Upset me. But apology accepted. And no more (munch) talk of armchairs, or stupid fucking essences. No more (yerm, yum) painting them, either. As for the candle, sticking up like that, it's positively phallic. Or do I take that as a compliment?' Paul laughed. He raised his glass. '*À la votre*. I mean, chairs, for fuck's sake!'

'Well, I like chairs, 'specially empty chairs. Charles Dickens's chair. I saw it in London. I love reading him, it brought me closer to his work.'

'*Oui*, and you love your own chair, Vincent, you paint it often enough, with your bits and pieces on the seat.' Paul rose, picked up the painting in question and studied it. 'Same question, though, where's *you*?' He grabbed a magnifying glass from the table, performing a mock inspection. 'So where did you put your essence? Invisible, like mine?'

Paul laughed again, uproariously, Vincent could only join in. Then, when they'd quietened down again, Vincent took the painting and placed it back on the pile.

'It's symbolic, Paul, a gesture. A symbol of us both, our being here, working together. My chair seen by day, yours by night.'

'*Bien*. That makes sense. But pity, with your chair, only thing it ever gets close to is your backside! You like painting boots, too, again 'specially your own. What are you, you sad specimen, a foot fetishist?'

Receiving no answer Paul continued. 'Anyhow, try one more dodgy picture of my favourite chair and I'll sit on it like this –' he rose and sat again, demonstrating, ' – but facing leeward, so you can't fucking *see*.'

Pre-empting Vincent, who'd also seated himself, Paul made a dive for the sausage.

Vincent gave a signal. 'Shouldn't eat that, Paul. We should sling it – it looks a bit off.'

'Well, I'll take just one bite. If I drop dead I'll save the rest for later!'

Paul laughed yet again. Then, with a grunt of satisfaction, he opened his mouth wide and crammed the whole sausage in. 'I – I mean (munch, yerm, blurp) if that's how you imagine painters work – creating imaginary portraits of people whose characters they completely misconstrue – then I think it's time you did ... something else! Like, what other talents have you got? Eh? Eh? If any? Sculpture? Engraving? Music? Or journalism, maybe? Tried it, myself, once, just the sort of boring job that'd suit you. Anything but painting. You said (munch munch, yerm) you can't paint without the subject being there – you've clearly proved it.'

At this point, there was a mild explosion under the table. Paul sniffed and glanced about him. 'Anyhow, you're totally deluded, sitting there, looking pleased with yourself, imagining you're a great artist, while farting – phew! What a pong! – smoking that filthy pipe and sloshing down the wine. Glug, Glug, Glug.'

'I didn't do it, that was you. I could see by your face. And I don't glug, I sip.'

'You do, you glug. You're a glugger.'

'I am not, I sip.'

'Glug.'

'Sip.'

'Glug.'

'Sip.'

'Glug.'

Vincent stared at his glass, a pause. Paul looked at him. 'Well, go on, say it.'

'Say what?'

'Sip.'

'Why?'

'So I can say "Glug."'

'Sip.'

'Glug.'

'All right, I glug. And I'll also give up sloshing.'

'I'll hold you to that. Why didn't you say so in the first place?'

''Cos I didn't know I sloshed or glugged, till you pointed it out.'

'*Bien*, we're getting somewhere.'

'But you, Paul, if you don't mind my saying, you make noises when you eat, like a pig at a trough.'

'That so? And you can't create, Vincent, 'cept with your arse!'

'And what's *that* supposed to mean?'

'I mean, it's you who farted – don't deny it.'

'Didn't.'

'Did.'

'Didn't.'

'Did.'

'Didn't.'

Another pause. Paul began to laugh. Vincent, looking cross, lunged at Paul, who sidestepped neatly. With a whoop of animal exuberance, Paul raised his hands, beckoning Vincent on. Vincent lunged again, at which Paul, laughing, did a perfect imitation of 'matador with bull'. Frustrated, Vincent dipped his brush in a pot of bright vermilion and flicked a splodge in Paul's direction. The splodge settled clown-like on the tip of Paul's nose, prompting Vincent to laugh, too. 'Suits you.'

'Right, I'll keep it.'

Playfully, Paul picked up his own brush and 'crossed swords' with Vincent. There was a shout of '*En garde*', as they squared up properly, followed by loud exclamations of 'Peruvian!' 'Dutchman!' 'Creole!' and 'Hah!'

Colliding with the furniture, they now duelled with boyish glee around the room, passing, feinting and parrying, as if their lives depended on it. The 'fight' then took them out on to the street, along past *Le Café de la Gare* and under the railway bridge, the whole time attracting astonished stares.

They continued with this game for some minutes more, until, back in the house, they 'crossed swords' one last time. After which, hurling the brushes away, they tensed up, fists clenched, ready for some sparring.

To any sudden visitor, seeing their fierce expressions, trying to stare each other out, it would have been difficult to know whether this were sport or serious. But, finally, they laughed outright, hugging and kissing with that easy, non-erotic *amitié* which two grown men, closely bonded in a common cause, may sometimes comfortably consider.

There was a last embrace, a shaking of hands and protestations of eternal friendship. They refilled their glasses, clinking them firmly. Then, with a warm exchange of '*Santé*' and '*Merci, mon p'tit*', they drank deeply, before shuffling back, each to his own business.

TWO

It was a clear Autumn day, an almost cloudless sky, more like late summer. But there, again by the window, stood Vincent, dressed in a simple blue peasant's blouse of coarse linen and armed with an almost full palette. He was humming tunelessly to himself, painting with his usual fixity of purpose. A glance at the sun told him it was lunchtime – wine, bread and cheese and a pathetically small ham were waiting on the table.

Another glance outside. Down the road, back from the fields, a familiar figure was approaching. Nearing 'The Yellow House', the figure quickened its pace, a timely bout of hunger driving it on. The clatter of clogs, too, in the street outside was familiar and, to Vincent, oddly reassuring. He looked up. Paul, perspiring and laden down with easel, board and paints, struggled over the threshold.

'Ça va, Vincent – aah, let me catch my breath – how's it going? Aren't you done with those damn sunflowers yet? How many more d'we need, for fuck's sake?' Paul unloaded his burden and moved across, to study the painting with critical eye. Vincent looked round.

'Pretty well, Paul. Nearly got them – despite this strange Provençale light. And it's difficult to capture them, too, even with tracing from the ones I did earlier.'

'They're fine. A symphony in blue and yellow!' Paul glanced again at the picture. 'Or, as of today, just green and yellow, terrific, I like them better than Monet's, no truly, *mon p'tit*, they're the flower, itself! But as I keep saying, you'd be better off if you painted them outside, instead of cooped up in here. We've still got sunflowers in the field by the river.'

'No, I went to check on them yesterday. They've done quite well this year, way beyond summer, but have finally started to droop.'

'Like you, Vincent, from what they tell me.'

'Miracle they've lived this long. Be Winter soon.'

'Thought I felt a chill. But more in here than outside. I mean, what's got into you? I've said it before, it's like you're allergic to daylight! We're in the country, why don't you make the most of it?'

'I would, it's true, be better working in the fields. But each time I do, it rains, or those wretched birds again, the gulls mostly, they drive me crazy, if I'm not already crazy. I don't know what it is, it's like they're lying in wait. Or rather, they come after me, seeking revenge for something, as if I've caused them offence? No, sod them, Paul, they won't leave me alone.'

'Bah. They never attack me, I'm lucky with those birds. Maybe you smell of worms?' Paul leaned forward and sniffed. 'No, not that, but you're still pretty high. Sorry to be tiresome.'

'You are, Paul, you are.'

'And the birds, they've stopped you working *al fresco*? Hmm.' Paul's tone grew ironic. 'Annoying, isn't it?'

'It's certainly a hitch.'

'Hitch? It sounds like a load of cock.'

'What?'

'Like I said, they don't bother *me*. Mosquitoes on the other hand...'

Vincent glanced again out of the window, then back at the painting. He sighed and shook his head. 'But bored, I'm *bored*, Paul. I wish to continue with my real vocation.'

'Real? What's real? It's an impression, *n'est-ce pas?*' Paul mopped his brow with another red handkerchief. 'Whew! I've been walking for hours. Or post-impression, if you like? As old Claude Monet tried to explain, when he gave a name to that stupid movement of his.'

'It wasn't Monet. He just did the painting, *Impression Sunrise*. It was an idiot critic Leroy, remember, who tried to lump the whole gang together? He meant to mock us.'

'Eh, what? Which "us"? What "us"? When, Vincent, were you an Impressionist?' Paul began to pace. 'But fact is, whatever we are, we all create, this new generation of artists, not what we see with our real eye, but in our mind's eye. Take me, I've gone beyond it. Away from the tyranny of mere appearances. Realism, Impressionism? Ridiculous, unfinished drivel, I've left it all behind. You've seen me, Vincent, known for a while what I've been aiming for: *le doit de tout oser*, the right to dare *everything*. To paint the sky yellow, the fields red, just to please myself – if that's how I see them at the time, if it's something I'm needing to say. You respect what I'm doing? I'm trying for a style that rejects illusion, searching for a still greater abstraction from nature.'

'That's not what I meant, Paul. Spare us your theories on Art. I meant that ... this is not my *real* work, this painting here. It's a stopgap, a passing measure, embarked on so I could get my bearings. You asked a few days ago if I had any other talent, something other than painting? Well, I have. My real leaning, *mon penchant animé*, the thing I've set my heart on, ever since childhood, is music.'

'Music? You mean, singing? Composing? *Zut*! *Sapristi*! Ha. Ha. You *must* be mad! I've heard that off-key humming, that tuneless tinkling of yours – I can tell you, from one *vieux ami* to another, in your *dreams*.'

'No, no, I can feel it. I've decided, the music is calling. There's a link there, convinced of it, that colour and music are closely related. Making music of tones with colour! Like painting, the inspiration, it's in my heart, too, my head.' Vincent moved towards the piano in the corner. 'I feel it strongly, just wait and see.'

'If you say so, Vincent, if you say. But forget my little jibe, about doing something else. In my opinion you should stick to painting.'

'Why, tell me, why? So I'll be remembered?'

'No, so you can do up the kitchen. Ha. Ha.'

'Funny. But I've made up my mind. Music it has to be.'

'*Bien*. I'll believe it, if others won't. We'll discuss it later. For now, let me clean the paint off my hands, grab a chunk of *valdebleu*, a slice of liver sausage, the last of the cheap plonk and I'm back in the fields. Maybe try those Roman ruins again.'

'We were having *bugnes*, Paul, local speciality. But I burnt them.'

'Now, how does that surprise me? But what's this?' Paul inspected the table. 'Ham? Not much, is there?'

'All we could afford. We still owe *L'Atelier Ginoux* for the wine.'

'See to it, will you?' Paul moved to the door. 'And when I come back this evening, I shall judge what you've written – from your head. Ha. Ha. *Au 'voir pour un instant, mon p'tit choux!*'

Paul went out, laughing. Vincent heard him singing '*Auprès de ma blonde*' in the yard, while splashing away at the pump. He gazed, hurt, through the open doorway, then clumped back inside. Roughly, he opened the piano lid, it broke from its hinges. He hurled it across the room.

Paul shouted something from outside. Ignoring him, Vincent seated himself on an orange crate and spread his hands. Dropping them heavily on the keys, he scrabbled around for the key of 'C' – or so he imagined. Then he hammered out a strange series of atonal chords, loudly, disconnectedly, with his paint-spattered fingers. The sound was excruciating. Vincent stopped, wiped his hands on his shirt and stared gloomily into space.

A few hours later. Vincent was leaning against the piano, an empty bottle of Pernod on top. He was smiling, pleased with himself, more relaxed now in the welcome cool, after the heat of the day. Paul's singing came again from the yard, followed by his heavy footfall. He entered, breezily.

'*Bon soir*, Vincent. Happy, are we? How's the composing? Ha. Ha. Coming along? As for me, out in the fields there, I had an epiphany. I saw, like a vision, that same South Sea island girl, basking in the sand. Gorgeous she was, *une belle nue primitive*. I have to find her − screw her! She is the one to inspire my masterpiece. I shall call it *Three Tahitians*.'

'Three? There was only one just now.'

'So there was. Ah. I was going to paint some of those dusky natives, maybe, as the Holy Family. That should please you, too, Vincent, transplanting Christian mythology to those distant shores! But think I'll get to know the locals properly first, making basic, very simple art with them. To immerse myself in their mysteries, their superstitions, to live their life. Creating, on wood and tree bark and makeshift canvas, in my growing closeness to them, my own savage *mise-en-scène*.'

Vincent looked at him, amused. 'And *The Three Tahitians*?'

'Scrub that. *Eh, non, oui*. Got it! It shall be "*D'où venons-nous? Que sommes-nous? Où allons-nous?*" Etcetera, etcetera, etcetera. What d'you think? What d'you see?'

'See? Think?' Vincent groaned. 'Hah. Very interesting. Congratulations. 'Specially "Etcetera, etcetera, etcetera". From sailor to stockbroker to broken-down painter, bankrupt, wife deserter, child molester − to exploiter of unclothed savages. *Monsieur* Eugène Henri Paul Gauguin anthologised. Ho. Ho. Well, all *I* can see, since you ask, is spots before my eyes. From the notes I've been trying to assemble. Crotchets and quavers, dancing off the keys!

But you, *cher* Paul, must congratulate *me*. I've finished it. My first *chanson*, a delicate but very real *chef d'oeuvre*. Unlike you, with that dark-skinned native girl, a pigment of your imagination!'

'Imagination? Bah. The girl was very real to me. *Une belle poitrine*, as I also said.' Paul raised his hands, outlining two breasts of approximate melon size. 'Grass skirt, kissable lips, long raven hair, all the rest of it. I'm going down to Marseilles tomorrow – booking passage, first thing.'

Paul paused and looked at Vincent. 'But come with me, *mon p'tit*, we go together? Some merry times, *hein*? Samoa? Bora Bora? The Marquesas? – no, first, Tahiti, I said it. It's paradise, the light fabulous. The Pacific, too, it's my destiny! Our best work, I promise. Renoir, Seurat, the old gang, they'll wish they'd come along!'

'Can't, Paul, can't. I'm a composer now, remember? What do I need with island girls, with their lustrous eyes and luscious breasts? Those red-gold sunsets on a coral reef and white waves lapping at the shifting sand? What I need is music paper and a good concert agent.'

'*Vraiment*? Ah.' Paul gazed at Vincent and shrugged. 'Very well, I'll miss you. As for the music, I'll give you my opinion, listen more carefully. I'm sorry for putting you down, maybe I'm wrong?'

Vincent looked longingly at the piano. Paul, afraid he was about to start playing, held up his hand. 'Not now – later.'

THREE

It was still quite early, a few weeks later, when Paul rolled out, or was rather ejected bodily with the other drunks, from *Le Café de Forum*. Regaining his balance, he blinked against the glare of the enormous yellow lantern, which shed its light on *le café terrasse*, casting an equal brightness over the paving stones. These had assumed a pinkish-violet tone, which, to a well-oiled Paul, looked unearthly in these otherwise conventional surroundings. In the distance, the streets stretched away under a dark blue sky and, casting his eyes above the rooftops, he tried to focus on the spangle of stars, which now seemed to draw him towards them.

Passing unsteadily around *La Place du Forum*, its gable-topped house fronts already bedecked with festive decorations, Paul turned south, inevitably taking his time. Then onwards, through ill-lit streets, to the outskirts of town.

This was not the first time he'd been removed from a favourite hostelry 'for behaviour inconsistent with the reputation of the house.' Now, bruised and humiliated by the handling he'd received, he seethed with indignation, ready to return to the scene, to 'sort a few people out'.

But he quickly realised, hampered as he was by a self-induced haze of cheap beer and 'absinthe chasers', that his far from negligible skills in the art of fisticuffs would this time scarcely avail him.

He wondered whether to continue the evening at another venue, popular with Vincent and himself. A more friendly house, *une boîte de nuit*, where he could pick up a *pierreuse* – all he could afford! – have 'a hair of the dog', or even take a nap in some quiet corner?

Failing to reach a decision, Paul stepped gingerly over the cobbles, wet and slippery from four days of rain, while braving the stares of the people he knew. Gazing blearily at a street lamp, almost tripping over a small dog, he tried to straighten, to assume a more dignified pose. Failing in this, he belched, then started to whistle, a misty version of '*J'en pense tous les soirs.*'

The song continued, as he made his way south. Growing bored with the tune, he now listened to the flat sound of his clogs on the cobblestones. It echoed back at him, deep, hollow and oddly powerful, just like the note he'd sought in his painting! Suddenly he stopped, since without really meaning to, he saw that he'd reached *les Alyscamps.*

In broad daylight, as a subject for his brush, this ancient burial ground had served him well. Now, by night, its stern, grey rows of stone sarcophagi, shadowed by twin lines of poplars, loomed ghostly in the moonlight. Paul shuddered and struggled on.

The air was scented with recently flowering laurels: in his present state it made him feel slightly sick. But, persevering, at the end of the avenue, he stumbled past the lantern-domed Church of Saint-Honorat, where a Christmas choir was rehearsing. He listened briefly, joining in '*Un flambeau, Jeannette, Isabelle / Un flambeau, courons au berceau!*' – but moving on again, he found himself beside the Canal. Deep and murky, not a ripple to be heard nor seen, it was the perfect suicide's grave! What now? Paul sniffed the night air and stared at the water. Walk a little further or throw himself in?

With a grim laugh, he turned abruptly, imagining (the inevitable post-inebriate melancholy now fast clouding his thoughts), that he might be happier, if he just re-crossed the Langlois Bridge and wandered discreetly back towards 'The Yellow House', where he knew that Vincent was waiting. Vincent had, of course, been invited to join Paul in the pleasures of the evening: a little carousing, a game of billiards, a strenuous bout of uncommitted sex and, maybe, a lively sing-song of old favourites from the Franco-Prussian War. But feeling the need to go out alone, Paul had been grateful when his friend cried off, due, he insisted, 'to concerns and creativity of a *superior* musical nature.'

This practice of Vincent's, to Paul's alarm, had grown ever more frequent, leading to an at least partial abandonment of his work as a painter. He still laboured furiously at his easel, whenever the mood took him, but had also taken to pressing Paul, on an almost daily basis, 'to listen properly' to his efforts at the piano and give 'a considered judgement'. Paul could postpone it no longer, so staggering just a little, still whistling and burping, he quickened his pace and lurched into *La Place Lamartine*.

As he continued to breathe in the chill December air, which had now all but cleared his head, Paul chuckled. He warmed himself in the notion that, though his friend's new 'skill' might be 'bad' for Vincent, it could well prove a fitting source of amusement both for himself and the sodden denizens of *Le Café du Forum*. It might even afford him the perfect excuse to return there and make peace with mine host.

Nearing the house, Paul caught his foot on the kerb and almost keeled over. But, catching himself, he offered full attention to negotiating the gate. Paul's spirits, as he crossed the yard, were raised by the sight of candles glowing within and Vincent's shadowy form in the window. Whatever their differences, they were still friends. Paul reassured himself that he'd rather spend time with Vincent, no matter how argumentative and touchy he might be, than with those boozy, dim-witted, false friend roughnecks that he'd recently had to tussle with.

Vincent was not at the piano, but busied himself, stretching fresh canvas on a frame. His already lit pipe made arabesques of smoke around the room, trapped indoors now by a window firmly closed.

Still garbed, almost defiantly, like some shambling middle-aged labourer, he was also wearing his straw hat and, to augment the small lamp on the table, had attached lighted candles precariously around the brim. This illuminated headgear gave Vincent sufficient light to work with, if also, one should add, a decidedly comic aspect.

Stopping for a moment, he glanced at the bale of coarse jute in the corner. It had been meant to last, but he and Paul had almost finished it. Soon they'd be painting on discarded bedsheets and bits of old sacking.

Vincent sighed, shivered, removed his pipe and carefully nailed the canvas. He placed it on the easel and lit another candle. Then squeezed out some tubes of assorted pigment, smearing and slashing it directly on to the surface. He then, with his palette knife, covered the whole area with a greyish-blue *ébanche*. He tried to concentrate, but every few seconds he'd twitch and turn away. Running his tongue over his lips, he looked longingly at the near barren table. He had the hunger, all right, but had lost the habit of eating.

He returned to his work, though his heart wasn't in it. At which point, Paul entered, more quietly than usual, taking Vincent by surprise. He dumped his coat by the door, swayed a little and sat down heavily. Noting Vincent's improvised halo of candles, he rolled his eyes and grinned.

'Ça *va*, Vincent, we meet again, everything okay?' Paul studied the painting. 'That's right, *mon p'tit.*' He started to sing. '"Paint your palette blue and grey, look out on a summer's day" … La. La. La.'

'Just about. Can't complain.' Vincent put the palette knife down and looked at him. 'You're back early. How come?'

'Sore point. Don't ask.' Paul rubbed his hands. 'But colder in here than outside, I can see my own breath. No, fuck you, Vincent, you've let the stove go out? We'll freeze our bollocks off!'

'We're right out of fuel, Paul. That's … a fact. And no light to work in, they've cut off the gas.'

'Could burn a few pictures? What? *Non*? *Eh bien*.' Paul glanced across. He saw there was food there, if again not much. 'So, no music this evening – what gives?'

'Nothing, really. I was simply wondering what we're doing for Christmas? It's almost on top of us, how are we going to spend it?'

'How would you like to spend it? How d'we *afford* to spend it? Speaking for myself, I abhor people's reliance on thoughtless bourgeois practices. This habitual celebration of the baby Jesus is one of them.'

'So you don't believe in it at all? You no longer believe in God?'

'Sometimes. Sometimes not. But I am afraid of Him.'

'That's a start, good for *you*. Anyhow, are we going *Chez Ginoux* or staying here? Be nice to get out.'

'For you, especially, who've stopped going anywhere. Drink a glass of decent wine – somebody else's! – go to the bullfight, maybe, and find ourselves a willing tart. What better?'

'Arena's closed, I think – out of season. And forget the tarts. I've set a limit, remember? For me now it's once a fortnight.'

'Ah, right, your little problem. "*Monsieur* Limpdick; or The Man Who Couldn't Come."'

'Not so, on either count. Rather, it's my first big nod towards the ascetic life. Painting and fucking too much, they don't go together. Nor do fucking and music. It softens the brain.'

'In your case, it wouldn't take much. Soft all round. Some chaps, Vincent, don't deserve a dick! But still, your choice. I'll be upstairs as usual, you stay and chat to *Madame*. Unless you'd rather go to church? Ha. Ha.'

'That, too, and it's no laughing matter.'

'Nor's Christmas, without the trimmings. By the way, what day's today?'

'Twenty-third. Two days to go.' Vincent glanced at the clock on the mantel, 'No, soon be Christmas Eve. One day to go.'

'Ah well, let's hope we win *Le Million*.'

'Have you bought any tickets?'

'No. Have you?'

'What with? You know I haven't. Panama Canal shares, that's all I've got left. Big scandal, they're virtually worthless.'

'Right, then. End of subject.'

Paul merely grunted. Vincent waited out the pause, then cleared his throat. 'So, what's it to be? Charity *Chez Ginoux* or carry on as normal?'

'Normal? This is *normal*?' Paul stared at the table. Pulling up his chair, he broke off some bread, grabbed a pickle and tucked in. 'Ah … (mmm yerm) … not too bad … for starvation rations. So what are you up to? *Mais oui*, you've started another canvas!' He glanced across. 'But slow down, you'll soon be back to rushing it, painting them too quickly!'

'Maybe you look at them too quickly? But vital to get things finished, what I came here to do. Complete a few more paintings, good enough to exhibit, enough for Theo to sell.'

'Bah.' Paul gave his habitual glance around the walls and floor, at the mass of paintings piled in every corner. 'So how many have you done so far? Since the day you arrived?'

Vincent hesitated. 'About … two hundred.'

'That's a hundred and ninety-nine more than necessary. Me, it takes all my time to complete *one*. It seems to me there's a fury in you, or surely was – you go at these paintings like the clappers.'

'Got to do it, till I run out of paint. So I can concentrate a hundred per cent on the music.' Vincent retrieved his knife. 'Just let me do the –'

'No, Vincent, no. Too dark, it's pointless.'

'I can still work by candlelight – do a still life or something.'

'No again, we're almost out of candles. We must keep them for essentials.' He gestured at Vincent's hat. 'Put them out now, a stupid idea, you'll set yourself on fire. Besides you look ridiculous, like some latter-day saint. Just finish, Vincent, why don't you relax? Can you relax? I mean, stop it, just stop. Give it a rest, go to bed or something. You're a man of extremes, existing at fever pitch. Music, painting, give it a rest. It's what I keep telling you.'

Paul helped himself to wine, awaiting Vincent's reaction. There was none. He just stood there, looking miserable, like an abandoned spaniel. Then, removing his hat, wincing slightly, he extinguished the lighted candles between finger and thumb. The lingering aroma of burnt candlewick filled the room. Paul sniffed his distaste.

'I mean, it's painful to see. Working at breakneck speed, slapping it on, stacking up canvases. And the mess you make, I've never seen a sloppier artist. You're like an active volcano, the paint splashing everywhere – an eruption of flying colours! For me, as you've seen, it's a slower, more careful rate, full of little details. I spend ages composing a scene.'

'I know you do. That's just as painful.'

'Not so much as you. It's like an ordeal. Punishing yourself, for what? These long hours you put in, the lack of sleep. You eat irregularly, how d'you keep your strength? And all this coffee you swill down, gallons of it.'

'Coffee, it's the artist's best friend.'

'Also his killer.'

'Not at all. Dickens said it was "man's best protection against suicide."'

'Fuck Dickens, fuck Balzac and all those other hacks you like. You read too much, you'll go blind. And it's not only coffee. It's the wine, too, the brandy, and always you're bloody smoking. Still, I'm not surprised. There's some psychologist chap in Vienna, I heard, claims addiction to tobacco is a substitute for wanking.'

'I don't go in for substitutes, prefer the real thing! And you smoke, too.'

'But not like a chimney, this terrible fug. Anyhow, I pity that whore of yours, young Rachel, those rare times you do it. How d'you expect to perform with all that lot inside you? Not to mention the absinthe?'

'She also takes it, Paul. It's fine, spectacular. You know what they say? "Absinthe makes the tart grow fonder."'

'*Eh oui* – but not in my experience. It makes them comatose.'

'Who, *les filles libres*? Ha. Ha. That's because you bore them.'

'So Ha. Ha to you.' Paul glared. 'Eh, what's this? Insults?' He paused. 'No, look, how can you do it? You're racing headlong to an early grave.'

Vincent placed the canvas on a chair. He looked at Paul and sighed. 'I admit it, I am, I do – I work in haste from day to day, like a miner facing disaster. I've told brother Theo as much. I can't seem to help it. But at the same time, to achieve this new style, the high yellow note I'm trying to attain, to remake the world as I see it, I've got to be pretty well keyed up. To clear my head of all else, almost to the point of lunacy. Cézanne said I paint like a madman.'

'You do. Ha. Ha. Degas said I paint like a wolf.'

In spite of his despair, Vincent laughed. 'And you? What did *you* say?'

'To Degas? "Get stuffed." Then I told him that story of the wolf who, unlike his well-fed friend, the family dog, simply starved to death 'cos he wouldn't wear a collar.'

'Again like you, Paul, very symbolic.' Another laugh. 'The story fits you perfectly.'

Paul joined in, then looked at Vincent gravely. 'But enough of this, we were talking of you. The way your friends worry, that includes me. And your intensity, it puts people off. I can say it, for your own good. But others are wary of you, they won't tell you things. The old gang, they were reluctant to come here – you intimidate them.'

Vincent gazed back at Paul, expression sorrowful. 'I'm sure I do. And I do find it awkward to communicate. Except with you, Paul, as you say. I've always been a bit of a loner, even at the Cormon studio in Paris. The other apprentices regarded me with suspicion and I had a fight with my instructor. Maybe it was my age, a late starter. An oddball, too, a little crazy, eager to break away. That's what Camille Pissarro once said, I would "either go mad or leave the Impressionists far behind."'

Paul chuckled. 'Far be it from me to agree with Pissarro. 'Specially now. But he was right, in his way. Take my advice. Slow down, go to bed early, eat more, drink less – and think before you speak.'

Vincent grimaced, he twitched again. 'Well, you're a fine one to talk. When do *you* eat properly, except when I provide it? When is your glass empty, whether we can afford it or no? When d'you ever edit what you say? If I weren't your friend, I'd find you offensive. And, as for the work, you're also at it, too, most days, out in the wind and cold without a topcoat, or else in full sunshine out of the shadow, soaking it up.'

'I am, I am.'

'But I learned my lesson outside in that boiling cauldron, or battling with the *mistral* in the weeks before you came. I was taken ill, nearly lost my sight. So never again, Paul, and I won't freeze to death now. In the cold Winter months it's better to work indoors. The elements can kill you, but still you go to it, you're just as obsessed as I am. As for me, when I'm out there, if I can keep the birds at bay and the days are promising, I enjoy it like a cicada!'

'And the composing? What about that?' Paul, reminded there was still a little food on the table, wrestled with a chicken leg. 'Mmm – aah. Just forget about me for the moment. I have faults, too (yerm, yerm), but ... we were still talking of *you*. You and that damn music.'

'I agree. I'm consumed with a passion to create. The

music, *c'est mon seul désir*, a compulsion.' Vincent sighed again and sat on the orange crate. 'But to please you, Paul, I'll try to approach it, as well as the painting, in less of a turmoil.'

'It's not just to please me, it's for you. Either way – music, painting, living this off-kilter life, I wonder how it'll end. You don't let up. You grind your jaw, your eyes pop out, your muscles tense – there's not a relaxed bone in your body. No wonder you have fits. And you treat the fermented grape like the oxygen you breathe. This way madness really lies!'

'If I'm not going mad already. There've always been problems, since I was a boy. I was a solitary child, with bouts of melancholia, which no one could fathom. Still have it to some extent. That and being lonely.'

Paul studied him ironically. '*Oui, je comprends*. Lonely, always, as a cloud. Except for our local peasants, and they don't count.'

'To me they do, they're more important than anything else. I may not speak their lingo and sometimes feel isolated. But when I look at them, they seem to be painted with the very soil they touch, perfect subjects for my brush. Whatever they are, these people, I try to see things their way.'

Paul spoke reassuringly. 'You do. You do … mostly. And the poor folk round here, they seem to love you for it.'

'Not what you said the other day, or are you taking the piss? You said I was – ?'

'That was then, this is now.' Paul laughed again. 'But you're right, nobody who's anybody comes near you, 'cepting me.'

'*C'est vrai*. But company? I do need *something* in my life, there isn't much. Like food, you said it's not deliberate, this gnawing hunger. Since when I do see food, if you haven't scoffed the lot, I sometimes can't face it. 'Specially with these stomach pains, or it's not the grub I like. Wish I hadn't given my painting of *The Potato-Eaters* to Theo. If it were here I'd eat it!'

'Your brother? Ah. But I thought he sent you some money, just the other day – an advance on your allowance?'

'He did, but I spent it. Grocer's bill, the wine we had yesterday, the wine today. New brushes and canvas, drinks in payment for models, that takes at least half of it. And then there's the gas and fuel for the stove – nothing comes cheap. The odd fifty franc note Theo slips in the envelope is almost my only support.'

'It *is* your only support.'

'And my brother knows it. He says I have talent, thinks I'm an investment. Poor Theo. Is he deluded or what? I'm a burden on him, no question.'

'You should push him more, Vincent. Chase after him with a sharp stick.'

'He does his best, if more for his conscience' sake than my need. And he sells the work of our friends. Ten paintings once for Monet, a good price, too, more than the cost of his house.' Another sigh. 'So, why can't he do it for me?'

'Maybe your work is just too unusual – like mine. But once an artist, always an artist, we paint what we see. What we are.'

'We do, you're right. And we can't help it. Paint, colour, it runs in our veins like blood.'

'And music?'

'In one's brain. Certainly *my* brain – fermenting there, just bursting to pop out.'

Paul laughed louder still. 'Like I said, you're in a bad way.'

'Don't I know it. Theo, Pissarro, that Dr Rey of ours, everyone who knows me, they think I need treatment. They think I should go away somewhere, get committed. If only for a while.'

'I say you should. At times, it's painful to see.'

'I'm *in* pain, Paul. P'raps I need it, for my creativity – to feel it?'

Paul chuckled, without humour. 'You want to feel pain, Vincent, just slam your head in the kitchen dresser, let the crocks fall down on your skull.'

'Maybe I should. Knock it all out of me?'

Paul sighed and changed the subject. 'Still, for the moment, at least, there's *some* money coming in, small amounts though they be. So stop worrying, *hein*?'

Paul looked at Vincent and hesitated. 'But what I truly think is … you ought to toughen up a bit. You're all sentiment, artistic sensibility, not enough cock and balls. With the women, first, don't be so fucking polite. With the tradesmen, stand up for yourself. But, mostly, concentrate on getting fit. Get out in the country more, be less confined, I'm tired of saying it. Go for walks, swim, climb trees, think of things other than food.'

'You can't exercise if you're hungry.'

'Well, you can. You can do anything. The secret is, distract yourself. You've no idea how not thinking about food can lessen the urge to eat.'

'I have the urge to eat, even when I can't eat.'

'Your problem. But me, I can go three whole days without a bite, and still step into *Le Café de la Gare*, to arm wrestle with the best of them.'

'Well, you sure ate well on Tuesday, Paul. Quite voraciously, I'd say.'

Paul chuckled. 'The food was there – that fifty francs. Pity there's so little left.'

'Nothing left.'

Both men stared at the table, the plates were now empty. Paul grunted.

'Anyhow, my three days were up. Reward for being a tough guy!'

'True, Paul, you're becoming more rough-hewn by the day, trying to identify with the Noble Savage. Rousseau was right. For those who seek it, there's a bit of the savage in all of us. "Free, sturdy and indolent."'

'That's it. I'm strong as a bull and lazy as a snake!' Paul looked wistful. 'Which reminds me, talking of savages, I'm off, Vincent, any day now, to that Pacific paradise. No, don't try to stop me, it's what I want to do.'

'You sure?' Vincent was now looking dismal. 'I mean, absolutely *sure?*'

'Couldn't be more so.'

'But couldn't you stay … just a little longer – at least until Spring?'

'No way, I've had it, got a life to get to. Sorry, *mon p'tit*, given it a lot of thought. It's not working, felt it from the start. Arles, this house, I've said it before – the dirt and grime, the lack of amenities. I can't reach my bedroom, without passing through yours! And that encourages your endless chatter, till well into the night. Then waking me up again with idiot questions. I mean, d'you ever stop talking?'

'Hardly ever. I do it so people won't hear me.'

'That's it, almost. They hear you, but don't listen. Or else it's the silent treatment, your mood swings and sudden rages, your aura of despair. You demand too much, you won't let me work. It's infecting me, truly, I just can't cope.'

'But – but, Paul, I don't –'

'You used to stimulate me, Vincent, get me on track, as I think I did you. At least in Paris, where we didn't have to live together. But now you irritate me, get on my tits. If I stick around, the way things are going, I'll end up like you. Hanging out with a loser, you become a loser – that's basically it.'

'Paul, you're the biggest loser there is. At least, I've never cut and run. Caused grief to the people who loved me.'

'Oh no? Well, what about that young woman, Margot or something, the one you dumped? You told me she took strychnine.'

'*C'est vrai.* A tragedy.' Vincent's eyes grew moist, he looked away. 'But that wasn't my fault, it was circumstance, she wasn't allowed to marry me. Anyhow, I've been dumped, too. Several times. My cousin Kee, for instance, turned me down. "No, never, never, *never*!" That's what she said. I was very cut up.'

Vincent held out his hand. In the centre of the palm was a dark red blemish, with loose skin around. It was faded, but visible. An old wound or a burn mark? It looked like a stigmata.

'That's when I held my hand in an oil lamp, an act of romantic daring. To love, what a business! She still wouldn't have me.'

Paul laughed. 'It's impressive, very. Awesome. But you've shown it to me before, too many times. Eh, poor Vincent. Had it been me in that young woman's place, I'd have thrown my arms around your neck and never let you go.'

'What? A big boy like you?' Vincent chuckled, in spite of himself, he fluttered his eyelashes. 'Paul, you'd have choked me to death.'

Paul raised an eyebrow, but didn't laugh. 'Well, I'm sorry for you. But if you smartened up a bit, lost that moth-eaten overcoat and bathed more often, as I also never stop saying, didn't act like a fucking loony, taking offence at the slightest criticism, decent girls – I mean, respectable – would have time for you.'

'Respectable? Who needs respectable? What one needs is someone warm and pretty and free with her favours, like the glorious Rosanette Bron.'

'Flaubert's lovely "Marshall"? Every adolescent's wet dream? You should be so lucky, Vincent. Just take a look at yourself.'

'Hah, you're a fine one to talk. With that huge moustache and unruly hair, the old seaman's jersey, greasy bandana and your shirt tails hanging out, you look like a Gypsy.'

'What I look like and what you smell like, Vincent, are opposite ends of the spectrum.'

Vincent opened his mouth to reply. He couldn't think of anything, so got on with his painting. Paul was beating a devil's tattoo on the table top with the tips of his fingers. He looked at Vincent and guffawed.

'So, all right. Your *chanson*, this masterwork of yours – is it really any good?'

'*Formidable. Extraordinaire.* Better than Auber. Greater than Massenet. As for Charpentier? He'll stop composing! Just wait till they hear it in Paris, they'll be green with envy.'

'Pink with embarrassment, you mean. Not to mention

instantly deafened. Or red with outrage, burnt umber for browned off, deep purple for high blood pressure, puce for dried vomit and yellow ochre for nausea – just like the colour of this house.'

'You know nothing, Paul. They'll be sorry they ignored me. They may imagine, the usual thing, that I'm insignificant – a bad painter. Well, let them. But the moment they hear me play? Hah. Sod art, give them music! I'll be like a little grain of sand in an oyster, growing bigger before their eyes – causing a reaction!'

Paul grinned. 'You'll never be a pearl, Vincent. But you're bound to cause a reaction.'

'And before that, *mon ami*, you'll be the first to hear it.'

'Okay, then. If you insist. *Mais oui*. I asked you, didn't I? Go on, then, get with it. *Étonnez-moi*, delight me – play, maestro, play!'

Vincent stepped to the piano, as Paul, rearranging his easel, began to potter. Vincent rapped the piano lid. 'Pay attention, stop pacing. Listen, I beg of you. Let your soul be stirred!'

'You mean, like soup?'

'No jokes, Paul.' Vincent raised his hands, with dramatic flourish, and prepared to play. 'Now, here it comes. It's in the key of "C Sharp Major" – I think. Or is it simply "C"? No, no, I changed it. So, Paul, listen carefully.'

Paul groaned and settled in his chair. Still a mite grumbly, he sighed and grunted, twisting his features into a semblance of concentration.

Vincent, meanwhile, played and croaked out the *chanson*, the light of 'inspiration' in his eyes offering ironic contrast to the ear-splitting racket which issued forth.

You may not know,
Where e'er I go,
I carry in my heart
A little town in Holland,
Why did we have to part?
My mother's there, my father, too
A horse and a cow with a plaintive moo,

I miss the sound of the water mill,
The barn owl's twit-too-woo.
Well, I think I'd like to die there,
When my life of toil is done.
Though I don't how I'll pass my time,
'Cos the dead don't have much fun.

Oh, I left my heart in Zundert
Zundert near the Zee.
I'd love to be in Zundert,
It's all the world to me.
Oh, Zundert, Zundert, Zundert,
The only home I knew.
Oh, can't you underzund-ert?
If I can, zo can you!

Finally, Vincent stopped. He raised his fingers from the piano and placed them on his knees. Then turned and looked at Paul, expectantly. The latter was staring at him, with a pained, even traumatised expression. There was an awkward pause.

'So', said Vincent, 'What did you think of it?'

'Think? I – ah, that is – well, er – um – ?'

'Come, come, truly, please. Don't spare my feelings, be perfectly frank. How much did you like it? Love it, rather?'

'Like? *Like*? Like is not the word. Nor love, least of all. It was – it was – you want me to be frank, *hein*? Very well, then, very well. If you must know, *c'est piteuse*. That is, it sucks. It has as much validity in terms of human enter- prise as balancing grapes on one's willie. In fact, it was … terrible. Painful. An affront to the senses, the lyric inane. Vincent, *mon pauvre ami*, don't humiliate yourself, *c'est un métier inopportun* – give it up now, while you can. It was frightful, doggerel, not at all pleasant. No, no, forget what I said, I changed my mind, remember? Do what you do best – paint! No, no, I assure you, you have no ear for music.'

'No ear? No *ear*! For music? Hah, so that's what you have to say? *Alors, mon Dieu*! So that's *it*? No ear? I have no ear? And you *do*, I suppose? Hah! Well, then!'

'Well then, what?'

'Well – well, I'll have you know, I did study singing and piano. Quite hard, in fact.'

'Not hard enough.'

'"Not" – "not" – ?'

'Also bad teacher.'

'"Bad" – "bad" – ?'

'And bad pupil.'

'Me? Who, me? You must be drunk?'

'If not, I've wasted the evening. Anyhow, it's the only way I could sit through your damn fool noise. An analgesic.'

'Right – right, that does it!'

Vincent, looking ferocious, picked up his wine glass and hurled the contents in Paul's face. He then rushed out. Paul, astonished, wiping his cheeks with his spotted bandana, could hear him scuffling in another room. But in moments, Vincent had burst back in with a cut-throat razor. He came at Paul like a whirlwind.

Paul ducked and weaved, as Vincent chased him round the table. Then, before Paul's appalled eyes, Vincent sliced off a section of his own ear. Paul swivelled abruptly, surging forward, as Vincent, still brandishing the razor in his right hand, clapped his left one over the bleeding orifice. Paul, kneeling down, scrabbled under the table for the severed portion.

'But, *mon cher* Vincent,' said Paul, now rising, 'I didn't mean it ... literally. Look, here – it's your missing ear. Let me sew it back on?'

Vincent, howling with pain, staggered towards a chair. Then sat down with a bump. 'Not on your life! Not on your bloody life! It's finished, you understand? Finished! Vincent, a martyr to his art! A human sacrifice! And you? You? Go! Go! Run away! *Le meurtrier a pris la fuite*! Eh? Hah! Holà! Welcome to my next *chef d'oeuvre*, a painter, again: *Self-Portrait of the Artist with a Bandaged Ear*! Ha. Ha. Ha. An ear that has no ear! Forget it – you said it! *You* have the ear, you imbecile – the one that has more ear than mine! Sew that on, if you will – throw the other bloody appendage away! Or give it to some woman, any woman, down at the Arles arena – a gift from Vincent, poor foolish Vincent, both Matador and bull! Then maybe hand her the other one! *Tiens, tiens*! Aagh! Aaargh! No, give me instead a Paul Gauguin ear, one that can judge my music better than the Paris critics, who – aargh! Ow! – now won't get to hear it! Ooh! Ooh! Aaargh! Aaargh! *Allez au diable*! – that is the one for me!'

Vincent, in agony, howled, then crumpled. But rising again, he made another lunge at Paul. Paul, sidestepping, terrified, charged from the room, still clutching the ear. Its owner, his free hand clasped tight to the bleeding wound, chased after him with the razor. There was a blood-curdling scream from Vincent, who promptly passed out. From the fearful Paul, rushing back in again, catching Vincent before his head hit the floor, there was a shocked silence.

It was twenty minutes later. Having put Vincent to bed, Paul set about washing the ear at the pump. Have to get Vincent to a hospital, see what they could do? It wasn't the whole ear, that was a good thing, but lots of blood. Meanwhile, he'd bandaged Vincent as best he could and sent a neighbour for Doctor Rey.

Once his friend was taken care of, that was it. He'd be off, Paul told himself, away from Vincent, away from this house. No sad '*adieux*', no tears nor embraces for a once firm friendship. He'd spend the night in a hotel and catch the first train. He'd tie up his business in Paris, drop in on his family in Denmark, then sail to those warm foreign parts. A new life was awaiting him, he'd never return.

Back in 'The Yellow House' Vincent had regained consciousness. He was again howling with pain, a terrible sound. Paul smiled grimly. Better or worse than that awful cacophony at the piano? It was a close-run thing, each equally bad. But, at least, the howling seemed human or, rather, like a man in wolf's clothing. Better a howling lycanthrope, thought Paul, than listening, even once more, to Vincent's ghastly music!

II

ST-RÉMY

The Asylum of
Saint-Paul-de-Mausole

ONE

The asylum, as Paul approached it, had off-yellow walls, balconies and green shutters, with tall trees dotted around. He had expected it to be dark and forbidding, not so pleasing to the eye, though the very thought of such a place, intended as it was for the treatment of mental patients, seemed as incongruous in this appealing landscape as a herd of cattle in the Tuileries.

The *diligence* juddered to a halt and Paul alighted. He stretched and breathed in the warm Summer air. Though still wearing his familiar Bohemian garb and Breton clogs, he had now added a black-and-white striped jacket. Around his shoulders hung a flowing Magyar cloak with silver clasps, on his head was a black, broad-brimmed hat *à la* Aristide Bruant, with a fluffy white feather at the crown, while his fingers toyed with a decorative *canne de jonc*, its handle carved in the shape of a couple making love. In this guise he looked jaunty, if not in any formal way smart.

Paul tipped the *cocher* at the gates, with instructions to

pick him up later. Briefly, he watched the carriage, with
its spavined, sway-backed horses, clattering past some
Roman ruins and a centipede of sun-dappled plane trees,
before crossing through dense fields of lavender on the way
back to town. Paul switched his gaze to the vast expanse
of wheat fields, the belts of cypress in the distance and the
violet *alpilles* of Arles.

With a feeling of dread, he trudged up a long path bor-
dered with iris, past some more tall trees and a merrily
splashing fountain. Pausing for breath, Paul took in the
long clay terrace at the side wall of the house, then a clump
of deflowered rose bushes on the edge of the parkland, its
red ochre soil scorched by the sun and covered with fallen
pine needles. After which, he removed his cloak, climbed
the steps to the great oaken doors and jangled the bell.

A minute or two passed. Should he try again, or turn
and race after the carriage? But, suddenly, he heard a
clanking and a grinding. The doors creaked open, he was
ushered inside.

Once there, it was again not so bad as he'd imagined –
not damp really and, as far as he could make out, when
led down a dimly lit passage from the vestibule, there was
just one solitary rat. It scuttled away at Paul's approach.
Possibly more of them somewhere, but at least he couldn't
see them. The place had a sour smell, of human sweat and
bad cooking, but compared with some other hospitals
he'd visited, it was almost bearable.

The man at the desk checked Paul's particulars and
handed him a pass. Then the same orderly who'd admitted
him continued to light him on his way. From some far-off
chamber, Paul heard the odd scream or two, a clacking
and scrabbling of feet on flagstone floors. But otherwise,
as they negotiated the labyrinthine corridors and climbed

the winding stairs, the building seemed as still and secret as a tomb.

Vincent had been here, at Saint-Rémy, since soon after that incident with the ear. That's when, acceding to urgent pleas from the local hospital, the oddly named *Hôtel Dieu*, his distraught brother Theo had smoothed things over with the police and come to collect him.

Faced with pressure from his landlord, the hostile townsfolk and with 'The Yellow House' mysteriously flooded out, Vincent required little urging to leave Arles and sign the committal papers himself. He was then prepared for the worst. The advice from the experts was for total restraint, shock treatment and a stay of at least one year. But within weeks, Vincent had already made progress, much more than anyone expected.

This seemed to be confirmed when Paul entered the cell. Well, not a cell exactly. The room was clean, if sparse, low ceilinged and serviceable, with grey-green wallpaper, sea-green curtains and a battered armchair.

It was, thought Paul, more like a billet in a military academy than a place of confinement. The only things out of place for a normal dwelling were the heavy chain 'restrainers' bolted to one wall, and the buckled straps, which hung around the sleeping area. They were evidently needed, Paul assumed, for the really difficult patients. Apart from which, the room had its comforts. There was even a small studio adjoining, with an easel and canvas prominently displayed.

Paul continued to look around. It was light in here, with a plain wooden table, a bed with mattress and pillows, some books, paintings and another easel, standing by the barred, though presently open, window. On the sill were assembled a siphon, empty bottles and a blue Majolica jug, decorated with flowers and leaves: they were no doubt intended for a still life. And there, over in the corner, was that old piano from 'The Yellow House'. Must be costing Theo a fortune, thought Paul, what with the treatment, meals and all, but that's what brothers are for.

He moved across, turning his head as the orderly mumbled something. On Paul's approach, Vincent looked up. Seated at the table, with a half-eaten plate of bread, cheese and pickled onion pushed to one side, he'd been busy scribbling on a scroll in front of him. He had a contented, almost childlike expression and, recognising Paul, seemed pleased to see him. Catching sight of the orderly, as if for the first time, Vincent smiled. '*Merci*, Georges, that's all.' The orderly nodded and left. The padded door was bolted from the outside.

Drawing nearer, taking Vincent's proffered hand, Paul saw the scroll was music paper. He peered at it more closely. Even with his limited grasp of notation, he could see that the scribbles were nonsense.

Vincent grinned, rose awkwardly and caught Paul up in an embrace. He held on to him tightly, as if afraid that his old friend, having suddenly reappeared into his life, might just as quickly vanish.

Gently, Paul extricated himself, twinkled briefly and studied Vincent's face. Vincent looked as well as Paul had been led to believe and, though his bad ear was heavily bandaged, he would seem, to the casual observer, almost like his earlier self. But Paul knew enough about mental illness to realise that even the most disturbed of patients can, at certain times, appear just as sane as the next man.

'You look fine, *mon p'tit*, in pretty good trim. *Oui*, best I've seen you in a long time.' Paul raised his voice. 'But can you hear me with just that one good ear, the bandage and all? How d'you manage with your specs?'

'Only need them for reading, Paul. As for hearing, it's well enough, and the bad ear's not bandaged too tightly. Dressing should have come off, but an infection set in, it's taking time to heal. That hospital they took me to? A nightmare, it ought to be closed down.'

'Heard you were chasing the nurses, trying to sleep with the patients?'

'I also washed myself in the coal bucket, I needed *some* distraction. One more day there, said Theo, they would've killed me!'

Paul grunted and gestured to the pictures on the wall. One was the *Bandaged Ear* self-portrait, executed in bright, clear colours. It was this which Vincent, writhing in agony at 'The Yellow House', had recklessly threatened to paint.

The Vincent of the picture was staring vaguely to left of frame, with the dressing round the right side of his head with his features pinched and corpse-like, though with little hint of martyrdom or self-pity, he was buttoned up protectively against an apparently cruel world, in a thick green overcoat. Vigorously brushed in, it covered almost half the picture area. This image was topped off with a woollen snow hat. Just behind Vincent, on the picture's greeny-yellow background, hung a Japanese print of jolly maidens in a mountain landscape. The presence of these girls, cheerfully cavorting under a reddish-pink sky, afforded the melancholic foreground figure a touch of unexpected lightness. It was almost, thought Paul, as if the storm had passed.

'Good, splendid,' he said, 'it's here as promised. And just like your flowers I can almost smell you!' He sniffed. 'Ah, I *can* smell you.' Then frowned. 'But it's the wrong ear, *mon p'tit*, bandage should be on the left.'

'It's my mirror image, I failed to reverse it.'

'Forgot to, you mean? Still, you've captured more than your essence. It's Vincent to a T, as the self-harmed suffering genius!'

'I *was* suffering then, it was done before I got here. And a cruelly truthful study, too, no doubt about it. The agony of Mankind, it seems, in red and green!'

'Agony? Don't see it. Hope, maybe, just a touch, and courage. Somewhere there, anyhow, aside from the sadness, to be able to undertake such a fine piece of work! In spite of all.'

'*Merci, mon ami.*'

'And do I also gather, from your real life expression and this encouraging hive of activity, that you're reasonably content?'

'When I'm creating something, terrific. But again, it comes and goes. Basking in the sunlight one minute, shadowed by storm clouds the next. Just like some of my paintings. You always said I was a moody devil.'

'Moody wasn't in it, a maniac more like. You at "The Yellow House", screaming fit to burst. Blood everywhere, crowds in the street and, to cap it all, those brain-dead *flics* arrested *me*. Lot of explaining it took, before they let me go. *Beauté du diable*! What a Christmas that was!'

'I'm sorry, Paul, truly sorry I frightened you.'

'Let's forget it, water under the bridge.'

'Don't know what came over me? Must have been mad. I *am* mad.'

'Not as mad as that. Daft as a brush, maybe, or should it be palette knife? But not truly mad. Back then, we were under a strain, too much confined, our temperaments incompatible. We're better, I think, taken in small doses.

And the house had a curse on it. It's quieter here, you're quieter.'

'It is, mostly. I am. And they do take care of you, even when bullying you back to health. But, too many bad days, when will I find peace?'

'When you find *yourself*.' Paul looked around again. 'Room's not too bad, bit like an artist's studio. *Mais oui –*' he nodded ' – there *is* the studio. And the country round here, the layout, I'm pleasantly surprised.'

'It used to be a monastery, from mediaeval times, a place of meditation.'

'Entirely suitable,' laughed Paul, 'to embrace your new asceticism. Vincent, the Mad Monk!'

He glanced at another painting, this time on the easel, an avalanche of roses in a country garden, which Vincent had been working on. 'And the music?' said Paul, 'I see you have the piano. That should distract you from your empty gut?'

Mention of 'empty gut' reminded Paul he'd skipped lunch. He gazed longingly at the plate on the table.

'Not so hungry now, most days they feed us well. Plain food, but nourishing, the kind that makes you fart!' Noting Paul's expression, Vincent winked and stepped over. He shifted the music paper, gesturing to the chair. 'Go on, Paul. You have it. Eat up, I've had enough.'

Paul needed no second bidding. He grabbed at the plate and wolfed the contents down. 'Long drive from town (mm, mm), *merci, mon p'tit*. Pretty hungry, actually, that was good.' He wiped his hands on his jacket, then grinned up at Vincent. 'Don't s'pose there's any wine?'

'Not even for guests!' Vincent winked again. 'I used to get half a litre with meals, by arrangement with Theo. But now, only as a special treat, much watered down.

Well, Paul, see you haven't lost your appetite?'

There was an awkward pause. The problem of two old friends who've bitterly quarrelled, but who, meeting again, having exchanged a few pleasantries, are now at a loss for words.

Vincent made the effort. 'So, how goes it with *you*? How's the painting? How's the trip – that tropical jaunt of yours? When d'you sail? I thought you'd gone already?'

'Well, I haven't. I mean, I was. I am. Going. When the time is right.'

'When you can afford it?'

'That, too. A hard nut to crack.'

'But in Arles, when you first mentioned it, you said "tomorrow".'

'Well, not literally tomorrow. Nor – precisely now. Maybe not next week, neither, nor in months. All that was hasty. For now I'm becalmed, in still waters. I mean, a few things to do. After that, nothing could hold me.'

'Well, careful, Paul. You know what the Chinese say: beware of what you wish for?'

'Don't worry. It's all taking shape, just thinking of it. The sea, the sand, the scent of hibiscus, those same dusky enchantresses. So, just suck on that! The blood is up and running, already in my mind's eye.'

'Ah, that famous "mind's eye"!' Vincent laughed. 'But aren't we mixing our metaphors?'

'Eh? What?'

'I said, be careful. Too much blood in the brain can lead to strokes.'

'Again, Vincent, not meant literally. But, like most things we wish for, it's on the edge of our dreams. If we wish it hard enough, bits of those dreams turn up. A healthy life, in spite of the heat. Swimming and screwing, decent grub, a perfect nirvana. And better than hanging on here, going the same way as those other clapped-out artists – starving, living with whores, sliding into forgetfulness with the aid of absinthe. Glad they've made *you* lay off "The Green Fairy". Worst thing for that complaint of yours – the fits.'

'So the doctors say.'

'They're right. Accept the advice and desist.' Paul looked grave. Then gazed absently through the window. 'Don't know how I'll fit in, though, in those unfamiliar surroundings, nor how I'll end up? Probably upset the locals eventually, I usually do. And die of pox, no doubt, in desperate circumstances. Have some stern Catholic bishop at my deathbed, in Tonga or Pago Pago, calling me "a contemptible individual named Gauguin, a reputed artist but an enemy of God and everything that is decent in the world".'

'Sounds like you.' Again Vincent laughed. 'You must be a prophet.'

'But before then I'll fill my life with beauty, broad forms and bright textures. Everywhere I go, there'll be orgies of colour.'

'Orgies full stop. Just like the old days.'

'You got it.'

Vincent looked contemplative. 'But be realistic for a moment, your plans are still in abeyance?'

'Again, precisely. Short of funds.'

'So what about those paintings you sold, at that exhibition in Paris? Pissarro told me about it, his last visit here.'

'A pittance, at auction. That's including the ones you gave me. Sorry, *mon p'tit*, I was desperate. I wouldn't have parted with them for the world.'

'Not to worry – what are paintings for?' A pause, Vincent stared at him. 'But the critics – at least, they praised you?'

'Critics? Bah. They don't put bread on the table.'

'And the cash our friends raised, I heard? 'Specially for the trip?'

'Another story. Anyhow, I've just enough to get there, the fare's a thousand francs. All told, I've raised about eighteen hundred. But that's not enough to live on, to buy materials, and … other necessaries. So, cap in hand, I went back to them. When I asked for more, they cut up rough. Said "Where's the money we gave you?" Accused me of drinking it away!'

'Did you?'

A grim laugh. 'Some of it, yes.'

'Then there's the inheritance – from your uncle? What happened to that? Enough for ten years, you said?'

'Gone. Expensive tastes.'

'But there must be some way. Have you tried Mette, your wife? Her family? Can't they help? They did before.'

'Not a *sou*. Not Mette. I asked her to come with me, by the way, to bring the kids. Big adventure for them, I'd have thought. But why live in poverty on a tropical island, when you can be comfortable at home? Like living "in a normal person's idea of civilisation", wearing decent clothes and seeing one's friends? Besides, she's left town, taking the little ones, too. We write, but I haven't seen her.'

'How was she – the last time?'

'Okay. Fine. In good nick. Always has been. Pissed off with me for going, though. Leaving home, deserting her, for my last big trip. And she never understood me, *pas du tout*. Even back then, when I was around all the time. With me trying to get my "innate feelings" on canvas – her words, not mine – when I should've kept on making money. She's busy, though, quite happy, a full life, translating Zola, running her salon. Nice woman, bit odd. Tall, blonde, attractive, smoking cigars, hair cropped like a boy.'

Vincent eyed Paul and grinned. 'Better to *have* a boy, *peut-être*? Not that I'm suggesting anything!'

Paul grinned back. 'Let's hope not.'

There was another pause. Vincent grew wistful. 'You know, you're so lucky, Paul. Or, at least, your women are. They go on to better things. Unlike mine.'

'All those that dumped you, *hein*? We're back to that again.'

'No, we're not. Basically, we were talking of your wife. You dumped *her*. Abandoned her. With five young ones, the whole family.'

'Not quite. I tried to get back with her, to make it work. But her people threw me out. It was only after that I said "Sod it, I'm off," and stuck to it. But believe what you want to.' Paul glanced away. 'Anyhow, we're in touch, as I said. The break's not … final. I'll make my own way, see a few things, do them, too – life, the world, all the breasts I can fondle. Then stockpile my masterpieces and come home.'

'Not what you told *her*?'

'Don't recall *what* I told her. Just took off, I'm like that. Even as a nipper I had a fondness for running away.' Paul laughed. 'A dirty dog, *n'est-ce pas*? We artists, a funny lot. A law unto ourselves.'

'*C'est vrai, c'est vrai.*'

'Still, that's all done. No more Mette.'

'*Tant pis.* It was a good marriage once?'

'Could be still, If I gave all this up. But we both know it's impossible. I miss the kids, though. One of the tragedies of my life is my children are no longer French. They're being raised in Denmark.'

'You're not so French yourself, Paul.'

'*C'est vrai, aussi.* I've the blood of Inca princes in my veins!' Paul grinned. 'Anyhow, that's it. Stuck here for now – the Pacific'll have to wait.'

Paul turned away from the window and reseated himself at the table. He stared at the empty plate and shook his head.

Vincent, meanwhile, sat on the edge of the bed. He gazed at Paul with the old affection and cleared his throat. 'How *were* the old crowd – before you fell out with them?'

'Not fell out, exactly. They're just … displeased with me.'

'Sod them. Their bad luck. So, how are they?'

'Successful, mostly, certainly the reviews. Except for poor Lautrec. Loafing around *Le Moulin Rouge*, doing the odd sketch or poster. And a number of lesser places. Much lesser, from what I gather, he's most at home with outcasts. If it weren't for that allowance from *Maman* he'd starve.'

'Just like us – the bad times.'

'It's still the bad times. But at least he has some fame, some powerful friends. He's frequently exhibited – when the censors allow – and he doesn't stint himself. That's despite his … imperfections. Poor Henri. Those funny eyes and tiny legs, what an oddity. When last I saw him he was all got up as a Japanese *samurai*, looking odder than ever.'

'A strange one all right. A fellow with singular tastes. Red hair, you know, drives him to ecstasy?'

'Who told you that?'

'He did, Paul. The night we first met.'

Paul laughed. 'Hope you watched your step!'

'He's never fancied *me* – likes the girls too much. And for me they'll never pose, those whores of his, as they do for him, *gratis* and for nothing.'

'Lucky bugger.'

'And he knows all the tricks of the boudoir, does Henri, he never falters. Concentrating for hours, each part of the body in turn, the same as when painting them. But to be so obsessed – with women's noses!'

'First thing he sees when he looks up at them. Red hair and noses. *Chacun à son goût.*'

Vincent shook his head. It was his turn to rise and gaze out the window. 'Wish I had Henri's way with women. In spite of his grotesqueries, it seems he can have anyone he wants. I toured *les maisons closes* with him in the early days. Henri *avec les cocottes – c'est phénonème*!'

'It's that outsize chopper of his. The proportions are astounding!'

'That's even for a man of normal height. As he's always said himself, "I'm like a coffee pot with a large spout!"'

'*C'est le destin, mon p'tit.* God takes away with one hand and adds something on with the other.'

'*Vraiment.*' Vincent was now staring at the piano. 'But look, Paul, since you're here, let me show you – I mean, play for you. Something I've written, my latest *oeuvre*. I hope you like it.'

'I – I don't think – um…'

'No, no, I *know* you will. Listen, do. What you're about to hear meets the perfect definition of great music: that it penetrates the ear with facility and quits the memory with difficulty.'

'Even bad music does that.'

'Shhh. Listen.'

Paul opened his mouth to protest. He thought better of it. Vincent had shuffled across, he raised the piano lid. Paul twitched a little, glanced longingly at the exit, but decided to tough it out. Whatever happens now, he told himself, he would not make the same mistake as last time.

TWO

A little later, with Paul's 'warm', if subtly edited *critique musicale* still buzzing in Vincent's brain, they were now outside. Paul had gained leave to take his friend for a walk in the grounds. Vincent had a stretched canvas and sketch pad under one arm, Paul a pain in both ears and something of a headache, but that was to be expected.

There were, Paul saw, several other patients outside. Gathered in twos and threes, some attended by their keepers, they were exercising a few yards away. A number of them, despite the warm weather, wore hats and topcoats, as if ready for a journey. These poor folk, he realised, were the ones deemed no longer a danger to themselves or others, though pathetically deluded, it seemed, in thoughts of imminent release. Vincent, too, was 'officially on the mend', to be trusted now with a short stroll around the estate, that's if Paul 'would keep a careful charge of him?'

The sun through the trees made a lovely *sous-bois* effect and all seemed at peace. So, turning their backs on the asylum, the two friends continued to recall the old days, the old crowd, the places they'd hung out in and all their younger dreams.

The gardens around them were planted with large pines, beneath which the grass grew tall and unkempt, with clusters of weeds in between. Not too far off, edging the wheat fields, stood that same line of cypresses, twisting and lowering like some dark jagged spot on the sun-drenched landscape. The scent of olive groves filled the air and the blue hills of Arles, under a suddenly troubled sky, loomed further in the distance.

Vincent sat on a low wall and began to sketch. Paul glanced over his shoulder. He frowned and shook his head. 'Vincent, *mais non*, you don't see. Look at the fields, the horizon, and position of the sun.'

'What sun?'

'That sun. Coming back from behind the clouds. It was sunny before, it's sunny again. You must keep tabs on what you see, 'specially in nature.'

'I am. All the time.'

'No, you're not. You keep turning your head, staring back at your prison. You'll get a crick in the neck, it draws you like a magnet.' Paul gestured towards the yellow stonework. 'Expect, when I'm gone, you'll be painting this place, too?'

'It appeals to the depressive in me. Cheerful on the surface, but filled with foreboding. My paintings are a metaphor of life and death. Like those cypresses there, planted as a screen against the *mistral*. Cut them down, Paul, and they'll never spring back. My own life, too, it's a broken branch, chopped and splintered beyond repair!'

'Vincent, you should look on the bright side. As in where we are now, more of a park than a hospital.'

'It's pretty untidy.'

'"Wild" is a better word for it. Wild and wonderful. So keep on painting the shrubs and the trees – see this one with the ivy? That should appeal to you! – the fountain and that stone bench.'

'I do, when I get the light right.'

''Cos there's some subjects should be left alone.'

'Not what Rodin said.'

'I thought,' grumbled Paul, 'it was Proust.'

'What? Which was?'

'You know? "Anything and everything is a suitable subject for art"? I mean it is, isn't it? Proust that said it?'

'Did he? Can't be. Couldn't have said it. Not poor whey-faced Proust. No intellect, poor chap. Ever the social butterfly.'

'Well, he will say it one day, almost bound to. There's more to Marcel, I'd say, than meets the eye. I'd stake my right hand on it.'

'We'll have to wait and see, then, won't we? But my advice to you Paul, is best start painting with your left! Anyhow, can't make the fellow out. Always reminiscing about his childhood, why can't he live in the present? It's unhealthy in one so young.'

'How young?'

Vincent thought for a moment. 'Eighteen, nineteen, can't be much more. Compared to us, that *is* young.'

'Bah. I'd sailed the Seven Seas by that age. Marcel should do the same, it toughens one up.'

'Too tied to *Maman*'s apron strings. But I'll give him your advice, Paul, if ever I see him. Did I tell you we nearly shared a lodging house in Paris? A most peculiar fellow.' Vincent chuckled, then looked wistful again. 'If Proust remembers time past in years to come, will he recall *us*, I wonder?'

'Doubt it.' Paul laughed outright. 'Any more than anyone will. Still, all this talk of past and future, I find it unsettling. How much does one remember of the past, how can we be certain of the future? Too difficult, strange. Like your painting, not to all tastes.'

'Not to anyone's taste.'

'And that music of yours, I'll agree to call it such – I mean, um, very good, Vincent, better than last time. *Incroyable*. Excellent.'

'Glad you enjoyed it. Maybe, back inside, we could play four handed?'

'Not me, I'm more of an organ man – the piano's not my forte. Ha. Ha.' Not yours, either, he wanted to say, but again quickly checked himself. 'Still, your music … it's pretty odd. Something for the specialised ear, like Marcel burbling on about being an infant and going to bed early. Oh, and all about his childish experience remaining valid enough to prompt adult memory. What's all *that* about? Now the bastard threatens to write it all down! Personally, I can't even remember last week. Too mystical, too mystical by far.'

'You've exercised your own share of mysticism, Paul. Or, at least, Christian mysticism. All those strange Bible studies of Breton peasants, a plethora of darkening brush strokes. That wasn't so cheerful, was it? How d'you account for that?'

'It was necessary, expected. Even if my preferred choice in Art is painting women *au naturel*!'

'I've never been into nudes. Well, early on, maybe. I envy you.'

'Ha. Ha. Poor Vincent. Another of your problems?'

'And you've gone the old Japanese route, too, Paul, in your time. Oriental exoticism at its most wonderful and weird. Just like me, the older stuff.'

'Very colourful, I'd say. You were something of a realist then. So don't castigate me, as you tend to do, for being unduly influenced. Lautrec was part of it, so was everybody. But a fashion, that's all. Don't knock our youthful enthusiasms. In order to move on, one first makes a start.'

'I won't. I'm sorry.'

Vincent had put the sketch pad aside. He picked up the canvas, which already had a few preliminary daubs on it.

He began applying colours, for the scene closer at hand. Paul glanced at this, too.

'*Bien*, that's it. Ensnare the light and throw it on the canvas! But listen, I dream, you know, of creating an art – a new art, that would be also Japanese, Oriental, with all those other influences – the Western tradition, Italian Renaissance – but filtered through the eyes of a Peruvian savage!'

'Like you, Paul?'

'Like me.' Paul grinned. 'But at the same time, as if such styles and sources could isolate some primitive essence of Man.'

'Bit fanciful, sounds like hard work. Think I'll stick to wheat fields.'

'And bloody sunflowers! Ha. Ha.'

Vincent grinned and looked away. Even during these moments, while listening to Paul's theories on art, he'd been busy. Looking out across the unkempt gardens, he now filled the canvas with simple black strokes on patches of bright green. The image was crowned by a narrow white path and a scattering of trees. But these, since the canvas was too small, had been cut off abruptly at top of frame, excluding the hills in the distance.

Paul grunted his disappointment and stared again at that strange blue mass. Vincent, meanwhile, squinted his eyes against the sun, as waves of just bearable heat drifted across the valley, warming his whole body through. Blinking, moving his head a fraction, he gazed at the plant and insect life, glimpsed through a haze of dancing flecks of colour. He wondered how he could capture it? With a whoop of enthusiasm, he retrieved his palette knife.

'I know, Paul, I know! I shall call this *Long Grass with Butterflies*.'

Paul followed his friend's eyeline. 'I don't see butterflies, like *where*? Why don't you paint that other stuff beyond, the scene you sketched just now? Or stick your head out the window some night, working *contre jour*, paint the stars or the moonrise, maybe both?'

'You don't see butterflies,' laughed Vincent ''cos it's *you* can't see. 'Cept those dark-skinned native girls in your so-called "mind's eye"! It's our task as artists, Paul, to make the invisible visible. I've heard you say so. So, butterflies it is! But I shall do "the other stuff", as you call it, tomorrow or soon after. And you're right, Paul. Sometimes, it seems to me, night is even more richly coloured than the day. A painting, then, *contre jour*. Next time you come, I shall give it you.'

'Can't wait.' Paul shrugged and continued to watch. 'The grass, though, is good, you've got it just right. Standing still but very alive. Or maybe about to blow down!'

'*Merci, encore.*' Vincent held the canvas away and studied it. 'But what we do is *really* odd. No wonder we're hated by the Philistines.' He paused. 'So what will it be called, this new movement of yours? An advance on that same … Symbolism, or Synthetism, they've been talking about?'

'Sort of. Or Modernism, if you like. My absolute reaction to Pissarro and all the earlier tripe.'

'Pissarro? But you were a devotee once, he helped you.'

'He helped himself.'

'And encouraged Cézanne.'

'Then he deserves the bum's rush.'

Vincent bristled. 'Does he? I don't think so.'

'We'll agree to differ.'

'But the Impressionists, in general … you had a lot of time for them?'

'Did I?'

'And at least you were exhibited with them. Unlike me.'

'Five times, true. But the link with them made me self-conscious. I regarded Impressionism as a stage to go through, not an end in itself. In time, I cut out.'

'Anyhow, Modernism? I like it, good word. As Rimbaud said, "one must be absolutely modern." Paul, I wish you luck.' Vincent paused again. 'So how would you describe *my* style? Impressionist, Neo-Impressionist, Post-Impressionist, Divisionist, or what?'

'Couldn't say, Vincent, you're a Movement all your own. One day, maybe, that uniqueness of yours will hopefully catch on.'

'Let's hope so. As well as this new experiment of yours.'

'Surely will, if the fates are on one's side.' Paul stepped away from the wall and began to pace. 'As I told you, they're not a sudden whim, these ideas of mine, they've been bubbling under the surface. Like whatever drives *you*, that "paint in the veins thing", well, it's in my soul.'

'We're two of a kind, Paul.'

'Too true. And I've always been haunted by the exotic, the life of the wanderer. Not in Martinique nor South America. Been there, done that, purchased *la chemise sans manches*. But Tahiti, that's the spot!'

Vincent was looking gloomy. 'So you're really off? Not just talking it up? This time you mean it?'

'Too right. Any day now.'

'But how could you do it? Survive that life, as things go at present? You're strapped for cash, we've established that. You mustn't believe all the "decent grub" stuff. Nothing is for nothing. It's a long way to Tahiti, what if you're taken ill? Look at it seriously for once! Do they have art galleries there, to sell your paintings? Free lunch counters? Banks? Bookmakers? Pawnbrokers? Money-lenders? Surely not?'

'Thanks for your faith, you know how to twist the needle. No, I've been thinking it over, these last few minutes, I've got it sorted, fully cooked, a lot clearer to me now. Firstly, art is my capital, also the end result. I predict a booming market, timing is of the essence. Secondly, I could live very simply, I've described it to you, like a native. Living off the land, picking fruit, catching fish, building my own hut, keeping a local girl or two, or having them drop by. I could do it quite cheaply, with only the moon and sixpence.'

'How much is that? I've forgotten my English money.'

'Nothing. A few *centimes*, that's all.'

At this point, Vincent gathered his materials. He glanced at Paul, noting the look of sadness, the restlessness that hung about him like a shroud, the growing consciousness of an unfulfilled destiny. He felt a sudden wave of remorse for that tactless jibe at Paul's poverty and the cynical view of his plans.

Reading him correctly, Vincent knew enough, from his own condition, that not only was his old friend still desperately yearning for those far-off shores, but that, in trying to reach them, his life and sanity depended on it. Vincent put down his bundle and tried to sound positive.

'So pay attention *mon ami*, the Pacific, these dreams you have? Pity to waste them, I've an idea. Why don't you work your passage, like that previous voyage you made? And then save some money for your stay?'

'Ah, the old days! Top rigger on a sailing ship, I'd broad shoulders then! Anyhow, as I said, got things to finish first.'

'Me, too.'

'*Oui.* Ha. Ha. Those interminable country landscapes.

But at least, up there –' Paul gestured behind him ' – you do have your windows to work from.'

'Thankfully, Theo insisted.'

'Facing east, too. Excellent.'

'I have. A perspective from which, alone in the morning through the iron bars, I can see a whole square of wheat and the sun rise in glory! Also, just like today, they let me out at odd periods, under escort. I can paint *en plein air*, as you always said I should. One gets tired of asylum walls, it's nice to hear the birdsong.'

'So you like birds now, do you?'

'Small ones. And sometimes they come to the window sill, I feed them when I can. And, whenever I can, I paint and compose to my heart's content. I even play cards with the orderly. Poor Georges. Ha. Ha. I kicked him up the arse once, mistook him for a cop.'

'What did *he* do, give you a flogging?'

Vincent chuckled. 'Not a bit of it, he was quite understanding. This is a hospital, after all, not like being in gaol. It's not a life sentence.'

'Ah, I know all about gaols. I recall, myself, when I was in Denmark, with Mette and those relatives of hers. Wearing a suit, going to the office, dinner promptly at seven. No escape from it, I was trapped in an endless routine. My wife was a gaoler and threw away the key.'

'And that's why you broke out? You had to.'

'I did. You know it, the whole damn story. Best thing I've done. Artists have to be free.'

'*Vraiment*. It's something I should do. Try to escape, climb over the walls. But mine's a different kind of gaol, more solid, reassuring than the one I've made for myself. And Theo would be so disappointed if I quit. He's paying through the nose, it's meant to be doing me good.'

'I'm sure it is. And work, they say, is the best recovery.'

'It is, when there's time for it.' Vincent seemed despondent again. 'But between all these doctors and treatments,
well, some days it doesn't come easy. I sit at my window or
outside here, and wait for inspiration. Then, when it hits
me, I paint away furiously, but none of it's any good and
Theo can't sell the damn things. I'm starting to accept that
the only person who'll have one of my paintings is *me*. No,
Paul, to quote Stendhal on the subject of a stalled romance,
I've drawn *le dead blank*. Somebody *wants* me to fail.'

'Not God, surely, you've worked so hard for Him?' Paul
was only half ironic. 'But this one –' He pointed to the
canvas ' – I think it's going to be great.'

'An exception. There's a few half-decent, like *The
Bandaged Ear*. But mostly, the finished work, I rip it all
up, or start again on the back of the canvas. I keep at
it, plod on a little, but what's the use? Don't seem to get
much right these days.'

'Twaddle, it's a passing phase. This environment,
dark, doomy – I mean, inside – great clanging doors, the
screams from the electric shock treatments, it'd kill off
any inspiration stone dead.'

'It is pretty hellish. Or it was, when I started, less like
treatment than torture! But at least they left me my paints
– they didn't know I'd once swallowed some, nearly died
of lead poisoning.'

'That's good. I mean, good that you've got your paints,
not that you nearly died.'

'*Merci*. But the doctors said at first I couldn't have my
brushes, they were a lethal weapon. That I could poke my
eye out or stick it in my bad ear. Again, Theo insisted.'

'Good for Theo. It's all that matters, really, that you're
still able to paint. I've seen you, Vincent, up or down,

hungry or no, beavering away, the bit between your teeth, turning out fine work. Sometimes I'm jealous, I seethe with frustration. There – Ha. Ha. – I've said it!'

'And the music? My new *étude*, you really liked it?'

'I did, I told you. But I do have some advice.'

Vincent looked edgy. 'What is it?'

'If you don't mind my saying, I think you could use a little *pianissimo*?' Paul caught Vincent's change of mood. He shook his head. 'No, *mon p'tit*, we'll forget about the music. I won't comment, let's not quarrel – don't want you hacking your other ear off!'

Paul saw Vincent relax, he grinned and looked relieved. 'But the painting, ah, Vincent, you're unique, one in a million. Single-minded in your dedication, making an all-out assault on the canvas. If only – if only, one can't repeat it enough, you weren't quite *so* intense, so damnably obsessive! A tortured genius with a quality of violence, an odd fish altogether. Don't take offence.'

'You're right again, and no offence taken. I really must settle myself, take life as it comes. That's what they've been telling me, Dr Peyron and the others. They're good folk, these doctors. But I don't know, Paul, I really don't. I've had my attacks here, four at least. And you've seen me, keep telling me, how I throw myself entirely into my work, rushing it through, like one possessed.'

'That's why it's slightly askew, Vincent. Your music, too. More than askew.'

'Is it? Are they? You're right, it is, I mean, are. Deliberately so. Since only in that way can I find release.'

'From what?'

'My demons.'

'Demons, eh? The thing we most have in common!'

'Or maybe it was Arles that did it, just as you said, the

heat, that strange light, the intensity of the south. It compelled me to paint, I couldn't slow down, and even the sun, when it sets, can scorch. Which is why I welcomed the Winter. Could be, when I'm better, it'll be time to think again. If I were a colour, I'd start afresh. But I'm afraid I'd never reach the heights to which the illness has to some extent led me.'

'Never mind that. A change would be good.'

'*Vraiment*, since I can't go back to Arles. The locals, you know, got up a petition – they ordered the cops to throw me out. The Mayor agreed with them. Said I was "a threat to public safety, a danger to the women of the neighbourhood!"'

Paul laughed. Vincent shot him a look.

'I'd be safer, too, I think, in a cooler climate, beneath the familiar grey skies of the north. I've been thinking of Auvers-sur-Oise, you must have been there? About twenty miles north-west of Paris?'

Paul shook his head. 'Not that I recall. Don't know it.' He paused. 'No wait a mo. I did hear something, when was it? – from Paul Cézanne. He stayed there once, that artists' combine of Pissarro's. Said it was quite picturesque, but infested with crows.'

Vincent grimaced. 'I've coped with gulls – kind of – I can cope with crows.'

'Hope you can. Or you'll be stuck indoors again.'

'Anyhow, crows apart, Camille Pissarro wrote me. He knows a doctor, a good fellow there, who's taken care of several Parisian painters, Cézanne included. Doctor's a painter, too, of sorts – an amateur.'

Paul grunted. 'I hate painters of sorts, especially amateurs. They're the worst.'

'Anyhow, that's why he takes an interest. He'll

recommend me, Camille, I mean. I might give it a try, let this chap suss me out. It's the real countryside, a place of peace and quiet, old Camille says, with a grave beauty. I should be fine, a more relaxed style, just as you suggest. The town, Paul, is perched on a hill. With lovely views, on one side of the verdant Oise valley. On the other, golden wheat fields, as far as the eye can see.'

Paul looked at Vincent, again ironic. 'Sounds ravishing.'

'It is, says Camille. Anyhow, I thanked him for his interest and dropped a line to Theo. To *Maman*, too, and my sister Lies, they're delighted with the plan. Soon, Paul, I shall be absorbed in that glorious landscape, covered by fields of wheat!'

'And fucking crows!'

''Fraid so. But it's a start, no more asylums. I'll also be at the piano as much as possible – it's my saviour. Composing, notating, singing my *chansons*. I mean, in the past, only when I stood there, painting before my easel, did I feel in any way alive. That was the lot I accepted. Now, it'll be different.'

'It will. Cheer up, your time will come. But before then, do what you've said you'd do. Take it easy, make a break, before you start again.'

'I'll try.'

'But also, your drinking. When you get out of here, no backsliding. It was out of control, you must promise. Give it up altogether – as I should.'

'But sometimes I feel I need it. 'Specially in this warm weather.'

'Bah. Just like a flower, forced to open its petals – Vincent takes wine when the sun comes out. Drinking and painting, what else? *Oui*, the sunshine is surely to blame!'

'I *shall* give it up – in Auvers.'

'Give it up now, all thought of it. We'll give it up together.'
Paul winked. He dug his hand into a pocket of his jacket
and extracted a flask. 'Jamaica rum, you don't get a drop.'
Paul glanced quickly over each shoulder, then downed the
contents in one. He winked again 'There, *mon p'tit*, I've
spliced the main brace – one last time!' He threw the flask
away.

Vincent chuckled. 'Did I tell you, Paul, that when they
stopped the booze in there, I almost drank turpentine.'

'*Mon Dieu*, as well as lead paint? Some very odd tastes,
I'm glad you're still with us. So, then what?'

'They restrained me, strapped the jacket on. Told me if
I didn't behave, they'd confiscate it – the turps, I mean –
and maybe my materials. Or, if they left them me, I'd have
to clean my brushes, mix my paints with something else!
My own piss or something, it was an object lesson.'

Paul laughed. 'I bet it was. We've all had a history of
being desperate.'

'We have.' Vincent eyed him, curiously. ''Spect you've
ingested some odd things, too, Paul, in your time.'

'Just so, Vincent, like you. Recall once in Paris, I was
eking out a living as a bill sticker. Putting up posters in *La
Gare St Lazare*. Around the time we first met, where was
that?'

'*Père* Tanguy's paint shop. Theo introduced us.'

'*C'est vrai*. We had a *pastis* and looked at the colours.'

'Drinking them in!'

'*Oui*. Odd free moment, it must have been, I was off to
sketch *Le Sacré Coeur, La Place Vendôme* or something.
Got hold of some honey and a pot of gum, to mix in
with paints for a *gouache*. Didn't get far, though. I was so
broke and hungry I ate it.'

'That's awful.'

'Not bad, actually, perfectly edible. I spread it on a *brioche*.'

'It's lucky you didn't stick your insides together.' A pause. 'So, what happened to the painting?'

'I had it for afters.'

They both laughed. Then another pause, as Paul eyed Vincent.

'So what's this fellow's name? *Le bon medecin* – the one in Auvers?'

'Gachet.'

'Gasket?'

'Gachet. Dr Gachet.'

'As you wish. Won't be much good. Country doctors? Bah. They're all the same. Take that chap in Arles, the one you went walkies with. Bleed a dying patient, soon as look at him – and worse. You've read your *Madame Bovary*?'

'Several times. But Gachet's different, according to Camille. General Practice, but also a Revolutionary, student of melancholy, he'll suit me down to the ground. Knows about ... physiology, nervous disorders. Another plus, with insights into the human soul. Nobody better, he's highly thought of.'

'He'd have to be. Probably suffers, himself, from melancholia, and everything else his patients have. Sad old bugger, I'd wager, most of these country sawbones are. And an amateur painter? God help us.'

'Well, they all say he's excellent. Pissarro, Monet, Cézanne – and they should know. Also a sculptor, engraver, collects stuff, too. Impressionists, supports the *avant-garde*. It must have rubbed off on him. Some fine unschooled talent. Or so they tell me.'

'Who? Who told you? Those artist friends of ours

– yours? They would. 'Specially to the wretched fellow's face. They'd say anything to a quack for a quick shot of something, an opium dream or two. Well, let's hope you're right, that he *can* do something, if you're not too far gone already.' Paul laughed, then serious. 'So how will you pay this character? He doesn't work for nothing? Tell me, Vincent, how *will* you afford him, this painting-mad doctor?'

'Same as our other pals – completed canvases in exchange for medical consultation. I'll also discuss art with him, advise on his progress.'

Paul laughed again. 'The blind leading the blind? Mind you don't fall in a ditch.'

Vincent ignored this. 'Maybe, with luck, I'll be able to put him straight on a few things. Improve his brushwork, his sense of form, all that basic practical stuff, and … give him the odd painting, too.'

Paul raised an eyebrow. 'He'll love that. Either grow rich or end in the poor house!' He paused, a mischievous grin. 'Um – does he have a daughter?'

'Who?'

'Doctor Whatsisname.'

'I think so. Son, too, somewhere.'

'Pretty?'

'The son?'

'No, dummy, the daughter.'

'How should I know? Haven't met her yet.'

'Well, be careful. I heard once of a medic with an unmarried pregnant daughter, whose lover had an accident on the railways. Not too bad, damaged one of his legs – not killed, thank God.'

'What happened … after?'

'Fellow went to this same medic, to get patched up. Doc,

still narked at the loss of his daughter's cherry and with her small mistake well on the way, made a pact with the chloroform and amputated both the chap's legs!'

Vincent looked at Paul with horror. '*Mon Dieu! C'est dégoulas*! So what did he do? The poor fellow, when he came round?'

Paul whooped with delight. 'He cried, "Aah – aaargh! Ooh! Oooh! Ow! Ow! Yowl! Where's the rest of me?"'

He laughed loudly, as Vincent sighed and shook his head. 'I fell right into that one, didn't I?'

'You sure did. Poor Vincent.'

Vincent groaned his irritation. 'Let's keep off the "poor Vincent" routine for a bit, shall we? Give it a break, Paul, it's pretty patronising.'

'You got it. Far be it from me to upset you. You, of all people. After all, you *are* my favourite painter.'

Vincent grinned again, the old eyelash flutter. 'Bet you say that to all the girls?'

Paul grinned back. 'Usually. Some of the new ones, most of the old ones. Well, all except Cézanne.'

'But I like him. Paul, you know that.' Vincent paused, he thought a moment. 'Paul? Ha. Ha. Paul Cézanne, Paul Gauguin, Paul Signac – too many Pauls, it's beginning to pall. But no, leave Cézanne alone. He's a genius.'

'Cézanne? A genius? This *is* Cézanne we're talking about? Or *you* keep talking about? Wish you'd mention somebody else.'

'It was you who mentioned him. Twice in the last ten minutes.'

'Did I?'

'You know you did. And don't disparage Cézanne. He's worked like the very devil to perfect his art, always a few jumps ahead. He's changed his style, and suffered, too.'

'About time he did. There is a road to Calvary we artists must tread. And that includes poverty?'

'It does.'

'Well, Cézanne's not poor, just under-appreciated. Anyhow, I still like him, he's got a good eye.'

'Good eye? Good eye? For what? For gazing at his own navel? Unlike poor Lautrec again, who, through some curious freak of nature, is forced to gaze at other people's! Cézanne? Cézanne! *Parbleu*! *Quel affreux*! *The Temptation of St Anthony*? Unspeakable. What a wanker! He's so repressed is Cézanne, I doubt he's been tempted by anything. That's why his painting's got no balls.'

'You know nothing, Paul. About Art, nothing. Cézanne is a great artist and he'll grow in stature. So's Toulouse, a fine artist, so are the others.'

'And I'm not?'

'Did I say that?'

'You implied it.'

'I did not.'

'You did.'

'Didn't.'

'Did.'

'Didn't.'

Paul sighed. 'Oh, please yourself, Corporal. But if anyone's an artist, it's me. The only artist.'

'How so? How d'you work that out?'

'Because I'm an original. An innovator. Something for the generations to come. Who was it taught the Impressionists to work freely, even madly from within, not merely the things that they saw? I did. And to interest themselves in the ability of Art not just to recreate a scene, but also to invoke a feeling?'

'Oh, yeah? Yeah?'

'Yeah. Too bloody right. No contest. To that end, my paintings *mean* something, they speak to nations, to the world. Triumphant brush strokes, full of shades of meaning. Not some vulgar daubs on an old cracked canvas. An assemblage of decaying dog turds, plastered on with a palette knife!'

Vincent began jumping about. 'What? What? Me? Me? You talkin' to me? You talkin' to *me*?'

'If the cap fits.' Paul reacted. 'No, hey, that's *my* line!'

'Cap? Cap? Hah. Hah. Right. *Mais, c'est une blague, n'est ce pas*? This is it? Enough, already! I'm glad you're going, Paul, to live with the savages. You've outstayed your welcome. Hah. Born a savage, still a savage and a savage you'll die! And don't come back to Arles, ever!'

'Eh? What? What's this? What are you trying to – ?'

'You go, right now. Go, go, go. This is my asylum. I mean, *my* treatment. My brother paid for it, as he did "The Yellow House". He did it for me, you odious creep, you were there on sufferance. Just as you're here, the unwanted guest! What were you doing, anyhow, cluttering up the Provençale countryside? The artists' colony was mine, not yours, I should have thrown you out! I mean, you *are* out – the door is barred to you!'

'To you, too, Vincent, remember? And who gives a rat's arse? Wouldn't see me dead there.' A delayed reaction. 'Artists' colony? Artists' colony? Did I see any artists? Did I see any? Only when I looked in the mirror.'

'Right. That's it. That's it. Off! Off you go! Go on, get out of here, this minute. Sail on the next tide! Off to Tahiti, anywhere but here, and never come back! May you spend the whole voyage with chronic seasickness or dysentery. Preferably both. Then rot down there, in some deep malarial swamp. Or get eaten by an octopus.'

'Octopuses don't eat people. They squirt ink.'

'Just like your paintings – a sea of murky squirts!'

'Murky squirts? But – but – what the fuck – ?'

'And to think I called you friend. You – you swarthy Creole! Peruvian halfbreed!'

'Bah. Dutchman! Lunatic!'

'Baboon-buttocks! Addlepate!'

'Nitwit! Flagellant!'

'Haemorrhoid! *Coquin*! Parson's nose!'

'Eh, what? Er – pig shit!'

'Oaf!'

'Penis breath!'

'Sympathist!'

'Synthetist. The word's "synthetist". Is that an insult? I'm proud of it, even if I've moved on. But what about you? *Impasto* merchant, palette knife scraper! Splodger and bodger! Fit only for plastering a ceiling!'

'Don't call me that, don't – I – I –'

'And you still stink, just as at Arles.' Paul gestured with his thumb. 'Don't they have washrooms in this place? You ought to be fumigated. Even when tucking into the stinkiest cheese, I'd still be able to smell you!'

'What about you, Paul, you're ridiculous. You *look* ridiculous. Talk about stink! With that hat and silly broad stripes, they'd mistake you for a skunk!'

'Better a skunk than a crackpot no-hope composer, who looks like a carrot with a hedgehog haircut! Did I say "composer"? Bah. You can't compose for crap, you can't play and you can't fucking sing.'

'Yes I can, yes I can!'

'No you can't. You can't do fucking any of it. None of it, full stop. Music? You're a bust. I'm not sure you can even paint. Vincent Van Gogh, quadruple threat, the enemy of Art as we know it!'

Vincent glared at Paul with venom. His eyes blazed, his body tensed, he raised his fists. 'All right, all right, Paul. *C'est fait. Fini!* It's what you've been waiting for. Come on, then. Come on!'

Before Paul had time to react, Vincent had hurled himself forward, pushing him, pummelling, then punching him in the eye. Paul staggered and pitched, trying to ward him off with his walking cane, as Vincent kicked him in the stomach with his heavy boot. This was followed by a crunching of toes and a bloody nose. The cane flew off into the bushes, as Vincent lunged at his stunned friend's throat. Grabbing hold, he began to squeeze.

Paul retched, choked and trembled, powerless to defend himself. As quite a strong man, relatively fit, he could have taken Vincent apart. But the element of surprise had been Vincent's ally, not to mention his powerhouse fury. Paul felt himself losing consciousness. But, just in time, Vincent relaxed his grip. Paul stumbled back, clutching at his throat.

'*Merde, alors! L'hooligan!* Bloody hell, Vincent –' Paul gasped and swayed ' – you've fucking killed me!'

At this point, the attendants, urging their patients forward, came bustling up from the far end, drawn to the ruckus more by curiosity than concern.

Drawing nearer, identifying the reason, the little group halted and hung back. The patients, who'd been rendered into passive zombies by their sedation and electric shock treatments, just stared at Paul and Vincent, without undue concern. The attendants, meanwhile, viewed the scrap with alarm, wondering what to do next.

Bloodily, the fight continued, as Paul, breaking free, got

in the odd blow on Vincent's chest. But his pain and injuries made any chance of victory remote. Help, though, was at hand. Also alerted to the conflict, four burly male nurses emerged from the building. They lumbered through the long grass, to break up the fracas. Grasping Paul and Vincent with strong hands, they managed to prise them apart. Struggling, still screaming abuse, Vincent let go of Paul and now gave battle to his captors. Then, protesting loudly, he was finally restrained, forced into a strait jacket and carted off.

Just as they reached the tall side doorway, Vincent jerked his head round to screech out one last insult. Over by the low wall, Paul was too far gone to hear him. Besides, he was fighting for breath, checking for broken bones, feeling dazed and sore.

But with a brief show of strength, ignoring his pain while still numb with shock, he straightened sufficiently to gaze after Vincent with tear-filled eyes. The doors clanged shut and Paul, in turning, began to lurch backwards. Catching himself, he scrabbled on his knees to retrieve Vincent's painting.

Clutching it to his chest, he succeeded in rising again, then tried to reach a decision. Whether, loyally, to see how his friend made out, maybe attempt a reconciliation, continue with the visits, then get him settled in with this doctor chap? Or else, to finalise his present plans and embark for Tahiti. A dilemma, certainly – which step should he choose? But History, as we know, has recorded the latter.

The effect of all this mental, as well as physical, effort was too much for Paul. He staggered again, his head swam, he dropped the painting. Then he clutched at his stomach, afflicted now with excruciating pain. He still felt choked from the near strangulation, the blood from his nose had stained his shirt and jacket, his toes and eye hurt like hell.

The attendants, to this moment as weirdly pacific, it had seemed, as their wretched charges, now sprang into action. They hastened the last few steps forward, as Paul, still swaying, with his good eye half open, tried to focus on the dizzying landscape. But he reeled and fell, ending in a crumpled heap on an iris bed. It was some minutes before his helpers had got him inside. By which time he was in need of urgent medical attention.

III

AUVERS

Chez Gachet

ONE

Dr Paul-Ferdinand Gachet was a tall, thinnish man of sixty-two. He had blue eyes, a bony face and flaming red hair, just like Vincent's, with a full moustache and small *imperial* in the centre of his chin. His features were ruddy, his hands somewhat paler, being those of a man who delivers babies. A glum mouth and drooping eyelids gave him a melancholic, haunted expression, which to some may have looked like a grimace. Despite this, he was courteous and concerned, and he at all times held himself with dignity.

Having just finished his evening surgery, he placed his instruments in the sterilising tray, washed his hands, dried them carefully and passed into the salon.

He now noted with satisfaction the tidiness of it all, the flowers in their vases, the shining brasses and stuffed birds, their glass cases dust-free and reflecting the light. There was even a pair of live canaries in an ornamental cage, warbling along to the strains of a *serinette*.

There was, indeed, a great deal of light in the room, which was just what his friend Vincent liked, as well as a pianoforte in the corner, which he liked even more. Dr

Gachet wished he could get rid of it, but that was something else. He turned, stopped and listened. Somewhere in the near distance, not quite drowning out the birds, he could now hear a somewhat tentative version of *Plaisir d'amour*, plinking out scratchily on the family's new cylinder phonograph – the maid must be playing with it.

Smiling, not as sadly as he looked, he eased himself into his favourite armchair, to skim the Paris journals. Before settling properly, he glanced, with even greater delight, at the pictures on the walls, covering almost every surface. Like the ones which filled the whole house, they were by famous painters, near-famous painters and those not so famous at all, jostling for attention with some paintings of his own. Those by Vincent, Cézanne, Monet and Pissarro were the most prominent. The contrast between the work of both an undiscovered genius and the three older artists, with that of a competent country amateur like himself, could not have been more marked.

He had read only a few lines of *Le Journal*, when he heard footsteps on the garden path. His heart surging with anticipation, Dr Gachet moved to *les portes-fenêtres* and threw them open. There was his daughter Marguerite, as pretty as the day was long, in a shimmering white dress and lemon-yellow hat, with an empty basket and a bright shine to her face. He kissed her on the forehead and ushered her inside.

Marguerite placed the basket on the table by the window and removed her gloves. Smoothing her skirt, dabbing at her face with a small lace handkerchief, she sat in the chair opposite her father and dazzled him with her most winning smile.

Dr Gachet beamed back. '*Alors, ma petite*, how was

your errand of mercy. Was *Madame* Le Pacquet pleased with the fruit?'

'*Oui*, Papa, and the magazines. Not that she'll have time to read them. To look at the illustrations, I mean, since she can't read. But she's worn out, poor thing. If only it were possible for these unfortunates not to keep having children, but that's God's purpose, I suppose?'

'There are ways to prevent it, as you know, but we won't go into that. I'd have the Church come down on me like the Spanish Inquisition, saying I deserve to be flogged! They'd call my views ungodly and say nature must take its course. I wish I believed more in that nonsense, but I don't. And if I *could* help "these unfortunates", as you call them, then naturally I would.'

'I know it, Papa. You're a good man, in spite of being a heathen.'

Marguerite caught her father's reaction. He frowned, but could see by the mischievous twinkle in her eye that she was teasing. It was a continuing pleasantry between them: his lack of faith, her making jokes about it.

'Anyhow, *ma petite*, that's enough of that. Surgery's over, I could have done with your help as usual, but now, let's think about supper.'

'Sorry, Papa, but you do understand? *Madame* Le Paquet having taken to her bed and those youngsters of hers getting up to their mischief, it was impossible. I would have been here for you earlier, if I could.'

'I know, you're a true doctor's daughter. But I do wish these people had ways to repay you. Not with money, perhaps, but a recommendation for sainthood!'

'Now, you're making fun of *me*, but I don't mind. Oh, by the way, how's *Monsieur* Vincent – I mean, Vincent, today? Did he come to have his dressing changed? Will his ear ever grow back?'

'It's not the complete ear, *ma petite*, just a portion. The lobe, mostly, and a bit at the side. I examined him, you remember, when he first came here, checking *all* his imperfections! I mentioned, too, that the wound might not be as bad as all that, but an infection had set in at the asylum – inevitable, I imagine, those places are grim, the treatment minimal. Still, he can hear perfectly well, when the pad's not on.'

'D'you have any idea where the rest of his ear is? Has he still got it? Has Vincent yet told you?'

'He has, but I wasn't going to say.' Dr Gachet turned away embarrassed. 'I hesitate to do so now, but ... ah well.' He turned back. 'You're old enough to know the truth, even though you may think less of Vincent as a result.'

'What is it, Papa? What happened? The ear, I mean?'

'Well, not to go into detail, but our poor friend decided, for reasons best known to himself, to wrap it in newspaper and give it ... to a prostitute.'

'*C'est vrai*? Oh no. That's terrible.'

'It is, rather. Vincent, I'd say, seems rather vague about the incident, whilst reports are widely divergent. But he claims he didn't actually hand it to her in person. He sent someone, *Monsieur* Gauguin, maybe, or another friend, to *la maison de tolérance* to seek the woman out – a person Vincent had visited in the past – with an instruction to "keep this object carefully." At first sight of it, the wretched girl fainted.'

Marguerite shuddered. 'I'm not surprised.'

'Where the ear is now, I rather dread to think.'

'Could be anywhere, then. I doubt that ... the woman

kept it? I mean, I wouldn't, if 'twere me. Seems an odd sort of present, a bit … grisly.' Marguerite shuddered again, she gazed at her father. 'But Vincent can hear well enough, you said, without the bandage?'

'Just as you or I.'

'Oh, dear.'

'How so? That's good, isn't it?'

'*Oui*, I mean, *non*. I'm referring to Vincent's music. I thought it was the injury, something missing in his apparatus that made him sing and play so badly. But this means he *can* hear all right? Like a man with normal senses? Except for his being tone deaf, without musical talent, since birth?'

'That's about it, afraid so.' Dr Gachet smiled again, sadly. 'No excuse, then, is there? Music is not where his future lies. Especially after that sorry trip to Paris, to launch himself on the public. A disaster, his friends say, though Vincent denies it and he does have his supporters. But he sets such store by these odd sounds of his, convinced he'll somehow succeed. Poor man, a total delusion.'

'We all have delusions, Papa. Mine *hurts*.'

'What? What's that?' Dr Gachet rose, then got distracted. Absently, he patted Marguerite's cheek. 'I know it does.' He moved to the door. 'Supper should be ready, surely?'

'It should, if that wonderful smell is anything to go by.' Marguerite rose, too. She inhaled the aroma and glanced towards the kitchen. 'I remember now, it's *ballotine* of partridge, with truffles and Armagnac sauce. With a Cherry Clafoutis to follow.'

'*Formidable*.' Dr Gachet wrinkled his brow. 'But can we afford it?'

'Not really, but it's amazing what *Madame* Chevalier

can do with just a few ingredients. The best of cooks, in the kitchen she's a genius.'

'She must be.'

'Anyhow, I'll go see.' As Marguerite passed the windows, she gave a little start. Then looked out and frowned. 'Oh.'

'What is it? What's the matter?'

'There's that poor man from the hill farm, Papa. *Monsieur* Tautain, the one with the club foot. Hanging about at the gate, I spoke to him earlier. He's wondering when you can do something for him?'

Dr Gachet sighed, he shook his head. 'You know I don't do procedural work? Not for years. It's something I – that is, I believe in alternative methods.'

'I know, but he is most insistent. Was the manipulation no good? I know you tried hard.'

'Too hard. He howled with pain, unhappy fellow, my heart went out to him. I thought of trying electric shocks, as I do with my venereal patients, combined with some simple pulling and stretching. Reducing the size of the foot, separating the clamped toes with … don't know what. But cutting, surgery, even under chloroform, I won't do it. Too risky. Haven't cut a patient since – don't remember when. Tell him to go away. I'm sorry, can't help him.'

Dr Gachet turned from the window. Marguerite drew nearer. 'A bit harsh, Papa? He relies on you so much, as do all your patients. He'll be most disappointed. He's so set his heart on being a clog dancer.' A short pause. 'Couldn't you recommend him, maybe, to a specialist? You know so many people in Paris, there must be someone?'

'I would if I could, but it costs money. Those wing collar and hair lacquer types, with their silky bedside manners, are not like me. They would not accept a few eggs from the farm, a fat capon or two, as this fellow brings me. No, if he wishes to be a dancer, tell him to be a big-footed one!'

Marguerite stared at her father appalled, hoping he was not going to laugh. He wasn't. Her face a picture of relief, she turned away to continue to the kitchen, then hesitated. She looked at him again.

'Papa?'

Dr Gachet returned the look. But, feeling guilty, he averted his gaze again to the pictures on the wall. A few moments passed, he turned back to Marguerite. 'Forgive me, *ma petite*. Just tell him I'm sorry? Too busy today. I'll get the books down, give it more thought.'

Marguerite smiled. '*Merci*, Papa.' Then paused again. 'Oh, where is Vincent now? Not coming this evening?'

'Later, perhaps. Off in the fields, I have no doubt, with his trusty easel. A canvas a day, at his present rate. Remarkable! Or beating out that same dreadful music, if that's what one calls it, over *chez Ravoux* – how do they stand it? It's putting off the other patrons, *Monsieur* Ravoux says. No one stays at an *auberge du pays* with that kind of clatter pouring forth.'

'But you do like Vincent? Truly?'

'You know I do. More and more each day, despite his awkward ways. And I know you like him, too. Your face lights up whenever you see him.'

'Yours, too, Papa. He's now our closest friend – isn't he?'

'He is, *chérie*. And long may he be so. It's a great comfort to think, after that business with his ear and being boycotted by the neighbours, the awful time he had finally at Saint-Rémy – his terror of the doctors, the other patients and even the local nuns! – that he seems fitter, happier than he's ever been. At least, according to his brother Theo, who should know.'

'I like *Monsieur* Theo, Papa. He's very good to Vincent.'

'He is, though it's we who now have the worry of him. His nightmares have largely ceased and, mostly, he's of an even temper. On the other hand, our friend still goes at it like the very Devil, painting or composing in many moods from serenity to hysteria. At other times, he seems … almost normal.'

'He does, as much as anyone.'

'And did I tell you, *Monsieur* Theo gave me his heartiest congratulations last time he was here? The day he and that pretty young wife of his brought the toddler? In fact, she agreed with her husband, told me she hadn't seen Vincent looking better. Let's hope he stays that way.'

'Papa. I think we –'

'The Ravoux have a lot to do with it, of course, all those regular meals, making sure Vincent gets to bed on time.'

'And he's stopped drinking?'

'He has, that's your doing. I couldn't persuade him, nor, they say, could *Monsieur* Gauguin. He was a lost cause, *Monsieur* Theo said. *Monsieur* Gauguin, meanwhile, now fully recovered from Vincent's vicious attack, will, I gather, be sailing round those Southern islands, as for some time he's been promising. Well, that's what I hear. He's forgiven Vincent or, at least, he writes. They were good friends once, most certainly.'

'As *we* are, Papa, as I said. Vincent likes coming here, an ideal refuge, and you've done a lot for him.'

'I've done my best. But your sweet smile did the trick. That delicious singing of yours, which he so appreciates, the way he listens to your comments on his work. Much more than he does mine. You're a wonderful influence.'

'You, too, I can't say it enough. You're very patient, very positive. Dropping everything when he comes. Nothing is too much for you, like sitting for the portraits, those sketches of his.'

'He paints you, as well.'

'But I have more time, and he makes me laugh. Too much, sometimes, he complains that I can't keep my pose! But you, Papa, it's you who's the saint. All those hours, sitting bolt upright, listening to his nonsense, when you should be doing your rounds. And Vincent, on his bad days, so intolerant, such a short fuse. How d'you put up with all that shouting? Those arguments?'

'We only argue about art. It's something we have in common and get very heated about. But our views are different and it's … inevitable. We respect each other, though, and Vincent's most contrite – for the less than kind things, sometimes, he says about my paintings! As for the music, I try not to discuss it. It would be unthinkable – I can't dissemble.'

'Nor should you, Papa. But what if he asks you outright – for an opinion?'

'Then I *should* dissemble. Vincent has a fragile temperament, he could easily regress. You know what it was like, you and your *chère Maman*, when your poor Papa had his … own troubles.'

'I do, and I'm glad you're better.'

'So am I. Less cranky and short tempered, my mind is now clear. Touching wood.' Dr Gachet now did so, upon the *escritoire* by the windows. 'I am myself again.'

There was an awkward pause. Marguerite frowned, not totally convinced. But she then brightened, for her father's sake, and changed the subject.

'But Vincent and his music? You're right, Papa, the awfulness of it echoes in one's brain! A pity you or someone couldn't order him to stop?'

'If only one could. But look what happened to *Monsieur* Gauguin. Just for telling the truth! He was stuck in some awful Provençale hospital for three weeks afterwards, then kept prisoner because he couldn't pay the bill. Another needless expense for Vincent's hard-pressed brother.'

'Poor *Monsieur* Theo. We really must –'

'No, no, there's only one person could conceivably urge Vincent away from this impossible course and return him to the path of True Art. And that's you, if you would – could see your way to do it? But I know I shouldn't ask you to risk his anger in this fashion?'

'And I wouldn't let you, you mustn't worry. I'd do it oh so tactfully, offering subtle suggestions that, since he's a great painter, anything else he does, no matter with how much skill, can only detract from his real talent. I would never be the one to undermine Vincent's slender *amour propre* by telling him straight out that he can't compose for toffee, nor even sing, that he's making a huge mistake.'

'I hoped you'd say that. Again, you're a true daughter. Worthy of being the daughter I've always dreamed of. *Maman* would've been proud.'

'I *am* the daughter you've always dreamed of. And *Maman*, I'd say, *is* proud – present tense. She's still alive, Papa, even if you sometimes forget? Just gone on a visit to *Tante* Francia in Lille.'

'Has she? So she has.'

'Along with my brother Paul. Your son, remember? That young chap you call "Coco", always clowning and joking.'

'Coco – ah? I *had* forgotten, a funny fellow. I thought the house was quiet. But for how long? No, doesn't matter. It'll all come out in the wash.'

'Papa?'

'Sorry, thinking out loud. I didn't mean, "wash", as in

laundry, I meant, *à beau temps*. But *mon Dieu*! Your aunt isn't ill, is she?'

'Not that I know of. Well, just a little. You know *Tante Francia*!'

'I do. Hypochondria is her middle name. But only "just a little"? Ah. Then *Maman* will be home … *toute à l'heure*. Or even *toute de suite*. That's right, won't she? Or, maybe, somewhat later, at least home 'ere long? That's it, isn't it? No, what *do* I mean?'

'No idea, You're waffling again.'

'Am I? So I am. Ah, well, sign of age, too much on my plate. Now, where was I? *Eh oui*, Vincent should concentrate on his painting. There's genius there, no doubt about it. As for the other thing – poof! A case of false pride and blind ambition, compromising his talent in a big way! And all these flatterers he meets, anticipating the drinks he buys them with his brother's money, wheedling and egging him on. In fact I –'

Dr Gachet broke off, alerted by a footfall outside, which he'd heard through the half-opened windows. It was accompanied by some tuneless humming. Nervously, the Doctor and his daughter busied themselves, trying to conceal the fact they'd been discussing Vincent.

TWO

Vincent now entered, jauntily enough, through those very same windows from the garden. He carried his paints and easel, looking calmer than when we last saw him, though with his bad ear still concealed by a cotton wool pad. It was affixed to the wound with medical tape.

'*Bon soir, mes amis*! Been a beautiful day. Not a cloud in the sky, *hélàs*. Difficult to get a perspective when it's all so clear! What's this? What's this?' Looking at his friends, he noted the air of forced activity, the sheepish expressions on their faces. 'Been talking about me again?'

'N – no. Not at all, *cher ami*. It – it –'

Marguerite giggled. 'We have, Vincent, very much so.' She nudged her father in the ribs. 'Best come clean, eh, Papa? Why lie about it?'

Dr Gachet threw a guilty glance at Vincent, then back to his daughter. 'You ought to say "fib", *ma petite*. Not "lie". *Maman* wouldn't –'

'*Maman*'s not here, I just told you. Don't be naughty now.' Marguerite turned to Vincent. 'We were saying nice things about you, mostly. Weren't we, Papa? With just a *soupçon* of vinegar to take away the sickly bits.'

Vincent nodded amiably. 'Ha. Ha. You two!' He smiled at Marguerite, depositing his things on the piano. 'Caught you at it then, have I? Always plotting something, making plans – for my doubtful benefit? I thought my ears were burning, what's left of them!'

'Oh dear, you poor thing! Is it hurting today, a touch of fever? Ear not doing so well?' Marguerite stepped towards him. 'Can I get you something? Some quinine? Another poultice?' She looked almost accusingly at her father, who shook his head.

Vincent drew close. 'No, it's fine, bit of a twinge, that's all. Headache, not a stabbing pain. Too much sun, maybe, despite this northern chill. Your Papa will look at it again later. Won't you?'

'Surely, *cher ami*. Any time but now.' Dr Gachet inspected his pocket watch, checking it with the ormolu on the mantel. 'If you'll excuse me, I'm due at a patient, I've just remembered. Bad case of dropsy, I shan't be long.' There was another awkward pause. 'So, I'll leave you two young people to it. To catch up on the day's doings, like Vincent's latest canvas – then maybe he'll play you his last night's composition?' There was an ironic raise of the eyebrows for Marguerite alone. '*Au 'voir, mon ami.*' Quickly, he shook Vincent's hand, then stepped towards the surgery to fetch his bag.

Marguerite forestalled him. 'But what about supper? We were just going in? You haven't –'

'No, no, it's all right. I'm sure they'll offer me a coffee and … a little something. You can leave a plate on the side for me, tell *Madame* Chevalier I'll have it cold. Oh no, the *ballotine is* cold.'

Dr Gachet was almost at the door when, again, Marguerite stopped him. 'Shall I get it for you, Papa, a coffee before you go? There was some already made.'

'Coffee? No. It's doubtless lukewarm or they've made it too strong. *Maman* does it just right. Where is she, haven't seen her for ages? But bring one for Vincent, see that he's entertained.' Dr Gachet grinned at Vincent. 'And do stand up to all his silliness – keep him here till I return.'

By this time he'd reached the other room and collected his bag. Coming back in, he now had on the shabby white *kepi* and officer's cape, which he'd continued wearing since serving in the Medical Corps at the Siege of Paris. He saluted – old habits die hard! – looked askance, grinned again and briefly turned away.

'Bit of a ride, but should only be an hour. Do hope that other wretched fellow has left?' He peered through the windows, glanced back at Vincent, then turned away again, passing on through. 'I hate being waylaid by poor beggars I'm unable to help. It's most distressing.'

Marguerite watched him go. She spoke softly, almost to herself. 'I forgot all about him, poor man – to give him

Papa's message. I hope he won't be cross. Should I do it now? No, he must have gone, already. I'll speak to him tomorrow.' Back from her reverie, she gave her attention to Vincent. 'D'you think you would like a coffee?'

'Don't bother about me, *ma chère jeune fille*. I try not to drink coffee at this time, not any more – I mean, not before a meal. It blanks me out for the evening, makes my head worse. Later, maybe, I'd welcome one.'

'Poor you.' Marguerite squeezed past him, about to leave the room. 'I really must get you something.'

'Not medicine, I hope?'

Marguerite turned back. 'Not without Papa. But something sweet, something hot? A lime flower tea and a *madeleine* cake? Very nice for dipping in.'

Vincent smiled. 'Nor that, neither. No tea, nor cake. You spoil me, better not.'

'No, really, do. They're very good, *les petites madeleines*. Fresh today from the corner shop?'

'I don't think so. I don't like tea and the combination of that and a *madeleine*, 'specially the dipping and tasting, may bring back memories I've no wish to recall. I'm only interested in the future, if ever I have one. The past I'm trying to forget.'

'Poor Vincent, you mustn't be defeatist.' Marguerite paused, reacted, then looked at him and frowned. 'But remembering things … from a *madeleine*? How's that?'

'Don't know. It's something – I can't explain. As if I'd read it somewhere, but hadn't. But would read it, should I live that long, into another century. The idea of recapturing memories, with just a simple key. Do I make sense?'

Marguerite laughed. 'Not much. You puzzle me sometimes.' She grew nervous, fiddling with her hair. 'So, no tea, Vincent. Nor cake. What, then?'

'*Rien, ma jolie*, just the sweetness of your smile.'

'What?' Marguerite again reacted. 'But that's ... uncanny. Papa said as much, a few minutes ago. You must have overheard us, or Papa's a prophet?'

Vincent chuckled. 'And *I* said something like that to Paul – Gauguin, before our split. About prophecy, the power of anticipation. *Oui*, it's uncanny. Life passes, someone is clairvoyant, you act as expected – it's one big circle! Or, maybe, a simple coincidence. What do *you* think?'

'I think ... I'd like – let's talk of other things?' Marguerite laughed once more, she began rearranging the flowers. Suddenly her face grew serious. 'That *Monsieur* Gauguin, you mentioned him, he hasn't come to see you?'

'No, nor likely to, I think. The break was pretty final.'

'But you were good friends, Vincent? It's essential to have friends.'

'It is, we'd grown quite close, Art and encouragement, a mutual need. I needed him, he needed me, a symbiotic relationship.'

'I don't know that word?'

'Don't trouble yourself, it doesn't matter. No more talk of Gauguin. Yesterday's dead, take care of today. It's a cancelled chapter in my life.'

'That's terrible.' Marguerite frowned again. 'A missing chapter, it must be hard?' She turned away, finishing her flowers, then brightened. 'So, what have you painted today, out in that beautiful sunshine? Show me.'

Vincent offered a shy smile. 'I'd rather ... play for you.'

'I'd rather you didn't – I mean, didn't right now. But later, perhaps – you *are* staying for supper?' She waited, as Vincent hesitated. Briefly, she touched his arm. 'You really must, it's a *ballotine* of partridge, our cold day. We've plenty to go round.'

'I'm tempted, delicious. It smells quite wonderful.'

'We can run a note round to the Ravoux, no problem at all, to say you won't be back? Papa would be delighted, he said to keep you here, he's got so much to talk to you about. His painting, his new experiments, and I'd be … much amused. As *Maman* would, too, were she here. Then, with good food inside you, some fine wine – no, you don't drink now, do you? – you can play and sing to your heart's content.'

Unthinking, Marguerite pulled a face but, catching a look from Vincent, she twisted it back into a smile. 'It'd thrill us to the very rafters, it really would, and our applause, our cries of '*Hourra*! Bravo!' – Papa's and mine – shall accompany you, like a heavenly echo, all the way home!'

'It sounds most inviting. I wonder if I should? I'd hate to intrude.'

'You know you should, you're always welcome. Just the hour when Papa likes company. These evenings with you mean a lot to him.'

'And … to you?'

Marguerite blushed. 'Me – too. *Oui* –' a small voice ' – me, too.'

Vincent, encouraged, moved nearer. Marguerite dodged past him, without his being quite aware of her stalling. He watched her during the silence which followed, she at first glancing down, then glancing up. She then looked away, but, finally, clearly more relaxed again, she turned to face Vincent, locking her eyes with his. She offered a small smile, parting her lips, as if she were going to speak. Vincent, tongue-tied, unable to do so himself, thought maybe she was about to make a declaration, to give him some sign of intent?

Marguerite failed to do so and glanced away again, embarrassed. Then looked towards *les portes-fenêtres*, listening out for who knew what? Vincent continued to gaze at her, yearning, but without hope, in his mind imagining the words he'd been longing to hear.

Regaining her composure, Marguerite stepped to the piano. She switched one of the canvases over, placing it on the polished surface, right side up. Carefully, she lifted it again and held it to the light. There was a brief look of puzzlement, even distaste. Again, she covered, quickly.

'But this is – I mean, what is this? *Where* is this? The valley?'

Vincent peered over her shoulder, slipping his arms around her, touching her, trying to get the canvas back. 'The wheat fields – it's the last weeks before the harvest. You see, I'm looking ahead! But ah, how I love to paint them! Coming to Auvers, it's what I'd most looked forward to.'

'It – it's – were there no wheat fields … at Arles? Provence?'

'*Bien sûr*, quite … big ones. Which I painted, in a magical light. Also cypresses, drawbridges and haystacks.'

'It must have been marvellous?'

'It was, for a month or two. A land of blue tones and gay colours, if levelled out somewhat by that hot southern glare. But marvellous … truly. I mean, for years I'd resisted landscapes, I'd doubts about their value. At least, when done simply for their own sake. And I occupied myself like Rembrandt almost exclusively with "Man". Faces, portraits, people in their daily lives. Only gradually did I see that a landscape can be made to mirror the artist's soul. Certainly in Arles.'

'I'm sure that's true. And Auvers?'

'Here, too. Though mostly wheat fields – an immense plain against the hills, as boundless as the sea!'

'Most poetic, Vincent.' Marguerite smiled and broke away, still clutching the canvas. Then she frowned once more, propping it against a vase. She pointed to the picture, still ready to keep it from him, should Vincent try snatching it back. 'And that's … the sky?'

'Meant to be.'

'Looks overcast, yet today the sun is bright?'

'Seemed dark to me, the way I saw it. Tenebrous, forbidding.'

'But – how sad. On such a nice day, too. Couldn't you have tried to make it more cheerful?'

'Hardly, with the mood I was in. I don't need to go out of my way to express sadness, the extremes of being lonely. This special torture a painter has to bear.'

'But I thought we – ?'

'No, not even here, *ma chère* Marguerite, away from the South, despite all the kindness you've shown me. A familiar melancholy holds me in its grip. My mind wanders wildly and I seem doomed to an unending series of recurrences. As I told my brother once, "In my own work I am risking my life, and half my reason has been lost in it."'

'Oh dear. *Poor* Vincent. I really did think you were better, happier? I hope you're not coming down with something, really depressed again. P'raps I should tell Papa?'

Yes, Vincent *was* depressed, but he now carried on false brightly for Marguerite's sake. 'No, no, I'm all right, really. Truly, I am. Forget what I said – don't disturb your father. He has more deserving cases than mine.'

'I'll mention it later, just in case.' Marguerite moved away a fraction, the canvas now under her arm. 'He's bound to give you a pick-me-up, you won't let me forget?'

Vincent's smile, coming back at her, was weak. 'I won't. I'll be the perfect patient. Every tic, each little symptom, faithfully recorded. And you, *ma jolie* … you'll be there, in the surgery?'

'Of course. If you like. As you know, Papa says I make a good nurse.'

'You do. I recall the time that – ah.' Vincent broke off, curious. He glanced towards the garden. 'But this other chap – the one you were talking about? He'd been hovering in the lane? Who was he? Is he? A … mental case? What's his problem?'

Marguerite gazed at Vincent puzzled. Suddenly, she twigged. 'Oh, *that* fellow. He's – no, mustn't tell you. It's doctor-patient confidentiality.' She frowned yet again, putting the painting back on the piano. 'Well, all right, then, since it's *you*. Unfortunate character, that, from one of the farms. A club foot, since birth, the blight of his life. Wants Papa to operate. Papa says "No". You know what he feels about surgery? Ever since he was a student.'

'How does he manage to – ?'

'Papa thinks there may be another way, or hopes to find one. But I know there's not. Not for … a club foot. What would *you* say, Vincent?'

'I'd say not either. Charles Bovary found that to his cost!'

'Charles – ? *Eh, oui*, Flaubert! *Bien*. Quite a *scandale*, wasn't there?'

'There was. The book that shocked a nation! They put Flaubert on trial, his work condemned as immoral. They wanted to ban it.'

'*Oui*, it even shocks *me* – they should have done. I don't know if I could live like that. *Madame* Bovary, so reckless, all those lies, she was a really bad woman.'

'Not too much, in fact, one has to feel for her. What

she had was a hunger – a hunger for an alternative to a dull husband, a commonplace existence, and a refusal to accept a life of unhappiness. That was all before you were born, things are different now, today's readers understand her better. But clever of you to know such tales, these old, old stories, *une belle petite comme toi*!'

'Don't talk down to me, Vincent, I don't like it. *Je n' suis pas une oie blanche*, a silly goose, I know more than you think. Papa saw to it that I had a good education – not too sentimental, full of facts. I enjoy reading and playing the piano, when I'm in the mood. Even if *chère Maman* would prefer to see me sewing or baking bread!'

'*Je m'excuse*, I take it back. It's because you know things, have interesting things to say, that you can talk to me, man to man, I mean, girl to girl –'

'Woman to man?'

'*Oui*, or vice versa!' Vincent looked nervous. 'That I – that – because of it – enjoy coming here so much. As much to spend time with your Papa, as with –'

'Tell me more about the painting?' Marguerite stepped back to the piano and once more propped the canvas. 'I mean, what are these? These red and green lines, snaking in and out among the yellow? Just here?'

'They're the paths leading into the wheat fields.'

'Mmm, so they are, but lost amongst the grain, like a wilderness, they just disappear?' Marguerite looked closely, she shook her head. '*Mais oui*, they do.' She glanced at Vincent. 'And the strange black things? Those squiggles in the sky?'

Vincent sighed, he was getting tired of this. 'Not squiggles. Crows.'

'But why? Why are they there? They're awful, they disturb me somehow.'

'Me, too. They're symbols of violence and death. The whole painting is the plain as I see it, but can't you see it, too? "The Plain of the Crows", stretching out beneath an endless Heaven. The colours sometimes rapturous, tumultuous even, but also threatening, a picture of absolute emptiness and chaos: a hectic sky clutched by the impending storm, with a maddened image of paths that lead nowhere.'

'Madness? Nowhere? How horrid. The whole painting? I hesitate to say it, Vincent, but –'

'And it is unfinished. I've tried to capture them, those marauding crows, but it's difficult. Especially with the palette knife – my silly style, *impasto*. New paint on wet paint, laying the pigment on thickly, as if it were sculpture. And ... um, well, Paul wasn't too keen on it, made fun of me a little. Though he admired my talent, such as it is. I'm thinking of giving it up, I *am* giving it up, painting, sketching, all of it.'

'But, Vincent, surely – ?'

'Anyhow, don't worry, *ma jolie* –' Vincent forced a smile ' – I shall finish your father's portrait, at least. Maybe in a day or two, pipe, hat, warts and all.'

'Papa will like that. Except for the warts!'

'But however it turns out, it may well be my last. Since I think, on reflection, by the end of the summer here, I shall switch exclusively to music. It's increasingly difficult to get a picture right. More and more, when I can't concentrate, when the sun is shining, yet I've dark thoughts in my mind.'

'No, Vincent, no, you mustn't. It's –'

'With composing, I can work indoors – as the muse hits me. No more waiting for a cloud formation or the wind in a certain direction, to get the wheat stalks standing right.

And those damn birds – sorry about "damn" – but same trouble as at Arles. There it was mostly gulls, but a few crows, too, and they just would keep menacing me.'

'Just like the picture?'

'Absolutely. All birds do that, it's something I have to live with. It slows me down, lowers my spirits. Not a bad thing, really – Paul said I work in a frenzy. But I seem to have lost my impetus, that white-hot rate of creativity driving me on, which I had when I got here.'

Marguerite was about to answer, or trying to think what to answer, when the dinner gong sounded down the passage. She sighed with relief – saved by the bell!

'Ah, supper.' Marguerite, too, forced a smile. 'Shall we go in?'

She took Vincent's arm. Together, somewhat shyly now in their close proximity, they proceeded to the dining room.

THREE

It was some time afterwards. The lamps had been lit, night was drawing in, Vincent and Marguerite were back in the salon. Dr Gachet, looking tired and defeated from his call, had settled in his armchair with a generous shot of Cognac. He felt it was needed, as he suffered through Vincent's impromptu recital.

It wasn't music as the good Doctor knew it. He hadn't much of an ear at the best of times, though could often recognise a catchy tune. Indeed, he was not above humming one on his daily rounds. But the incoherent babel of disconnected sounds, which Vincent was wresting from the keys, had no tune at all – it seemed unlikely to obtain one. At the same time, he kept up a grumbly harsh-sounding vocal refrain, which progressed through ear-splitting stages into a high-pitched whine:

The fields were green, the skies were blue,
Her cheeks were fresh as the morning dew.
I wandered there, by the river view,
To catch her face, well wouldn't you?
She smiled at me, but did she care?
When I looked again, she wasn't there.
But came a day that I tossed the hay,
With my feet all bare, and my shirt astray.
And she brought me wine, with some
      bread and cheese,
And a spark in her eye that was bound to please.
Then she murmured soft, in a warming way.
And I knew as we kissed, she'd not break away.
Oh, ooh la la! Oh, ooh la lay!
Since I knew in my heart, she was there to stay.
Oh, how I kissed her, ooh la lay!
For I knew in my heart she was there to stay.

Vincent continued, repeating the phrases, with a gleam in his eye and a bumping of 'chords'. Dr Gachet, resisting the temptation to clap his hands over his ears, fell to puzzling why this daft, outmoded lyric, with its limp banalities *au genre de la poésie pastorale*, should be further scuppered by such a heavy-handed accompaniment? Even the canaries, cheeping and skittering in their cage, were showing their evident distress! And why the servants were not screaming and running into the room, fearful of a new Revolution, was something he could not fathom. He glanced at Marguerite, who was standing by the curtains. She was staring at Vincent with a look of bemusement, or was it simply horror? She had heard him play before, several times, even heard him 'sing'. But this was worse, far worse.

Dr Gachet tried to catch Marguerite's eye, but she seemed rooted to the spot. Finally, the cruel punishment Vincent had been wreaking on the instrument ended on a thudding, nerve-jangling climax. He lifted his hands from the keys, wiped them on his trousers and gazed at his friends with an expression of enquiry.

Taken by surprise, Doctor and daughter both jumped into action. Dr Gachet leapt from his chair, as Marguerite stepped forward, her spirits and eardrums restored, spared at last from this terrible ordeal! If the applause at first seemed muted, the clapping and cries of approbation now rushed towards crescendo. To the unfortunate pair, only too conscious of their false enthusiasm, these sounds of approval were as strident, to their own ears, as the piece which had deafened them.

'*Très bien! Très bien! Magnifique! Bravo! Épatant*! It's totally brilliant, astonishing! Good show!'

They now exchanged glances, each waiting for the other to stop. Vincent rose also, preening and pressing down the piano lid. '*Merci, merci.*' He gave a mock bow. 'You loved it? *Bien*. I hoped – I knew you would. Ah, I'm ... truly encouraged.'

There was an awkward pause. Marguerite spoke first. 'Does it have a title – this little piece of yours?'

Vincent beamed, he bounded towards her. '*Chanson de l'été à Auvers: un hommage à Marguerite.*'

'For me? Me? A dedication?' Marguerite looked doubtful. '*Merci* ... Vincent, I'm flattered.' There was a beat. 'You really mean it? Me?'

'*Oui, mais oui.* You're my inspiration – *ma jeune fille*

inspiratrice!' Vincent turned to Dr Gachet. 'She is, isn't she?'

'If you say so, Vincent.' Dr Gachet sighed and reseated himself.

'I do. She is. Ah.' Vincent's face lit up. He moved back to the piano. 'Would you like to hear it again?'

Marguerite threw an anxious glance at her father. '*Oui*. I mean, we would. We would – but –'

'It's past Marguerite's bedtime.'

'Is it?' Marguerite frowned, then nodded to her father, another moment of relief! 'It is.'

Vincent gazed at her, deflated. He opened his mouth to speak but, with a small head shake, shut it again.

Dr Gachet looked firm. 'Off you go, *ma petite*.'

'*Oui*, excuse me,' Marguerite offered a fake yawn and a little stretch. '*Vraiment*, I *am* … a little tired. But you stay here, *cher, cher* Vincent, another pipe with Papa? A nice intense chat, I know you've been dying to?'

'Chats can never be intense,' said Dr Gachet, 'discussions, conversations, disputations can be intense. Chats are merely –'

'Now, now don't be naughty again, Papa. Or roguish. It ages you. And you won't get your goodnight kiss.'

Dr Gachet laughed, offering up his cheek. 'I'm sorry, truly. Here.'

'I forgive you, as always.' Marguerite moved to her father, leaned down, hands on his shoulders, and kissed him on the forehead. '*Bonne nuit, cher* Papa, sleep well.' She turned away. 'And you, too, Vincent, don't get lost on the way home!'

She hesitated again, then stepped towards him, brushing her lips on his cheek. Unseen by Dr Gachet, who was laying out the chess board, Vincent spread his hands towards her. Lightly, she skipped away. A giggle, she was by the door. Glancing back at her father, she took in the board and the chess pieces.

'Now, you two, don't stay up half the night. I'd stay, too, if I could, but I need my beauty sleep. I'll leave you children to your games! Sweet dreams, Vincent … Papa … when you have them!'

Smiling, one last time, Marguerite hesitated a second and was gone. Vincent gazed at the empty doorway with disappointment but, on a word from the Doctor, he seated himself on the small chair opposite. There was a low table between them, the chess set by this time laid out.

They had only just established the order of play, moving their pawns, murmuring in low voices, when they heard a heavy knocking at the front door. They looked at each other with surprise, listening out as the maid, still pottering somewhere downstairs, hurried to the hallway. She pulled back the bolts and opened up.

Dr Gachet rose again and stepped towards the passage. Vincent followed at a short distance, straining to hear what was said. None of his business, really, but it might be someone from *L'Auberge Ravoux*, wondering where he'd got to. He and Marguerite had failed to send that message, his hosts might be worried?

No, it was more likely a patient or some other emergency. Vincent was about to return to his chair, when he heard voices. Edging to the passage, he proceeded to eavesdrop.

'Apologies for the late hour, *Monsieur le Docteur*, but one did try at the Inn. The people there told me *Monsieur* Van Gogh might be here? Again, my apologies.'

'He is, certainly, my good fellow, right at this moment. Nothing serious, I hope? Who needs him?'

The second speaker was clearly Dr Gachet. The first? It could be anyone. There were some further words from the stranger.

'The good *Monsieur* being here, as you say, it would oblige me, I'd be grateful, *Monsieur le Docteur*, if you'd present me?'

Vincent, hearing these words, fearful the visitor might be a debt collector or some girl's irate father, flattened himself against the door of the salon. But the next exchange reassured him.

'*Monsieur* Van Gogh,' said Dr Gachet, 'is – he's not in any trouble? If he is, then –'

'One would surely hope not. But Special Delivery from Paris, express rider straight to the Post Office, we had to open up. Evidently important, we've brought it straight away.'

As Vincent appeared in the doorway, he saw a uniformed Messenger. The man was holding out a large yellow envelope, which someone, himself or the Doctor, was expected to sign for. Dr Gachet did so, taking the envelope from the relieved fellow's hands. Dr Gachet turned, registered Vincent, smiled and handed the package over. 'For you, Vincent. From Paris.'

'I know, I heard. *Merci, mon ami.*'

As Vincent retreated to the salon, Dr Gachet thanked the visitor, then murmured to the maid, a young woman evidently curious, instructing her to 'take this good fellow to the kitchen, give him something, some bread and cheese, a hot drink, maybe, to see him on his way.'

The maid and the man, who'd been making eyes at each other, retreated down the passage. Dr Gachet turned again. It was then he spotted Marguerite, who, disturbed by the commotion, had appeared at the foot of the stairs. She'd already donned her night clothes, now covered by a *peignoir*.

Dr Gachet raised an eyebrow at his daughter emerging thus, especially with a guest in the house. But, admitting to himself that times, indeed, were changing, he tactfully said nothing. Instead, he ushered Marguerite back into the salon, where Vincent, having found a paper knife, was frenziedly slitting the envelope. This task completed, he dived his hand in.

'What is it, *cher ami*? Who's it from?' asked Dr Gachet, as he and Marguerite waited.

Vincent, of course, received letters and parcels all the time from his family and friends. But nothing before, the Doctor told himself, had required delivery at this late hour. He still hoped it wasn't *bad* news.

By this time, Vincent was seated on the piano stool, revolving slightly back and forth, now reading the enclosure. His friends watched nervously, afraid to interrupt.

In turning the pages, Vincent's expression veered from puzzlement to doubt, through disbelief and various allied states, till his already pinkish, freckled face – that curse of being one of nature's redheads – finally suffused into a great ruddy glow. His eyes lit up, he clapped the letter to his chest and erupted from the stool.

'*Mon Dieu*! *Mon Dieu*! I do not believe it! *Mon cher docteur, ma jolie Marguerite*!' Vincent brandished the letter above his head, vigorously shaking it. He then jerked his arm down, to squint anxiously again at the words, as if fully expecting them to vanish.

'What is it? What is it?' cried father and daughter, together.

'It – it's –' Vincent thrust the letter towards them ' – here, read it, both of you. Tell me if it's true? *I* can't believe it – but is it … true?'

With amazement at their friend's exuberance, Dr Gachet grabbed the letter. Marguerite drew close, as her father held it up. Vincent reseated himself, looking expectant. But before his friends had time to focus, Vincent let out a whoop of jubilation. There was a fluttering of the hands, followed by a sudden jerk back on the stool. He bashed the piano in the small of his back but, so excited was he, he seemed not to feel it.

'It – it's just not *possible*! There's some chap here, in the letter, that is, who's heard about my music! You recall those few frustrating weeks I spent in Paris this Spring, after my first spell in Auvers, trying to earn my living as a *chanteur*? Singing my own songs in the cafés of Montmartre, accompanying myself, too? Well, whatever I told you, it didn't go down so well – those tin-eared twits! – but this fellow in the letter, a *Monsieur* Jean-Paul Dombasle, has heard all about me, he's been trying to track me down. And here – here it *is*!' Vincent snatched the letter back. 'I have to journey to Paris first thing in the morning, for an interview!'

He rose again and looked at his friends, grinning a broad grin, then turned to go. '*Merci, mes amis*, I'm grateful for everything, your friendship, the treatments, your warm encouragement, all the rest of it. And I'll see you again shortly, I know I will. But I must get back *chez Ravoux* this very minute – sorry about the chess! – and pack up my things. Get to the station as early as possible, book my ticket, first train in the morning, and go!'

Dr Gachet took a step forward. 'But, Vincent, your

painting, your – I mean, are you really sure about this?'

'Couldn't be more so. That whole thing about all art aspiring to the condition of music is very significant. Ask any artist what he'd like to do – write, paint, sculpt, act the classic rôles, they'd most of them say the same: "Go on stage and sing!" Well, here's my chance.'

Vincent moved away, he was almost out the door. Then, as Dr Gachet and Marguerite exchanged stupefied glances, he bounced back in.

'I say, *mon cher docteur*, I'm a bit short of – that is, I mean to say, Theo hasn't yet sent me my, um – I – er, I mean, you couldn't oblige me with – ?'

'Surely, Vincent, you know I could, you don't have to ask.' Dr Gachet moved to the *escritoire*, opened it and extracted a small wad of banknotes. 'Will these do?' He glanced at Marguerite. 'Not a lot I'm afraid but, as you know, the folk round here don't believe much in cash payments!'

'*Merci, merci*,' said Vincent, 'that'll do nicely.' He grinned broadly. '*Alors*, I'm off then, to conquer Paris. Shine while you can, that's my motto!' He then seized the money and, still beaming, was out through the doors without another word.

His friends heard him whistling another tuneless something, as he clattered down the path in the moonlight, on towards the road. Dr Gachet and Marguerite exchanged further glances. It was quite extraordinary, their expressions implied, that Vincent should have caught the attention of someone important.

Dr Gachet locked up, as Marguerite stared at *les portes-fenêtres*, her movements fidgety, manner uncertain. 'Bravo, Vincent! Bravo! Or should that be – ? No, I wonder, *cher Papa*, will this be the making of him?'

Dr Gachet gave a slow head shake. 'His ruin, more like.

Sorry, I do hope I'm wrong, but life must be very cruel to encourage him like this – in a skill for which he has no talent.'

'D'you really think so?'

'I know so. Having heard Vincent's dreadful *oeuvres* first-hand, I fear he may be in for another disappointment. False optimism is a worse killer, one feels, than a clear realisation of failure.'

'But you're so sure he can't succeed?'

'Aren't you?'

'I – I –'

'Still, let's be cheerful. Stranger things have happened.'

'Have they? I mean, *oui*, Papa, if you say so.' Troubled, Marguerite made for the door. 'Are you coming?'

'No, a last pipe, perhaps, while trying to think things through. Principally, what this strange news from Paris really means? And why our friend has been singled out for especial interest, when so many musicians of real talent have long been woefully ignored? An ironic contrast with Vincent's struggles as a painter, wouldn't you say? But once I've pondered a little and come to some conclusion, I trust we can talk of it again?'

'*Oui*, Papa, I'm too keyed up to discuss Vincent's new adventure, unexpected and unlikely as it seems … at least until morning!'

With a grim smile, Dr Gachet escorted her to the hallway. Another brief kiss on the cheek. 'There. *Bonne nuit*, see you tomorrow?'

'Tomorrow, Papa.'

Marguerite lingered a moment, a few more brief pleasantries, then ascended the stairs. Dr Gachet, dejected, returned to the salon. Let Marguerite sleep sweetly, if she could, his own mind was in turmoil.

Settling in his chair, he dimmed the small oil lamp beside him, leaving just enough light to see by. Then, sinking back in the cushions, he stared into space for a moment, before reaching for his pipe. But after a few minutes, having considered the above questions, coming to no conclusion, Dr Gachet extinguished the light altogether and followed his daughter to bed.

IV

PARIS

ONE

As the lights slowly rose, the audience that night at *L'Opéra Garnier* was restored to its familiar view of neo-Baroque luxury: decadent, extravagant, and well-nigh overwhelming – a feast of red plush, crystal and mirrors, ornate gilt, swirling balusters and multi-coloured marble.

Meanwhile, the unholy symphony, having lurched from one unmentionable movement to another, perforating any number of innocent eardrums along the way, ground and clattered to a halt. With no noticeable pause, a riot of whooping and cheering broke out, the sound of clapping was thunderous.

At the side of the stage a surprised theatre manager orchestrated the applause with grins and gestures, while a lively *claque* in the gallery added loudly to the 'Bravos!' and cries of '*Vive le vrai Vincent*!', as if their lives depended on it.

Grinning through yellowed teeth, though his beard was neatly trimmed, Vincent stood there in the limelight's glare. He was dressed in white tie and tails, somewhat tight-fitting and rented for the occasion, and awkwardly took his bow. His words of thanks were drowned out by a fresh burst of clapping and some even more baffling cries of 'Encore!' His spirits surged and soared – he was a success at last! – but in an entirely different field from the one which had so long obsessed him.

The applause reached danger point and the vast chandeliers rattled and shook. Approval was all but unanimous – only the orchestra seemed doubtful. There was a bit of hostile muttering among the brass section, drowned out fortunately by the clamour from the audience, while an elderly cellist and the relief triangle player miserably shared a hip flask.

The conductor, mopping his brow with an outsize white handkerchief, looked rather more shocked than triumphant. He glanced blearily about him, as if he'd just gone twelve rounds with the Heavyweight Champion of the World. He poked the life back into his ears with the point of his baton. Then, neglecting to take his own bow, he clapped his free hand over his mouth and, vanishing beneath the stage, rushed off somewhere to be sick.

The theatre manager melted away, as the spot swung back on Vincent. He bowed and grinned, grinned and bowed, while the applause rose and died. He still stood there, the lights fading once more, finally enveloping him in darkness. It was truly, for whatever reason, an evening to remember.

A few, but only a few in the audience that night, though politely clapping with the rest of them, found themselves bemused by their fellow concert-goers' rapture. To their ears the 'music' they'd endured seemed like nothing at all. A very loud 'nothing', to be true, but nothing is nothing, whichever way you look at it. Or hear it, rather: the object of the exercise.

These chaps were even more bemused by the reviews they read later in *Le Journal*, *Paris Illustré* and *Écho de*

Paris. Especially since those same *critiques* offered encomiums so wildly complimentary, so lacking in restraint or even a modicum of good sense, that the bemused ones wondered if they'd been snatched at night by Jules Verne's moon creatures and been reawakened on another planet.

Biographers and commentators, writing in subsequent eras, have been equally baffled by this peculiar interlude in Vincent's life. Did it happen or did it not? And, had it happened, had Vincent been *truly* involved in the incident, should the subsequent chroniclers of Western Culture still not slavishly record it?

The easy answer to the first question is 'Well, maybe' – since the evidence, if you search for it, is there. In the second matter, all true *aficionados* of the troubled genius Dutchman have striven strenuously to 'airbrush' this absurd occurrence from the history books.

Thus, Vincent's brief career as singer, composer, lyricist and concert star has been consigned to the dustbin of half-fact, urban myth and 'biographical' theorising, along with Beethoven as a black man, Mae West as a gentleman and Elvis Presley being alive and well and living in McDonald's.

The effect of this concerted act of cultural censorship has left Vincent with his reputation intact. His reputation, that is, as a painter, rather than musician: one whom at least a few contemporary detractors had already proclaimed 'tone deaf'.

And so, for succeeding generations, Vincent, the abysmally inept, yet briefly popular 'composer-star', has been totally subsumed into his lasting fame as, arguably, the most acclaimed visionary painter of the 19th Century. Not to mention, as a consequence, the 20th Century, 21st Century or any century yet to come. For all that, this specific and, indeed, limited approach to the man who was Vincent may represent for us, certainly in the present writer's view, one of the most shameless revisionist exercises of all time.

You can say that again. I mean, look at it this way. For the purposes of my narrative, I had taken it upon myself to comb through all known records of Vincent's life and work. The books, the articles, any number of elderly press cuttings, exhibition notes and auctioneers' catalogues – all for some hint of this little-known moment in Vincent's tragic story. That's not to mention the visits to galleries, travelling far and wide, watching and studying the many TV and film documentaries, the small and big screen features devoted to Vincent's life.

But, in spite of that massive, time-consuming labour of research, little of the 'musical' Vincent has come to light. Nothing, indeed, but that he had genuinely studied piano and voice and received some small enjoyment from it. As for the rest, how true was it, really? Did Vincent Van Gogh truly become the nine-day wonder which those inconclusive rumours imply? And why, exactly, has the 'musical' Vincent been so effectively excised from the history books?

I leave it to you, the reader, to decide, since, apart from a few tattered copies of some surviving Paris journals, still kept on dusty shelves in the obscurer archives, the words of a single, long out-of-favour French biographer are all we really have to go on.

TWO

It might now be instructive to recall this once-celebrated author, writing some years after the event. A good man, he afforded Vincent's musical 'talents' a brief airing, while at the same time predicting, quite rightly as it turned out, that reputable historians would one day come to soft-pedal the surprising 'musical' turn for the better in Vincent's fortunes.

A stringer for *La Vie Parisienne* and other journals in the early 1890s, our man was a pen and ink *écrivain* of moderate talents. A fellow who meant well and often told the truth, according to his view of it. As I say, he was famous once. But to protect his descendants, we shall call our helpful penman 'Hercule Petitpoint', in reference to his small nib.

Monsieur Petitpoint knew Vincent, he said, or rather, had entertained him in a circle of other scribblers – critics, chroniclers, petty wordsmiths and the like. He was not a little puzzled by the fawning and the flattery, the further exclamations of 'Bravo! *Formidable!*' – the words seemed quite sincerely meant – to support the almost general view of the time that Vincent Van Gogh was proclaimed a genius. A genius sadly not in the one art for which later generations would applaud him.

Seeing no alternative, in the company of this overly enthusiastic band, than to cast his doubts aside and join the general approval, this the good fellow did. So convincingly, in fact, that he almost convinced *himself*. As to his motive in resurrecting, for the benefit of a some-what nugatory readership, this least-recalled interlude in the life of Vincent Van Gogh, only *Monsieur* Petitpoint could have told you. Less elusive, though, is what he had to tell one about the matter at hand. Namely, the travails of Vincent 'Composer', as opposed to Vincent 'Great Artist'!

Let us eavesdrop, then, on that very same gentleman, an observer young at the time of Vincent's 'triumph', but

still lucid enough, in later years, to have talked persua-
sively to his relatively small audience, via the wonders of
the printed page. *Monsieur* Petitpoint did not answer all
our questions directly, but he offers us what he likes to
describe as 'an exercise in biography'. One feels sure it
will inform, elucidate and entertain. So, to help you make
up your minds, or to set the record straight on what may
well prove to be but a fleeting controversy, I have pleasure
in presenting *Monsieur* Petitpoint:

The lights go up on our interview, to reveal that gentleman, now very, very old, behind his desk. There are copies
of *Le Figaro*, *Paris Match* and other French journals laid
out in front of him. Along with a small marble bust of
Vincent Van Gogh, next to *Monsieur* Petitpoint's own
early biography. This latter is opened on the appropriate
page of a pre-selected chapter. *Monsieur* Petitpoint starts
to read, smiling from time to time at some invisible listeners. The latter clap, inaudibly:

'*Merci. merci. Bienvenu, mes ami*s [*Monsieur* Petitpoint
glances at the 'listeners']. *Je commence, oui? Eh oui, c'est
ça!*'

Monsieur Petitpoint clears his throat. His English,
when he once more speaks, is excellent. No halting, no
Franglais, no solecisms, nor grammatical hiccoughs, so
no need here, either, for a literal translation.

'In writing a great man's biography, as I have done, the
biggest decision one has to make, keeping it in mind at
all stages of the work's creation, is what to leave out.
Most great men offer material for a hundred books, in
some cases more. In the matter of Vincent Van Gogh,
the key to the man, his life and loves, his viewpoint and
increasing madness, resides surely in his painting? All
else, those little anomalies and enthusiasms which do not

colour one's view of him as a pictorial artist, are therefore irrelevant.

'I refer, principally, to his very minor skills as a musician. A success, certainly, to some misguided folk in the early 1890s, even to a handful of reputable critics. But, in the context of what we now recognise as Vincent's greatness as a painter, contrasted, despite some limited critical success, with an inability to sell his works in his lifetime, that cursory foray into the world of the concert hall, allied to his corresponding status as a social lion, was simply a stop-gap in the greater plan.

'In the matter of the queues for his recitals, the headlines in the gutter press, the phenomenon of that best-selling but now long out of print sheet music, we may compare Vincent with such subsequent unskilled "musical" chancers as Florence Foster Jenkins. But *Madame* Jenkins was exposed to ridicule in her own lifetime and in no way was she seriously considered. Her sell-out recitals were filled to bursting merely by the jeerers and mockers, less interested in music than cackling at this poor, self-deluded woman's failure.

'Vincent, on the other hand, really did take Paris by storm. He received, as I say, considerable *éclat* in the musical journals, which so hoodwinked the general public through some lavish imputations of genius, that they flocked to the recitals in droves. The way Vincent was hailed, the way he was *fêted*, and I witnessed it myself, was, surely, in the retrospective view, undeserved. Yet ironically, despite his posthumous fame as a great painter and life force, or the fact that, in later years, his work would fetch the highest prices at auction of any artist living or dead, the "musical" Vincent was, back then for a brief moment, the one that chiefly held sway!

'Taking note of his fame as a whole, based on his consummate skills as an imagist, this sorry musical interlude – we must veritably call it that? – is such an embarrassment to those who admire Vincent the painter, that the tactful biographer leaves it out.

'This, in general, is what I have done, so let these brief paragraphs [written for publication only in the smaller magazines], clue us in, partially at least, to that very odd period – less a matter of months than of weeks – when Vincent Van Gogh, "singer", "arranger", "pianist" and 'composer', was, indeed, the toast of the town.

'And so, with the clear understanding that what follows should in no way confuse or be held up as the authorised view of a man who is now bigger, in death, than his tragically under-appreciated life could possibly have anticipated, herewith are the facts of the case: that mystifying moment when the ears of an entire city were gravely assaulted, and those selfsame ears seemed to welcome the assault. This, *mes chers amis*, is how it happened.'

Vincent had been making little headway with his questionable musical talents, he was growing despondent. The few good reviews he'd received for his paintings, though he still couldn't sell them, did not alleviate his despair. This was now exacerbated by the bleak indifference to his composing, the widespread antipathy to his public performances.

These latter took place in various cafés and artists' hang-outs in Montmartre and Montparnasse. There, with his appalled listeners clapping their hands over their ears and assuming expressions of extreme anguish, he would clear the *ateliers* in no time. But why, oh why? Vincent had, indeed, studied singing and piano, with a gentleman called Van der Zande. This much the biographers agree on. So why could he not parlay that recently acquired skill into measures of public approbation? It really was too bad.

The depressions were beginning again, too, and Vincent's correspondence with the still concerned Dr Gachet pointed towards the fateful relapse which the good man had predicted.

Then one day, a dubious concert promoter, apprised of the weird 'music' emanating from the cafés, not to mention the notoriety of its progenitor as both an aural menace and laughing stock, decided on a visit. However bad, however excruciating to the ears was the 'music' in question, our man would see for himself.

Neither impressed nor appalled, the promoter thought he saw something in the performance, even though, being as tone deaf as Vincent, he was no judge when hearing it. Returning in the *fiacre* to his back-street office near *Le Quai d'Orsay*, the promoter thought things through. Whether Vincent were good or bad at what he did was scarcely important. Since, as ever, with many public performers, talent was the least of it. Many *une grande vedette*, reasoned our promoter, had attained fame and fortune through only minimal ability, while artistes of real skill had fallen by the wayside. But this odd man, with his carroty hair and beard, his intense, at times maniacal gaze and a voice and piano style which, according to the promoter's informants, could drive a mad elephant madder, certainly had *something*. Call it personality, call it a misunderstood talent or *un numéro effronté*, if a reputation can be harnessed to the truly awful and get so widely talked about in a negative way, could not the reverse be true? That, just through insisting the awful is *good*, a solitary voice might well sway the multitude?

With this thought in mind, opting to be that very voice, the promoter signed Vincent on the dotted line, then set about promoting. Just as the man suspected, Vincent would find an audience. Not only an audience, but critics to bat for him, newshounds to interview him and fans queuing at the stage door for autographs. Virtually overnight, Vincent took Paris by storm.

With each recital, the critics raved even more, following each others' example, unwilling to expose themselves as narrow-minded or living in the past. Each one too ashamed to admit he'd been missing out on a development so strange, so unfamiliar and so truly revolutionary.

The public, equally reluctant to be caught napping, fearful of being dubbed 'retrograde', offered its own plaudits. The theatres and concert halls were packed, Vincent and the promoter were 'made'. The money poured in and a new kind of 'music' had been born.

Mais oui, mes amis, it was a flash in the pot. The audiences were still eager, booking well in advance for each and every recital. The lectures and magazine articles on the subject of this 'new musical form' continued unabated. But, for Vincent, after just a few weeks, the wild euphoria, the loud adulation, the parties, picnics and intrusive attentions – offered by admirers of both sexes – had finally started to pall.

Vincent thought he should be happier than he was, that success and artistic satisfaction were what he had long been seeking. Alas, his health and mental state did not keep pace with this sudden burst of recognition, especially for a skill which was not his real forte. He grew *un peu distrait*, the anxieties returned and so did his need for change. Intending to resume his concert engagements later, while letting a short sabbatical out of Paris whet his audience's appetite for more, he found himself back in Auvers. Here Dr Gachet, his daughter Marguerite and all of Vincent's other acquaintances seemed more than delighted to see him.

The days passed into weeks, but Vincent's fame and earning capacity were kept at a white-hot pitch through the phenomenal sales of his sheet music. Not that there was much to put on the sheets in the first place, since whatever it was that Vincent had offered on the concert platform, it seemed to come straight from his head. Conjured mint new, I mean, at the moment of execution and then, by its conjurer, just as swiftly forgotten.

Meanwhile, he continued to respond favourably to the ministrations of Dr Gachet and the gentle Marguerite, as well as the routine of life in Auvers. He even tried a little painting again, till his already fragile personality was struck by a fresh crisis. This was, it turned out, a problem beyond Vincent's control. In his attempts to overcome it, he fell victim to 'the final tragedy', which prematurely robbed us of his genius. His genius for painting, I mean – nothing more.

As for that brief 'musical foray', unimportant, I would say, in the greater scheme of Vincent's life, may these paltry paragraphs suffice. To be read and considered by those who are curious. After which, one should cast them aside. Let us continue to rhapsodise over a great man and his paintings. But, concerning that other matter *ce prodige bizarre mais pas si musicale* – let us now maintain a discreet silence.

[*The present writer has ignored this advice. There now follows, in our remaining chapters, a further clutch of insights into the strange musical life of Vincent Van Gogh. They will be climaxed, as history still tells us, by 'a tragic denouement'. But, in relating the causes of that denouement and the events which followed, the official history and some less remembered 'facts' will again be seen to diverge.*]

V

AUVERS

Chez Gachet

ONE

Dr Gachet refolded his newspaper and gave a long-drawn-out sigh. Set perceptively in his sunburnt face, his pale blue eyes scanned the middle distance, taking in the extent of the pretty, overgrown garden. There was an aloe, with marigolds, white roses and cypresses, vines, poppies and plants of a colourful Southern variety. These jostled together in a kind of left-to-its-own-devices, yet meaningful, tangle, which, to the true country dweller, resembled how a garden should try to look at all times. Dr Gachet felt proud that Vincent would turn up two or three times a week to paint it.

Adjusting his focus nearer, his gaze settled on Marguerite. She was down there, not too far off, and had just finished feeding the pets. Dr Gachet was a member of The Society for Protection of Animals and the family owned several dogs, a pea-hen and, until recently, a monkey. This was Marguerite's, it had sadly died, and though she'd washed the body daily, her father said it would stink out the house and gave the poor thing away. But they still had their goat called Henriette, which the Doctor took for walks around the village.

This was not the sole reason he was deemed to be eccentric, if not a little mad. But for some folk, firm in the view that goats should not be afflicted with leads and collars, it was enough. The good Doctor was glad, though, that his daughter supported him in his endeavours and gave full attention to the creatures in their care.

Her task completed, Marguerite paused to pat the goat, which did not seem to mind. Then, smiling indulgently on the familiar edgy friendship between rabbits, pigeons and sleepy-looking cats, she moved away and skipped towards the terrace. She saw her father sitting there, rocking gently on the swing seat, and hurried up the steps. Noting his anxious expression, then the paper on his lap, she sensed the cause of his distress. Marguerite placed a hand on his shoulder.

'*Alors*, you've read it? The critics said he was good – more than good, and his recitals were sell-outs.' She pointed to the paper. 'There's a piece in there, by a *Monsieur* Edouard Dujardin – you must have seen it? – who calls Vincent "a bright original flame, crackling in the embers of what once was French music".'

Dr Gachet shook his head, he sighed again. 'I read it, *ma petite.*'

Marguerite sat. There was iced coffee, or tea, for preference – it was that time of morning, it could not be bettered. Marguerite handed her father his glass, picked up her own and reached for a biscuit. 'Bit odd, is it not? I like Vincent very much, but I don't understand this ... triumph of his.'

'Nor I, nor I.' The Doctor sipped his *demitasse*. 'His failure as a painter was almost too sad to be true. His success as a composer is unbelievable. Yet, he has such confidence in his strange musical "talent" – *faux* talent, I'd call it – that, in its offering only brief respite from his suffering, I fear for him. His life is a disaster and whatever the critics may say, however much his reputation gets pumped up, however many recitals they manage to wring out of him, this new musicality can be but a nine days' wonder. It will be found out one day and shown for what it's worth.'

Marguerite munched on the biscuit. 'It is (yerm, mmm) very bad, Papa. Almost deafeningly so.' In spite of her concern, Marguerite giggled.

Dr Gachet gave her a look. 'It's a tragic case of self delusion. A handful of noted "experts", some woolly-minded professors at *La Conservatoire*, say this new movement in music, this wretched "Dissonance", is a stroke of genius – an *ars nova* for our time, the most revolutionary change in the laws of composition, or non-composition, rather, since the caveman!'

'Did cavemen write music?'

Another look. Marguerite blushed, made an effort to seem contrite.

Dr Gachet continued. 'And everyone who's anyone pretends to agree with them. To me, to you – and who are we two hapless sufferers among so many champions? – it sounds like a riot of un-neutered tomcats on a slate roof, having sex and dying at the same time. *Je m'excuse, ma petite*, for saying "un-neutered" in your presence. Not to mention "sex".'

Marguerite laughed. 'I excuse you, Papa. I'm a doctor's daughter, remember? I've read your medical books and been around farms. I also help with your patients, so there's little I don't know about … that side of things! "Un-neutered cats"? Ha. Ha. You should have been a vet!'

'Not I – people are bad enough! Though the way things are going, it may come to that.' Dr Gachet looked gloomy, then just as quickly brightened. 'And I know you know, *chérie*, I was pulling your leg. Again, forgive me?'

'As ever.' Marguerite laughed again. 'Why not?'

'But I do worry about Vincent. He seems to have regressed.'

'He's also started drinking again. I caught him snaffling your Cognac.'

'I'll get rid of it, or lock everything up. I hope you told him off?'

'I did, but very gently. He was most apologetic, with that forlorn, whipped-spaniel look we know so well. If I hadn't been cross or so anxious for him I'd have laughed outright.'

'I'm glad you didn't. Last thing we want is to have him think we're not serious. About his resisting the things which are bad for him.'

'Too many things are, Papa.'

'I know, I know. But what ails the fellow? I thought there was a definite improvement. That our warm ministrations were really helpful. Or that this unexpected success of his would change him beyond measure.'

'It hasn't, has it?'

'I don't think so. The pressures of what, surely, can be but a transitory fame, with all the work involved, the effect of that overwhelming flattery, the inevitable socialising and carousing, seems almost to have unhinged him. Or certainly made him worse. Since, despite his making a little money at last, his long ingrained sense of insecurity won't let him enjoy it. The same old clothes, same small room at *L'Auberge Ravoux*? I mean, it's wise to be cautious – *Monsieur* Dombasle, Vincent's so-called impresario, is said to be a crook! – but Vincent acts as if he, too, fears the fame and adulation, so tremendously encouraging at first, must be bound to vanish in an instant. These recurring periods of depression – why *isn't* he happy with his success? It's just what he wanted.'

'It was, Papa, but now he seems most troubled. No wonder he's returned to Auvers – for a rest, he says, but for how long?'

'Poor Vincent, he's back in his old ways. Not eating, not taking care of himself. The Ravoux put food out for him, but he doesn't touch it. You saw him yesterday. He's like a haunted man, with that fixed stare of his. Sharp featured, making him look ever more skeletal. He seems weary, intense, his face an unhealthy colour.'

'True, Papa, some days I don't recognise him.'

'And for one who left here just a few weeks ago, looking so well. It's reflected in his painting, which I'm glad in a way he's returned to. But all those jagged brush strokes, a sky that seems louring and grey, even with the sun shining brightly, well, it makes me uneasy, wondering how to act? Simplicity's not so easy – most artists know that to their cost! – but for Vincent it seems impossible, he complicates everything so.'

'He showed me a painting once, just before he went to Paris. Some terrible thing with crows in it. A dreadful mess – so very depressing.'

'Crows, they say, are the harbingers of death.'

Marguerite started. 'Vincent, too, said words to that effect.'

'Oh, dear. I hope it doesn't mean something? Another suicide attempt, like that incident, not the first, I gather, where he swallowed lead paint? He told me the other day he'd given up on things, it was all too much, he wanted to die. The next day he couldn't have been jollier. I fear, though, whenever he talks of ending it all, he's convinced he's serious.'

'I trust not, Papa. And you mustn't say such things, that last time was awful, touch and go. Our unhappy Vincent, I'm terribly afraid.'

'I, too. But his euphoria, the childlike enthusiasm when somebody praises him, is now countered by a deep despair. Even more so, when somebody doesn't. We all feel like that at times, everyone has his sensitive side, but not in the extreme way that Vincent suffers. I wonder what it is this time? I must talk to him. Love, perhaps? Hmm.'

Dr Gachet looked at Marguerite, he pursed his lips. 'Unrequited … love? Or his lack of success at the painting, now that he's back to it? Why, I wonder, is recognition slow for him? Is that always to be the artist's lot, even for the ones with talent? After all, Corot never sold a painting, Manet was frequently laughed at and mocked. It'd be a tragedy if Vincent is never appreciated fully for that one supreme talent – he needs it so badly.'

Marguerite said nothing, Dr Gachet continued to study her. 'But tell me, *ma petite*, you and Vincent – you've never – ?'

She blushed again. 'Of course not, Papa. You know me better.'

Dr Gachet turned away, embarrassed. 'I mean – pardon, *chérie* – you and Vincent … when you've been alone … in his company … he has never – declared himself?'

Marguerite offered a thin smile. 'Like a – a proposal of marriage?'

'Something like that. Or … anything else?'

'No, nor likely to, I imagine. But … what else? You mean – ?'

'*Oui, ma petite*, has he … never … tried to – er, showed excessive – ?'

'Affection?' A small head shake from Marguerite. She took her father's shoulders and gently spun him round. Then raising her hand again, she lightly stroked his cheek. 'Like kissed me, in a non-fraternal way? Touched me? Embraced me? Never.'

'Good. Good.' Dr Gachet smiled his relief.

Marguerite looked wistful. 'Though sometimes I wish he would. To see if I feel for him what I sometimes think I feel. Then I imagine those innocent kisses, when he greets me or says "*Au 'voir*". And I think how scratchy his beard is, that he's missing several teeth, that his *toilette* is not always of the first order, and he's nearly as old as you. Then I realise, for all our fondness together, the way I admire him for his gifts, that anything more would be unthinkable.'

'It was as I hoped. You see, I and your *chère Maman* – *Maman* … ? Um – ah, remind me, where is she at the moment?'

'Back at *Tante* Francia, Papa. This time it's serious.'

'Eh *oui*. I forgot. *Tante* Francia. It's her – her – ?'

'Her heart, Papa. You know, we discussed it?'

'So we did. So we did. Poor woman, how long has she – ?'

'Oh do stop it, you know you're not interested. I get the impression, sometimes, that if something or somebody doesn't affect your immediate concerns, that you think it's an irritant, invented to annoy you. If you were concerned, not always so *distrait*, my poor aunt, I'd tell you, is not expected to live. But *Maman* and brother Paul are helping all they can.'

'That's good. Excellent.' Unaffected by the criticism, Dr Gachet continued. 'But, getting back to Vincent, you must assure me, promise me, really on your honour, as the loving, dutiful daughter you always are, that you would tell me straight away … if anything of that sort transpired?'

'And … if it did?'

'Then, perhaps, he would not be welcome. Or I would have to warn him it's impossible, it could never be.'

Marguerite frowned. 'But you still … like him, Papa?'

'Very much so, but he's not for you. He's too old, as you say – he may be successful as an artist one day, or he may not, should he live that long. But, if you were really desperate for such a man and told me you couldn't live without him, I'd try to be indulgent – with an admonition.'

'You mean – ?'

'There's his mental state. This morning he seemed stable, tomorrow, what then? The insane can be dangerous company. It must preclude, for all time, I fear, any virtues he may offer as a husband.'

'Can he not change, Papa?'

'I don't know, I'd have to be a fortune teller. But, in my experience, my long, informed studies of the neurasthenic condition – especially in artists – I would have to say "no". They are all a little mad and madness is not like measles, a sickness you pull through in a darkened room, with all the correct treatment. Your poor Papa suffers from his nerves, too, as you know, and when the dark clouds lower, chasing out one's good mood in a flash, there is no cure. One must bear with it and wait for the shadows to pass.'

Marguerite took his hand. 'I'm sorry, Papa.'

'*Merci, chérie.* I'm all right at present. A doctor's work is hard and it makes one – a little absent-minded. But poor Vincent is another matter – your Papa's problem is minor compared to his.'

Dr Gachet paused and cleared his throat. 'There's another reason, too, though it may be unseemly to talk of it. It's an illness of a … more personal nature, a reason why Vincent is unsuited to the married state. Why the kind of alliance of which we speak … would be inadvisable. It's an ongoing infection that – that – no, let us close the subject, forget I brought it up. I'll speak of it no more.'

Dr Gachet looked embarrassed again, as Marguerite gazed at him, frowning. But she'd grasped what he meant, since, as ever, being a doctor's daughter, an efficient nurse for the more treatable patients, she knew more about his work here in the village than the good man thought she did. Dr Gachet turned back and looked at her once more, studying her expression.

'And this is the truth, you'd really swear to it? You'd not contemplate … an understanding with *notre cher ami* should the subject come up?'

'No, Papa. If not for that reason, then the various others we've discussed.'

'I'm glad. Since, to have sent Vincent away, it might have prompted his total mental collapse. We brighten his day, as he brightens ours, he relies on our friendship, as we do his, and I try to think of him as a son – to encourage him in every way.'

'You do, Papa, in most things.'

'So, if there's nothing more serious in Vincent's presence here than some dark paintings on the walls and that infernal racket he inflicts upon us, then all will be well. Though I have to say, that this odd secondary talent of his is beginning to wear me down. If we cannot tactfully dissuade Vincent from his misconceived course, then my dwindling flock of patients will cease coming here at all! Something must be done. I asked you to speak to him?'

'I did my best.'

'I'm sure you did. And – ?'

'It's been difficult, Papa. To get Vincent in the right mood, to take the criticism. Even worse now, after his success, it's difficult to get a word in. All that talk of his about the connection between colours and music. "I can *hear* the colours, just listen to them! Blues and greens and even reds!" That's what he says and insists all good musicians do the same. It's something about chromatics versus diatonics, or maybe … maybe, oxytonics? Another silly word, it sounds like a cure for stomach ache. I'm sure I never hear any of that nonsense while sitting at the piano. As for what Vincent claims to see, all I see before me is the music paper. Still, I wouldn't like to argue.'

'We'll leave it then, let sleeping dogs lie. Along with those un-neutered cats!'

Dr Gachet chuckled, as Marguerite joined in. He grew serious again. 'And there really is nothing to it – between you and Vincent?'

'Nothing, Papa, nothing. You keep asking, I keep saying. Don't worry so.' Marguerite avoided his eyes. 'It is the truth. I love him … like a brother – an older, crazy, amusing, infuriating older brother, but … as *un grand amoureux*, a man to spend my life with … no.'

At last, Dr Gachet accepted. He moved over, to kiss Marguerite on the forehead. Then took his seat.

'*Bien*, excuse me once more, for my indecent probing. An awkward moment between us, no? A tiresome old father, questioning the secret motions of a young girl's heart! This, too, you do forgive me?'

'*Oui*, Papa, yet again. And *merci*, from the fullness of that heart. You understand me so well.'

Once more, Dr Gachet looked away, the slightest

suggestion of a tear. 'And from my full heart, also, *ma petite!*' He glanced at his pocket watch. 'Ah, it's time for luncheon.' Quickly, he rose again, a little stretch. 'So barring interruptions, a sudden errand of mercy, the gong today shall be greeted with alacrity!'

'No gong Papa.' Marguerite smiled back. '*Madame* Chevalier is paying a visit. But everything's prepared, cold again today. *Noix de veau*, with *bouchées à la reine*, and a *salade niçoise*. Then a rich chocolate *mousse* to follow – mouth watering, truly! – made with ten eggs.'

'Oh, dear, do we have to lunch so lavishly? The eggs from one of our patients, I suppose?'

'*Oui*, Papa,' Marguerite giggled, 'it's all he could afford. Shall we go in?'

'Let us, *ma petite*. Come on, come on, I could eat a horse!' Dr Gachet laughed. 'I mean, that'll do nicely – no horse meat, thank Heaven, we haven't come to that! – but, um – whatever it is you just said?'

'Oh, Papa, you're impossible.'

Marguerite smiled teasingly up at him, then rose, too, and took his arm. They began to leave the terrace. But her father's fear of interruption proved justified. At this precise moment, there was a shout from the gate. It was Vincent, damn him! Not that his friend was ever unwelcome, but Dr Gachet, with much on his mind and an unusually full surgery later, had awoken with a yen to take the day quietly. Still, he waved and forced a smile, as Vincent waved back at him.

Then something else caught his eye. Not too far off, under the trees across the lane, stood *Monsieur* Tautain, the man with the club foot. Dr Gachet groaned his irritation. What's wrong with the fellow, he asked himself? It's as if the man had taken root, turning up, several times a week it seemed, just hovering there, begging attention, his very presence a constant reproach!

No, mused the Doctor, he'd given his answer, there was nothing to be done for the man, could he not accept it? His condition was a tragedy, that went without saying, but if it carried on much longer, this continual watching and stalking, *Monsieur* Tautain would have to be restrained. As Dr Gachet considered this, *Monsieur* Tautain, crossing over, shuffled heavily towards Vincent, as if to waylay him.

The man, noted Vincent, was thickset with reddish hair like his own, but untidy, with wisps of loose straw caught up in it. Vincent nodded agreeably, unable to resist a glance at the fellow's malformed foot. Then, sidestepping neatly, he made it to the gate. Vincent clicked and entered. *Monsieur* Tautain shrugged and stumped away.

Vincent came bustling up the path, brandishing his latest painting. He moved one of the rabbits aside with his toe, collided with the sundial and nearly tripped on the steps. With a shrug and a brief exclamation, he gestured again at his friends and was finally beside them.

Marguerite and Dr Gachet were gazing at him, trying to assess his mood. Vincent looked thin, true, his cheeks were pallid, but he seemed by no means as desperate as the Doctor had implied.

As Vincent hesitated, Dr Gachet stepped away from *les portes-fenêtres*, trying to conceal his impatience. There were brief greetings from father and daughter, another glance by Dr Gachet at his watch, then Vincent was ushered inside, with as much warmth in their welcome as his friends knew how.

'Come in, come in, Vincent,' said Dr Gachet, 'it's good to see you. Sorry about that fellow at the gate.'

'Oh him? *Oui*, I've seen him loitering. Rather more than

usual, since I came back from Paris. Usual thing, is it? That wretched foot of his?' Vincent grinned. 'Or maybe, *mon cher docteur*, you owe him money?'

'Were it that simple,' said the other, unsmiling, 'but, sadly, the poor man's obsessed. So convinced there's a cure for his affliction that he won't give up on it. I'd hate to have to report him, thus adding to his misery, but he hangs around there like a secret agent, noting our comings and goings, in the vain hope, it seems, I'll relent. Well, I can't and I won't. There is no cure for what he has, so why should I lie –' he glanced at Marguerite, 'I mean, fib, about it?'

Vincent nodded sagely, but didn't answer. What could he answer? He, too, had his obsessions, he knew about affliction, the poor chap had his sympathy. He glanced at Marguerite, then back at Dr Gachet. The latter took a step forward.

'Still, enough of our problems, we mustn't bore you with them.'

Vincent made to protest, but Dr Gachet, brightening, held up his hand.

'So, Vincent, tell me, what about you? What've you to show us? Your new masterwork? Hand it over.'

Vincent, with a grin and a quick, shy glance at Marguerite, gave Dr Gachet the canvas. He seemed to be brimming with enthusiasm, but at first said nothing, awaiting with anticipation, the good Doctor's verdict. Dr Gachet continued to study the picture, bringing one side nearer to his eye, then the other. Holding it even closer to the light, he frowned, then nodded, at last beaming in Vincent's direction.

'But that's good, Vincent. Excellent. It's a definite return to form – it's as if you were trying to capture the rhythmic vitality and sheer dynamics of nature. Splendid, splendid. It's the countryside around Auvers as I'd not previously seen it. It's alive! And the style so individual, one could not mistake it.'

Dr Gachet, still studying the painting, moved nearer to the windows. 'It's a very marvellous thing, to look at something closely and realise it's beautiful.'

'*Merci, merci.* It's just what I needed to hear.' Vincent chuckled. 'I've an ear for painting, too, *n'est-ce pas?*'

'*Oui.* A pity those fools in Paris don't take notice of your gift, the way they do your music. It would buck you up no end, confirm one's faith in you ... the conviction in your talent ... the belief of all those who love you.'

Vincent edged forward. He mumbled, a whisper, no more. 'You mean ... Marguerite?'

'What? I'm sorry?'

'*Rien. Rien du tout.*'

Vincent glanced again towards her. Marguerite was smiling at him, a little shyly, too, though she'd failed to catch, it seemed, the previous brief exchange. Vincent smiled back, then took a breath and spread his hands before him.

'But they *are* taking notice. I've been exhibited, at last! My brother sent me a cutting, only this morning. A critic called Aurier, in some Symbolist magazine, *Mercure de France*, spoke highly of me. Quite reputable, says Theo, both magazine and critic. Anyhow, this fellow Aurier, listen to this!'

Vincent grinned again, withdrawing a now much-thumbed cutting from his pocket. 'He writes that "*Monsieur* Van Gogh – blah blah blah blah and so on and so on and so forth –" this first bit's a trifle dull "– is not, thus, merely a great painter; – he is also a dreamer, a fanatical believer, a devourer of beautiful Utopias. Living on ideas and dreams."' Vincent's grin grew wider. 'So how's about that, then? This'll fix it!'

'*Très bien. Magnifique!*' exclaimed Dr Gachet, with genuine delight. 'That's more like it. You must be very pleased? Very proud, too? I know I'd be.' His grin now was almost as wide as Vincent's.

'I am. I am. It's a step. Painting, I've tried to tell myself, is a faith and it imposes the duty to disregard public opinion. I've done my best to conquer its indifference through perseverance and by not making concessions. Now, with opinion moving my way, I feel almost humbled by it, as much as I'm encouraged. And to think, just before I went to the asylum, I was seriously thinking of joining the Foreign Legion!'

Marguerite laughed, hesitated. Then moved in and kissed Vincent on the cheek. 'And I'm proud of you, too. Pleased even more that you changed your mind.' She caught her father's look of disapproval. 'I mean, we … both are. Had you been in North Africa, we might not have known you.'

Vincent gave another grin, wryer this time, tinged with a touch of melancholy. 'But they … still won't *buy* my paintings.'

'They will, in time,' said Dr Gachet. 'One branch of … fame so often leads to another. But, *cher* Vincent, if you don't mind, if you'll excuse us, our luncheon is waiting.' He paused, a quick glance at Marguerite. 'You will join us?'

Vincent laughed. 'Seems I always turn up at meal times. Must be a compulsion, I eat better here than at the Inn.'

'One should hope so. You have *Madame* Ravoux. We have *Madame* Chevalier!'

Vincent thought for a moment. '*Chers amis*, I'm sorely tempted. And *merci*.' He looked longingly towards the dining room. 'But I find, as time goes by, I need less and less food. Besides, out in the fields there I caught a tune, running through my head. In no time it had transformed itself into an aria and that, in turn, sowed seeds for an opera. I must get back … to complete the whole work.'

'As you wish.' Dr Gachet looked relieved, then doubtful. 'But *bonne chance*, *mon cher* Vincent, with … the opera. Look forward to hearing it.'

'Me, too,' said Marguerite, '*bonne chance*.'

Vincent thanked them, retrieved his things and they waved him off down the garden. Pulling faces at his usual tuneless whistling, they watched him pass through the gate. Father and daughter then turned back to each other, communicating, initially without words, the anxieties they still felt.

At last, Marguerite spoke. 'Is this more bad news, Papa?'

'I'd say so. Painting, *ma petite*, is Vincent's saviour – it's keeping him alive. Music, I believe, will be his undoing.'

Marguerite, though she wouldn't have put it like this, was clearly thinking the same. With a look of sadness, she moved closer to her father and reached for his hand.

Vincent, meanwhile, retaining his lively mood, failed to notice *Monsieur* Tautain, still out there, sitting on the grass verge opposite. The poor man, now massaging his club foot with horny peasant hands, looked thoroughly sorry for himself. But, catching sight of Vincent, his mood, too, seemed to change.

With a last glance at the square, red-roofed house – no sign now of the Doctor or his daughter – he re-booted, rose with difficulty and lumbered after Vincent.

TWO

L'Auberge Ravoux

Vincent's small attic room at *L'Auberge Ravoux* had flaking paint, rough wooden floorboards and minimal decoration. It had a grimy bull's-eye window, set in the deep outer wall of the building, which afforded far less light than any good artist might feel he'd a right to. When he opened it, however, Vincent could look out on to the thatched-roof cottages he liked to paint, with an appealing view, besides, of their neighbour's flower-filled garden.

Back inside, in spite of its Spartan appearance, the room seemed almost cheerful, uncannily like every other bedroom Vincent had lived in and painted. The iron bed was narrow but serviceable, flanked by a small table and rush-seated chair. There were canvases packed untidily, an easel and canvas always set up, and Vincent's old piano in the corner. He was now sitting on a stool before it.

Still feeling buoyant, Vincent raised the piano lid, about to continue with his 'opera'. He struck a few chords, if they could loosely be described as such, when there was a loud hammering on the door. It must be the police or, more likely, feared Vincent, a writ server!

Vincent glanced through the window at that convenient beech tree outside, wondering if he should make himself scarce. But instead of bursting in to seize him or God knows what, the person or persons outside kept hammering ever more loudly, as if intent on shaking the building to bits.

Taking his courage in both hands, Vincent shuffled across the room, opened the door a fraction and peeped through the gap. There, on the landing, stood a young man, moustached and bearded, in a state of high agitation. He was somewhere, thought Vincent, in his early to mid twenties, with a face red and twitching, eyes blazing, body shaking and fist raised, as if for the final blow.

Opening the door wider, Vincent was obliged to duck as the fist crashed down, narrowly missing his bad ear. Instead, it connected with the blank space between doorway and door jamb, before falling impotently to the young man's side. The fist was followed by the rest of his arm, which now just hung there, looking rather useless. The young man stood and stared, his angry expression transformed into one of deep anguish, while the gloved fingers, on the end of that same limp arm, scratched at a thigh which seemed to be itching.

Vincent observed his visitor. The young man had rather thick, twisty lips, a sensual greedy nose and bright, though presently stricken, eyes. He was somewhat shabbily dressed, his hair floppy, shoes unpolished and everything about him showing the signs of frustration and despair. The fingers doing the scratching had now worked their way through the tips of his gloves, a further clue that this youthful unfortunate was on his beam ends. There, but for the grace of *L'Opéra Garnier*, mused Vincent, go I!

As Vincent stepped back into the room, the visitor took a few steps forward. Then stood gazing at his unwilling host, his mouth opening and shutting like a goldfish. Though no words initially came out, it seemed evident to Vincent that the young man had much on his mind. He continued to study him, then pointed to a chair. The young man shook his head. Vincent shrugged.

'*Eh, bien*, stand if you like. But who are you? And why d'you you make such a racket? Could you not have knocked more gently? You're disturbing the drunks downstairs.

What's up with you? What are you doing here? How did you get in?'

The young man glared, then answered. 'The street door was open and, ferreting around, I earmarked your room from the ugly off-key noises which shrieked from within. I have a few words to say to you, *Monsieur*, things which you may not like. But I have arrived here, direct from Paris, with one aim in view.'

'And what aim is that?'

'I've given this matter some thought, weighing one consideration with another. But I must strike while the fury is white hot and my distaste for your so-called talents seems not, at this precise moment, to be at vomiting point. I asked at the Doctor's down the street where I might find you and – here I am. My name, if you're interested, is Satie. A composer.'

'Suttee? Suttee? What's *that*? Sounds like a Hindu ceremonial, burning young widows on the funeral pyre! Hah, I've never heard of you. Who are you, exactly? You make a lot of noise, yourself, you're not French? You must be German?'

'Half-French, half-Scottish. But that's irrelevant.'

'Sounds relevant to me. I'm Dutch. And proud to be so.'

Vincent stuck out his hand. *Monsieur* Satie ignored it.

'I know. And you'd have to be double Dutch to listen to that awful din you make. Or read all those stupid critics who write about you. It – it's quite … offensive. So is – so is –' *Monsieur* Satie sniffed and glanced around him ' – what's that bad smell? You?'

He took a step back. Vincent looked at him, stung.

'That's my problem, not yours – on both counts. I thought you said you were a composer? A creative artist. Not a critic? Or an expert on bad smells? Maybe it's the same thing, sniffing out success or failure! I mean, critics don't create, that's why they're critics. What are you up to?'

'You, *Monsieur*, are my undoing. I'm here to have it out with you.'

'Out with me? But I don't even know you.'

'*Mais oui*, you do. Or would do. If they hadn't cancelled my recital, the one that was going to make my reputation. To put me on the musical map. Now, they'll never hear the name "Erik Satie" and it's all your fault!'

Vincent stared at the man in some perplexity. What exactly was *he*, Vincent, supposed to have done? It made no sense, whatever it was, but was evidently serious. He tried to imagine how Paul would have handled this? Act firmly, dismissively, with irony and courage? Something like that. Intent on brazening it out, Vincent stepped forward again. He took a breath.

'How can that be? *C'est incroyable*. Where *was* this recital? Paris? I haven't left Auvers for weeks. Trying to get fit, before my next engagement. And I don't know any of these critics you've mentioned. They write about me, true, I get the cuttings, but I've no wish to meet them.'

'And why, may I ask, is that?'

'An artist meeting a critic, it's like shaking hands with a turkey one's about to have for dinner. Or swapping sex talk with a eunuch. You can do it, *he* can't. He'd like to do what you do, but you know he never will. So out of revenge, he passes judgement – there's no common ground. I compose, they praise me. Or not, as the case may be. My duty ends there. As for you, how could you and I have had an influence on each other, or me be responsible for anything which concerns you, when, before today, your name to me meant nothing?'

'And shall continue to mean nothing. To you or anyone else. You've ruined me and I can't forgive you. You've knocked me in the bud –'

'You mean *nipped* you in the bud?'

'Nipped, *c'est ça* … before I've really started. *Monsieur* D'Indy who's been sponsoring me at *La Conservatoire*, teaching me modal harmonies, and *Monsieur* Roussel – of course you've heard of them – ?'

Vincent shook his head.

'*Alors*,' said *Monsieur* Satie, 'they both agreed I had a certain promise. Were ready to push me forward. Expose me to the public – and the critics – with some modest little pieces of my own, the, um –'

'All right, then. Name one – name just one of your works, *Monsieur*, something I might have heard? What are you famous for?'

'Nothing much, as yet.' Satie looked at Vincent, he hesitated. '*Eh, oui*, there is one piece, a series of pieces, it's had some success. Limited, at least. "*Gymnopédies*".'

'Oh? Ha. Ha. *Gym no pédies*? It means "Exercise without Feet"! How does it go?'

Satie hummed a snatch. Then folded his arms, gazing at Vincent smugly. Vincent shook his head again, then suddenly remembered '*Oui*. I know. "Tinkle. Tinkle". I've heard it. Played in some café in Montmartre.'

'Probably by me, a pianist there. Or later, at *Le Chat Noir*. It's how I started.'

'Just like yours truly – but I escaped. Maybe you should've stayed?'

'You can joke about it, but we all have beginnings. What, may I ask, was yours? And "Tinkle. Tinkle"? That's a *canard* by the ignorant to denigrate the – no, don't worry, I'm used to it by now. You may say what you like,

Monsieur, but I've already been praised by some critics, by established composers. *Monsieur* Massenet called me "a bright spark in a minor key."'

'Minor is right. And spark? Ha. Ha. Don't burn down any concert halls! Anyhow, Massenet's a fool, an enemy of progress. So must you be, if you compose crap like that.'

'Crap? Enemy? Well, let me tell you, despite my penchant for Mediaevalism and a serious interest in pagan rites, I'm as innovative as the next man. Opposed to orthodoxy, sometimes violently, Wagner in particular. Berlioz, too. But not at the expense of the melodic line, or with a total disregard for harmony, the basic rules of music.'

'But I like Wagner. And Berlioz. Are you eccentric?'

'I may *be* eccentric, as some men call me, my approach to composition unsentimental, even satiric. But music is music, it has form and function, it may soothe or stir, elevate or provoke. To do none of these things, to be disharmonic, disjointed, sounding like nothing on Earth or in Heaven, it is no longer *bearable.* I mean, there's no beauty in it. Art always has to have beauty, or we might as well not have it. It reveals, especially great Art, the truth about Man and his finer aspirations.'

'Art is also capable of concealing the truth, as much as revealing it.'

'Maybe so, I'm sure yours does.'

'Oh, sod that. But, ah well, I take your point.' Vincent looked at his guest more kindly. 'But forgive me, I'm forgetting myself – a terrible host! Would you like a drink, a bite to eat? You must be famished after your journey, I'll nip down and fetch you something. There's *chateaubriand,* venison on the spit, casserole of hare, I think, in red wine and fresh lamb from our local pastures, cooked for seven hours in its own juices. If you'll excuse me, I'll –'

'Most kind of you,' said *Monsieur* Satie, sounding just a mite pompous, 'but I only eat white food.'

'What, like roast polar bear?'

Monsieur Satie failed to crack a smile. Vincent shrugged and stared at him. 'So, what's the problem?'

'You are. *You*. I really thought I was getting somewhere. I mean, on something of a roll. But that – that – it's just a pipe dream, a whole future shattered. I'd big plans.'

'Like what?'

'If you must know, I've been working on an epic of minimalist repetition. It consists of the same piano passage played very softly and slowly 840 times. I was going to call it *Vexations*.'

'Very apt, I'd say. And you dare criticise *me*?'

'Well, anyhow, it's not going to happen. Not now. And it's all your fault, no doubt about it. You've scotched it, you bastard, stuck your big Dutch foot in!'

'Eh? What? Quite average size, really – my foot. And not so much of the "bastard"! Not true, as it happens. My ear, on the other hand –'

'Damn your ear! I don't want to hear about it! I mean, can *you*? Hear, I mean? That horrendous row you make?'

Vincent chuckled, leaning back against the piano. 'You *are* a critic, then! And the word is not "row", though spelt "row", but "roe". R-O-E. And my music? It's a unique version of the twelve tone "roe", as in "row of peas", inspired by German models.'

'"Tones?" "Models?" What tones? I heard no tones. Even half-tones or quarter-tones. While "peas" is right, fit only for boiling. It's miserable, nothing, the Emperor's

New Clothes of modern music. It bears no relation to the world around us.'

'You mean, your world or mine?'

'*Mais merde, merde, merde, alors*! Please take me seriously. You, at least, who're responsible! You owe me that much. You erupted there in Paris, from some field in the provinces, with these terrible compositions of yours, these ugly dissonant *chansons*, that half-baked tuneless symphony they wrote up so encouragingly in *La Vie Parisienne* –'

'Tuneless? Half-baked? Anything else?'

'*Oui*, it was noisy, endless. It went on and on and on, like a Jewish wedding. And now, that frightful discord is all anyone listens to. "Dissonance!" "Dissonance!" "Dissonance!" It's all I ever hear!'

Monsieur Satie began to pace, though with rather small steps in a room this size. 'It's the talk of the salons, the humble *estaminets*. A Niagara of ink pours through the popular press. *Le Figaro* runs editorials and it's hotly debated in all the best clubs. So what's the result? *Monsieur* Gounod has taken to his bed, *Monsieur* Delibes has fled the country, *Monsieur* Saint-Saëns is talking of suicide, *Monsieur* Franck has succumbed to a street accident – and your abject visitor, myself, a mere novice compared to those beloved, insouciant giants, has every door slammed in his face!'

Vincent gazed at him, concerned. 'Bad as that, eh?'

'It is. Worse. So what do they say to me, these musical experts? The critics who've taken you up – you and your wretched "Dissonance", praising it to the skies?'

'No. What? Tell me.'

'They say "Go away *Monsieur* Satie!" "Get lost, *Monsieur* Satie!" "You're redundant, *Monsieur* Satie!

You write *tunes*! They're pleasant. They're simple. They're repetitive and easy on the ear. But who wants music where there's no *work* involved? Work on the part of the listener? Music like yours, *Monsieur* Satie, where there's form and structure, a pretence at instrumentality, with bars of equal time value, the correct number of beats to the bar – who now wants *that*?"'

'It varies, I gather?'

'What would *you* know about it, you musical moron? You know nothing. Of major or minor, crotchets and quavers, *andante* or *allegro*, according to the rules of notation? Music, I'll have you know, is a science, all based on the rules of phonometry –'

'You what?'

'Phonometry. A small device of my own. And quite evident, from your own sorry efforts, it would be beyond you.'

'How can you be sure? Since I've never even heard of it. What *is* it?'

'In brief, it means this. That it's not enough to compose or play the notes, they have to be *measured*.'

'Measured?'

'*Oui*. It avoids the elemental mistakes made by inferior musicians. Inferior like yourself.'

Vincent laughed. 'And *you're* a cut above – is that it?'

'Absolutely. I work very hard. Measuring, studying, drawing conclusions. Matter of fact, it gives me more pleasure to measure a sound than to hear it. And vital when one's composing. For instance, the first time I used a Phonoscope for that purpose I examined a B-flat of average dimensions.'

'And?'

'I can assure you I never saw anything so repulsive. I had to call a neighbour to come and look at it.'

'I still don't understand.'

'Don't understand? Don't *understand*? But what if I hadn't *found* it? What if I'd left it in? *Quel désastre!*'

'Sounds pretty complicated.'

'*Vraiment*. But essential, as I said. Phonometry is the only way.'

Vincent let out a low whistle. 'And they dare call *your* music simple and old-fashioned, that there's no effort involved? *Mon Dieu! Quelle ordure!*'

'It is, and *merci*. But anyway, that's all irrelevent now, so they tell me. They fail to see that what I've been doing *is* entirely new. Quite revolutionary, in fact. But now, according to the critics, since your own presumptuous elevation, it's already past its sell-by date. "It's old hat, *Monsieur* Satie, your kind of music! *Finie, passé*, dead as old socks! Please tour *les écoles Provençales*, *les lycées du Midis*. Invade the girls' finishing schools in Switzerland and Alsace. Your fripperies, these silly little nothings, will be appreciated there!"'

Monsieur Satie stopped pacing and waved his arms about. This, too, proved difficult, the ceiling being so low. Vincent dodged the flailing limbs and took refuge on his bed. *Monsieur* Satie continued.

'Your stuff, *Monsieur* Satie, is old, old, old! The new style – we're coming up to *la fin du siècle* – is "Dissonance". A revolution in musical form! Or, rather, an alternative to musical form. A breakthrough for the modern ear! Get with it or change your tune! I mean, *no* tune, *Monsieur* Satie! We don't need one, won't have one, won't *listen*! "Dissonance" – that will be the rallying call for the new century! The days of trifling little melodies for the newsboys to whistle to went out with hooped skirts and carpet bags!'

Vincent rose quickly, assuming a look of distress. '*Mon Dieu*! My poor young man, it really *is* bad.'

Monsieur Satie, catching another whiff of him, just as quickly moved back. 'It is, it is. I'm ruined. I can't let any more people tell me I've already composed enough. No, not again! Oh, *Monsieur*, why couldn't you leave it be? Why did you have to encroach on my territory, the world of your betters? Painters paint, composers compose, that's surely the preordained plan?'

'Don't agree. There are several ways of skinning a cat.'

'But why *my* cat? My art form of choice? Why couldn't you stay in the countryside, painting away, doing what you do best? You and that friend of yours – a wise man, it seems, who had no pretensions to composing?'

'Which wise man? You mean, Gauguin?'

'Gauguin. So they tell me. But not so wise, then, after all, now I come to think of it, to be an ally of yours. Gauguin? More like "Go again"! A really *suitable* friend. That libertine! Wife-beater! Child-abuser! A Bohemian with no sense of family! What else can one expect in a society like ours, where adolescent boys receive their sexual education in the beds of elderly women?'

'Eh? What? Not *me*.'

'Degenerates, both of you, since an early age.'

'I wouldn't know about degenerate, it's a matter of degree. And Gauguin's women have always been on the young side. For the rest, libertine, *oui*, and not so hot on family. Plus a lot of other things you could say about him. But wife-beater? Not that I know of. He simply left her.'

'How? Left her? His wife? Explain.'

'He stepped from a carriage in the street, one day, and

just … left. To follow a life of Art with a capital "A". Good for him.'

'"Good"? I hope he rots in Hell.'

'Never. Gauguin's indestructible. He's like the dog that gets hit by a *fiacre*. It gets up, licks itself clean, pads away and keeps on padding. That's Gauguin personified. Anyhow, he said his wife imprisoned him, she was stifling his talent.'

'As you've stifled mine.'

'Have I? I'm sorry. So you said.'

'You should be. But *Monsieur* Gauguin had responsibilities. We all have responsibilities. You, me, everyone, the whole world.'

'Do we? Really? I think, *mon ami*, you're a bit of a prig. If a rather young and dull one.'

'I am young, *oui*, maybe dull – I don't have quite your worldly sparkle – but old enough to know what's what.'

'Even worse.'

'But you do … have responsibilities. I'll ignore "prig". You and your whole parcel of arty pals. You disgust me, make me depressed. You have to face up to the fact that people rely on you, need your support, you can't just opt out. You seem not to know that fact?'

'Eh? Is it a fact? Who says so?'

'God – for one.'

'Hah. Don't talk to me of God! Don't even presume. I know all about Him. I'm the son of a minister, I studied at the seminary.'

Monsieur Satie raised both eyebrows, he looked incredulous. 'You're a priest?'

'I failed to qualify. But I spread the Word. Lay preacher to the miners. Grew obsessed with their lacerating poverty, identified with them wholesale, offered them the clothes from my back and took up painting to depict them. If people wanted God, I gave them Him, too – what's more responsible than that? To cap it all, I've translated the Bible into four languages – that's three languages, apart from Dutch.'

'Right. English, Yiddish and rubbish, that's more your style.'

'Do not mock me, *Monsieur*, or my religion. God means a lot to me.'

'Religion? God? You truly mean it? For one, I hear, whose life and manners are so ungodly. That's really rich, I'm astounded. I mean, just look at you – you, with your scabby face and bad teeth, your breath assailing the nostrils like corked wine. How could God possibly make a world that has people like you in it?'

'We mustn't judge God for the world, it's just a study that didn't come off.'

'That, *Monsieur*, may be the fault of organised religion?'

'*Vraiment*, an abomination! I've said as much, far too often, and it led to a break with my father. But notwithstanding, my belief in the Divine presence is as strong as ever, give or take some minor details. I'd lost my faith, I admit, but found it again in painting. And it's the same God, I'll have you know, who made me a painter, not a plaster saint. I cracked that one, too, thanks to *Him*. So what did He do? Pleased with my artistic sensibility, he showered me with a further gift. Told me to focus on music and the public lapped it up.'

'"Music"? He'll have to think of a new name for it, if that's what you compose! To my ears it's more like a curse than a gift.'

'Curses only have power when you believe in them. I don't.'

'You don't seem to believe in anything – not even God, if truth be told – except your own selfish talent, misguided and all the rest of it. Is there nothing to which you owe allegiance, can show a modicum of respect?'

'To Art. *Mon Dieu*, you're thick! Art is what we're *really* talking about. To what else should I owe allegiance?'

'Mankind.'

'Mankind? But that's what Art is, after all. A great, unified soul, blessed on its highest level by this God of ours – you implied it yourself – to which Man pays lip service. One could even live without God, but never Art. Art, that is, as an alternative to Christian salvation. With Art one has something to live for – Art gives hope. Take that away and what have we got? Nothing. Gauguin believed that, too.'

'Gauguin again? Don't give me Gauguin. They say in Paris that where most men have a heart, Gauguin has a black hole. I mean, is he mad?'

'I don't know. Only inasmuch as all artists are mad. They say I am.'

'Oh, we know all about *you*.'

'If you know all about me, how come you didn't know I'd prepared for the ministry?'

'That's something else.' *Monsieur* Satie sighed and shrugged. He was looking truly dismal. 'What I do know is what you've left *me* with. Nothing. You and your off-key plonking.'

'Plonking? *Tu parle?*' Vincent whistled. '*Mais c'est monstreux!*'

'*Oui*, nothing. An art stillborn, almost before it could breathe – because this new "style" of yours has cancelled out centuries of melody, the purest of pure emotions, that form and structure I was talking about. Traditional ideas of musicality: modulation, instrumentation, orchestration, syncopation, concord, vibrato, tonality, whole-tone, semitone, harmonics, dynamics and – and good taste.'

'Good taste? Hah! Heaven preserve us!'

'As for your painting, well! The talk is you do too much to too little effect. It is hard not to think of your work as the Japanese Knotweed of modern art. Both a blight and ineradicable.'

'You said it was what I did best?'

'For *you*, certainly, if simply judging by standards.' *Monsieur* Satie gestured airily around the room, his eyes coming to rest on a painting by the window. 'So what's *that* supposed to be? A postman? A *zouave*? It's as grisly a looking object as I've ever seen.'

'Full marks for the observation. I'll have you know –'

'Anyhow, that's the story.' *Monsieur* Satie let out a big sigh. 'My fall coincides with your rise. I had dreams, ambitions, thought I was really getting somewhere. I saw myself as a prodigy, a social lion, a future fulcrum of elegance, intent on distinguishing myself from other people, being original, having "tone". Placing myself at the centre of things, since in Paris, remember, once in society you are always there. *Oui*, a life of fine foods, fine friends and *armoires* full to bursting, with a sartorial style all my own. Bowler hats, velvet suits and smart umbrellas, one for each day of the year! No more, *hélàs*. I've fallen out of fashion before I properly clung on to it. You and your so-called innovation has cast me in the shadow. Whereas *my* innovation – the genuine article – is already a back number.'

Vincent thought about this. He furrowed his brow, he really wanted to help. 'But how much does it actually matter? We're both artists in our way. The art of creation is not a competition, or ought not to be. We're each equally gifted in God's eyes, no man better nor worse than another. That goes for all His creatures. If God sent us into space with a mouse and an elephant, we'd all of us weigh the same.'

'That's stupid, how could we?'

'We could, I think, where there's no gravity. But that doesn't alter the present problem. Let me see...' Vincent thought some more. His face lit up. 'You know, there is *one* solution. You could always copy me, you have my permission. Do what I do and you'll be fine.'

'You mean, plagiarise?'

'Not exactly, only minor composers plagiarise. Great composers steal outright. To some people plagiarism is an art.'

'Not to me it isn't. I'd rather starve.'

'An idealist, eh? And a hungry one. More fool you.'

'Fool, am I?'

'Though I'm truly sorry to be the cause of your distress.'

'You can be as sorry as you like, but that also solves nothing. So, *Monsieur*, let me tell you something – and for God's sake stop patronising me, I'm not a boy – this is a battle of the artists and there's not room in the concert halls for both of us. One of us must go.'

Vincent looked at him, amused. 'Which one?'

'You, hopefully. First because you've ruined me, second because my ruination is based on a false premise – your unholy lack of talent, linked with an undeserved success. But enjoy it, this is the time to do so, your vogue will be brief.' *Monsieur* Satie paused and stared glumly at the wall. 'Though how, in Heaven's name, will that help *me*?'

'All right then, how will it?' Vincent grinned. 'You're already ruined.'

'I am, totally. Recovery will be slow, if at all. So this is what I propose. Because of the ill you've done me, the humiliation given and total truncation of my gifts –'

'Humiliation?'

'Nothing is more humiliating than the success of another when oneself has failed. For that, and those other reasons, I demand satisfaction – and I'll have it!'

With that, *Monsieur* Satie removed one of his visibly frayed gloves – two of his fingers now well through the fabric – and flicked it fiercely at Vincent's cheek. 'There! Take that! Consider yourself challenged!'

He gazed at Vincent defiantly, fixing his eyes with his own, almost as intensely as Vincent fixed him back. Vincent, mumbling something, stroked his cheek, then spoke to the composer softly, not unkindly, choosing his words with care.

'But look, *Monsieur*, you struck me first. The code says I should challenge *you*. This makes me the aggrieved and you the aggressor.'

'Fuck the code, forget the ritual, do you accept? I mean, what's it to be, death or dishonour?'

'Sod that, too. Questions of honour, in our time, have surely been ceded to reason?'

'Not in my book.'

'In that case, young man, and it's not a course I, myself, might have chosen, instruct your seconds to call – first thing in the morning.'

'Seconds? Which seconds?'

'Your seconds, the friends who'll support you. They have to arrange things. The weapons – it's your choice, I believe? – the rules of engagement, as in how many shots to be fired, what signals given, the number of paces, that's twelve, I believe, the statutory number? Though I've never fought a duel – I assume you mean pistols? – I've read and heard enough, I've a grasp of what's needed. So if you do have friends to act for you, send them here. Or I'd be happy to meet them at your hotel, whichever you prefer?'

'No friends. No hotel. I arrive, I go back – once my job here is done.'

'But you must have friends? You'll need them. As I say, I'd not have recommended this – this drastic action, and I have to tell you I'm quite a fair shot, potting at crows and such. But since you insist, let's at least do it right. You – er – have thought this through?'

The composer looked at him sadly. '*Monsieur*, I have no friends. The people I knew, whom I called my friends, were happy to hang out with me when I was a budding genius, one who might have scored. But all that's changed, thanks to you. Fair-weather friends, dropping me like a hot potato, the moment this "new music" caught their ears. They knew I'd not succeed, that's your fault, too.'

'Again, I'm sorry.'

'You will be, it's pay-off time. You've made a tit of the public – the critics, too. But you won't make a tit out of me! And, in final answer to your question, as I've no chums in Paris and know no one locally – no seconds.'

Vincent gazed back at him, almost with compassion. 'Maybe I could help? Suggest somebody? Take you to the café downstairs, ask around, get you fixed up. Seconds for both of us and a doctor. We'll need a doctor?'

'No doctor. When I get my shot in, which I fully intend to, you'll die like a rat. No bandages, no patch-up jobs, no doctor. And I don't need help, least of all from you. They're all your cronies, I have no doubt. What chance would I have?'

'Every chance. They'll examine the pistols, see that

they're clean and loaded. Mark out the ground, hold the coats, act as lookouts, make sure that it all goes like clockwork. I'll insist upon it.'

'Insist? You *are* mad. Barking.'

Vincent growled, but said nothing.

Monsieur Satie continued. 'I wouldn't trust you further than – well, I won't insult you any more than I have already, which is what you deserved. It's scarcely etiquette, is it, to tell a man what you think of him when he's just about to die?'

'I appreciate that. And you're really set on this? This odd revenge of yours?'

'Very. Sticking to it – like glue.'

'But what if I kill *you*?'

'So be it. I can no longer live in an Age where you have everything and I have nothing.'

'Bit defeatist, I'd say. Sounds more like suicide.'

'I've thought of that, too. Maybe bypass the duel and do it to myself. But God would scarcely approve.'

'Ah, God again.'

'*Oui*. And He will give me justice. To stop your sad excuse for music, once and for all.'

'*Eh bien*. God decides.' Vincent twinkled. 'But let's make a pact, save lives all round. You ask God's help and I'll cease composing, the moment He arrives!'

'You're making fun of me – I don't like it. And I have to tell you, *Monsieur*, having failed all calls to your better nature, a duel it must be.'

'*Alors*, that's it, then, pistols at dawn. Or evening, if you prefer.'

'Evening will be best. Less chance of being … seen.'

'Or seeing the target. Ha. Ha.'

'Oh – ah, d'you think it'll be too dark?'

'"When I'm in the dark, I don't *think*."'

'Eh? Is that a quote? Who said it?'

'Claude Monet.'

'The painter chap? What did he mean by it?'

'You choose. Or come up with a quote of your own.'

Vincent laughed again, still hoping to soften the mood. *Monsieur* Satie again did not laugh. He barely twitched, his face was immobile. He just stared at Vincent as if he were, indeed, as mad as everyone suggested, to make so light of this fateful step. As if suicide and a longed-for forgetfulness were this man's sole motive in accepting the challenge.

The consideration did not take long. *Monsieur* Satie straightened, drawing himself up to his full height, an inch or two above Vincent's head. He stuck out his hand. Vincent, briefly, was taken aback, then grinned hugely at the gesture. He seized the proffered member, shaking it with vigour.

'*Bien*,' said *Monsieur* Satie, 'that's done. This was the first, only, and I insist, the very last time for any hand shaking between us. We are now at daggers drawn.'

'I thought we agreed pistols?'

'*Monsieur* Van Gogh, if I may say something, a little word of advice – though you won't need any where you're going. You are too flippant, too flippant by far, and that is part of your trouble. It puts people's backs up. Several of the crowd who knew you say the same. I have heard them complaining – it grates.'

Vincent bristled. 'What crowd? Which crowd? *Who* of the crowd?? Sisley? Cézanne? Toulouse-Lautrec?'

'Maybe. Could be. I won't name names … specifically.'

'Bastards. I knew it. Accepting my hospitality, the warmth of my welcome and then – a stab in the back.'

'The other way around, if my information is correct. I doubt that you've ever welcomed anyone. But let that be, we won't pursue it. I'll leave you now, see you this evening. Twenty thirty sharp. Come armed and ready, the copse by the bell tower. Pistols loaded, shirt unbuttoned and, if you even possess one, a prayer book. You will need it.'

With that, *Monsieur* Satie straightened again, turned on his heel and marched straight out. Vincent stared after him in disbelief, then began to chuckle. The chuckle transformed itself into a laugh and that's where, at this moment, Marguerite, dropping off a basket of fruit, found him, cackling away at some jest or other. But because poor Vincent refused to elucidate, she concluded, knowing her friend and his *louche* ways, that it must be too indecent for repetition.

Marguerite smiled. 'A joke, Vincent?'

'*Oui, ma jolie*, but a very bad one.'

VI

AUVERS

Chez Ravoux

ONE

In the hours which followed, Vincent made his preparations. But the nonchalance and cynical good humour, which had first graced his acceptance of the challenge, had vanished by stages through moments of tension, nail-biting anxiety, juddering nerves, a deep depression and mounting dread.

He ran the forthcoming duel through his mind, conceiving every possible excuse to avoid it. The urge to do so was enormous, but the coward's way out was not for him.

For a while he lay on his bed, the straw from a split in the pillow tickling his one good ear, while a fat bluebottle on the ceiling transfixed his attention. A strange insect, he thought, oddly constructed, like so many of God's creatures. Not to mention an alarmingly short life, if not an unhappy one?

Closing his eyes, despite the apprehension he felt, Vincent found himself drifting off, slipping through wakefulness and dreams in equal measure. There were recaps of his life, his failures at art and friendship, his success at music and getting up people's noses.

He saw those he knew and had no wish to meet again,

and characters he'd never met, whom he'd quite have liked to, but now most probably wouldn't. He saw, in no particular order, *Le Borinage* in Belgium, 'with its dark awkward beauty' and the long beach at Scheveningen, lapped by a dishwater-coloured sea. There, too, the asylum of Saint-Rémy and *Le Cloître Saint-Paul-de-Mausole*, where he'd painted *Starry Night*. Then his father's pulpit and also his father, a stern, if now ethereal figure.

In a host of flickering memories, he glimpsed his younger self, following in his father's footsteps. There was a vision of the Thames, looking hazy through the trees at Richmond, the dour fenlands of Hoogeveen, the weavers of Nuenen and the peasants in their hovels, staring up at him with desperate eyes. And surely, he could just make out the thatched cottages of Brabant, reflecting the honest simple folk whose homes they were? Or now, just coming into view, the fishing village of Saintes-Maries-de-la-Mer, with its Mediterranean seascape the colour of mackerel, gradually changing from purple into green? He'd loved to paint it, especially the sail boats, for somehow it reminded him of the old country.

He saw the Latin Quarter, from a tiny studio under the roofs, with a view of grey houses as far as the eye could reach, then the Seine and Notre-Dame by sunset. And, away in the distance, he could just make out *la butte sacré*, that sacred hill of St Denis, a place both of pleasure and pilgrimage. And there, indeed, were Lautrec and Pissarro, Monet and Cézanne, now barely visible in the rising mists of evening. Also, if he tried really hard enough, there were the cafés of Montparnasse, rustling with the murmur of poets.

Further into his thoughts came the poppy fields of Arles and the crows at Auvers, transmuted into giant size. Also, the women he'd bedded or, more frequently, failed to bed, and the street girls he'd painted while starving in Antwerp. They were mostly of a certain type, like so many others in his portraits, a certain battered and broken kind of woman, whom life has rolled over and scarred.

In among the memories, Vincent's thoughts became words, as, taking each in turn, he acknowledged these flickering shadows: '*Maman*? Papa? Theo? And Henri? Camille? No, ah, Margot, where are you? Why did you – did you – ? Are you there? No, it's Marguerite, *ma jolie Marguerite*. I'm sorry – sorry. Truly I am.'

Vincent groaned and turned on his side, but the scramble of words persisted. 'What? What? *Eh oui*, it – it's – another candle, Georges, light another candle, is that too much to ask? Can't see – can't you see? The light is fading, one must finish – important to finish. Listen, it's an opera, greater than Massenet, greater than Verdi. Verdi is through. I – I –'

He turned on the bed once more, grunted and yawned. 'I'm hot, it's hot. No cold, I'm cold.' He sang quietly, 'Starry, starry night, shadows on the window pane...' then hummed the next few bars and stirred again. '"The Yellow House", my best work – best work. And all the old friends, are you coming to see me? Too late now – too late, those bloody birds! No, listen, my music – music ... they've heard it in Montmartre, that's almost a home to me...'

Vincent ended on a sigh, then yet again turned over. He now heard voices, one in particular, growing louder it seemed, quite near to his bed. In a blur of puzzlement, mixed with inertia, Vincent yawned and looked up. His eyes beginning to focus, he assumed they must be open. But, again, maybe not, it could as well be his dream.

He now glimpsed a strange glow moving nearer, a figure was starting to materialise. 'Ça va, mon p'tit, how goes it? Hear you've having a bit of trouble?'

Vincent started. No, it couldn't be, could it? Yes, it was! Paul Gauguin, as alive to him as if he were present in the room. But having no inkling that his friend had quit the Pacific, nor even touched harbour in France, he knew, in the recesses of his muddled mind, that it was, indeed, a vision.

A very live vision, though, of *cher* Paul. Benign, three-dimensional, fit and tanned, grinning and waving, brimming over with a bearish *bonhomie*. For some reason – this, too, puzzled Vincent – he had a full beard and shoulder-length hair and was got up in boots and buckskins *à la* Buffalo Bill. Was this some kind of a joke? And there, too, was a familiar twinkle in the eye. But, peering closer, Vincent noted something else odd about his old friend, as if this cheeriness were a front, a false impression, constructed simply to reassure him.

'Is that you, Paul? Is that you?'

'It is I, *mon p'tit*. Come back to haunt you.'

'Torment me, you mean. You're not dead?'

'Not quite. But I come from far away.'

'Hah, the man who comes from far away and *will* go far! Mm, maybe not. But nice outfit, Paul. Ride 'em, cowboy! Or should that be "How"?'

Vincent raised his hand in a Redskin salute. Paul grinned and looked sheepish. Then doffed his battered stetson and bowed. Vincent studied him.

'You know, they told me you were on your travels. Doing things, adventures? So you're back home, sort of – from wherever it is you got to? Tahiti, wasn't it?'

'The Marquesas, I've moved on. But I'm still there,

becalmed in the tropics, with the fabulous sunsets, those light-brown native girls. I'm in your dreams, Vincent. You see, you once painted me *in absentia*. Now you've my absent presence present.'

'You ... seem real enough?'

'Reality is relative, you've heard me say so. Just like painting, an impression, a mood. The work of our friends, of artists everywhere. It's not real, not representative. An illusion, merely, of what one sees. Ridiculous, isn't it?'

'It is, rather. But I don't understand. Someone I spoke to, Degas, perhaps, said he'd seen you somewhere, at *La Gare du Nord*, going off to Denmark or – or – so how can you be in Tahiti, or the other place, when you're a ghost right here, if your real person, when you have one, is not even *there*? In the South Seas, I mean, instead of here. Here, this minute, instead of where ... you can't now possibly *be* ... if Degas has seen you, since he's also *here*? Do I make sense?'

'Perfect sense. I think. Just put it down to magic. Black magic, maybe. It's become all the rage in Paris, so they tell me.'

'The cops are on to it, Paul, you'd best look out.'

'I shall make myself invisible. But not to worry, *mon p'tit*, this is not precisely *now*, but somewhere in the future. My future, not yours. You're still in the present. I *am* the future.'

'But – but do I believe this?'

'Whether you do or not, it makes no odds. None. Still, let me see now?' Paul studied him. 'Y'know, Vincent, you're looking pretty seedy, like the Arles arena after a bullfight! Sure you're not working too hard?'

'I am, but it's fulfilling. I thrive on it.'

166

'So I gather. And all this success – the music? That does surprise me.'

'It surprises everyone.'

'I'm not surprised. Not surprised that I'm surprised, nor that everyone *else* is surprised. Surprises all round – Ha. Ha. And so, Vincent, you're getting good notices at last, for both your talents?'

'Small for the painting, huge for music. It's wonderful, but –'

' – Your triumph in Paris has got you into a scrape, *hein*? Well, it's to be expected. Foolish failures are always jealous of another chap's success. And, as a result, this fellow Satie is giving you a hard time?'

Vincent was growing irritated. 'If you know so much about me, Paul, and what I've been doing, as in who's been praising me or giving me stick, why all these questions?'

'Just checking. And now, it seems, the sore-headed Satie, with you having stolen his thunder, has challenged you to a duel?'

Vincent gazed dolefully at Paul. 'Seems like it.'

'Ah.' Paul beamed at Vincent, he spread his arms wide. 'So let's see what we can do. Or, rather, what your *vieux ami*, Paul Gauguin, can do? If it's advice you need, I'm your man – ghost.'

'*Monsieur* Satie also offered me advice, but in a somewhat unfriendly fashion. Full of irony and threats.'

'Stands to reason, in his case. But this … is different. So, tell me, how's your gunmanship? Been practising on those birds again?'

'Just a bit, just a bit.'

'*Bien*, you've seen sense and got yourself a weapon. You evidently need it.'

'It has its uses.' Vincent paused. 'You mentioned advice? With guns?'

'Fencing's more my line. That and boxing. Except – Ha. Ha – when taken by surprise! But here's my tip. You must get a shot in first.'

'Oh, do I have to? It is all my fault. *Monsieur* Satie is ruined, he seems so abject.'

'Bah, you're not feeling sorry for him? He's the one that gave the challenge. Heaven forfend, but what if he kills you?'

'I'll have deserved it.'

'So will he. Gaol or the guillotine, once the cops turn up.'

'Then, I – I'll tell them what happened. That it was I started it – my crazy longings, selfish ambition, my recent successes and putting paid to this poor chap's career.'

'Ah, you *are* sorry for him? So much the worse! *Cher ami*, you're too saintly by far. Anyhow, what good can you do if you're already dead? A secret message from the grave? Or turning up as a ghost – I mean a *proper* ghost, not like me, to have a word in *le Procureur's* ear. "Écoutez, *Monsieur le Procureur*, it wasn't his fault, this other fellow, it was mine – mine for getting shot"? Ha. Ha. Ha.'

'Paul, you have a point.'

'I do, I do. So how d'you expect to save him when the evidence is on the ground, with a bullet through the heart and a pistol in the murderer's hand? One bullet missing from the chamber and a face as guilty as sin?'

'Will it really be like that?'

'Just a touch of poetic licence.'

'But *Monsieur* Satie? Maybe – maybe he can get away quickly. So that, when they turn up, the people who've heard the shot, they'll see me lying there and think I did it myself. My gun, too, it may also be missing a bullet? *Oui*, I'll see that it does. I've had a bit of practice at self-harm, it can't be that hard to fool them? No, I know, I'll leave a suicide note.'

'Another bad idea. You know what our friends will say? That because you fail at everything else, you can't even kill yourself without help. Besides, as a suicide you'd be denied a Christian burial, you thought o'that?'

'I hadn't. But God will understand, I'll have to chance it. The idea, though, Paul, it *could* work?'

'Hardly, there'll still be witnesses. Like … who are your seconds?'

'No seconds.'

'No seconds? Too bad. Wish I were real, I'd surely be there for you.'

'I know you would, Paul, but I'd not put you through it. If the victor were guilty of murder, the seconds would be accessories. Thanks, though, for the offer. You're a good friend, despite our differences.'

'Differences? What differences? I mean, no worries, don't give it a thought. We're the same, you and I, maybe too *much* the same. Volatile, impatient, self-destructive, hyper-adventurous and lovers of beautiful women. We believe in perfection in Art.'

'*Merci*, Paul. You know how to say the right thing. And do it, too. Sometimes. I wish they all did.'

'Who? The old gang? They did, in their way. Still could. I talk now of Art, Vincent – but the mighty franc outweighs all else. Take Renoir. His paintings are full of false optimism, soaked in a perennial summer and showered with undeserved coin.'

'But a superb draughtsman. Theo thinks I should be more like him.'

'Bah. Bad advice. Renoir was an Impressionist once. Now he's a photographer. A deluge of bland designs for the tops of biscuit boxes.'

'No answer to that. But the Impressionists or lapsed Impressionists, our old friends, we got on quite well?'

'That was then. Our salad days when we were green in judgement!' Paul, to Vincent's amazement, appeared now to conjure the Impressionists, as in a vision, though one to which Vincent, himself, seemed not to be party. A vision *having* a vision? *Oui*, typical Paul, bizarre or not?

'But look,' said Paul, 'there's Monet, *le vrai Papa*, smudging his way through *les grands jardins de Giverny*, not to mention those bloody poplars!'

Vincent squinted, trying to focus where Paul was pointing. All he saw was this room, with his own things in it, and Paul standing there before him. 'But it's sad, very,' murmured Vincent, 'they say he has cataracts.'

'That so? Poor Claude. I shut my eyes in order to see.' Paul did so. 'But God closed Claude's, his painting's a blur. Tell me, is life at all fair? And then – ah, there are the others. Look hard, Vincent, hard. D'you see?'

Again Vincent tried, but saw only what he saw. Taking his cue from Paul, he now closed his own eyes shut. No, nothing. Total blackness. Whoever said 'darkness can reveal the brightest light' was an idiot! He opened them again.

'But there, over there,' urged Paul, 'it's silly old Sisley, nothing but endless landscapes. And Redon's unsettling symbolism – blue faces in profile, with stupid white blobs, and a nightmare of giant floating eyeballs! Paul Signac, too, with his muddy mosaic patches, and Seurat dotting the canvas like a multitude of pinpricks – one big prick and a million small ones – who needs it?'

'Certainly not the man in the street.'

'*C'est vrai, tout a fait.* Then, Degas, who became fascinated, it seems, with twisting the female body into awkward contortions … though I'm not so sure he really liked women.'

'Nor did he seem to find a settled style. Said it bored him to death.'

'*Vrai encore.* So that's Degas. A very tricky gentleman. And still we have Cézanne. Bah. What did they once call him? "The Poussin of Provence"? He should be so lucky!'

'There, Paul, you're doing it again. You're knocking Cézanne.'

'Who deserves it more? He didn't like *us* much. Said he scorned all living artists, 'cept Renoir and Monet.'

'That apart, I told you it upsets me. He's an important painter.'

'You don't say? The most important thing about Cézanne, give or take his aloofness, or the insults and rages if you dare contradict him, is his own anxiety. He may be able to paint, after a fashion, but the man is his own worst enemy.'

Lost for a comeback, Vincent went on staring, making every effort to envision this portrait of their old companions. But whatever the picture Paul had wrought, with these new ghostly skills of his, frustratingly he now turned away from it.

'*Alors*, those *were* the Impressionists. Living and dead, original or otherwise, good, bad, indifferent and sometimes bloody awful. God help them all.'

'God *has*, in spades. 'Cos each has enjoyed his moment in the sun. And at least they most of them sell.'

'Except Cézanne, who won't sell.'

'That's his choice. The others do.'

'So do I. Or have done.'

'Who to? Where? Apart from that measly auction of yours?'

'It wasn't measly, just badly lit. And the workmen there attacked me.'

'Poor Paul. So, who did you sell to?'

'Eh? What? Um – to Degas. And my brother-in-law.'

'Disciples, Paul, disciples.'

'And others.'

'Ah.'

'So, you see, I do sell.'

'Me, too. Now I come to think of it.'

'Since when?'

'Since … recently.'

'How many?'

'Apart from those of mine you sold, yourself, then kept the cash?'

'Aha. Now we come to it. You said you didn't mind?'

'Well, I did. They were a gift.'

'Sorry, my need then was great. Anyhow, I sold them on – second-hand. As it wasn't you, doesn't count. So, other than that, what else?'

'What else what?'

'All right, then, *who* else? Who else has bought your paintings?'

'Um – er, let me see now, there was this chap who looked like me. Man called Reid, Glasgow art dealer. Dead ringer, I'd say, same red beard and hair, we could have been twins. We shared lodgings in Paris.'

'Get to the nub, Vincent, what about him?'

'He acquired two of my paintings.'

'What d'you mean "acquired"?'

'He had them.'

'Had them?'

'Up to a point.'

'"Up to a point"? Ho. Ho. Bet he still has them. Propping up a table.'

'Not at all. His father disapproved and sold them.'

'Sold them *on*?'

'*Oui, c'est ça.* So, *ergo*, a sale.'

'So, *ergo* – how much?'

'What?'

'How much did they go for?'

'Five pounds in English money.'

'More than I'd have paid. But it's second-hand again, still doesn't count. What I want to know is how ... many?'

'How many what?'

'Paintings.'

'Paintings what?'

'How ... many ... paintings ... have ... you ... *actually* sold. You, yourself, deliberately ... from your own hand?'

'How ... many?'

'*Oui.* Is the question so difficult? Are you deaf as well as suicidal? Your bad ear playing up?'

'No. Not difficult.'

'Then answer me. How many?'

'Um, I haven't – don't physically sell them ... myself. Theo does. In his gallery.'

'Right, then.' Paul let out a groan. 'How ... many ... has Theo ... sold?'

'How *many*?'

'*Oui.*'

'To date?'

'To date.'

Vincent assumed a small voice. 'One.'

'What? Speak up. Can't hear you.'

Vincent spoke louder. 'One!'

'One. Right. Ha. Ha. Thought so. Which one?'

'*The Red Vineyard.*'

'Don't know it. Who to?'

'Who?'

'*Oui.* Who bought it?'

'Eh, what?'

'Again, can't answer? Cat got your tongue? Who owns it now?'

'The painting?'

'*Oui. The Red Vineyard.*'

'My brother – Theo.'

A pause. Paul shook his head. 'He bought it *himself?*'

'*Oui.*'

'Doesn't count, either.'

'Does.'

'Doesn't.'

'Does.'

'How so?'

'Still a sale. Money changed hands.'

'Bah. So it did with that whore of yours, in the village at Arles. But after you'd done what you had to do – somewhat too quickly, from what I gather! – she was her own property again.'

'Not the same at all. Theo gave me money. He still has the painting. Money mine, painting his. *Quod erat demonstrandum.*'

'And one day you'll get it back – 'cos he can't ever sell it. Ha. Ha.'

'Well, he can. A woman called Anna Boch – she's made an offer. 400 francs.'

'Who she?'

'Sister of an old friend.'

'Old friend? Sounds like charity. Again, doesn't count.'

'It does. She'd have bought it anyway.'

'From your brother, who's already paid you up front? So the profit will be his.' Another pause. 'Besides, he's always giving you money. The allowance for "The Yellow House". Presumably your lodgings here. *Oui, ce petit chambre simple*! Tell me, what is this dump?'

'*L'Auberge Ravoux*. They're nice people.'

'Have to be.' Paul sniffed. 'Still not taking a bath, Vincent? Pretty gamey, you smell something awful.'

'Ghosts can't smell.'

'No?' Paul backed away. 'Well, I told you, I'm a live ghost, not a dead one. I can smell and so do *you*.' He sniffed again. 'Really, Vincent, phew!' A thought. 'Or maybe you can't? That's it, isn't it, you can't smell … *yourself*? But this place is pokey, there's no avoiding you. Reason, probably, you don't lodge with Dr Gasket.'

'Gachet. I told you.'

'You did.' Paul glanced around. 'Bad light, too. Not like the other place, the two of us. We had room to swing a cat. An incontinent cat – but a cat.'

'Right. In that house, that very house, which you failed to help with the upkeep of.'

'I'll ignore that. And don't end a sentence on a preposition.'

'Conjunction. I was a teacher, remember?'

'Then why don't you learn to speak properly? Anyhow, I paid what I could, *when* I could.'

'Almost never. Or the food. Or the wine.'

'Aw, put a cork in it. I wasn't there long enough for "Never". Only nine weeks, though it felt like a century. Most of them freezing or in a hair's breadth of getting murdered! Eh? What? What food? We were fucking starving. You can live without Art, without food you die.' Yet another pause. 'No, leave it, it's old hat, to me it'll always be a house of fear. We were talking of your wretched painting. *The Red –* ?'

'*Vineyard.*'

'*Vineyard, oui.* Painted, I'd guess, in your cups? Like everything else one sees on the canvas. All the detail, the definition, probably, hidden away by great *impasto* splodges. Vincent Van Gogh, splashing it on like gravy, so one doesn't have to see it. And still, I say, it's no sale.'

''Tis.'

''Tisn't.'

''Tis.'

''Tisn't.'

''Tis.'

''Tisn't.'

A final pause. Paul tried to stare Vincent out, daring him to continue.

'*'Tis!* Hah.'

Paul sighed, then studied him closely. 'Okay, Corporal, a sale. Congratulations, you're winning. So, what else is new? How are you otherwise?'

'*Comme ci, Comme ça.* But still the old melancholy, that's even without the duel hanging over me. *La vie est une connerie*, everything's shit. Paul, I'm at the end of my tether. I try to seem cheerful, sometimes I am, but the gloom remains.'

'You should be a Russian.' Paul now declaimed in a strange comedy accent, making appropriate gestures. '"*Do svidaniya, malchiki*, I so happy I kill myself!" Ha. Ha. Ha. It's a national characteristic.'

'Very suitable for my composing, then. There's no such thing as happy moments in Russian music, ever.'

'What about *The Nutcracker*?' Paul hummed a snatch of "The Sugar Plum Fairy". 'Hear that? Sounds happy.'

Vincent gave a grimace. 'You're splitting hairs. Tchaikovsky shot himself. Stone dead. Where's *happy*?'

'No, he recovered.'

'What? Did he? You sure? *Eh bien*, he'll no doubt try it again, those who are prone to it usually do. Poison or something, that's best.'

'So this is your advice to Tchaikovsky? Bah. Pathetic. You must write and tell him.'

'I wish I could. And it's still pretty sad.'

Paul was gazing through the windows. 'So how's Auvers? How is this physician of yours? Dr Gasket – Gachet. Helpful is he? Not yet in the loony bin, living up to Pissarro's recommendation?'

'He is. A huge help.'

'Another surprise. Camille, as we know, has his errors of judgement. Crusty old twit.'

Vincent frowned. 'That's unkind, Paul. Uncalled for. If it's not Cézanne with you, it's Pissarro.'

'Well fuck him, I say. Last time I was in Paris he gave some of my new work the once-over. He called it "a step backward".'

'He's got a bit set in his ways. But you used to respect his judgement?'

'More fool I.'

'You know you did. Were in awe of him, too. His talent, his drive, his selfless guidance, he was like a father to us all. Made us feel we were better than we were.'

'Bah. That's when my enthusiasm for those weird ideas Camille tried hard to instil in us – poor lousy beggars! – began to pall. I needed stretching, given a jolt. I'd had it with that Impressionist crap, too middle class by far. I was drawn instead to the contemplative character of Cézanne. Much more my style. There, that'll please you?'

'It does, Paul. I knew you'd come round. It must be a miracle.'

'At least, it was then – Cézanne had his moments. As for the others? Admired them all. Still do in my grudging way. Maybe I've mellowed.'

'In just five minutes?'

'Could be, ghosts are like that. Or else, I'm no longer envious?'

'And some of the earlier chaps. You always praised *them*? Millet and Delacroix, Ingres, too, "The Great French Masters?"'

'The *old* French masters. *Les peintures de nos grand-pères.* The Italians, too, and naturally, Rembrandt. I admired him enormously.'

'I *love* Rembrandt, Paul. It's more than "admire". The portraits – *magnifiques*! 'Specially the self-portraits.'

'Now you're talking. The face of human nature at its most monumental.'

'It's also more than nature, a kind of revelation. Those people we speak of, they had the vision, the all-embracing eye. Being an artist is not just about fine paintings. It's creating a whole view of the world and making it work. "Painting is a feat of alchemy." Some Englishman said that. If we go to the place, itself, we will see it through the eyes of the painter who best heard it and sang its song. You see, Paul, the connection once more between sounds and colour?'

'Ha. Ha. That word "song" again. *La belle chanson.* My poor Vincent, you're still dying to regale me?'

'I am. And you'll find me much improved.'

'*Alors*, nurse your frustration. I *shall* listen, I'll be all ears. I still have two!'

'*Merci.*'

'But the painting?' Paul nodded sagely. '*C'est vrai, n'est-ce pas?* Painting, great art, it's just like women. You can't love them all, but those you do love, you love 'em to pieces. *Eh, cher* Vincent, we both had our fancies.'

'Our dreams, too.'

'*Mais tout se change*, we're old now, you and I. Soon be losing it.'

'Not that old.'

'Old enough. What age are you again?'

'Thirty-seven. And you?'

'Forty-two. Just look at us! Two old crocks. We should have come to it earlier – all that wasted time.'

'I said as much to Theo, when was it? Something to the effect that "Not only did I start painting late in life, but it may be that I shall not live for many years, between six and ten." Looks as if it's about to come true.'

'Cheer up, may not be as bad as you think. Let's remember the good times.'

'Too few. But it forged us.'

'Forged us? Bah. Maybe it did. Me in my dull old bank, my non-stop round of starched collar dinner parties, you in your pulpit or those wretched coal miners' hovels? I'd rather have been forged in a metal worker's smithy and taken some heat from that!'

'Same for me. I'd like to have altered things, but it's what I am.'

'And what, pray, *are* you, in fact?'

'Not just a late starter, a late developer.'

'Slow developer, more like.'

'If you say so. Too many distractions in the early days.

Holland, Belgium, England, they were a useful learning curve, but I wasn't a real artist.'

'Are you now? No, sorry, course you are. I've always said it.'

'Sometimes you have.'

'I do. And to be an artist you need to have lived, to travel.' Paul looked at Vincent, he reacted. '*C'est ça*, I forgot you'd been in England. How come?'

'Surely, Paul, I told you? You know all my adventures by heart?'

'Ghosts forget. Remind me.'

'Like a drowning man recalling his past?'

Paul nodded, while Vincent, sitting on the edge of the bed, moved his weight from one buttock to the other, taking his time.

'*Alors*. Two of my uncles were dealers with international connections. I worked for *Goupil & Cie*. For five years, in fact, before I had to quit and followed my father into the ministry. Enjoyed London at first. I was fit, then.'

'So why *did* you quit? What happened with those art dealers?'

'They sent me to the Paris office, for my health's sake – mental, that is – after an unhappy time with my landlady's daughter. I was drawn to her, it got me nowhere, it was affecting my work.'

'*Mon Dieu*, young Vincent and his women! Having them or not having them, it's always been your trouble.'

'Preferably having them. To be cut off from female companionship is a lonely pilgrimage – I must have a woman or freeze. It's the story of my life, Paul, forever veering between the unsuitable and the impossible. This time the rejection proved hard. It changed me completely.'

'I won't ask you how!' Paul, disconcertingly, laughed. 'So 'twas then you got religion?'

'Always had it, never really lost it. The prayers, the family business, the old traditions. It was that caused the break with *Goupil*.'

'How so?'

'They called me "a religious maniac" – I insisted on going home for Christmas.'

Paul chuckled. 'That all? *Mon Dieu*.'

'Well, I also told them art dealing was a form of organised fraud. They fired me on the spot.'

'I'd have fired you, too. 'Specially for telling the truth! So, then what? You stayed in Holland?'

'No, I returned to England. Teaching and preaching in Richmond and Ramsgate. That didn't work out, either, I soon moved on.'

'All over the place, eh? And nowhere near the sun! Is that a sad story or no?'

'As sad as yours, Paul, in the early days? You on *La Bourse*, a tiresome interlude?'

'Let's not milk it. City men, investors – as bad as your peasants. I'd made a killing in the boom years, but was relieved in '83 when the Crash came. It wiped me out, the domino effect. I said, "Now it's time for a change."'

'An instant decision?'

'Not entirely. I'd already been a well-regarded amateur – *oui*, me too, to my lasting shame, a Sunday painter! And to Mette, who could never get the point, it was a just barely tolerated hobby. But, as I wrote to her later, I fully intended to make some money from it. I'd embark, come what may, to more favourable climes. And, whatever they say, I didn't ditch my family to lead a wild life of travel. I'd been travelling since childhood, it was my twelve years in an office I saw as the aberration.'

'The way you describe it, Paul, it sounds almost logical.'

'It is.' Paul laughed. 'So off I went.'

'Without a second thought? You always had guts by the barrel-load.'

'True, true. Never afraid of scandal, always ready to uproot myself. Paul Gauguin, the eternal globe-trotter!' He grinned. 'Still, I'm glad you also saw the light. It wasn't a job for you. Teacher, preacher, the other thing. Art dealer? Bah. Not for a born *artist*. It's the fourth lowest rung from the top.'

'How d'you make that out?'

'When you can't create, criticise. When you can't criticise, collect. When you can't collect, sell!'

Paul roared. Mildly, Vincent joined in, though laughter was the last thing on his mind. At this point, the vision faded. Vincent stared hard at the spot where Paul had been, but saw nothing. He lay back on the bed and began drifting off again. 'Mustn't fall asleep,' Vincent told himself, 'must force myself awake –' he yawned, trying to sit up ' – I have a date with destiny. Mmm.' The effort was too much. Breathing heavily, he again lay back. His eyes flickered shut, his head sank into the pillows.

TWO

Opening his eyes, Vincent glimpsed Paul once more, coming back into focus. Just like the Cheshire Cat, he thought, here one minute, gone the next, then back again when one least expected it. How long had Paul been gone? A glance at the clock told Vincent no time had passed at all, though it felt like some minutes since the last 'sighting'. As the vision grew stronger, Vincent sat up. Paul was inspecting him closely.

'Ah,' said Vincent, 'I thought I'd lost you.'

'No chance. So what happened next?'

'Next? My life, you mean? You know what happened. Art happened. Studying in The Hague and Antwerp. Or else, roughing it with the miners, a missionary to the destitute. I caught them on canvas, best work I'd done. From that moment all was transformed for me.'

'And then?'

'Then on again, back to Paris. Hanging out with you and the other fellows, being part of the group, if not quite fitting in, at the same time eager to learn. And though the stresses and stimuli of the city became intolerable, it was there I found my path, and that inspiration led to Provence.'

'It did, for both of us.' Paul was looking wistful. 'But the lure of the exotic was always too strong. Me, I needed that other life, my drug of choice. Away from everything and everyone I knew, relieved of responsibility, except to my art. Screwing, canoeing and getting fat. Civilisation? I was well out of it.'

'As you don't stop telling me.'

'*Oui, c'est une idée fixe.* I was being choked. Freedom was my goal.'

Vincent thought about this. He took a breath. 'Your break with Pissarro caused him great sadness.'

'Who told you that? Pissarro?'

'A little bird.'

'One of your crows again? Ha. Ha.'

'Still, that's all past. But *mon Dieu*, Paul, the example you set. I, too, began to loathe the self-doubt and squabbles of the Impressionists, seeing myself, as I said, somewhat outside the frame. I had my own idealistic dreams, vain though I see them to be now, of artists *en commune*, working to a unified goal, fed by visions of the South. As if one's physical removal from Paris could be the crucial instrument in transforming one's style. For the better, one hoped.'

'Maybe, for a brief time.'

'Arles, you know, was Lautrec's idea? A pity he didn't come.'

'*Oui.* You always clicked, you two. And he encouraged you.'

'We encouraged each other, a mutual admiration society – though our styles and subject matter were opposites. He told me, did Henri, that he doubted I could paint as well as he did, those girls at *Le Moulin de la Galette*, the night-life and human flotsam, frequenting the backstreets and *les maisons de passe*. But he said he couldn't paint my wheat fields, either, "all hot with the sun of Provence. A man can stare at one of Vincent's canvases," said Henri, "and go blind with delight".'

'Another twit. But a good egg.'

'He is, too. D'you know he once challenged another painter to a duel, for daring to slag me off?'

'What happened?'

'It fizzled out, but Henri's a fine shot. I wish he were here, I could use him.'

'Being on the short side does have its advantages. He'd be right in line with this Satie fellow's balls.' Paul chuckled, then crossed his legs and winced. 'Ooh, doesn't bear thinking about!'

'He's a loyal friend, Henri, odd though it seems. Different as we are.'

'Very different, I'd say, but you both found what suited

you. Only for me, it was Panama and Martinique. And now, the South Pacific. A search for new subjects. Much good it did me.'

'Really? But the work you brought back last time was pretty fair.'

'*Merci*. The critics were kind. But it didn't sell.'

'You just said it did.'

'It sold, but not well *enough*. No more talk of selling. Close the subject?'

'*D'accord*.'

Paul looked around again. He began to inspect Vincent's paintings. 'Quite good some of these. Don't like this dark one, though. That louring sky, the grubby-looking crows. I take it they *are* crows, not accidental drips?'

'Crows. And you're right, Paul. No one likes dark paintings. Theo says it's difficult to place them, when everything in Paris is bright.'

'Always has been.' Paul now examined a more colourful landscape, stroking the frame, his ghost hands clearly slipping through. 'Ah, this one is better. Bit garish, I'd say, like noise for the eyes. But vivid, truly alive.'

Vincent beamed. 'My grip on the brush has never been stronger. I did it for the people round here, trying to make them open their minds to the miraculous force of life. It's Auvers – the fields and the houses, as they ought to be seen! *C'est une juissance, n'est-ce pas? Oui*, virtually an orgasm, with one great ejaculation of emotional energy and paint!'

Paul chuckled. 'That's what I go to the knocking shop for. 'Cept for the paint. But, Vincent, I like it.' He picked up another picture, protruding from under the bed. 'So who's this odd party with the dinky beard? Looks a bit sad.'

'Dr Gachet.'

'Your present mentor, that's what he's like? Miserable bugger.'

'In that respect, Paul, the painting's accurate. I've given it the heartbroken expression of our time.'

'Then it's worse than I thought. And here's your brother, Theo.' Paul had picked up another painting. 'Good likeness.'

'I think so.'

'Losing weight, is he? Problems?'

'He has his worries, I'm tormented by it. Keeping the business going, mouths to feed, including me. And the new baby.'

'*Eh, oui.*' Paul turned away, not much interested, then thought he should make an effort. 'And how is the little one? Thriving?'

'I think so, one keeps one's fingers crossed. I wrote to Theo immediately. Said, since they were good enough to name him after me, I'd "like him to have a spirit less unquiet than mine".'

Paul laughed again. 'Poor kid. He'd be extra lucky without your red hair! Not to mention the so-called music.'

'Eh? What's that? "So-called?" What d'you mean – "so-called"?'

'What I said.'

'But – but I was just about to play for you? To illustrate my success. Last time you heard me you said you liked it.'

'And then I said I didn't. You belaboured me for saying so.'

'Did I? I don't think I did?'

'You know you did. At Saint-Rémy. You nearly fucking killed me.'

'Oh. Oh, that? A friendly disagreement, it was nothing.'

'Nothing? You nutcase, you menace, it was almost a massacre. You put me in hospital, your brother paid the bill.'

'Did I? Did he? Sorry, my memory, it's – you're all right now?'

'It seems so, in that respect, no thanks to you. Or, rather, if you hadn't relaxed your grip, I'd have been a goner. I could barely get a blow in, otherwise I'd –'

'I really *am* sorry. Those last days at Saint-Rémy, I was – I was painting like a madman, it all stemmed from that.'

'You mean, the other way around? First you were mad, then you painted like – no, no matter. There's no need to dwell on it.'

Vincent looked at him, pleadingly. 'And we're still friends?'

Paul nodded. '*Oui*, Vincent, we go back a long way. But you do understand, I couldn't stick around? Some folk blamed me, ostracised me even, saying my desertion of you, soon after that ear nonsense, precipitated your madness. But, in my view, you were almost there. The state you were in, I feared the very sight of me might prove fatal to you. I'd have been crazier than you to have stayed. Crazier still, after Saint-Rémy.'

'You're right, it must have been terrifying.' Vincent hesitated, then stared at his knees and spoke. 'So now you *really* don't like my music?'

'Never did. It's horrible. Can't help it. Don't want to hurt your feelings, but ghosts tell the truth. Ghastly, that's the word. Tuneless, toneless and an insult.' Paul grinned. 'To the ear, that is.'

'Right. Right! That does it! That bloody well does it!' Seething with fury, his eyes ablaze and almost popping out of their sockets, Vincent leapt from the bed to assume a fighting stance. 'You've asked for this! You've really asked for it, you – you – you – ! You're dead, okay? If not dead, already – else, I'd – I'd eat your liver and piss on your grave!'

'*Mahua no varua ino*,' laughed Paul, 'the Devil speaks.'

Vincent gave him a look and began moving forward. But nonplussed for a moment that Paul was just standing there, hands in his pockets, apparently unconcerned, he pulled up short. The fact that his old friend, despite Vincent's threats, was also twinkling and grinning at him, treating it all as one big joke, served only to infuriate him more. Raising his fists higher, Vincent took another step forward.

'You – you – you – ! Come on, then, come on! You big swarthy coward, you arsehole of a Peruvian! What is it, you afraid? Can't make your fingers work? You're this close to extinction, put your mitts up – come *on*!'

'Can't. Won't. 'Specially *can't*. It's yet another peculiarity of being a ghost. If you go for me, you'll just shoot out the other side and fall flat on your kisser! And if I try to parry, my fists won't connect. So, let it be.'

Vincent looked doubtful, but gradually lowered his fists. Paul still stood there and grinned.

'I'd even shake hands with you, kiss and make up, but that wouldn't work either – whole thing would be one big blur. As the natives say, "*No te ahia oe riri?* Why are you angry?" Forget what I said, I spoke out of turn. Others like your music, quite a few, so why worry about *me*? My opinion's nothing. I'm not here for long. 'Twas good to see you.'

'Me, too.' Now quietened down, Vincent sat on the end of the bed again, gazing at Paul, with a tolerant smile.

'So, it's just a fleeting call, this, your ghostly visitation? You'll wake up in your own hammock, eh? In some frond-roofed *faré*, with the hair or shoulders of a lovely *vahiné* brushing your cheek, the sun twinkling through the palms and some haunting native chants calling you to your easel. You've got it all worked out, I'd say? Notwithstanding every obstacle, Paul Gauguin remains true to himself.'

'What d'you know about it, Vincent? You know fuck all. I'm the one that's sailed the seas and come into contact with the rough and primitive. What have *you* ever done?'

'Nothing, really, that's just it. I still envy you, Paul, in this new world of yours.'

'*Alla o feii*? Why are you so jealous? It wouldn't be your scene at all.'

'But I did get it right?'

'Just the way you picture it, just as the travel books say. A beguiling landscape, crystal-clear sea and women coming out of one's ears.' Paul offered a thin smile, but his eyes were troubled. Or, as much as a ghost's eyes *can* be troubled, Paul's, indeed, were. He sighed, staring out sadly. 'But with the sweet, I have to tell you, there also comes the sour.'

'I don't understand, I – ? You mean, trouble in Paradise?'

Paul looked grim. 'Exactly. That's what I do mean. I'd seen my self-imposed exile as a search for excitement, for ecstasy, calm and art. But it's not turning out that way. Except, maybe, art.'

'That's all that matters.'

'Could be. But it's not how I'd imagined it. It's more like ... Paradise Lost, the fall from Eden.'

'So, what gives? Tell me, if you have to?'

'I do, Vincent, it's falling apart. I really thought I *was* in Heaven, I'd been to the islands before, remember? The vibrant colours in a translucent light, the vanilla-scented air and hillsides ablaze with flowers. Again, just so. I could immerse myself in nature, see no one but savages and live their life. Meanwhile, I'd be the master of my palette, using those same colours to strip away the veneer of civilisation and find True Being. At the same time, raise the horizon higher and higher, till it was all but out of the frame! How on earth, I asked myself, could it now be different? I arrived there, after an untroubled voyage, with a 30 per cent discount, a grant from the Ministry of Fine Arts and some high expectations.'

'Lucky Paul.'

'Lucky? Mmm. At first I was lionised, invited every-where, living like a true colonial. But I came to dislike the town, which was dirty, run-down and corrupt.'

'Corrupt? As in licentious?'

'Hardly, more's the pity. One's movements were restricted, the women forced to behave. So I moved along the coast – to find a life that suited me. And I found it. Everything I'd ever wanted, everything I'd ever dreamed of, 'specially the women. In a free love culture, where the gift of the body is deemed a sacred duty.'

'Sounds like you fell on your feet, Paul?'

'There was one in particular, well, not a woman, exactly – you know *me*, she was barely into her teens! – a beauti-ful nutbrown maid. My model, later my mistress, I might have mentioned her? Teha'amana, her name, gorgeous, just like the one you describe. I liked her, she also liked me, or so I imagined. Anyhow, I'd left her in a delicate con-dition. Sailed back to France, without a second thought. *Oui, d'accord*, anyone would say so, I acted like a shit. But, setting sail again, I told myself, all that way back to Tahiti, this time I'd make an honest woman of her.'

'True love, then?'

'Love? Love? I don't know love. Not at all, really. Never did, not even with Mette. To say, "I love you" would break all my teeth!' Paul laughed, bitterly. 'But still, I'd made my decision. To live in connubial bliss and see the kid grow big and strong like his Papa. It was then I found, in my absence, she'd married an islander.

'That was the first thing, it blew me off course. Second, cash for materials soon ran out, payments from Paris took months to arrive. Another dream shattered. I was reduced to painting on wood or tree bark, old cigar boxes, bits of sackcloth. All knots and wrinkles, terribly rough.'

'But that's how you were *going* to paint? With makeshift materials, in nature's own way. It's what you wanted, I recall you saying so.'

'When was that?'

'At Arles. "The Yellow House."'

'*Eh, oui*, I did. Thought it might be romantic, to paint like a native, but not so romantic as I'd thought. Remember, I told you, two natures reside within me, the civilised man and the Indian savage. But on this occasion, the civilised side was fast gaining ground. I mean, what was I doing, in that ragged end of nowhere, slumming, I felt, even more so than usual? I also had a girl, another girl. Posed as my Virgin Mary – Ha. Ha – in a Tahitian Nativity scene. Luscious she was, I was overwhelmed by the sheer irresistible beauty of her!'

'Paul, you *are* lucky!'

'We had a daughter, too, I've always preferred daughters. Delighted when she was born, but she died a few days later. Another great blow, it almost unhinged me. On top, that is, of missing my family back home. You know,

I'd always intended to return? To re-marry Mette, even, I
wrote and told her so.'

'I think you should.'

'Should I? It's not to be. I mean, fate says otherwise. For
to cap it all, after several other privations: the curse of the
islands: it's set in for real.'

'Curse? I still don't – ?'

'*Oui*, curse. You remember that talk we had once, of
leaving the natives as they were. Making friends but not
trying to change them?'

'I do, vaguely.'

'*Hélàs*, not all the visitors to Paradise are quite so
high-minded.'

'But what – ?'

'It was they, Vincent, those fucking French missionaries.
Brought death, disease and a dread of the Hereafter. If
not them, it was the sailors. And those silly native girls,
naive and trusting. Getting religion on the one hand and
a sharp dose of pox on the other. Well' – a wry grin ' –
not on the hand, exactly, but *you* know? That dreadful
malady the Europeans gave them, as their initiation into
the civilised life!'

'I do, I do.' Vincent looked glum. 'In fact, I –'

'Until the white man came, they'd never even heard of
it. Living in a state of cheerful promiscuity, happy and
healthy, from one day to the next. But syphilis? The
scourge of sin? For me, as well, it got me in the end.'

'You mean – *eh, mon Dieu*. But Paul – ?'

'*Oui*, Vincent, I'm dying. I went there to escape the
disease of civilisation, but there it was, catching up on
me, in both senses of the word. We may be done with the
past, but the past is never done with *us*. Either way, I'm
fucked. The shadow of Manao Tupapau, the Great Evil

Spirit – his revenge on the unwelcome guest. Bah! May they rot in Hell!'

'The Spirit, the girls or the missionaries?'

'Take your pick. And don't make bad jokes. Anyhow, I'm done for.'

'I'm truly sorry to hear it.' Vincent looked genuinely distressed. 'But you seem so well, a picture of health.'

'I do. But this is my dream person – *te rerion*, the natives call it, the life you live while asleep. The *real* person looks terrible. Pink blisters all over, you should see the sores on my legs! Ghastly, the locals now avoid me, they think I've got leprosy. When they've fought as many battles as they have, they can smell death. So, I'm on my own now, and the only way to ease the pain is by rubbing arsenic in the open wounds. I start my day with a shot of morphine, followed by Cognac. The illness is working through my body, corrupting my brain. Reminds me of something you said about my paintings: it's like I've fornicated with the Devil!'

Paul sighed and shook his head. 'Besides, you don't look so hot yourself. Pity you don't also have a ghost side, to wander in and out of people's dreams. It'd give you a better image.'

'You're right, since I too have had my doses, gonorrhoea, "the curse of Venus", suspected syphilis – my madness, they say, may be due to that. Rather more, I've been told, than "*La Fée Verte*". And I know what it's like, Paul, to be under sentence of death. It really *is* bad luck.'

'Chance makes a plaything of a man's life.'

'It does. But look, we must get you to a hospital. Is there no hope?'

'None, they tell me, too far gone. And we can't – a hospital? No good. I'm a spirit, remember – a figment?

Were I here, in some corporeal guise, instead of just my "essence", as you once called it, even the best specialists in London or Paris couldn't help. I know that all too well. I'm like the Marquesas, Samoa, the whole of the fucking Pacific, a victim of the fatal impact. When I did ask for assistance, from that crap priest we've got there, all he could do was object to my nudes, not offer to pay for a doctor! I'm doomed, Vincent, doomed, just as I'd once predicted.'

'I'm doomed, too, Paul.'

'Not on your life! You *must* snap out of it. Go see that *Monsieur* Satie, tell him you're sorry. Make it fulsome, contrite. Tell him you'll give up your music, your recitals, that you'll leave the whole field clear.'

'Can't, I'm successful now, I couldn't go back. Not to the old ways, before Auvers, begging for handouts. Or back in Paris, shivering in my cold-water flat in *La Place du Tertre*, surviving on stale bread and soup. With no money for models, cadging discarded canvas from my friends. Then sketching folk without asking, pulling at their coat tails in hopes that they'd buy. They never did.'

'But at least you were alive.'

'Just.'

'And you're alive now – just. So best find this Satie character, tell him you'll desist and try to patch it up.'

'Still can't. No dice. That is, I tried to apologise, negotiate. But it's a matter of integrity. Of commitment – to my art. The art of Music. If you were in my place, Paul, would you give up painting?'

Paul looked away, he thought for a moment. 'Probably not. It's in the blood. You said it.'

'There you are. I was like that, too, before I found the other thing. Going at it like a madman – your words,

Paul, not mine – a painting locomotive. Devouring paints, burning up the canvas, full steam ahead! Besides, wasn't it you who told me to get a gun, to scare away those birds? And what'd I say?'

'What? Again, remind me.'

'I said, "No, Paul, I'd be afraid of turning it on myself." You see, it's almost the same, a prophecy come true. I borrowed the gun from my landlord, now I must use it. This way, confronting Erik Satie, I can die with honour. Or maybe not, who knows? We artists are like ships, I've heard you say so, we do not decide on our fate. So you see, Paul, we're both fucked.'

'I didn't quite mean it like that. But stick to your commitment, do, it's been keeping you going. But honour? Integrity? Bah! They're just a fart in the wind. You must get away from here, now this minute. Forget your good friend *Monsieur le Docteur* and his stupid treatment. This duel, it's pretty dicey, they may not believe the suicide crap. So the rate you're going, if by chance you survive, you'll end up on Devil's Island. Along with poor Captain Dreyfus and all those other wretches.'

'Devil's Island? Would it come to that?'

'Surely.'

'But what can I do? Where should I go?'

'You must travel, Vincent, come with me. We talked once of a "Studio of the Tropics", come on, let's do it.'

'You said it wouldn't suit me.'

'Fuck that. Desperate times call for desperate measures. It'd be like Arles again, but somewhat hotter, if you promise not to nobble me! Not that it matters now. There's nothing remarkable about dying, it's a bad break, that's all, the dark night of the soul. But you, Vincent, have a chance. Come with me, as I say. Or else, there are

195

other islands, go to them. All it needs is to make good sail, with a following wind and the Gods to smile kindly on one. But far away, the world is your oyster, take your pick! Forget the curse, keep your nose and your todger clean and you'll be fine. But now – *now*, before it's too late! Make up your mind, know where you're going, and go. You'll be happier there! And … *still* alive.'

Vincent stared down again, a groan of despair. 'How so? To know where you're going is to know where you'll end. I'm already one of the walking dead.'

'In that case, get something decent inside you. You can't fight a duel on an empty stomach. "Eat well, shit strongly and you need have no fear of death." Old Catalonian proverb. Ha. Ha.'

'I shall dine on a piece of dry bread and a glass of beer. That's what Dickens advises for those on the verge of suicide.'

'As you wish, but semi-starvation, then topping oneself, which is what it amounts to – I wouldn't advise it. If 'twere me, I'd build an advantage.'

'That so? Maybe you'd like to fight the duel *for* me? Since the bullet, just like everything else, would sail on through?'

Vincent looked up, to test Paul's reaction. But the vision had faded once more, as unexpectedly as it had come. The awful awareness of being alone again hit Vincent like a hammer blow.

To distract himself from his present desperation, Vincent rose slowly and shuffled to the table. Reaching for pen and paper, he composed the aforementioned suicide note. Then he opened the chest of his belongings and withdrew the revolver. He cleaned and loaded it and laid it beside the note. He now had to choose the clothes he would wear. Simple, he would not change a thing.

This, then, was Vincent's resolution, there was no turning back. But his agony continued, combined with a feeling of dread that was now overwhelming. His apparent conversation with Paul, the actions of these past few minutes, had served only to increase his anguish. They'd been no distraction at all.

VII

AUVERS

[Continued]

The Copse by the Bell Tower

ONE

Vincent set off, nervous yet determined, to be some minutes early for his appointment. *Bien*, it would soon be over, one way or the other. What it needed, as Paul had said once of fencing, was *de tête* (a cool head). A moment's distraction can change a duel's outcome. The result? Defeat or death. Must concentrate on that.

He walked briskly, through the old part of town, then on past a line of quaint stone, thatch and plaster houses, set back from and flanking the river. On the farther side of the water, tall, weather-beaten cedars stood out against a pinkening sky, beneath which the grassy banks and meadows had assumed the colour of absinthe.

Vincent taking it all in, smiled briefly at a group of children on a nearby patch of wasteland, playing 'Prisoner's Base' with merry cries. He'd now reached the Church and heard the *Dies irae* emanating from within. Outside were carriages, horses with black plumes, dark-clothed men in frock coats and top hats, attending a hearse hung with crape. A funeral? Indeed. It could have been his own. And, considering the circumstance of the forthcoming duel, should he, Vincent, not also be wearing black? He shivered, despite the warmth of the day. Then crossed himself and hurried on.

He now passed down the red lane to the wheat fields, stopping for a moment to gaze at the luxuriant *Val d'Oise* in the distance, before pressing on again. No time to savour it now, he told himself, but should he survive this ordeal, he swore that he'd paint it as never before!

Though still not quite dark, there were few people about. But approaching the outskirts, the sky now glooming over, Vincent grew uneasy. He felt sure that someone was following. He turned to see and there, sure enough, he saw a figure coming after him, briefly illuminated a little way off by a flickering vestige of sunlight.

The figure stopped also, paused a moment, then followed on down. It was a man with a strangely off-balanced gait, if an oddly speedy one, not quite hampered, it seemed, by the need to jerk one leg heavily after the other. Drawing closer to Vincent, the man was now revealed as *Monsieur* Tautain, the unfortunate with the club foot. Vincent turned away again, ready to quicken his pace. But something – a fellow feeling, perhaps? – made him hesitate.

'Can I help you? I think you're following me?'

'I am,' said *Monsieur* Tautain, a mite breathless, 'an' not so easy, you bein' sich a fast walker. 'Twas a bit of a chase.'

'*Je m'excuse, monsieur.* Sorry 'bout that. I mistook you for an anarchist.'

Monsieur Tautain looked blank. He scratched his head.

Vincent gazed back, agreeably. 'Bad joke. *Je m'excuse encore.* No anarchists here in *Île de-France*, I'm glad to say. We may safely leave that to the streets of the capital.

But by all accounts it's now reached epic proportions, there've even been plans to blow up the Paris *Opéra*.'

'The *Opéra*?'

'Banks and restaurants, too. So "*Vive le son de l'explosion*", as that new song goes!'

Monsieur Tautain looked blanker still.

Vincent was about to hum him a snatch, but thought better of it. He also regretted the pleasantry, he was scarcely in the mood. 'Still, here you are. Here am I.' He made as if to go. 'I'm in rather a hurry, but can I help?'

'You can, *oui*,' said *Monsieur* Tautain, moving forward again, with a distinctive waddle of the lumbar regions, 'for I know ye to be a good man. An' it may be y're me only hope.'

'I don't see how,' said Vincent, kindly, 'since I hardly know you – least, only by sight. But maybe, if my evening's business has been completed and I'm still – no, briefly, what is it you require? Money? I have a little.'

'Not money, though that's also one o'me problems. But it's a delicate matter, if easily dealt with. It revolves around your friendship with a certain party and –'

'Which party? Friendship? I have few friends.'

'But you do. I talk of *la famille* Gachet and, in particular, your *bon ami, Monsieur le Docteur*. You're close to him, it seems, an' are bound to have some influence – ?'

'I don't quite – influence? Again, I've less than you think.'

'*Oui*, you do. Sure of it. How could you not? The amount o'time you spend with him?'

'Ah.' Vincent looked serious. 'Spying, eh? Not just on *mon "bon ami"*, as you call him, but myself. I have to warn you that –'

'*Mais non*, not spyin'. Not 'xactly. Just lookin' out for

me interests, who can blame me for that? This complaint o'mine – this Devil's foot! It's the bane o'me life, the source of all misery. You must have discussed it? Eh? Eh? You and that Dr Gachet o'yours?'

Vincent shook his head and, growing edgy, glanced away at the burgeoning shadows, fearful now that he might be late.

'*Oui*, Dr Gachet, your *bon ami*,' continued *Monsieur* Tautain, 'that great healer an' friend of all the world! But not to me. He *could* help, but he won't.'

'Maybe he can't? No, I know that he can't. No, *Monsieur*, I'm sorry. I don't see what I can do for you, either? And look, I'm late – it's … getting late. I've business to attend to. Please let me pass.'

Monsieur Tautain had stepped in front of Vincent, blocking his path. 'Late? Business? What business could you have? I've seen you, I see you, ye're makin' for th' woods.'

'The woods, *oui*. Or rather, the copse by the bell tower. That's where my business is, just let me pass.'

'*Bien*.' The man stepped aside. 'But *when* your "*business*", so called – 'neath the trees, of all things, bah! – has been completed, mebbe we can speak again? If not tonight, then another time. Meantime, please be so kind an' deliver a message. Tell your Dr Gachet, if you will, I shall *not* give up on it. There has to be an end to me suff'rin', he *must* agree to help me.'

'I don't promise that he will,' said Vincent, relieved to get away, 'but I'll deliver your message, gladly. I don't see any further discussion between us could possibly help, either, but that could also be arranged. Since you're so fond of following people, you'll not find it hard to track me down.'

'I'll seek ye out.'

'I'm sure of it.'

With that, Vincent, mumbling an '*Au revoir*', turned once more and hurried on his way. Reaching the fields, he glanced back a last time. The man, he'd decided, had an interesting face. He would like to have painted him. Another day, *si'l plairait à Dieu*?

Idly swatting at a swarm of midges, which buzzed and flitted in the warm evening air, *Monsieur* Tautain stared after Vincent, his expression haunted, though not without hope. Then he also turned, as if to go back into town. But just as suddenly, he changed his mind and, though presuming it advisable to keep a distance between them, he now, less energetically, limped his foot-dragging way in pursuit.

Losing sight of his quarry, the poor man put on some speed. Swinging his mismatched member in front of him, his passage was now interspersed by a series of odd little jumps, as he sought to catch up. At the same time, a family party, out for its evening stroll, observed *Monsieur* Tautain with amusement, mixed in, it is only fair to add, with a redeeming show of pity.

In the copse by the bell tower, Vincent and *Monsieur* Satie, immobile as statues, stood back to back. 'Let's start if you're willing?' said *Monsieur* Satie, in an echo of Pushkin's doomed duellist. Twitching back to life, acting on their own signal, they took the correct twelve paces, then turned to face each other. One – cock pistols. Two – aim. Three – fire. Vincent got his shot in first. But in the gloom of this darkening woodland scene, the twigs of a tree branch obscuring his vision, the bullet went wide.

Monsieur Satie, on the other hand, with the moon

behind him, the lights from the local château casting their glow on the greensward ahead, had no such problem. The shot rang out. Vincent gave a sharp cry, clutched at his side, then fell to his knees. A brief moment, he keeled over.

The victorious *Monsieur* Satie blew some imaginary smoke from the barrel of his gun, twirled the weapon on his trigger finger and pushed quickly through the undergrowth. He found the path again and strode on. Re-entering the town, he passed a small bunch of villagers, rolling tipsily out of a local bar. 'Man near the tower,' he mumbled, 'badly hurt – suicide!' He hurried on his way.

The men looked at each other, puzzled, wondering why the stranger was moving in the opposite direction, not leading them to the scene of the 'accident'. After a muttered consultation, they shook their heads and hastened to the copse. There lay Vincent, a bullet apparently lodged in his chest, groaning and lying limply on the ground.

By the beam from their lanterns, the men recognised him all right – a sometime drinking companion, strange but chatty, a bit argumentative when sober, foul-tempered when drunk. But, as a past frequenter of their own watering place, not above cadging the odd drink or two, he was basically one of themselves.

Besides, the fellow was hurt. They lifted Vincent up and, dodging overhanging branches, carried him out of the copse. Negotiating some deep furrows at the edge of the nearby field, they managed to manhandle him without further mishap, up towards the crossroads.

Dr Gachet had, himself, been abroad that night, visiting a patient. At one point, returning home, he glimpsed a young man rushing towards him, evidently heading for the station. It was that same young fellow who'd called on him earlier. As the man drew near, he stepped briskly from out of the Doctor's path. Averting his face some-what guiltily, he tipped his hat, murmured '*Bonne nuit*', then quickened his pace and was gone.

Perplexed, Dr Gachet stared after him. Then, a little later, he came upon the 'stretcher party' and realised instantly it was Vincent. With a feeling of shock and mounting apprehension, he led the way to his house and opened up the surgery. He was relieved when, offering some small payment to the men for carrying his friend thus far, they indignantly refused. Promising to let them know how Vincent made out, he saw the little group to the door.

Back in the copse, there was silence. Then a sudden move-ment. *Monsieur* Tautain emerged from the bushes, his badly enlarged foot clattering loudly on broken twigs and branches. Anyone who now saw him, even in this indis-tinct light, would sense that he'd also had a shock!

Baffled by the end of an evening that had started off, to his own mind, surprisingly well, he began, once he'd taken the situation in, to reflect bitterly that the serious wounding of *Monsieur* Van Gogh – at least he knew the man's name – had been 'specially engineered to flout him. To remove yet another brief chance for the sad, much derided Hippolyte Tautain, to have his birth malforma-tion seen to. That is, cured, normalised, smoothed and straightened, made – it had long been his fervent wish – to seem all but invisible!

His surprise at the duel, which he'd only vaguely heard and witnessed – though the twin shots had made him tremble! – pre-empted, so dazed was he, any misplaced urge to join the 'stretcher party'. Just as well, he mused later, since who would believe that his own presence in the copse was entirely innocent, or that his failure to go to the victim's aid was based on the very real fear of being shot at, himself, by the victim's young assailant?

Monsieur Tautain was not to know, either, as would subsequently come out, that the duel was to be deemed not a duel at all, but the build-up to 'suicide'. And that the victor, whose name was unknown and whose flight was slick enough, was already 'like a man who had never existed'.

Dragging his club foot over one last obstruction, a rotting tree log at the edge of the clearing, *Monsieur* Tautain peered about him. There may have been blood on the grass at his feet, but he could not now see it, nor any other real evidence that a duel had taken place.

But then, the one thing he *did* see, glinting a few feet away in a sudden shaft of moonlight, was the wounded man's revolver. Easing himself forward again, *Monsieur* Tautain bent down painfully and picked it up. Hushed and fearful, he held the gun close to his nose, sniffing the lingering scent of cordite. Then, wrapping it carefully in the scrap of rag that posed as his handkerchief, he placed it deep in his pocket.

With a last look round, *Monsieur* Tautain made his way laboriously over the fields and back towards town. His mind now working furiously – or as fast, indeed, as a simple fellow's can – he tried to think of a way in which both his knowledge of the duel and discovery of the weapon might happily merge towards his own future benefit.

TWO

Chez Gachet

The good Doctor lit the lamps and busied himself. He stared at Vincent, bloody and unconscious, lying there on the examination couch. Dr Gachet shook his head miserably and took out a clean towel. He pressed it to Vincent's wound, then turned and moved away. He must choose his instruments with care. At this moment, Vincent, wincing, also reaching for the wound, narrowly opened his eyes.

He peered about him. There was his jacket, on a small table beside him. With difficulty, he sat up, reached out again and rummaged in the pockets. He found his pipe and grasped it. Forcing it between his teeth, wincing even more with the pain, he extracted his tobacco pouch and with difficulty filled the pipe.

There was a small flint lighter on the same table, fashioned like a derringer. He managed to get hold of it, twisted it into the right position and lit up. Sucking in, though with much reduced vigour, Vincent got a glow. He leaned back, in agony though he was, with a look which suggested contentment.

Alerted by the sound of the flint, the sudden aroma of pipe smoke, Dr Gachet turned. Should he remove the pipe from his patient's mouth? No, let him be – for now. It might be the last pleasure Vincent would have. He watched for a moment, inhaling the familiar smell of his friend's cheap tobacco, then stepped towards the bed. Vincent was staring up at him. Manipulating the pipe to the side of his mouth, he tried to speak. 'Wh – where I am I? All right … if I smoke?'

'If it relaxes you. Especially since – no, do so, if you wish.'

'Since? Since – ? But where *am* I? Is it night? Dr Gachet?'

'*C'est vrai, cher ami*, it's night, and it is I. You're here among friends, the friends who love you. Now, lie still and I'll have a proper look at that chest.'

Taking the pipe from Vincent's hand and placing it on the table, Dr Gachet tried to make Vincent comfortable. Trying hard, also, to conceal the anxiety he felt, he moved nearer to Vincent, cut away his bloody shirt, cleaned and cauterised the wound, then examined him with a professional eye. Vincent twitched and groaned as the Doctor's probe made contact.

'But how – how? Why here? Your surgery? Did you – did you – ?'

'I saw you on the road, being carried by the townsfolk. They brought you in. Don't worry, you're fine now. Let me take a closer look.'

'But what … happened? Did they tell you – ?'

'No, I guessed. That is, I saw a young chap running off, he was brandishing a pistol. Or rather, he almost collided with me in the street – I was returning from my rounds. I'd seen him earlier, I believe, he dropped in upon you? I'm sorry, I gave him your address.'

'Can't … be … helped … no blame … attached … to you.'

'*Merci*, but *mea culpa*. It was … a duel, I take it? Where were the seconds? Was there no doctor present? Why did you not call me? I'd have tried to talk you out of it, but would have come.'

'No … seconds. No doctor. A personal matter. And I don't want – er, want – but – *mon Dieu*, it hurts! – hurts! – to get … that … young man into trouble. Your promise

please? You've been so good to me, you and Marguerite,
I'd like – like –'

'Try not to talk, Vincent, you'll need all your strength.'

'Too late, too late. I'm … aaagh … done for.'

'Not at all, you'll be fine. *Courage, mon ami.*'

'I mean it. I know it. You're wasting your … time.'

'Ah, Vincent, ever the gloomy one. A little faith, a little
faith.'

'I – I – do mean it. I'm done for.'

'No, just let me try to patch you up, at least remove
that bullet. Then we'll see. But don't talk, I mean it, too.
Afterwards, I must call the hospital and the police. It's my
duty, it's the Law. Duelling's illegal, whatever the cause.'
Dr Gachet looked about him. 'Now, I ought to have a
nurse, you'll need cold compresses, there may be fever.
But Marguerite will be so – I mean, *cher ami*, she musn't
see you like this.'

The Doctor frowned for a moment, trying to remember.
'*Eh, oui*, Marguerite – she's not here, a sudden call this
evening from *Maman* in Lille, to be with *Tante* Francia.
It's bad, bad. *Tante* Francia has just – ah no, let me see…'

He busied himself again, cleaning his instruments, pre-
paring the bandages. Meanwhile, the shock for Vincent
had lessened the pain, but not altogether. He groaned
once more and tried to massage his side. This time the
effort was beyond him.

'Now,' said Dr Gachet, 'be *very* brave, which I know you
are, just do your best. I'm going to give you chloroform.
Let me apply some antiseptic to that wound. I mean,
bathe it with iodine. It'll hurt at first, but when you drift
off you won't feel a thing. The bullet is lodged quite deep
– well, deep enough, it's right inside.'

'*Monsieur* Satie was … aiming at my heart.'

'That would have been the finish of you. Anyhow, it's lower than I first thought, somewhat lower than the chest. It seems to have passed on through, at something of an angle, not touching any major organs. A tricky one, we'll see if I can find it. I don't promise but I, too, will do my best.'

'But you don't operate ... any more. An aversion, you said ... to surgery?'

'I know how to, I've not forgotten and needs must. Lie still, don't talk.'

'No ... no, I said ... don't bother yourself, it – it – I'm going ... going.'

Dr Gachet lightly squeezed Vincent's shoulder, by way of reassurance. He then applied the chloroform and Vincent drifted off. But even with only cursory probing, the Doctor could see that the case was hopeless. The bullet was in an awkward position, now lodged near the base of the spine, it might well be pressing on a nerve? Even to have tried removing it, rusty in procedure as he was, would surely have meant fumbling and hesitation. There'd be a grave danger of driving the bullet in further, prompting an instant seizure, a massive shock to the system.

Dr Gachet considered this. No, best leave well alone and try alternative means – if there were any. There weren't, of course, and the good Doctor felt his failure keenly.

When Vincent came round, the effects of the chloroform still deadened the pain, but for how long? With an expression of concern, Dr Gachet gazed at Vincent, trying hard to smile.

'I'm sorry, Vincent, can't remove it. Thought I could, but I can't, intervention would be fatal. On the other hand, there may be –'

'It's fine, fine, don't worry.' Vincent was peering at him, through half-closed eyes. '*Timor mortis non conturbat me*. I know how hard you tried.'

'*Merci*. Is there anything else I can do for you? Let me give you a shot? A compress?'

'No shot, no compress. Just my pipe again, fill my pipe – on the table.'

Dr Gachet looked at Vincent strangely, but did as he was bid. He picked up the pipe, sucking what was left of the smouldering tobacco into life. Then he placed it between Vincent's lips. Vincent drew in, even more feebly than before, yet managed to get a glow again. The same look of contentment suffused his face and he seemed to be at peace.

Turning away to hide his tears, Dr Gachet left Vincent for a moment. The latter was now resting back, propped against the pillows, quietly smoking. But, after a few more weak puffs, the pipe fell from his mouth. When Dr Gachet returned, the patient lay hunched and groaning on the bed. Suddenly, he rallied, trying to sit up. Dr Gachet again made him comfortable. Vincent's thoughts, muddled though they now were, seemed primarily centred on Marguerite.

'You're right … it's best – best … she … *doesn't* see me. Tell her – tell her –' Vincent's face was ashen, he was losing blood, fading rapidly, his body growing weaker by the second ' – no tell her nothing, Marguerite, she – she … aagh … knows how I feel … about her.'

Vincent paused for breath, his face contorted with pain, trying to continue. 'And no police … I beg of you. Let *Monsieur* Satie be. He was not to blame, I made him suffer so. He's a young man, he has a chance … huge chance. With all his life before him a … major talent. But listen – listen, there's a suicide note … that should clear him. In my coat pocket – show me.'

Dr Gachet frowned again and went through Vincent's jacket. He found the note, sealed in an envelope. 'This it?'

'*Oui – oui*, that's the spirit. Take it to the –'

'No, Vincent, no, it won't do. It goes against everything I've believed in. Professional honour, medical ethics – I mean, to lie, to fake a death certificate? It's –'

'Not lie – no lies. Omissions … not lies. For me, *mon cher docteur*, for me? You'd surely do it for *me*?'

'For you, Vincent? Not even for you. I don't think – that is, I –' a pause, then despairing ' – very well, then. For you, Vincent, what else can one say?'

'Say nothing. But that I died by my own hand, shot in the chest. *Merci, mon ami*. Since I was desperate, the long days ahead … could see absolutely nothing, there seemed no way out. And Theo, tell him I wish it … for the best. Explain to him, ever supportive Theo. The only one who understands me – he'll know what to do and … make up a story.'

'But, Vincent, a suicide, your faith, you still *believe*? They'll claim, the priests, you died not in a state of grace, but had departed this life impenitent? Forgive me, that *is* the expression they use? It's not for me to say, to me it's nonsense, but surely, to die without their prayers? And then, your reputation? You don't want, you really must – ?'

'Mine? Reputation? None … that I can think of. The priests – what does it matter? Who are they to judge me? I'm finished here. Poor … questionable Vincent. But – but a real gift, they say, has … *Monsieur* Satie, or rather … did. A great swathe of beautiful music … dying to get out.'

'You, too, Vincent, you too. Some fine work to come. Don't give up, you still have so much to offer. I'll get you through this, you'll see. I mean, the hospital, a specialist. You've lost a lot of blood, but if you can make it through the night there's a chance – you have it all to live for. Your painting, music, all your old friends around you.'

'No friends, Doctor, just you and Marguerite – and Paul, of course, I've just ... seen him.'

'Paul Cézanne – here?'

'No, Gauguin. He – he –'

'He's back from Tahiti. Then that's – ?'

'No, no, in my mind's eye – the old ... mind's eye. A dream, a vision. I've seen him. A good friend, despite ... our quarrels, though we shall not meet again. Theo, too, a real friend. And Johanna, *la jolie Jo*, and the little one, *le petit* Vincent. Poor Theo, he did his best for me, he did try. I'm sorry I ... didn't sell.'

'But you're a brilliant painter, *cher ami*, musician, too. Your time is present and future. I'm sure of it.'

'Too late. Too late. As for the music ... I – I – ooh, can't *breathe* – I realise it now. It's just as Paul said, as everyone ... *should* have said. You, Marguerite, those stupid critics. That I have ... no ear, not even part of an ear. Unlike my real ear which has more of an ear than the bits that got lost! Ha. Ha – ooh, ooh, *oui*, it hurts – I mean, that's funny. No ear, but part of an ear. No ear for music, a wreck, that's me.'

'No, Vincent, no.'

'True, true, I feel it. Death you know, opens one's eyes. They'll soon forget about my music, realise their mistake. Just as if – as if that whole thing ... never happened. History shall ... be my judge ... if maybe I'm even remembered. "Once he was a notable madman, now an insignificant one." Or else, it's "Vincent the painter ... a modest talent. Vincent, the composer – who he?" A non-entity – a non-person. Famous for a day ... then *rien*.'

'Better famous for a day, than nobody for – I mean, *cher* Vincent, please be hopeful, just let me –'

'I – no – no – it – it's dark. I'm sinking ... sinking ... ah, no, the sorrow will never end. Theo, oh Theo, *c'est fini*, the pictures I might have made! I wish it were all over, wish I could ... go home now. If you see ... Paul ... again ... tell him ... "Nevermore."'

With that, Vincent, delirious, in great pain, his breath like a sigh, closed his eyes and just seemed to fade away. Gently, with tears rolling down his cheeks, Dr Gachet wiped Vincent's face with a clean cloth, washed away the blood and dried him. He struggled to remove the soiled shirt, then managed, moving him into various positions, to dress him again in one of his own. It was a decent fit, lint-white and perfectly laundered.

Vincent, now lying straight and flat on the couch, looked almost respectable, as if he'd come to the house, clean and spruced up for a formal visit, then fallen asleep after dinner.

Brushing the moisture from his cheek, Dr Gachet gazed at Vincent's seemingly lifeless body. He gathered up the instruments, placing them in the sterilising tray. Then washed his hands at the sink in the corner and reached for his coat.

The good Doctor had now come to a decision. He would carry out Vincent's wishes to the letter. *Monsieur* Satie was safe. He slipped the suicide note in his pocket – he must take it to the police, sign the death certificate, tell them as much as he knew. Well, just as much as he *wanted* them to know – everything, but not quite.

First, though, he must rouse the undertaker. Marguerite could return at any time. She must not find Vincent as a corpse, nor hear of his death from anyone else. She would be devastated at the news, *pauvre petite*.

The Doctor thought, maybe, he could just tell her that Vincent had gone away, to join Paul at short notice in the South Seas? But girls that age are wiser than they seem and news travels fast. Especially in a small town like this. There would be no big secrets in Auvers, except one: that Vincent did *not* die by his own hand, even though everyone but Dr Gachet thought that he had.

The Doctor's version of events should hold. No one but himself knew about the young man's part in Vincent's death. Vincent, besides, had fired a bullet from his own gun. Evening was a less likely time to be thought of for duelling and, to cap it all, there was the suicide note.

The Ravoux family son, whom the Doctor had bumped into earlier, had seen Vincent leave, going off to the woods, armed, some time after seven. Or certainly thought so – it was already twilight. But they'd not glimpsed the person he was meeting, and would assume their friend had been going alone. Probably to kill birds? That's it. As for the men who'd carried Vincent to the surgery, Dr Gachet knew, if it were he himself who requested it, that they would, even though suspicious, keep the true facts to themselves.

Thinking it through, Dr Gachet felt Marguerite should not hear the whole story either, or at least no more of it than he'd be telling *les flics*. There was too much at risk in revealing the truth to anyone, even his own daughter – his promise to Vincent came uppermost. Marguerite might think less now of Vincent as a fake 'suicide' than as a 'real hero', a man of honour slain in a duel, but that was the chance he must take. Though Dr Gachet hated having to lie to her, it would surely be for the best?

Vincent's death, too – he cursed himself for thinking so – was also for the best. They were both fond of the poor man, this brilliant but blighted artist, hopeless musician, unhappy genius and self-destructive force.

But, and they'd even discussed it, Vincent would not have been a suitable match for a well-brought-up doctor's daughter. Since all the torments he had suffered, the sadness and instability had he lived, which he'd no doubt suffer still, would be more than a wife could endure. For a girl as loyal and loving as Marguerite, it would have been torture. Anyhow, for those who believed in such things, Vincent was in a better place.

Quietly, Dr Gachet closed the door, proceeded down the passage into the salon and stepped on to the terrace. Here, to take a moment's respite. The moon was rising, stars already bright in a darkening sky, though a soft pinky glow was still just about visible beyond the hills in the distance. As a picture for painters to paint it was as blissful, as beautiful a night as the Doctor could remember. Vincent, he knew, would have loved it.

THREE

As Dr Gachet turned and re-entered the house, he thought he heard a sound. Uncanny, there was surely nobody there? But, passing through the salon, he heard a groaning, some disconnected words, then a clear voice – Vincent's! – calling softly to him. The good Doctor started. No, no, he must be dreaming? Unlike Vincent, he scarcely believed in ghosts. Pausing in the hallway, he took a deep breath and entered the surgery.

Dr Gachet relit one of the lamps and moved to the couch. Then started again, on sighting his own shadow on the wall. He turned his eyes to Vincent. The poor man was now lying on his stomach, not as the Doctor had left him, but with his right hand across the small of his back, gently rubbing the skin. His head was turned to one side, he was trying to look down, his face racked with pain, but the Doctor had a clear glimpse, even in this dim light, of a brave determination in Vincent's eyes.

'*Mon ami, mon ami*,' said Dr Gachet, with a great surge of joy, 'by what extraordinary miracle do I find you thus? Your pulse had stopped, and so had your heartbeat. Indeed, I was sure of it, totally convinced we had lost you.'

'Not me,' gasped Vincent, 'not *me*...' though equally astonished to find himself alive! 'But come – come here, quickly, see what I've found.' Vincent's forefinger, his wrist bent awkwardly just above the waist area, sought out a certain spot, dangerously near the spinal column, though in the fleshy area to the side. '*Oui*, I've found it. The bullet. I felt ... a great pain. It was that which woke me, I think, from my unconscious state and – as you say, a miracle, it ... somehow revived me. Look here, my finger's on the spot, a small lump ... the bullet, it must be working its way through?'

'If that's true, Vincent,' said Dr Gachet, eagerly stepping forward, 'then it changes everything. If I can finally remove the bullet, we may yet see you, in due course, firmly on your feet again!'

Vincent chuckled. 'I'd given up the ghost, *cher ami*. Now, *grâce à Dieu*, I'm alive again, a veritable Lazarus! Or at least, like poor Paul, a live ghost, able to breathe and communicate for just a little longer...'

'That may certainly be the case. Move your hand away and let me take a look.'

Vincent did as he was told, while Dr Gachet lifted the shirt tails, which his friend had already managed to pull from his belt. The flesh around the now exposed protuberance was darkened, with a clear sign of trauma. Unfazed by this, Dr Gachet sat on a stool beside the couch and, as delicately as he could, pressed his fingers to the aforesaid lump. Yes, surely, it *was* the offending bullet! Bringing the lamp nearer, he saw the shell's outline, the point plainly visible, near enough the surface for a quick removal!

Dr Gachet grinned. 'Bravo, Vincent, well done! If you can stand the pain – or would you prefer more chloroform? – I may be able to massage the bullet through the subcutaneous tissue, in order get at it. It should be a simple procedure, a small incision, that's all, though there are, of course, risks. Shock for one, infection is another. But once that little devil is removed, you will at least be on your way to recovery. Convalescence afterwards, not too long, one hopes, may bring you back to full health. It could also revive you in other ways, quite unconnected with this terrible … accident.'

'*Merci*,' murmured Vincent, 'do what you can. My fate is in your hands, you have … my fullest confidence.'

Dr Gachet raised a finger, a quietly uttered 'Shhh'. He relit the other lamps, prepared his instruments, laid out a pile of lint, waxed thread and a veritable pyramid of bandages, then stepped back to Vincent and applied the antiseptic.

Vincent flinched, as Dr Gachet's hands came into contact, so chloroform, indeed, was again deemed necessary. But more confident than earlier, since he could already see the end of this new beginning, Dr Gachet set to with a will. With massage and manipulation, the bullet continued to work its way through. In no time, the good Doctor felt himself ready to remove it.

A little while later, Vincent had recovered consciousness and was smiling cheerfully at his friend. Dr Gachet, eyes gleaming in triumph, held up the bullet at the end of his tweezers, offering it for Vincent's inspection.

'You should have it mounted, *mon ami*. As spoils of war – a trophy.'

'Mounted?' Vincent chuckled, then flinched.

'Or, rather not,' smiled Dr Gachet. 'The less said or shown about this whole matter the better.'

'*Comme tu dit*. It shall be as if it never happened.'

'*Bien*.'

Dr Gachet, still smiling and nodding, tidied his things away, dropped the bullet into an open drawer and proceeded to wash his hands. At the same time, he conveyed in hushed tones his delight at the operation's success and how this might be the precise time for a little light refreshment. Vincent agreed, with the proviso that Dr Gachet should assist in feeding him.

This done and Dr Gachet having once more cautioned Vincent into silence, he offered him a *calmant*, washed down with water, checked his bandages, readjusted the pillows and tried to make him comfortable.

Then, after a few further platitudes, he bid him a cheery '*Bonne nuit, cher Vincent*' and extinguished the lights. Leaving the door ajar, so he could hear his friend, should he call out in the night, Dr Gachet smiled again, congratulating himself for a job well done. He now repaired to the salon and poured himself his usual Cognac.

Through the rest of that evening, and the days which followed, Dr Gachet remained ecstatic. This was buoyed by the fact that Vincent, himself, seemed so jolly. Maybe, the Doctor reasoned, the very fact of his being drawn so miraculously from the jaws of death, had given Vincent pause to take stock, to consider himself luckier than most. Whatever the reason, Dr Gachet was exultant in his friend's new-found demeanour and the rapid recovery from that potentially fatal wound.

Now, having moved him with difficulty to one of the smaller bedrooms, thus leaving the surgery free for his decreasing number of paying patients, Dr Gachet would sit up till well into the night with Vincent, discussing life, art, family, friendships, literature, music, current affairs and the happy phenomenon of his friend's resurrection.

There was also an account by Vincent of Paul's strange visitation on the afternoon of the duel, relating how Paul was now dying or at least predicting his own death, horribly indeed in that South Seas exile. What could the story mean, wondered the good Doctor? And could it have any genuine significance outside of Vincent's own fevered imaginings?

It was during one such conversation that Dr Gachet, ever patient with Vincent's thus far much slowed-down delivery, revealed to him that he had not yet told anyone in the village about his friend's strange recovery. Not even the men, in fact, who had carried him to the house, each of whom, the good Doctor reassured Vincent, had been sworn to utmost secrecy.

A couple of them had called to enquire, but Dr Gachet simply parried their concerns with 'The patient is doing as well as can be expected. I shall relay your good wishes and keep you posted, whatever should transpire.' By playing down the nature of Vincent's injury and his own efforts in dealing with it, Dr Gachet hoped that the business of the duel and Vincent's involvement would simply blow away.

The men had kept their pact of silence and, though one or two of them, at least, might still let something slip – to some loose-tongued neighbour or a fellow inebriate at the local taverns – the police, it seemed, had not got wind of the incident. Or if they had, they'd scarcely felt it worth investigating. There were enough poachers, wife-beaters and falling-down drunks around town, to be cautioned already on a daily basis, for the cops to bother with some pointless duel, in which no one had actually been killed!

VIII

AUVERS

[Continued]

Chez Gachet

ONE

It was a late afternoon or early evening, about two weeks after the duel, and Dr Gachet was out on the porch. He was enjoying an aperitif, listening to the birdsong, the buzzing of the bees, while browsing through *Le Journal* and bubbling with the news that Marguerite was coming home.

Tante Francia's health had not improved, but with the poor woman doggedly hanging on and *Maman* and Coco well able to cope, there was no reason why Marguerite, too, should remain in Lille. Hopefully, also, with Vincent progressing in leaps and bounds, he could soon be transferred *chez Ravoux*, where his other good friends could then keep an eye on him.

Dr Gachet had said nothing to *Maman* or the children about the episode with *Monsieur* Satie, least of all the matter of Vincent's wound – they had enough to worry about. The Ravoux, he'd decided, should likewise be kept in the dark, being told only that Vincent was unwell, that he might be infectious – no visitors! – and that he, Dr

Gachet, would be coping with the patient for the time being. The boy bearing the note was also instructed to bring a few of Vincent's things over from the Inn, as a way, explained the Doctor, of 'making him feel more at home'.

Madame Chevalier, too, was kept in the dark, Dr Gachet merely informing her that his friend Vincent was not to be disturbed. His breakfast and luncheon trays would be borne into him by Dr Gachet, himself. Hortense the maid and the twice-weekly cleaning woman would also be kept at arm's length. If there were any other enquirers, who might arrive to put a spanner in the works, they, too, would be diverted from Vincent's sickroom with a polite, but brooking-no-argument, firmness.

When Vincent did, finally, make his reappearance in the neighbourhood, it would be as one who'd been convalescing from something no more serious – though, in those days, such things often *were* – than chickenpox or German measles.

During his thoughts on the above, Dr Gachet paused for a moment, suddenly aware he was being watched. Looking up, casting his glance past the fruit-packed *espalier*, squinting his eyes against the dying sun, he observed a figure leaning on the fence, down at the bottom of the garden.

It was that damn fellow again, *Monsieur* Tautain, the man with the club foot. He was a now all-too regular visitor, who just stood or ambled there, his voice silent, manner uncommunicative, but his eyes and presence, as ever, in constant accusation. Still, Dr Gachet wished he could help. Still, he knew that he couldn't. He wished, too, that the fellow would go away.

He did not go away and, as Dr Gachet's feeling of guilt

transformed itself, as it generally did, into a sense of grudging admiration for the fellow's persistence, he saw the man's hand was on the gate. In a trice, catching Dr Gachet's eye, he pushed the gate open and, with only a second's hesitation, to avoid stepping on the somnolent, sun-lazing creatures on the lawn, he clumped his way up the path.

Dr Gachet, surprised, then wary, rose to greet him. '*Ça va bien*, nice evening. Can I be of service?'

'You can and you *could*,' said *Monsieur* Tautain, his manner surly, though he still kept eye contact, 'but the trouble is you won't. You call yourself a doctor, the only doctor here'bouts, but doctorin's not what you *do*. I've heard 'bout you, *Monsieur*, and what I hear *is* – your game is quackery, the patients few and your usefulness less. That's 'cos you don't do surgery. You prefer paintin' an' spoutin' forth, 'specially to that strange one wi' the red beard – the other red beard, we're *all* of us red beards! – that odd chum o'yours. I've heard 'bout *him*, too, I knows 'bout him, *vraiment*, much more than you'd think. And a lot one could say 'bout *that*.'

Dr Gachet looked perturbed. 'What on earth d'you mean?'

'We'll not go into it ... not for now. Later, mebbe.' *Monsieur* Tautain tapped the side of his nose, musing on this last remark with the trace of a leer. 'The strange one, did he give you my message?'

'Message? No I –'

'No, why would he? What would *he* care? But let it pass. *A ce moment*, we're talkin' of you.'

'My poor chap, what was this message?'

'Forget the message, and don't "poor chap" *me*. You told me some time back ye'd "get the books down" – or rather, that's what your daughter led me to believe – and that ye'd mebbe think again 'bout that disappointin' verdict you once gave me. You said there's no cure for what I got? Well, that's what *you* think. I knows it, sure as the sun rises an' sets an' the world goes to sleep, that surely there is one.'

The man pointed down, with all due solemnity, to his unfortunate *pied-bot*. 'See that? Look bigger to you? Like a dray horse's hoof? It does to *me*. But I knows in me heart, there's things can be done. And could I afford them Paris doctors, I'd make the trip. You knows my case, an' you knows deep down you can cure me. So how's 'bout it, then? Are you game or are you sorft? A great deal – all, in fact, depends on what you say.'

'*Mon pauvre ami*,' said Dr Gachet, 'I've told you what I think and you must accept it. There is nothing I know, nor anything in the books that details satisfactorily what one can do with a club foot. Not one, I mean, as advanced as yours.'

'That jus' ain't true. There's de – ? Developments. I sees it … in a journal.'

'It is, believe me. You mustn't believe the journals.'

'That so? Well, it says, this paper o'mine, it *can* be done. There's words I don't know, foreign an' sich, but I gets the drift. 'S the truth, I knows it. A cure. No more diff'rent nor painful, it says, than a little blood-lettin' – jus' like takin' out corns. 'Sides, there's instruments, machines, 'specially for the purpose.'

Dr Gachet sighed, murmuring, almost to himself, 'Ah, these abominable Paris inventions! So-called specialists with too much time on their hands, feeding old wives' tales to the truly desperate! It cruelly preys on the susceptibilities of those who know no better. No, it isn't right.

The Government should do something, it really should.'

'That's as mebbe, *Monsieur le Docteur*, but that's what it says. You can't fool *me*. There's pages of it, read the journal, I have it here.'

Monsieur Tautain withdrew the paper, limp and frayed through too-frequent study, and offered it to the Doctor. The latter shook his head, he waved the object away.

'No, no, I won't read it, I know what's in it. Just the latest in a whole history of theorising on what can or cannot be done, with complaints that are genuinely hopeless. It's witchcraft, despicable, it has no relation to proper medical knowledge, nor the way that it should be practised. No, I beg of you, do not read this nonsense. It will just make your situation worse. Filling your head with ideas that have no basis in fact or science. Please, listen to someone who knows.'

'So you *do* know, then, do you?'

'It happens I do. This condition of yours, I've already told you, is congenital. It's due, often enough, to a baby's bad positioning in the womb or, maybe even, a nervous disorder. In the most common type, one may deal with the problem at birth. A mild deformity, if simply positional, can be cured by the use of wrappings, plaster casts and sometimes a special splint. That's if treatment's immediate. The foot, with proper manipulation – torsion, say – can then correct itself, by the time the child starts walking.'

'You *see*? 'S jus' what I says.'

'You don't – did not. And *I* said "immediate". But a more serious form, the rigid type, a *varus*, say, tending strongly to *equinus*, as yours is – ah, more foreign words for you! – requires surgery, to free the tendons, reposition the bones. I'd not recommend it, not so late in the day as this. I'd gladly refer you to someone for a second opinion, if that would help, but –'

'Why don't you, then?'

'Because I know it would be pointless. I've every sympathy for your terrible claudication. But a club foot is a club foot, and in such a long-standing condition, intervention would be dangerous. Agonising, debilitating, the shock alone could kill you! With scarring as a given, arthritis a strong possibility. No, I'd not attempt it, not in any circumstance. Reducing, straightening, cutting the Achilles tendon? There'd be no more success in the enterprise than trying to straighten a hunchback!'

The man again made to interrupt. Dr Gachet forestalled him.

'No, *mon ami*, that's all I can possibly say. Please, don't be disheartened. Many men, you know, even worse cases than yourself, have made the most of it. Famous men, too, Lord Byron for one, a noted English poet, who swam the Hellespont and wrote some of the finest verses in the English language. For such a man, an impediment like his was the goad that spurred him to greatness!'

'Poet? Who cares 'bout poets? What 'bout my fuckin' foot?'

'You should stop worrying about your foot. As I say, *accept* it. Be grateful you're otherwise well and alive, that the evenings are warm and that I am not about to report you to the police for this constant harassment. Not to mention your immoderate language, it really *is* too bad. That said, I'd offer you a drink and something to eat and we could discuss the matter further, but my evening surgery's about to start and I have to go inside.'

'So that's it, then?' said *Monsieur* Tautain. 'It's easy for *you*, ain't it? You in that nice house o'yours, with its paradise garden...'

'Ah, you like it! *Très fleurie, n'est-ce pas?*'

Monsieur Tautain ignored this feeble attempt at an olive branch. 'You in your so-called *Castel*, with your wife and pretty daughter, wi' good food on the table, your cats an' pigeons, that stupid goat and all them bloody rabbits! Lordin' it over the less fortunate, the poor an' diseased, the old an' the dyin', the halt an' the lame, like meself. *Alors*, you've had your chance to help me, and this is where it *ends*.'

At that, *Monsieur* Tautain, from the deepest pocket in his topcoat, produced a gun – Vincent's, or rather the Ravoux gun, which he had found that night in the woods. He brandished it in front of Dr Gachet's face, as the latter took a nervous step back.

Dr Gachet held up his hand. 'But, my dear fellow, you can't do this! In cold blood, to someone who once tried to aid you? They'd hang you for sure. Or, maybe the guillotine. Hand me the gun, please do. I'll say no more about it and you be on your way. This is foolish, I assure you.'

'Foolish? Hangin'? The big chop? Mebbe. So, that's it, then. Ye're right, I see. Why should I honour you with a merciful death, when it's my life, *my* death that's the matter here. Me lost ambitions, this wretched foot. Folks all laughin' at me, e'en worse than when I was bein' schooled –'

'I'm sure you exaggerate. You must be – ?'

'No, no. "There goes King Clumper," that's what they says, "Ol' Leadenhoof, him o'the outsize boot!" Or, "The Off-Balance Kid, ol' dot an' carry one" – that's for the sound I useter make – "quick, keep out o'his way.

Ow, what a dreadful sight! Clump, clump, clump! He's stumpin' on agin – oops, oops, he's jest squashed a stray cat!" *Alors*, I've had enough of it – enough, you understand? I saw you as my saviour, the man with the cure. But call y'rself a doctor? – ye're a fake. A fraud an' a man without principle. *En nom de Dieu*, where's your humanity? But you'll know how to sign a death certificate? That small thing, at least? So there's *another* chance for ye!'

Before Dr Gachet could stop him, the man had raised the barrel to his own temple. Then, before the Doctor's horrified eyes, *Monsieur* Tautain squeezed the trigger. The gun was near enough to kill him instantly and the shell, with a huge spurt of blood, took a portion of the man's head away with it. Dr Gachet tried to catch him, but he fell, a well-fleshed dead weight, there at the shocked doctor's feet.

Dr Gachet glanced around him, wondering what to do next, relieved for the moment that no passer-by had appeared in the lane, nor even heard the shot. The pets on the lawn, though, had woken and scattered. They were now cowering by the shrubbery, eyeing the body on the grass with an awful, almost human fascination!

Still in shock, Dr Gachet bent down to feel the fellow's pulse – a superfluous act, he reasoned, prompted more by reflex than necessity. He rose slowly, again looked about him, gazed down at the body and scratched his head. At which point, he heard a low voice behind him. It was Vincent.

The Doctor spun round.

'What is it? Who … is it?' Vincent stumbled forward. He had been well enough, these past days, to propel himself awkwardly from room to room, but had not ventured before into the garden.

'*Mon cher* Vincent,' remonstrated Dr Gachet, 'you shouldn't be out here, down on the lawn, too far, too far. Besides –'

'No, no, I'm feeling quite fit.' Disconcertingly, Vincent chuckled. 'But I see you have a visitor. *Oui*, I know him, there he is again, our ubiquitous *strephopode*, the chap with the club foot! We spoke that day – the day of the duel. He accosted me, I remember. Very cut up he was, or so he told me, that you wouldn't operate.' Again, Vincent laughed. 'Not necessary now, *le bon Dieu merci*.'

'Vincent, this is no laughing matter. The man is dead, absolutely. A suicide – genuine, not like yours – and a former patient. Dead in my own garden, after an argument about that wretched foot. I thought he was going to kill me, but you see what happened? He turned it on himself.'

'That's in his favour, then. No one deserves to die, and surely not you. But at least he had a choice, don't worry so. Here, let's get him indoors, I'll give you a hand.'

'But, Vincent, your wound?'

'*C'est fait*, much better, we'll manage, the two of us and – ah, that looks like my gun? It is, I see, so that's where it got to? *Alors*, I'll take care of it.'

Vincent, with effort, bent down, picked up the revolver and stuck it in his belt.

Dr Gachet shook his head. 'Bad idea, that's evidence. It's now in your possession, it has your fresh prints on it.'

'Prints? Ha. Ha. Been reading again your well-thumbed Gaboriau and his clever detective Lecoq? This is Auvers, *mon ami*, not *le Quai des Orfèvres*. The *flics* in this town wouldn't know a fingerprint if it jumped up and bit them on the bum! But quick, before anyone comes by – we'll drag this poor chap inside, cover up the traces, all this mess – a hosepipe to the blood and all – put up the sign, to cancel your evening surgery and … I may have an idea. A good one. You'd be surprised, *mon cher docteur*, how convalescence can freshen the mind!'

TWO

With the dead man safely installed in the surgery, slightly cleaned up and a white sheet over him, a now physically tired but oddly exhilarated Vincent led Dr Gachet back into the salon. The servants were away from the house, it seemed, and the supper that evening was catch as catch can. Vincent did the pouring, arming the good Doctor with a generous slug of his favourite Cognac, 'then something lighter for himself.'

For some minutes they discussed the events in the garden, the terrible suicide, Dr Gachet's sense of shock and Vincent's more sanguine, almost light-hearted reaction in the presence of death. How they had then struggled up the path, to the steps of the terrace, bundling the unfortunate visitor through the house to the surgery. How Vincent, moving surprisingly swiftly, had readied the corpse for its present perch on the examination couch and how, calm and persuasive, he had taken command.

This, thought Dr Gachet, was again a new Vincent – new to himself, that is – as if the recent wound and its rapid recovery had afforded his friend not only a more cheerful aspect, but a new outlook on life altogether. Vincent, indeed, had assumed a character more determined, more decisive and, in his present actions, a manner more dominating than at any time before.

Finally, in a pause in the conversation and their glasses replenished, Dr Gachet cleared his throat. 'But tell me,

Vincent, something you said in the garden? That you had an idea, a good idea, d'you mind telling me what it is?'

'Not in the least. I meant to. It's this. *Mon cher docteur*, you know how much I appreciate your friendship, all that you have done for me, you and your family – in particular, *la jolie Marguerite* – that you recently helped bring me back from the edge of the grave and for some time have tolerated my little stupidities, my music and all the rest of it – ?'

'Not as stupid as that.'

'*Merci*, too kind. But now – and I know it will be a blow to you and you mustn't hate me for it – I'm afraid I'm at last going to leave you. This time, it's for real. All these days I've been laid up, trying to get my strength back, thanking my lucky stars again, the miraculous removal of the bullet and my present good humour, that I have decided to take a drastic, irrevocable and no doubt surprising step – I am going to commit suicide.'

'What, you – you – but *mon cher* Vincent, surely you don't mean – ?'

'*Mais non*, I don't mean that literally. What I mean is, in the eyes of the world, *only*. As I said, I've had time to think – about myself, about you and Marguerite, my brother Theo, poor dying Paul and all those others I cherish. Paul I can help by being with him, down there in that illusory paradise of his. Turning up to take him by surprise, laden down with bags of hope, and my own will that he should live.'

'But Vincent, I don't quite – ?'

'Theo I can help by pushing up the value of my paintings, based on the thesis – no, it's more than that! – that the works of dead artists, just like writers, composers or what have you, sell far better than live ones. Or, at least, are worth more than the price of their paint! My brother shall be free from worry and *le petit* Vincent, my nephew and godchild, shall be guaranteed what I desperately crave for him, a life worth living. You and Marguerite, too, can think highly of me, that I have begun to think not merely of my own vain ambitions, but of those to whom I can be useful.'

'You already are.'

'And Marguerite – don't say it won't be a relief to you? – she'll be all the better, won't she, freed from my unfortunate attentions – ?'

'Oh no, Vincent, no, when have I ever said that?'

'It's true, though, isn't it? I'm no fool, *mon ami*, I know you must have warned her about – *mais non*, no matter, leave it be.'

'Very well. *C'est ça*. But then there's your friends, your family?'

'They can learn to live without me. Especially my family. Even when I was with them they regarded me with annoyance, afraid to take me into the house. The same kind of dread they'd feel for some big shaggy dog, running about, leaving wet footprints on the floor and climbing on the furniture! "*Mon Dieu*, what a rough fellow it is and he barks so loudly!" As for my friends, they could only ever take me in small doses. They may miss me for a little, but not for long, and may even benefit. *Monsieur* Satie, too, will profit wholesale from my absence and so, I'd imagine, would the ears of my detractors, who will now have just my humble paintings to contend with!'

'Not humble, literally works of genius.'

'Again, too kind, but we shall see. And so, this is my plan. As soon as I am truly fit and able, though continuing to conceal myself, should you be so willing, in your house, I shall book passage to the Marquesas. I still have a little bit put by from those wretched recitals and –'

'Vincent, you must realise, this is very big step – ?'

' – I shall settle all my debts to you and, if you will also be so kind, you shall purchase for me a consignment of bandages, ointments and necessary medicines, not to mention every available pamphlet on poor Paul's condition. Any new drug you know of that will help him – potassium iodide, compounds of arsenic and so on – that, too, I shall ask you to provide. I shall then arrive at my destination and fight to my last breath for my good friend Paul's survival!'

Dr Gachet looked at him, shaking his head. Was Vincent really finally, incurably mad, or was this plan of his a conception so brilliant that only the truly brilliant could fathom it?

'This is all very praiseworthy, Vincent, and I'm more than grateful to be a beneficiary in your plan. But you spoke of suicide. How can you do all these things if you're already dead? *Monsieur* Satie, *oui*, that might work. The increased value of your paintings, great works from a dead artist, true. But trying to cure Paul Gauguin, far gone from that disease with the loathsome name – or so your strange dreams seem to tell you – I mean, shouldn't you check on him first? A letter, even to telegraph some passing ship? Your friend's illness – it may just be a fantasy. Paul, you say, was a ghost!'

'Ghost, yes. Fantasy, no. I believe every word of it. And a letter? No time. Do they have telegraph? Doubt it. By the time it's all sorted, poor Paul will be dead.'

'But – but – just for the sake of argument, this strange tale of yours? Paul Gauguin dying: let's say he is. Then you, Vincent, a suicide, ministering to him from within the depths of your own grave? *Mon cher ami*, impossible!'

Vincent laughed loudly at this. He leaned in, patting Dr Gachet playfully on the cheek, and spoke in confidential tones. '*Mon cher docteur*, when I talked of suicide, I said in the *world's* eyes. I did not say in the eyes of yourself or mine. I shall be as alive as you see me now, but, as far as anyone else knows, I'll be as dead as the proverbial doormat.'

'Doornail.'

'Doornail. *Merci*. But a suicide shall be reported and a suicide shall be buried. One could fake death to reach a star, I'd imagine, or anywhere else for that matter, just as easily as one takes a train to reach a black dot on the map! But I'll need your cooperation in this, *cher docteur*, and I trust that once more, for my sake and those others I've mentioned, you can see your way to bend those precious ethics of yours one last time?'

Dr Gachet was not so obtuse, he was relieved to consider, and during the above he had twigged what Vincent had in mind. 'You mean, *cher* Vincent, our man with –'

' – the club foot? *Oui*. Bravo! *Exactement*. He shall take my place in the funeral plot, concealed from all eyes by a solid oak coffin, with brass handles and suitable inscription, which I myself shall have paid for. Say what you like over my – I mean his interment and – he has no family, I take it?'

'None. I'm sure of it.'

'*Bien*. Just another of life's unfortunates, buried in an unknown grave. Only this time, it will be *my* grave, with all the pomp and ceremonial my friends and admirers think fit.'

Dr Gachet gazed at Vincent, both aghast and excited by the plan. But why not? He had bent those same precious ethics already and, for Vincent again, of course. But it would scarcely be as simple as Vincent implied.

'It shall be so, *mon ami*. I, myself, will see to it. Or *would* see to it, were this not a total mirage. Vincent, have you really thought it through?'

'In every detail. Lying inactive on my convalescent daybed, in your cosy spare bedroom, I have had many hours to think. Indeed, I've thought of little else. And our dead friend in there, more fortuitously than one could have imagined, has presented the perfect solution!'

'But your painting, your music? How will you – ?'

'My music? Rubbish. I seem to remember saying so. In my delirium, when sure I was dying, or words to that effect? And my painting, one hopes, will live on. My death, or presumed death, will happily see to that.'

'It surely will. But – but – the dead man. The *real* dead man, he – ?'

'*Eh, oui*, I know what you're saying? That he looks not at all like me? But I've not met the undertaker, either, at least I don't think so, and he won't know my face. "*Voici mon pauvre ami* Vincent Van Gogh," you will say, "an unhappy suicide, so do what you can for him, your best in the circumstance etcetera etcetera" and –'

'*Monsieur* Tautain, though, *may* be known to the undertaker?'

'A risk we must take. I'll think of something.'

'And he has a club foot. Should the undertaker mention that fact about town, those who know you will smell a rat. Especially since the only club-footed one hereabouts is our poor friend in there.'

Vincent laughed again and slapped his knee. 'Then cut it off!'

'Off? The foot?'

'*Oui. Très simple.* You will say that in the course of my hoped-for recovery from the gunshot, gangrene set in and you had to excise it.'

'Gangrene takes longer than a – I mean, you weren't shot in the leg?'

'I wasn't. But I *was* shot. If you say the foot had to come off, it had to come *off*. You're the doctor, you should know!'

Dr Gachet shrugged. '*Oui*, Vincent, it's just about possible. But the operation? A grisly job, and I don't usually do –'

'Procedural work? Just so. Not even on the dead?'

'The dead … maybe. I'm not a religious man, as you know, Vincent, but surely – ?'

'I see where you're going, but just think of it as an autopsy – hah, that should ease your qualms! Come, I know you can do it, I've still every confidence. You – um, do have a hacksaw?'

Dr Gachet blanched beneath his high colour. 'If not in the surgery … then, the garden shed.'

'Capital.'

'Are you certain about this, Vincent? It'll be pretty messy.'

'Not *too* difficult, eh? The blood has surely stopped, *rigor mortis* now set in?'

'Long since.'

'The patient will be quiet … and we won't need an anaesthetic!'

'*C'est vrai. C'est vrai.*'

'And if the cops, afterwards, wish to see the body for themselves, I, your *bon ami* Vincent, am not known to them either, though some folk may think that I ought to be!'

Dr Gachet looked doubtful. 'But can we be sure? About

your not being known? You did present your papers at the *Mairie*, when you first arrived here? Someone may recall you, Vincent, yours is not a face one forgets. No, it's taking a chance, too big a chance – one glimpse of that poor chap, and someone at least may know it's not *you*?'

Vincent thought for a moment. 'Let me see now. Ah. Got it. To be on the safe side, we'll keep the lamps deliberately low – just say it's a fuel cut! – the corpse, with its singular deformity, will be hidden under a sheet. The cops'll only need to see his face – and examine the wound. A horrible sight, that's the forehead and temple, they'll scarcely linger long! Our dead friend, meanwhile, shall play a part for us, with a little help from myself.'

'But, Vincent, I –'

'*Corpora non agunt nisi fixata!* "Bodies do not act unless fixed." Therefore, we shall *fix* him! *Monsieur* Tautain already has a beard, a small reddish one. Some further modest tinting with the burnt sienna, a pinch of *amoretto* dye, mixed in with the *Trypan* red, a little discreet face painting – and his features shall resemble mine!'

'Extraordinary.'

'*Oui*. The whole idea appeals to me. It touches strongly on a fantasy I've long entertained of merging with a double. In the same way I once dreamed, but failed, of twinning myself with Paul. *Monsieur* Tautain shall be *me*, I shall be – who knows? With luck, as the German poets have it, his more nimble *doppelgänger*! The deadly double from mediaeval folklore, who, transported from the spirit world to confront his human counterpart, warns him of approaching death. Only, in this case, the victim is already dead! So, what d'you think of that? A veritable brainwave. My newest self-portrait, the last on French soil. *Oui, mon cher ami*, one can see it now – Vincent's farewell masterpiece!'

'But d'you think it'll work, the make-up and all?'

'Without question. "Art is a lie to which we give an accent of truth." Degas said that. By the time I've finished with him, *Monsieur* Tautain shall be more like Vincent than Vincent, himself.'

Dr Gachet mused on this. He looked at Vincent and smiled. 'You know, it's all fitting into place. You really have been thinking things through.'

'I have.'

'It grows on one. It's a good ruse.'

'Terrific.'

'And this new Vincent, this new self-confidence of yours? I say it again, it's truly remarkable.'

'We are at our best when we are boldest. I've been given a second chance in life, I'm confronting it head on!'

'Good for you. I can't tell you how pleased I am.'

'*Bien.* And we'll do as I say?'

'*D'accord.*' Dr Gachet offered a mournful grin. 'And in bringing it to fruition, I shall have taken leave of any moral scruples I have left.'

'All in a good cause.'

'Indeed. But tell me, Vincent, how will you cope, in that distant tropical refuge? Being alive still, yet aware that everyone here who knew you must imagine you dead?'

'I should be used to it by now. Did I tell you, *cher docteur*, that I once had an older brother, who died – a stillbirth – the year before I was born? I was named after him. "Vincent Willem". I inherited a ghost. Later, nothing ever disquieted me more than, when walking to my father's Church to attend the services, I would pass the small grave of my late baby brother and find my own name on the tombstone! A sobering thought, you'd agree?' Dr Gachet was about to reply. Vincent, with a gesture, laughed and forestalled him.

'But come, let's get cracking. *Alea iacta est* – the die is cast! Off with that poor fellow's foot!'

The Doctor, to whom Vincent's enthusiasm was infectious, also laughed loudly. '*Oui*, off with it, I say!'

And the two friends, happy in their firm and continuing friendship, repaired to the surgery to do full honours to the first step in Vincent's great plan. At which point, Dr Gachet, already with instruments in hand, stopped short. He gazed at the form of the dead man under the sheet. Then frowning, turned back to Vincent.

'No, no, this won't do. It won't do at all. I cannot do it – it chills me to the bone.'

'But – but you promised...? It's what we – ?'

'What I mean is, Vincent, I've a better idea, a better plan, less drastic than the one you suggest. Even though that, too, goes against the grain! *Monsieur* Lestiboudois, the undertaker, is a friend of mine, in spite of his all too evident rapture whenever I lose a patient! But I did save his wife's life once – let's not go into detail – and he swore to return the favour. If he can accept the enormity of what we're asking, then this may be his chance. If he can, likewise, be persuaded to prepare a man for burial, who is not the man he is said to be – substituting a dead *paysan* for a very live painter! – then this could be the answer to our problem. You agree?'

'*C'est formidable!*' Vincent clapped his hands. 'My unfortunate double shall keep his foot! He shall enter Heaven, not maimed and minus, like that hapless Captain Ahab, vainly questing the oceans for the Great White Whale, the devil which snatched his missing limb – ah,

"*Thar* she blows!" – but, give or take that small piece of *Monsieur* Tautain's head, "the whole man" again!'

'Anything else?'

'Don't think so. Minor details only. We can make a list.'

'No lists, Vincent, let's keep things simple, we must cover our tracks.'

Vincent nodded, then had another thought. 'Aha, one last thing. You still have the suicide note?'

'*Hélàs*, I have, it's been burning a hole in my pocket.'

'Keep it safe, at least for this evening. Tomorrow morning, first thing, go to the cops. Say you found the poor fellow – *votre cher ami* Vincent! – lying in the garden. You brought him into the house, trying to save him. He died and, when you searched his pockets, to find if he'd left a note, you came across it.'

'But it's dated, Vincent? Surely they'd – ?

'I'll tear it off! The date. Or rather, a new note. Then sign it a second time, "*avec mes regrets très sincères*, Vincent Van Gogh", and for the sake of authenticity, I'll try to smudge it up a little. That should do the trick, I mean, why would anyone imagine that a suicide note in a dead man's pocket is from any man's hand but the man that's supposedly dead? Oh, and once again, make sure those chaps who carried me in that other night don't breathe a word about the duel.'

'All shall be done.'

'Meanwhile, I'll make myself scarce – for a few hours at least. When I return, I'll start making plans to sail away.'

'Sail away, Vincent? *Oui, c'est ça.* The object of the whole exercise! But I'll surely miss you.'

'I'll miss you, too, more than I can say. The only doctor, *mon ami*, who's ever made a difference to my life! *La jolie Marguerite*, of course, and all my friends. But Paul's need is great and so is my brother's. He's in dire straits, almost on the verge of bankruptcy, maybe losing the gallery and all. I was a worry and danger to him, I know that, living at his expense. So I'll render myself to Theo – the brave martyr, Vincent, who "died" with a smile on his face. *Et hop, merci, c'est fini*! From this moment on, I'm incognito – like the great mythic hero, intent on his quest, whose fate is unknowable yet certain! But my prediction is, in almost no time – once my "end" has been affirmed – that the interest in my paintings will increase a hundredfold.'

'A thousand.'

'*Merci, mon ami*. Let's hope so.'

'You'll be famous, Vincent.'

'And the price of my fame will be death. Or *mortis imago*: an appearance of death, the living variety. *Je serai un revenant du Pacifique* – one day you see me, then you don't!'

'Wonderfully cynical, wonderful.' Dr Gachet chuckled, then stopped abruptly. He gave Vincent a troubled look. 'Will I *ever* see you again?'

'For the plan to work? Never. But think of me sometimes, and know I'll be fine. Mine will be no bleak Ovidian exile, living only one step short of extinction, but a cleansing and salvation – rewards for a selfless spirit! I'll think of you, too, *cher ami*, and remember you in my prayers.'

Dr Gachet nodded, sadly. Holding back their tears, the two friends embraced. After which, this time at last, they set about busily, intent on bringing off this daring deception!

IX

AUVERS

[Continued]

Chez Gachet

ONE

As it happened, Vincent decided not to risk implicating Dr Gachet, for fear the police were cleverer than he thought. Instead, yet another plan was set in motion. Using his original 'suicide' and that remark about 'staggering home from the fields' as inspiration, he set off the following evening, armed with the revolver and a handy blood capsule, offered up from the good Doctor's medicine cabinet.

Immediate events coincided very much with what came to be known as 'the authorised version'. That Vincent, lingering by a wall of the local château, some time after nightfall on the 27th July, either deliberately or accidentally shot himself. Then, some time later, with blood on his body and shirt, he stumbled back to the Inn. Without a word to the Ravoux, he took himself upstairs and climbed into bed. But the Ravoux, 'realising he was in pain', sent for Dr Gachet.

Avowing that he had 'a bullet' in his chest, Vincent allowed Dr Gachet, aided by a somewhat befuddled village doctor called Mazery, to bandage him up. Then, according to Dr Gachet's testimony, he himself tried to extract the bullet but failed. The following morning, he sent for Theo, the artist's brother, who arrived post-haste.

Early next day, the 29th, with Theo in attendance, Vincent 'died'. Whereupon, Dr Gachet made a sketch of him on his deathbed. The day after that, Vincent's coffin, closed and decorated with flowers, was placed in his room, with his easel, stool and painting utensils close beside it. By this time, distraught and loyal to the end, Vincent's good friend and paint supplier, the saintly *Père* Tanguy, had travelled especially from Paris to lay Vincent's most recent pictures round the bier. They could thus be admired there or on the walls by various of his other friends, as they came to pay homage.

That was how it was reported. What was not then known, except to Vincent, Dr Gachet and *Monsieur* Lestiboudois the undertaker, was that the stiffened body of *Monsieur* Tautain, already wrapped in a winding-sheet, had been bundled in the back way, substituted for Vincent's very live form, and was then laid in the waiting coffin with the lid screwed down.

After a touching farewell between Vincent and the Doctor, watched over by a fearful, yet oddly manic *Monsieur* Lestiboudois, Vincent, in heavy disguise, was reacquainted with his baggage (earlier placed in wait for him two stops down the line) and then entrained for the coast.

Dr Gachet and *Monsieur* Lestiboudois were joined by the pallbearers, who now bumped the coffin down to the hearse. This latter, since the Catholic priest in Auvers had refused to permit the community's own vehicle for a suicide case, had to be borrowed from the neighbouring town.

The mourners had been waiting and the funeral followed hard upon. Theo was acting strangely, as if he knew or suspected something. But only two of the witnesses (Dr Gachet and *Monsieur* Lestiboudois) had any inkling that the occupant of the coffin was anyone other than Vincent himself.

Meanwhile, the small group of hardened drinkers, who, on that previous occasion, had carried the badly-wounded Vincent from the copse, did manage against the odds to keep their secret. Even though, so mystified were they by 'the weird delayed outcome' of their strange friend's story that they would forever afterwards refer to Vincent in private as 'The Man Who Died Twice.'

Some days later, Marguerite returned. The young woman, Dr Gachet had by this time decided, should know the truth – the whole truth, unvarnished by lies or half-truths. It would be his chosen self-curative, alleviating, at least for the present, the crisis of conscience which still consumed him.

But changing his mind, he offered only the sequence of events already agreed upon with Vincent. That is, the duel, his miraculous recovery and the final 'suicide'. The young woman's evident distress, when her father told her of the poor man's 'tragic end', came near to breaking his heart. The good Doctor almost changed his mind again, but decided to leave it there.

The deception would always haunt him. But he knew, with certainty, that were Marguerite to know about Vincent's false passing and subsequent departure for the South Seas, it would not be the end of the matter. Her sweet nature and saintly inclination would virtually impel her to embark for those sunnier shores. There to assist Vincent in the relief and preservation of *Monsieur* Gauguin, a person she'd only heard of and surely never met?

Before Dr Gachet could elucidate further, to lay out some more 'facts' before her, there was another blow. A late-night messenger from the Post Office once more arrived, with an urgent communication from Lille. *Tante* Francia had died peacefully that afternoon and Marguerite's presence was again requested. Within the hour she'd set off, for the second time in a month, to be with her brother at her grieving *Maman*'s side.

While Marguerite was away, there was Theo to be dealt with. At first reluctantly, he'd agreed to recognise Dr Gachet's record of events, now fully accepting, like Marguerite, Vincent's 'suicide' at face value. The wound, when he'd first asked to see it, had been, of course, the original one – that from the duel in the copse – though subtly 'redesigned' to make it look 'new'. Vincent's performance had, likewise, been convincing, despite his being squeamish about putting something over on the brother he adored.

Indeed, immediately prior to Theo's arrival, Dr Gachet had suggested to Vincent that he try recalling elements of the scene in the surgery, as 'a kind of dress rehearsal'. So that, for the benefit of Theo, the Ravoux clan or anyone else who should chance to come in upon him, he'd be able to convince them.

Vincent acceded to this and, with much relish in his own thespian efforts, he re-enacted certain incidents and emotions, with winces, wheezes, groans, the feeble pipe-smoking, gradual 'weakening of body and spirit', and even his actual 'dying words' from that original ordeal!

Dr Gachet was truly admiring. As he told Vincent later, 'You have a gift for acting, *mon ami*, which I did not know you possessed. You could have been another Mounet-Sully or Coquelin. Though the talents you're already known for,' he added with a grin, 'are in my view quite talent enough!'

He could also have added that, without a painful *aide-mémoire*, his friend might not have been as 'naturalistic' as he was. And, for his part, the Doctor doubted if his own attempts to play 'the concerned physician, tragically unable to save a dying friend' had been anywhere equal in quality. He feared, indeed, that he'd let Vincent down. But everyone seemed taken in – Theo, in particular, manifesting a genuine (not acted) sorrow at 'the decline' of the brother he loved.

At one point, the police paid a visit, but, insisted Dr Gachet, his patient 'was not up to answering questions'. Then, following Vincent's 'death', they barely showed an interest. 'A suicide? *Oui, naturellement*, it happens all the time. Put that on the death certificate.' The officers shook their heads and departed. 'Just one less possibly troublesome citizen for us overworked officers to worry about!'

It was with some relief, then, having written his false report, that Dr Gachet was able to divest this and Vincent's 'suicide' note quickly from his hands, placing them with the proper authorities. Further, that it was left to Theo and *Monsieur* Ravoux to make the declaration for the death certificate, signed jointly by them without argument, before the local Mayor and Registrar, *Monsieur* Alexandre Caffin.

All well and good, the Doctor told himself. Yet later, with Vincent already some days absent and his convenient double laid to rest, there was a setback. Going through Vincent's things, prior to packing them for Paris, Theo came across another letter, addressed to himself. It had been written by his brother four weeks before, though for some reason not sent. Had Vincent changed his mind about the letter, or simply forgotten to post it?

According to a perplexed Theo, the letter referred to 'a duel with a certain young composer'. It implied that Vincent, fearing the worst, was also offering his fond goodbyes and laying out his 'last wishes, as to the disposal of property and paintings'.

On being confronted with this 'surprising news', Dr Gachet went a deep brick red (redder, indeed, than his normal ruddy hue!) and tried to stammer his denials. But no, there was no reason, averred Theo, to doubt the letter. Why would Vincent make it up? What on *earth* was it about?

Dr Gachet knew that he had to 'come clean'. With a deep breath and no little amount of further stammering, he explained to Theo why nothing had before been relayed to him, either about the duel or Vincent's near-fatal wound. Vincent had not wanted to worry his brother, nor bring him needlessly from Paris. There'd been no reason either to post the letter. It had been held back, presumably, while Vincent was fighting for life, then deemed of little consequence after his recovery.

Vincent had other reasons for keeping things quiet. Chiefly, said Dr Gachet, 'the illegality of the duel, in the first place' and the Doctor's 'own lapse of ethics in the cover-up'. There was also to be considered Vincent's fellow feeling for the young composer, who had suffered from the older man's success.

Theo gave this some thought. He'd been puzzled and

angry, but now seemed inclined to accept that 'silence is
the best policy'. Vincent's suicide was sufficient 'shame'
for the Van Gogh family, he agreed, without adding to it
'the extra stigma of an earlier criminal act.'

Further, clinging to the old-fashioned notion that 'a duel
has long been accepted as a private dispute between two
parties, to be enacted on equal terms and by no means
comparable to murder,' he would follow the Doctor
in adhering faithfully to Vincent's 'dying request' – the
one he had made that particular evening on the Doctor's
surgery couch. Namely, 'just to let us recap', said Dr
Gachet, 'in the awkward matter of *Monsieur* Satie'.

To enable that gentleman to keep as much possible
distance between himself and the circumstance of the
duel, Theo agreed to let matters rest. 'But that does not
signify, *Monsieur le Docteur*, when taking into account
my poor brother's wound, his great pain and the fact that
he might have died even before he *did* die, that, were I ever
to run into this Satie character, somewhere on the streets
of Montmartre or thereabouts, I should not hesitate to
punch him on the nose!'

As for Vincent's more recent 'wound' and the widely
reported 'fact' of his 'death', it was absolutely necessary
to establish 'an agreed pattern of circumstance'. So Theo
and Dr Gachet cooked something up. This was the soon-
to-be-famous story that two whole days had transpired
between the shooting and Vincent's 'actual expiry'.
Further, that Theo, arriving, as he did, the morning after
the incident, had gone not to Dr Gachet's, but directly to
L'Auberge Ravoux. There, he had raised an eyebrow to
see his brother, sitting up in bed and smoking his pipe,
acting, moreover, as if nothing were wrong.

Then, a little later, Theo welcomed the 'news' that 'by

some miracle, following "the accident", his brother had been given two more days to live.' Well, that was the story he now told. While the police, still unconcerned, had conveniently moved on to other things. In the precise matter of Vincent's 'death,' when accosted by reporters and suchlike, they would neither confirm nor deny.

It was Theo, writing to his sister Elizabeth, who first posited the 'official' account that, despite his trying to convince their brother that he would, in fact, be saved, the patient had replied, very calmly, that 'He, himself, wanted to die. Among his last words were [as related to Theo by Dr Gachet] "I wish I could go home now." And thus it happened. In a few moments he found the peace he had been unable to find on earth.'

And so, too, the above version – 'the botched suicide', progressing through Vincent's much weakened decline, before slipping finally into a painless release in his brother's arms – would be accepted by biographers as 'the true one'.

TWO

Within the fortnight, Marguerite came home, some days ahead of *Maman*. Since, as the tender-hearted daughter she always was, her own mourning for *Tante* Francia and, especially, their late friend, had been swiftly elided into 'a greater concern' – the comfort and consolement of her father. And so we have to leave them. But before we do so, one last scene.

Dr Gachet and Marguerite were sitting on the terrace on a sunny afternoon, watching the world go by. The Doctor dipped *la petite madeleine* into his lemon tea, recalling Vincent as now he'd always hope to do, each day at this same time. Meanwhile, somewhere upstairs through an open window, Hortense the maid could be heard singing '*Le Roi d'Yvetot*', that nice old song by Béranger. Quite a tuneful voice, mused Dr Gachet, unlike poor Vincent's. The song, with its sweetly satirical refrain, combining itself with thoughts of their absent friend, could not fail to move him.

Marguerite glimpsed the tear forming in her father's eye, and then another. She was not to know that these were less for Vincent's 'death' than for his permanent removal from France. The truncation of Dr Gachet's friendship with the now-vanished painter was also a sort of death: he felt the loss profoundly. Marguerite reached out, to grasp her father's hand.

'I miss Vincent, too, Papa. More and more each day. Let us hope the future, that uncertain new existence of his, treats him more kindly than the past or present?'

'Let us do so, *ma petite*. Let's hope it with all our hearts. But, you know, I'm encouraged. The funeral had a goodly turn-out, despite the cancellation of the church service. All those Impressionists, Post-Impressionists and Neo-Impressionists, the Modernists, Symbolists, Synthetists, Divisionists, Cloisonnists, Petit-Pointillistes, Vingtistes, Constructivistes and all the rest of them. The great and the near-great, the bad and the good, as well as some younger up-and-coming talents, who'll no doubt waste their lives from now on in a spirit of total abstraction. They were all out in force, along with the neighbours and Vincent's other friends, in fact all the people who'd loved him. He was so good and human, one could not have expected less.'

'That's wonderful, Papa. But what of the ceremony?'

'*Alors*, the eulogies were reverential, but with humour,

too. Much talk, from his admirers, of the bold forward thrust he had given to Art, the great projects that had always preoccupied him. I, myself, choking back the tears, spoke of Vincent's achievements and noble aims, and of my own great affection for him. The words, in general, were almost as congratulatory to our poor dead friend's painting, as they had been for those recent recitals, in the brief time that they'd made him famous.'

Dr Gachet sighed and looked away. A pause, as Marguerite took it all in.

'I wish I'd been there, Papa, it must have been beautiful? But with *Tante* Francia dying, *Maman* was most insistent. I came as soon as I could.'

'I know you did. And it *was* beautiful. We climbed the hill above Auvers, *en plein soleil*, talking of Vincent the whole time. And when we arrived at the cemetery overlooking the wheat fields, they were all ready for reaping. We stood there, bareheaded, beneath a wide blue sky, which Vincent would have marvelled at. Then, scattering sunflowers on the coffin, we lowered him into the grave.'

Marguerite, for her part, had accepted her father's version of Vincent's death; the result of a duel, rather than suicide, as otherwise reported. So, though her father still felt guilt over the deception, he comforted himself with the knowledge that the story was now more to do with omission (in that later part of his account) than with a more sinister attempt to cover up the truth. In this, he tried to convince himself: it was all for the best.

Dr Gachet glanced at Marguerite, just as she was brushing away a tear of her own. She increased the pressure on her father's hand. 'But there should be something else, Papa, something to commemorate him? Not just a gravestone with the usual cold inscription, but something living to remind us of Vincent and the things he liked best.'

'What did you have in mind?'

Marguerite thought for a moment. Her face lit up. 'I know, ivy! It has to be ivy! That was his favourite. *Oui*, that's what we'll do – Vincent asleep, in an ivy-covered grave.'

'*C'est magnifique*. Couldn't be better. *Merci mille fois, ma petite*. I'll put it to Theo, I'm sure he'll agree. We can take a cutting from this very garden. And the good news is that Vincent's good friend, *Monsieur* Bernard, is organising an exhibition at Theo's home in Montmartre. To be followed by a more important affair, next April in a small gallery in Paris.'

'That's wonderful, too, Papa, even though it's too late for Vincent to benefit.'

'*C'est vrai*, but at least it'll help put his paintings on the map. It's a step long overdue and will go some way to erase that peculiar interlude with the music.' Dr Gachet grinned. 'Thankfully, there was barely a word among the mourners of that other side to him. We were spared, too, the ordeal of a valedictory *chanson*. Too difficult to stage, I'd hazard, for the lack of Vincent's caterwauling and his eccentric gifts at the piano!'

'It *was* rather awful, wasn't it? Vincent's music?'

'Truly, it was.'

'But maybe it'd be different sung by somebody else?'

'I doubt it. I mean, *who* else? Who on earth would have the nerve? No, I blame the critics. How could they say *notre cher ami* was a master of musical composition, when the reception for his paintings has, till now, been so sparse and grudging?'

'I don't know, Papa. It says more about the critics, I think, those so-called art lovers … than it does about Vincent. It's very sad. I mean, the neglect of his true talents and the terrible effect it had on him.'

'*C'est vrai*. Vincent was like a rare orchid, which withers if left in the shade. But now, at last, he's justified.'

'*Oui*, Papa. In spite of the rumours.'

'Rumours?' Her father looked askance. 'Which rumours?'

'Vincent had noted, Papa, some folk in the newspapers cruelly say, that dead artists sell better than live ones. So he thought, and it's clearly a calumny, to increase the value of his paintings by killing himself. A sacrifice, as it were, to save his brother from bankruptcy.'

The Doctor shot her an anxious look. 'But we know that not to be true. What we do know is that Vincent's paintings, his already immense talent, will surely grow in reputation. While his music, a brief fad at best, will be mercifully forgotten.'

Dr Gachet paused, exchanging glances with his daughter. He turned away, embarrassed. No, this was awful. These lies of his, they were growing too smooth for comfort. If he weren't careful, he'd begin to believe them, himself. *Oui*, lies and then more lies, stacked up on each other, the pile growing bigger by the day! Just for keeping Vincent's secret at all costs, now and forever, even from those one loved best.

So, what was it to be? Loyalty to Marguerite, or loyalty to Vincent? A dilemma, certainly, since the tragedy of it, the greatest dishonesty of all, is in finding you cannot live *without* your lies, so you have to see them through!

Dr Gachet sighed again. He was still dying to tell Marguerite the truth. Risking her displeasure at the falsehoods – the tale of a death that never was, a funeral that wasn't Vincent's – though confident in her manifest joy at learning of their dear friend's survival. *Mais non, ce n'serait pas possible*. He could *never* tell her. Since, for all those reasons he'd already told *himself*, what other choice did he have?

Dr Gachet cleared his throat. 'Oh, by the way, I spoke to Theo seriously. He now knows what happened – what *really* happened. About the duel. Shocked, of course, almost suicidal, I fear, but he'll keep our secret.'

'*Bien*. The young composer is safe. And so, now, is poor Vincent. In Heaven, I hope?'

'God willing. That's if one believes in the afterlife, or even God – which, as you know, I don't. But I'm glad for Theo that Vincent may finally receive the *éclat* which both of them longed for. Life weighed heavily upon him, since despite that strange interlude in Paris, he knew in his heart that painting was his one *true* gift. And now, as it so often happens, everyone is full of praise for his talent.'

'Poor Vincent, it would have solved all his problems.'

'*Peut-être*.' Dr Gachet grew pensive. 'You know, I really thought at one point he was going to pull through?'

'I wish he had, a great pity. But he's gone now, Papa, at the very moment his life is vindicated. You mustn't blame yourself.'

'Well, I do. If I'd managed to extract the bullet, maybe he – oh, I don't know, with my lack of practice, the very nature of the wound, I might have killed him, anyway. Vincent knew that, he said I'd done my best.'

Marguerite nodded. 'It's what I'd expect. But you were with him, Papa, the whole time? Could Vincent speak to you? What did he say?'

'Several things.' Dr Gachet smiled his relief. In *this*

account, he could tell her the truth! 'Despite Vincent's agony, which I tried to alleviate, he was moderately lucid. I don't recall it all exactly, but most movingly, when I tried to reassure him that he was bound to recover, he shook his head and said, shortly before he died, "The sorrow will never end."'

'Nor will it, Papa. But we must look on the bright side. Think what he left us. Friendship, humanity and the memory of a loving spirit.'

'*C'est vrai, aussi*, he did, *ma petite*, and a huge capacity for truly fine works. His skill and imagination were vast, with an ability – mere words seem inadequate! – to transform the pain of his existence into moments of ecstatic beauty. Let us remember him as an honest man and consummate artist. He wished to create paintings, he said, which would strike later generations as masterpieces, "revelations to people in a hundred years' time." They are, *sans barrière*, masterpieces already, though few men yet know it – indeed, a victory over madness and death. History, Vincent said it himself, will be the judge. Art mattered to him more than anything else, the paintings were his children and he will live on in them. As Degas declared on the passing of Manet, "He was greater than we thought." Vincent, too, just see if I'm right.'

'I'm sure you are. But, come, let us go in, it's getting rather chilly.'

Dr Gachet rose sadly and helped his daughter from the seat. Linking arms, they crossed the terrace and passed inside.

Way up above, the sun was now behind the clouds, the sky had darkened and a flock of crows flew from over the rooftops, flapping and cawing, studying the ground beneath. It was as if they were searching for a man with a straw hat and a red beard, who had now mysteriously vanished.

But, in moments only, the crows had also gone and, from behind those same clouds, the sun once more peeped through. The clouds cleared completely and, across the town and over the wheat fields, it beamed its scorching rays. Caressing the fields, the bright yellow stalks, the sulphur sun in a pure cobalt sky beat down with a fierce intensity. Even to the most untutored eye, the scene looked like the work of a very great painter.

X

AFTERMATH:

The Vincent Phenomenon

The veteran tramp steamer Second Class, *á Bientôt, Mon Ami*, pulled away from the quayside in Marseilles, to an accompaniment of funnel bursts, ships' hooters, cries of '*Au revoir*' and, for the apparent benefit of a large cruise ship nearby, a tinny town band. Not to mention the screech of seabirds and a clanking of chains! It was a fine day, outlook fair, the sea calm, they'd be bound to make Suez in no time. Thence, making trading stops down the East Coast of Africa, across the Arabian Sea, the Indian Ocean, through the Malay States, full steam ahead to those Southern islands.

Vincent was standing at the stern, looking back at his adopted homeland for the very last time. Or that's what he now intended. He'd a bit of cash saved from his brief success in the musical world, if not all that much. Enough, though, to preclude his working his passage, if insufficient for a more luxurious berth.

Gazing at the waving crowds, the hive of activity in the harbour, he felt a frisson of regret for the friends he'd left behind and the possibilities in terms of Art, which the world, finally, had now been opening up for him. But he felt no nostalgia for his failures, the illnesses he'd suffered, nor the lack of appreciation that had plagued him, till just a short time before.

As land became an ever-decreasing speck, Vincent turned away, intending to make for his small but comfortable cabin. He'd have a brief nap before deciding what to do next. Keep a diary, maybe, paint a picture or two, though seascapes were not really his style. Anything he could think of, to make the long voyage pass pleasantly. Soon, with luck, he'd be seeing Paul again, determined to be his loyal friend and saviour. A spare bag packed with medical supplies, books and treatises on syphilis and other lingering diseases, accompanied Vincent, just as he'd promised, in his firm intention to live a healthy life and at last do some good.

Vincent smiled to himself, then nodded agreeably at the second officer, who was grinning down at him from the bridge. Dodging the burly seamen busy on deck, almost somersaulting over a guy rope, he descended the companion way, in the region of the cabins.

This was the last anyone saw of Vincent – in France, that is. No one, not even his friend Dr Gachet, heard from him again. Nor should they ever, for the plan to work.

To ensure this, Vincent had purchased his passage and signed the ship's register 'Jean Passepartout', the surname meaning 'Master Key'. It was a joke which the skipper, far from being a literary type, had signally failed to pick up on. Several name changes later and Vincent, as at first he'd hoped, had obscured himself from the scrutiny of doubters and sceptics. Anyone, in fact, if that were now possible, who might still believe him alive.

There were stories, of course. A French journalist, seeking a scoop, had spotted someone looking very like Vincent, red-bearded, with broad shoulders, shambling gait and wild-looking eyes, at some port or other in the Malayan archipelago. Then, on or around those far Southern islands – Fiji, maybe, or was it Western Samoa? – dwelt an old sailing type, who'd known the original Vincent 'back when.' He duly reported 'a genuine reincarnation, holed up with a native beauty, in a palm hut on the beach.'

Someone else, a trader in copra and phosphates, in the years when Vincent's name was becoming more familiar to the art lovers of Europe, sent word that he'd seen something strange. A chap, who *could* have been Vincent, 'hanging out with that even stranger painter fellow, *Monsieur* Paul Gauguin. In Dominiha, on the Marquesas, it was. I'm sure of it. Yes, that's right. Gauguin, if that were he, had gone native – long hair, loin cloth and all, but sick as Hell and *persona non grata*, except to the Dutchman. The cause of it, I wouldn't care to tell you, not in polite company, but the island talked of little else.'

'Still friends, then, are they,' asked the trader's interlocutor, 'I mean, those two, after all this time?'

'Good friends, *oui*, or so it seemed,' though at that final stage in *Monsieur* Gauguin's sorry life – a catalogue of debts, arrests, lawsuits and suicide attempts – 'they were more like a nurse and his patient.'

Indeed, 'that same red-bearded man was with *Monsieur* Gauguin when he died, in May 1903 of a double heart attack, "having made," according to the French Colonists he'd so frequently slandered, "a Hell out of Paradise". Meanwhile, his true friends, the natives who'd loved him – simple creatures, really, frightened by the striking of a match! – set up a wailing chant of "Gauguin is dead! We are lost!"'

Yet another source, some time afterwards, had stumbled

on a Vincent lookalike in Wellington, New Zealand. He'd been got up in leathers and a jaunty peaked cap, sitting behind the wheel of a bright green Darracq. His time on the island was brief, his spell at chauffeuring reputedly briefer. The sad demise of our driver's chief casualty, the new Premier's adored pet dachshund, came near to causing a diplomatic incident.

Then, another sighting came up, thousands of miles to the north, 'in Jakarta, or it could have been Borneo.' But how could that *be*, since a trio of seafarers, homeward bound from the Orient, on the long voyage back to France, had glimpsed some rather similar types in Macao, Yokohama and the backstreets of Shanghai?

'Fellow I saw,' said one, 'seemed keen on sketching, not that he kept anything, mind. He'd swap sketches and paintings for meals or a berth, and seemed to live very simply. Said he'd been in the South Pacific and, by a roundabout route, was working his way back to Europe. Each year getting nearer, whenever the homesickness drove him. But in small stages only, you understand? He said it wasn't that easy, few skippers would take him. A bit of an oddity, I wasn't surprised. But I promised to speak to *my* people, helping to get him a passage. We were sailing on to Aden. It'd bring him a little ways closer. But the fellow, afore I could fix it, just vanished.'

Then the trail, aided and abetted by hazy photos in the popular press and cheap reprints of paintings like *Self-Portrait Dedicated to My Friend Paul Gauguin* (1888), made everyone with a reddish beard and hair, and a rather queer look about him, seem like an analogue of 'that famous Dutch artist chap'. Various Vincents of one kind or another now presented themselves to the eagle-eyed view, everywhere, it seemed, from Hangchow to Hobart, from Cape Town to Calcutta.

One time, still some years before the Great War, a First Class passenger, doing the Far Western tour, clearly recalled a man very like Vincent, discussing literature and the art of navigation with a certain Mr Joseph Conrad. They were leaning on the taffrail of a British cruise ship in the Bay of Bengal, 'missing all meals and the ship's entertainments, so intent were they on their talk and the pleasure of each other's company'.

There was even another voyager, a Yank this time, himself an art lover. He claimed to have 'spied some guy, a dead ringer for Mister Vincent Van Go [*sic*], though now grey-haired and stoopin' a bit', playing 'Stride' piano and singing in a low dive in Cairo. 'Collossal', enthused the Yank, 'a real humdinger. He shoulda bin on Broadway!' So not 'the *real* Vincent' then? Not unless the listener had no ear at all, or Vincent had improved his questionable musical talents, somewhere beyond the realm of recognition.

TWO

Back home, tragedy persisted in the Van Gogh family. Theo, grieving, in dispute with and quitting his employers, suffered a mental breakdown and died of a paralytic stroke, complicated by syphilis, barely six months after Vincent. He was laid to rest beside his 'brother' in Auvers. (And who but the good Dr Gachet was to say that the man in the next grave was not Vincent himself?) It was now left to his beloved widow Jo to see that the Vincent legacy would be carried on and appreciated, which very much it has been.

Further tragedies struck. Vincent's youngest sister Wilhelmina, diagnosed with schizophrenia, was confined to an asylum, for thirty-eight years until her death. Their mother outlived all her sons, the youngest of whom, Cornelis (known as 'Cor'), served in the Boer War. He either committed suicide or was killed in action. Another Theo, a student grandson of Vincent's brother, later refused, during the 1940s, to sign the loyalty oath to Holland's Nazi occupiers. He joined the Resistance, with whom, among other activities, he helped forge papers and hide many Jews. In 1945, shortly before the end of hostilities, he and his group were arrested, tried and executed. This took place in the dunes near the North Sea, which Vincent, as a young artist, had so hauntingly painted.

Then, in Amsterdam, November 2004, the artist's great-grandnephew made world headlines when he was murdered by gunshot and machete, while riding his bicycle on an apparently peaceful street. A right-wing film director and talk show host, this Theo Van Gogh had met his end at the hands of a Dutch-Moroccan extremist, for making a film which 'blasphemed' Islam. At the time of his death, the victim had been planning a documentary on Vincent, to be called *The Golden Brush*. Vincent, with his darker side, might well have enjoyed the irony.

As for the actual Vincent, whether he ever did return to France, whether those aforementioned shadows were, in fact, the genuine article or mere coincidental doubles, is another question entirely. Suffice it to say that the fascination with the artist and his work, his personality and psychological condition, has continued unabated. To the extent, complained the critic Dr Jacob Baart de la Faille, that 'We are no longer far removed from a veneration and interpretive activity which extends to everything he touched in his life, an adoration *ad absurdum* which only Goethe before him experienced.'

The rise in appreciation of Vincent's work has been slower in some countries than others. In England, despite the best efforts to promote him by the likes of Roger Fry and the Bloomsbury Set, Vincent's paintings were initially attacked as 'lunatic' and 'shocking'. While observers, elsewhere, expressed themselves bemused by the ever higher prices those paintings seemed to fetch.

The Americans, meanwhile, have not only insisted on pronouncing Vincent's surname as if it were a quick-speed removal company, but, in the Summer of '44, for no strategic reason, the US Air Force blitzed 'The Yellow House' off the face of the Provençale map!

But the Van Gogh boom of 1945 and the buying spree which followed were soon being accompanied by a world-wide wave of interest, as for no artist before or since. Books, films, plays and operas, TV and radio documentaries, critical tributes and full-scale exhibitions have also played their part. Indeed, long after the cruel neglect and trials of his early years, the myth-forming phenomenon of Vincent, as the artist everyone loves and professes to know, has 'found no contradiction to the turn of the tide – it [has simply] confirmed it.'

Along the way, while the facts of the artist's life have been exhaustively exposed, the legends and conjectures regarding the same have been seized upon with vigour. These include stories, in passing, of a 'secret son' from a street girl Vincent looked after in The Hague, as well as an affair with his landlady in London (subject also of an excellent play), the result of being spurned by her daughter.

Rumours, too, have been noted of an 'actual' sexual

liaison between Vincent and Marguerite Gachet, or at least 'something cosy going on' with the artist's young model, his landlord's daughter Adeline Ravoux. Vincent described Adeline to Theo as 'a girl of about sixteen'. And then there's that stuff about '*Monsieur* Vincent' and his nightly task of tucking up her thirteen-year-old younger sister Germaine, before reading her bedtime stories, then 'kissing her good-night in her bed so that she could sleep'. Innocent? Maybe. Vincent, in his own writings, fails to elucidate.

As for Marguerite, Vincent was again commendably circumspect, though his attentions to the girl apparently caused a rift with Dr Gachet. The latter barred him from the house and their friendship ended soon after. Notwithstanding the revisionist approach of Maurice Pialat's brilliant 1991 film on Vincent's last days (which proselytised a full-blown sexual affair between the couple), Marguerite's brother Paul long insisted that, although Vincent was fond of his sister, the artist's affections were not returned.

Even more spurious is 'the strong possibility' (considered at the time, but again now 'firmly' posited) that it was really Paul Gauguin, and not the victim, who had bloodily sliced off poor mad Vincent's earlobe. This, according to the same ludicrous theory, had been the gruesome climax of a duel with razors, out and about in the night streets of Arles. It was Vincent's amnesia, combined with Paul's 'faked-up memoir' (*Avant et Après*, 1903), which had jointly conspired to obfuscate the truth.

Paul's recollection is inconsistent, unreliable, boastful and, in relating to their quarrels, frustratingly evasive. He refers to 'happenings' he could not have been present at and attributes unflattering 'opinions' to Vincent on the character and work of other painters, which run counter to Vincent's own written view of them.

As to the ear-cutting, Paul's account of the incident is usually the accepted one. That, out at the night café, the friends had quarrelled. Vincent had thrown absinthe in Paul's face, whereupon, said Paul, he had wrestled Vincent bodily across *La Place Victor Hugo* to 'The Yellow House' and put him to bed. He then, not waiting till morning, took himself off to a hotel. Only later did Paul learn that, during the night, Vincent in desperation had sliced off part of his own ear and his bedding was drenched with blood. By which time, the neighbours had called the police and a crowd had gathered. Apart from the fact that there is no *Place Victor Hugo* in Arles, Paul's story seems logical. Whether it's the true one has frequently been questioned.

In 2008, two Hamburg-based academics, Hans Kaufmann and Rita Wildegans, published a book on the incident, which Martin Gayford, amongst others, dismisses as 'a leap into wild conjecture'. The authors claim, for example, that, during their dispute on the night streets of Arles, Paul, an expert fencer, sliced off Vincent's earlobe, while defending himself from attack with his fencing sword. But Paul had only foils at Arles, which are basically thrusting weapons with no cutting edge. I know from my own early experience as an amateur fencer that you may well be able to concuss a caterpillar with a foil, but the likelihood of removing a human ear is well-nigh impossible.

There are several other speculations in the book, intriguing but far from conclusive. It is said by the academics that Vincent, to protect his friend Paul from opprobrium and possible arrest, conspired afterwards to give the incident a different reading. In other words, making out that the ear-cutting was self-inflicted. Paul went along with this, hence the version we find in his memoir.

Though the 2008 book does offer a handful of fresh insights, the key revelations are again far from original. The suspicion that Paul was, indeed, the culprit goes back a long way, to the aftermath and official investigations of the time.

So was Paul really responsible for the ear-cutting? Who knows? But look at it this way: Vincent had a thing about razors. Apart from threatening Paul (twice) he is also said to have brandished such an implement at Dr Rey in Arles. Who is to say he'd not have used it on himself? Added to which, we have another incident, when Vincent came at Dr Gachet with a loaded revolver. For this and other reasons, Vincent was not safe to be around!

Explanations for the ear-cutting are as varied and ingenious as those given for Vincent's 'madness'. (And who can deny that slicing off bits of one's own ear is the act of an at least 'temporary' madman?) There's the theory that Vincent, increasingly edgy and hearing voices in his head, had grown depressed over spending Christmas away from his family. Or, obsessed with homoerotic yearnings for Paul, was upset that he'd grown 'deaf' to Vincent's needs and had talked of leaving. The razor episode therefore, had distinctly 'gay' origins (Bradford Collins p. 226). My own personal favourite is the idea that Vincent, striving to paint a self-portrait, could not get the ear quite right, so he angrily cut it off! If that's not artistic perfectionism carried to extremes, I'd like to know what is.

More likely, though, it was all due to the clearly claustrophobic, verging on catastrophic, situation at 'The Yellow House': two strongly conflicting personalities who, by the end of nine weeks in each others' pockets, could barely tolerate each other. Not to mention the thesis that self-harm for Vincent (the hand in the candle flame, his imbibing of oil paints and kerosene, a taste for flagellation, some very public nude appearances made in all weathers, and those eccentric hair-shirt deprivations at Nuenen and Antwerp), had for him become a byword.

In 2011, two Americans (Steven Naifeh and Gregory White Smith) came up with a lengthy tome (*Van Gogh: The Life*) which, among other startling 'revelations', claimed that Vincent had actually been shot 'accidentally' by a young boy, one of several to have been tormenting Vincent in Auvers. 'Something went wrong in the scuffle between the tearaway and the eccentric outsider. The pistol went off, Van Gogh was wounded but, in a noble desire not to get the lad into trouble, he pretended that it was a self-inflicted wound. He died thirty hours later with everyone assuming that it was suicide.'

It's an interesting enough theory and the authors (aided by a formidable team of researchers) do provide chapter and verse. True or not, it is significant, they also mention, that the gun which caused Vincent's death (whoever did fire the final shot) was never actually found.

Together with the various motives and other contradictory reasons given by 'experts' for Vincent's 'suicide', sources also seem to differ as to the precise entry point of the fatal bullet. Dr Gachet, as witness and attendant physician (though not the only one), swore to 'the fact' that it was Vincent's chest which received the wound. And the good Doctor, if anyone, should have known? But since 'side' and 'abdomen' have also been offered as possibilities and the exact moment of Vincent's demise is, likewise, in doubt, could Dr Gachet, himself, as yet other sources suggest, have been wilfully confusing the issue, to divert official gaze from his preferred herbal remedies and implied inadequacies as a surgeon?

Paul Gauguin wrote in 1903 that Vincent had shot himself in the stomach. But, of course, he wasn't there and knew only what he'd heard. Paul's was just one of many 'accounts'. Alexander Barnett, writer and director of both a play and film on Vincent, may come closer than most as to what actually happened re the artist's 'suicide'. He insists that Vincent 'died slowly and languished for days, because he had shot himself in the (upper) abdomen rather than the chest, which had been his intention. The wound he suffered would not necessarily have been fatal, but he no longer had the will to live.'

As for the causes of Vincent's mental suffering (aka 'madness') the speculations have been endless. Was it genetic, self-induced, of obsessional religious origin, maybe due to persecution mania, his being haunted by the past or simply 'the fault of Society'? (P. Cabanne p. 189). There are claims, too, for a cerebral lesion at birth, a family history of nervous instability, autism, epilepsy, sexual imbalance, metabolic attacks, hallucinations due to absinthe and other alcoholic excesses, tinnitus, mal-nutrition, advanced syphilis (and/or mercury poisoning from treatment for same!), and a report from the hospital at Arles that he was suffering from an 'acute mania with general delirium'. Recent researches posit the possibility that Vincent was suffering from Asperger's Syndrome, which led him to being 'a workaholic loner' in later life.

There also seems to be evidence pointing to Paul's insistence that Vincent paint from memory, rather than from models, and this, too, had contributed to his mental breakdown. Brother Theo maintained that Vincent's madness was due to obsessive painting with colour, while at least one biographer (W. Uhde 1951) put it down to the sun, which Vincent loved more than anything else [and 'glorified in his pictures'] but which tragically 'robbed him of his reason and killed him'. The Anti-Sunbathing League could well use this fantasy in its advertising.

So, you take one possibility, painstakingly mull it over, then replace it with another. None of which accounts for the times (quite frequent, actually) when Vincent's behaviour seemed perfectly normal. 'My fear of madness has considerably lessened,' he wrote to Theo in May 1889. And at such times he also painted fine pictures, which fact seems to make redundant the nonetheless frequently asked question, 'Would Vincent still have been a genius without his madness, or would he be an even greater genius had he been sane?' (Cabanne pp. 161, 236–7.) Since Vincent, as in many aspects of his life, was so wonderfully inconsistent, one trusts the answer either way would be 'yes'?

Psychologists the world over have written 'informed' studies and even book-length treatises on what they imagine was wrong with Vincent. And these without even meeting or analysing the poor chap. Think what they might have come up with, had they ever *had* that dubious pleasure! (Vincent's letters, we have more recently been told, reveal he was 'most probably suffering from Bi-Polar disorder.' And the epilepsy he apparently suffered from was likely to be Ménière's disease.)

Whatever the truth of the matter, novelists, filmmakers and 'cottage industrialists' have continued to exploit the credibility of such speculations. While, at the same time, Vincent's influence and legacy are assured, with the one proviso that our admiration for those paintings which survive must be set against the indefensibly vast number which are lost to us.

Between 1884 and 1891 Vincent completed around 900 paintings and 1,100 drawings. Those from Arles alone, including Gauguin's, and currently valued at about $1.5 billion, represent 'one of the greatest artistic outpourings in history'. But many of Vincent's works were destroyed by their original owners, who thought them worthless. For instance, a quarter of Vincent's entire output was painted at Nuenen and although some of these paintings and sketches went with him to Antwerp, or were sent forward to Theo for safekeeping, the bulk of the work left behind in his studio was later sent to the paper mill to be pulped, or simply scattered by junk dealers.

Ironically, too, in both The Van Gogh Museum and *La Musée Estrine* in Arles, there are no original paintings by Vincent. Indeed, only one, says the latter's curator, still remains in the whole of Provence: *Railway Carriages* in *La Musée Angladon* (Avignon), which is not one of Vincent's best. And that's from the over 300 Vincent painted in the eighteen months he lived there! Though many of these do still survive in other galleries and private hands, sadly, quite a number do not.

Added to this, many of Vincent's surviving pictures have been subject to colour fading. Chiefly, because the paints supplied to him by his friend and *avant garde* mentor *Père* Tanguy were not of top quality. This meant that some of the more exotic shades, chosen by Vincent himself, had darkened or absorbed those colours with which they were mixed. Tanguy also stored a quantity of Vincent's and other artists' pictures in his attic. The room was mildewed and they suffered accordingly. Vincent became aware of this and harangued poor Tanguy for keeping his work in a damp place (Cabanne p. 275). The loss to art lovers on all these counts is unforgivable.

There were other losses. Many contemporaries, even those who had offered him friendship, saw little value in Vincent's work. Dr Félix Rey in Arles considered Vincent 'a fraud' and viewed his later fame as 'a passing craze'. Intensely disliking Vincent's portrait of him, he kept it in a loft, then used it to plug a hole in his chicken run. Later, apprised of its value, he astonished his sceptical family by obtaining 150 francs for it.

Dr Peyron from the asylum at Saint-Rémy also saw no merit in a painting Vincent had given him ('What the Devil could I do with that mess?'). The Mother Superior from the nearby Convent is on record as likening Vincent's painting style to 'swallow droppings', while the artist's own mother referred to her son's efforts as 'ridiculous'. To cap it all, the blinkered Peyron son (yet another Paul!) kept the works Vincent left at Saint-Rémy for rifle practice. Other paintings, too, were damaged in the two World Wars, or fell into Nazi hands, their whereabouts still unknown.

Luckily, many people of taste saw the merit in Vincent's work and enough of it, gifted by the artist to friends or exchanged for square meals and other benefits, has been left to posterity. Dr Gachet's son Paul, in 1950, bequeathed several paintings from his father's own collection to the Louvre, while The Van Gogh Museum in Amsterdam contains more than 200 paintings, plus many drawings and letters: one of the largest collections of a single artist's work anywhere. No doubt there are still other paintings in private ownership, lying around in some vault or closet, awaiting that moment of rediscovery?

Thieves, also, acknowledged the value of Vincent's work, though sometimes they had an ulterior motive. Several paintings, including works by Vincent and Paul Gauguin, were stolen from Manchester's Whitworth

Gallery in 2003. The thieves, when caught, claimed that they were merely highlighting 'the woeful security', since the paintings were found abandoned later in a public toilet nearby.

Nor is this all. Had he not been a great painter, Vincent would be hailed, as since he has widely been, as a gifted writer. Various anthologies and even 'complete' versions of his voluminous correspondence have been published over the last century. Finally, a huge (said to be 'definitive') six-volume collection became available: *Vincent Van Gogh: The Letters – The Complete Illustrated & Annotated Edition* (6 vols) Thames & Hudson Oct 2009.

Mostly addressed to brother Theo, his confidant and lifeline, though to other family members too, as well as to favoured friends and famous contemporaries, the letters (902 in all) are a revelation. Complete with more than 2,300 of Vincent's own wonderfully descriptive illustrations in the margins, they deal with everything from his works-in-progress, plans and instructions on same, his daily doings, current enthusiasms, views on art, literature, music, the people and places he'd seen, his touching love and respect for the everyday, to notes on his emotional and mental states, complaints about his want of success, lack of money, his hurts and grievances and the growing awareness of an almost wished-for tragic destiny.

Not since the days of James Boswell and Jacques Casanova have the personal writings of a brilliantly observant force so accurately fixed the inner life of a writer amid the rhythm and vibrancy of a specific time and place. This may be the greatest collection of thoughts and opinions left by any artist in history.

Further, the letters, extensively cross-referencing Vincent's life and work, form a major part of his assimilation into World Literature. In this, he has had a huge impact on the likes of Henry Miller, who claimed Vincent as an influence on his novel *Plexus* (1952) and confessed to the part the artist played in his own 'Apocalyptic view of life'. Or Antonin Artaud, who, after viewing Vincent's paintings in 1947, called him 'an artist suicided by society' and cited Vincent later as the direct inspiration for his 'Theatre of Cruelty'.

On the other hand (referring back to the title of this book), one has to ask oneself, how bad really *was* Vincent's music? Vincent had, indeed, been tutored, first by the family governess, Anna Birnie, later by Hein Van der Zande, organist at St Catherine's Church, Eindhoven. Irritated by Vincent's persistence in trying to learn 'how colour and sound relate to one another' (especially in reference to Wagner and 'Prussian blue'!) a despairing Van der Zande, according to Vincent's own painting pupil Anton Kerssemakers, 'thought he was confronted with a lunatic, and grew so afraid of him that he called a halt to the lessons'.

There's no accounting for taste, yet it is more than just an urban myth that certain 'long lost' Vincent song sheets have been turning up in recent years, clear of all copyright and entering the public domain. Their contents have been 're-arranged' and orchestrated, providing moderate success under the imprimaturs of present-day composers. *Par example*, as the great Hercule Poirot would say, it takes but a rudimentary amount of detective work to recognise that the original birth name of one modern musical genius is a perfect anagram for 'Vincent Van Gogh'!

As for Erik Satie, he did achieve his own measure of fame. Ballets, sonatas, *études* and great experimental works were all grist to his musical mill. He died, aged fifty-nine, of cirrhosis of the liver, having never married nor invited anyone to his apartment for twenty-seven years. Friends discovered a cache of unpublished compositions throughout his belongings. Some were deemed valuable indeed, yet, not averse to taking Vincent's advice, he'd no longer believed originality to be the sole key to success.

For those experts with time on their hands, it's easy to see how Vincent's eccentric themes and chord structures have found their way into the works of Satie, Milhaud, Boulez and several other hugely innovative composers. Even in the lighter vein, it takes but a cursory aural examination of Don McLean's famous 'Vincent' to glean that this evocative hit single *hommage* to the Great Artist is, in essence, a simple remix of *Chanson de l'eté à Auvers: un poèsie pour Marguerite* – only this time made bearable by being played backwards!

So, finally, what, again, of this odd idea that Vincent survived his reported fate and sailed for foreign parts? That there *were* further rumours, history records. Especially when the prices paid for Vincent's paintings at auction began to go through the roof. Had those rumours been true and Vincent's Pacific idyll been confirmed, Lord knows where such prices might have gone? Through the stratosphere, one thinks, as many years later they seemed to. Just compare, if you like, the modest £10,000 paid by Samuel Courtauld in 1928 for *Self-Portrait with Bandaged Ear*, and the astonishing $82.5 million (£44m) for *Portrait of Dr Gachet* some sixty years later!

But with little to back up or confirm the various stories, interest in this particular chestnut lapsed again and the papers gave up on it. Said one weary Editor of *Le Figaro* in a brief, somewhat dyspeptic editorial:

We have each of us, somewhere, glimpsed our living counterpart, *notre sosie de nous-même*. Maybe more than once, surely? Since that is God's way: He delights in confusing us. But all this stuff about Vincent Van Gogh as a world traveller, a man of multiple identities, who pops up everywhere, painting his pictures in Tonga, Togoland or Timbuktu, is hearsay, arrant nonsense. We know him to be long dead. Indeed, I, myself, as a callow cub reporter, attended the poor fellow's funeral! There was no doubt on that day that the man in the coffin was Vincent. There is no *real* doubt about it now. Let us have no more of this. Let us enjoy the paintings and reflect, if we must, on the Great Man's tragic end. But to live in hopes that he will once more materialise on the streets of Paris, to greet his old friends, claim his artistic birthright and all the hard cash, which that same claim might imply, is a pipe dream, a fantasy – *all sensible people know it*. There will be no more reports of such nature here, not so long as I'm Editor. I am irritated by these stories, thoroughly tired of them. And so, dear reader, should you be. "Each artist," pronounced the great Edouard Manet, "creates his own myths, he scarcely needs others to help him?"

POSTSCRIPT

Paul Gauguin (1848–1903) was laid to rest in the Calvary Cemetery, Atuona, on the island of Hiva Oa, French Polynesia. His grave is a mere stone's throw from that of the great singer-songwriter Jacques Brel (1929–78), who spent his last years there. Their tombs look out on the town and Tahauku Bay and have long been a place of pilgrimage.

According to local superstition, the ghosts of these two get together of an evening to discuss art, music, politics and everything under the moon. The anti-bourgeois, anti-clerical tone and poetic versatility of Brel's best songs obviously appeal to the older ghost, while Paul's wanderlust, iconoclasm and artistic sensibility are more than appreciated by the younger. Added to which, both men had shared in their work and deeper thoughts the idea that death, during much of their earthly existence, was a thing they could well come to terms with.

There is talk now of forming their own combo, since Brel's talents in the music department remain unquestioned and Paul, in his day, was no mean guitarist. But it all depends on (1) whether they can work out a way of playing without their ghostly fingers slipping through the instruments and (2) keeping their plans secret from the ever-watchful Vincent.

He died there, too, finally, of old age, unnoted by the world media and is buried in an unmarked grave. His ghost, regressing to the more delusional, musically unself-critical side of Vincent, would love to join in the fun. (He even has some new 'songs' to try out.) But that, say his friends, would spell disaster.

Acknowledgements

The book is exactly what the title suggests: an alternative history, rather than an assemblage of dry, already well-ordered facts. Facts, of course, are important in any work of historical fiction, even one which strays far from the accepted circumstances of a subject's life. But this is a story of what might have happened to a certain group of characters, had those circumstances been in some ways different.

'Name me one writer,' wrote the great critic Saint-Beuve, 'who does not prefer fiction to reality.' A not entirely true comment, one should add (then or now), since many authors are perfectly happy assembling factual portraits of their subjects. But, given that there have been at least five novels already based on Vincent Van Gogh (one Dutch, two German, two American), each moving on in various small ways from the absolute gospel of the artist's life, I have taken it as my cue (why not?) to take it even further. So accustomed did I then become to establishing my own version of Vincent, with more than a little help from the genuine biographers, that the Vincent of my book became more and more alive to me. To the extent, so enjoyable was the game I caught myself playing, that the 'real' Vincent, for my purposes, may now no longer be found in the many historic versions I have read, but in the preceding pages!

That said, it was entirely necessary to ferret around among the 'true' facts, even half and quarter facts, to increase my own knowledge and understanding of the subject of our tale. Indeed, as any self-respecting author will tell you, to get the facts right is essential, before one can even begin (deliberately?) to get the facts wrong! For instance, having already taken liberties with the 'truth' I have made, for convenience' sake, a few additional adjustments.

The relationship between Vincent and Paul here portrayed was not as friendly as all that, nor would Vincent, if their story here shown were the true one, have really taken off to the South Seas to tend his ailing friend. He would have been too selfish and/or impecunious for that. Similarly, Dr Gachet, in real life, was a widower at the time of Vincent's extended visit. I merely introduced a live *Maman*, albeit *in absentia*, to give their daughter Marguerite a logical reason to leave the Gachet household near the end of the book. This was to let her aid *Maman* in looking after a sick aunt in Lille. The existence of the aunt and her final illness were, though, quite true, while Marguerite's brother Paul, not seen but referred to in the text, survived to outlive them all.

So, here's another quote, this time from Mark Twain: 'The only difference between reality and fiction is that fiction must be credible.' To this end, I should like to credit and offer my gratitude to all of the following sources for, in many such cases, unknowingly, helping me in my task:

First off Vincent's own *Letters*, mostly to his brother Theo, a work *in toto* that, more than anything else, justifies claims for Vincent as a literary force and stylist almost equal to his skills as a painter. Essential, too, was Taschen's monumental full-scale biography, with gorgeous reproductions of virtually every one of Vincent's paintings now known to exist. I read *The Yellow House* somewhat late in the day, but it's a beautifully written account of Vincent's time with Paul Gauguin at Arles and proved invaluable for a bit of late-day 'fact checking'. A list of other volumes I found especially useful follows below. Many others were consulted, at least in part, for the purposes of cross checking and elucidation, so to all those authors – distinguished fellow Van Gogh and Gauguin enthusiasts! – my good wishes and warmest thanks:

The Art of Van Gogh Nathaniel Harris (Hamlyn/WH Smith 1982).

Avant et Après Paul Gauguin (1903; first publ. editions G Cres, 1923; Librairie Julien Cornic, 1989). Contains unreliable, self-justifying detail on the Arles interlude, including the ear-cutting & Vincent's supposed dislike of Ingres, Cézanne, Degas etc, which is contradicted by his own letters to others.

Dear Theo: The Autobiography of Vincent Van Gogh ed. Irving & Jean Stone (Houghton Mifflin, Boston 1937; Plume 1995). Selection of Vincent's letters to his brother, sharing his outlook on life & art. Based on some of Vincent's edited writings etc.

Flora Tristan's Diary: The Tour of France 1843–1844 Publ. Peter Lang (ex Cornell University, 2002).

Gauguin by himself ed Belinda Thomson (Little, Brown & Co Boston/New York/London 1993). With lavish colour plates, text based mainly on Paul's letters to his friends.

Gauguin 1948–1903: The Primitive Sophisticate by

Ingo F. Walther transl Michael Hulse (Taschen, Cologne 2006).

Johanna: a Novel of the Van Gogh Family Claire Cooperstein (Scribner, NY 1955). Entertaining story of the unsung 'hero' of the Van Gogh saga, Theo's wife, Johanna Van Bonger ['The brother who ruined my life has *become* my life'].

The Letters of Vincent Van Gogh ed. Ronald de Leuw, transl. Arnold J. Pomerans (Constable 2003).

The Love of Many Things, A Life of Vincent Van Gogh by David Sweetman (John Curtis/Hodder & Stouhton 1990).

Lust for Life: A Novel of Vincent Van Gogh Irving Stone (Heritage Press, New York 1936). Book [and film] which more than anything sparked the modern revival of interest in Van Gogh.

The Moon & Sixpence (novel) W. Somerset Maugham (William Heinemann 1919; George H. Doran, New York 1919). Paul Gauguin re-imagined as a middle class English stockbroker/dropout.

Murder in Amsterdam: The Death of Theo Van Gogh & the Limits of Tolerance Ian Buruma (The Penguin Press, London 2008). Three US feature films have apparently been produced.

Noa Noa: The Tahiti Journal of Paul Gauguin (orig. Charles Morice, La Plume Paris 1901 [abridged, minus illustrations]; publ. US 1919; Gauguin woodcut edition, ed. John Miller, with a 1967 introd. by W. Somerset Maugham, Chronicle Pubs, New York, 1994, 2005). Vivid, if at times fanciful memoir of Paul's first two-year stay in Tahiti, with the artist as classic South Seas wanderer-sybarite.

Paul Gauguin: A Complete Life David Sweetman

(Hodder & Stoughton, 1996; as *Misadventures in Paradise: Paul Gauguin, a life*, Simon & Schuster US 1996). Rejecting hard & fast feminist assertions on Paul's lifestyle. The author challenges the traditional view of the artist as simply a 'syphilitic paedophile', setting himself up with child brides.

Der Roman eines Gottsuchers (a novel) Julius Meier-Graefe (Vienna 1932). This distinguished art critic, historian and gallery owner again juggles fact and fiction, reprising our suffering artist as 'a man in search of God.'

The Studio of the South Douglas Druick, Andreas Buhm (Thames & Hudson, 2001).

The Sunflowers Are Mine: The Mystery of Van Gogh's Missing Paintings Martin Bailey.

Van Gogh Pierre Cabanne (editions Almery Somogy, Paris 1963; Thames & Hudson, 1963).

Van Gogh W. Uhde (Phaidon Press Ltd UK/US 1951; reprinted 1972).

Van Gogh & Expressionism Jill Lloyd (Hatje Cantz Verlag, 2006).

Van Gogh & Gauguin: Electric Arguments & Utopian Dreams Bradley Collins (Thames & Hudson, 2003).

Van Gogh & Gauguin: The Studio of the South Bradley Collins (Thames & Hudson).

Van Gogh 1853–1890 Authors uncredited (Grange Books, 2007).

Van Gogh in Provence & Auvers Bogomilla Welsh-Ovcharov (Arts Guild 2009). With 300 colour plates, illustrating Vincent's most prolific years, leading up to his suicide.

Van Gogh: His Life & His Art David Sweetman (Crown 1990; Touchstone 1991).

Van Gogh's Ear, Paul Gauguin and the Pact of Silence Hans Kaufmann & Rita Wildegans. (2008). Controversial study, laying the blame for Vincent's ear-cutting on poor old Gauguin. An idea heartily dismissed by most in-depth researchers, including the present author. Well argued but inconclusive.

Van Gogh's Table at L'Auberge Ravoux Alexandra Leaf & Fred Leeman (Artisan 2001).

Vincent: a Biographical Study (novel) Julius Meier-Graefe (R Piper Verlag, Munich, 1921; The Medici Society, London/Boston 1922). 'Romanticised & dramatically overheated' effort, in which the author introduces a German Expressionist note into the writings on Vincent. This work did much to increase the artist's popularity. [In a foreword to the 1925 revised version, Vincent is likened to Dostoevsky.]

Vincent by Himself ed. Bruce Bernard (Orbis 1986).

Vincent in Der Haag (novel) Theun de Vries. Vincent's life semi-fictionalised between the years 1881–1883.

The Vincent Van Gogh Atlas Nienke Denekamp, Rene Van Blerk, Teio Meedendorp, transl. Laura Watkinson (Yale University Press/Van Gogh Museum, Amsterdam 2015). Lively, detailed, beautifully illustrated trek through most, if not all, the places Van Gogh visited and/or resided in, and how they influenced his work.

Vincent Van Gogh: A Biographical Study Julius Meier-Graefe (1922).

Vincent Van Gogh: Between Earth & Heaven: the Landscapes Authors various (Hajie Canz, Konstmuseum, Basle UBS updated, 2009).

Vincent Van Gogh: His Paintings & His Drawings J-B de la Faille (Wiedenfeld & Nicholson, London;

Meulenhoff International, Holland 1970 revised from 1928).

Vincent Van Gogh: The Landscapes Hatze Ganz (Konstmuseum, Basle UBS undated).

Vincent Van Gogh: The Letters – The Complete Illustrated & Annotated Edition 6 vols, ed Leo Jansen, Hans Luijten, Nienka Bakker (Van Gogh Museum, Amsterdam; Thames & Hudson Oct 2009).

Vincent Van Gogh: The Lost Arles Sketchbook Bogomilla Welsh-Ovcharov (Abrams 2016). All 65 drawings in VG's rediscovered sketchbook (1880 to 1890) reproduced in facsimile with editorial comments. Invaluable as an insight into the artist's life & work at this time. Alas, this 'long lost' work (once placed, with them all unknowing, on a shelf of the Ginoux family in Arles) would cause controversy. In early 2019 it was denounced by a number of distinguished experts as a fake. Welsh-Ovcharov stood firm.

Vincent Van Gogh Visits New York drawings by Greg Constantine (Chatto & Windus 1983).

The Way to Paradise Mario Vargas Llosa transl. Natasha Wimmer (Faber & Faber, London 2003). Significant novel based on Paul Gauguin's life.

Without Feathers ['If the Impressionists had been Dentists'] Woody Allen (Random House, New York 1980; New English Library, UK 1981). Amusing story which parodies Vincent's letters to Theo.

The Works of Vincent Van Gogh JB de Faille; introd. AM Hammacher (Weidenfeld & Nicholson, London, 1970; Meulenhoff International, Amsterdam 1970).

Monumental study, from beginning to end, of Vincent's paintings & sketches.
The Yellow House: Van Gogh, Gauguin & Nine Turbulent Weeks in Arles Martin Gayford (Little Brown & Co, NY 2006; Penguin 2007).

A number of additional writers (in-depth articles, critical pieces and insights) have been invaluable: Jad Adams, Rebecca Allison, Jane Anderson, HH Arnason, Andy Barker, Frank Barrett, Will Bennett, Michael Billington, Caroline Boucher, Tania Branigan, Mark Braxton, Richard Brooks, James Burleigh, Jonathan Calvert, Jeffrey Camp, Rachel Campbell-Johnston, Jonathan Calvert, Maurice Chittenden, Rupert Christansen, Susannah Clapp, Pete Clark, Steve Connor, Charles Darwent, Andrew Davies, Gareth Huw Davies, Alain de Botton, Nicholas de Jongh, James Dellingpole, Andrew Graham Dixon, Celia Dodds, John Dugdale, Geoff Dyer, Kieran Falconer, Deirdre Fernand, Nick Fielding, Maxine Frith, Martin Gayford, Linus Georgiadis, Michael Gibson, Gerard Gilbert, Brenda Gilhooley, David Gillard, Richard Godwin, Andrew Graham-Dixon, Fison Guner, Ed Harris, Douglas Heingartner, Clare Henry, Philip Hensher, Henry Hitchings, Christopher Hudson, Mark Hudson, Kathryn Hughes, Dave Itzkoff, Waldemar Januszcak, Jonathan Jones, Laurence Joyce, Louise Jury, Michiko Kakutani, Janine Kelso, Ted Kessler, Sally Kinnes, Richard Lay, John Lichfield, Joy Lo Dico, Sarah Lyall, John McEwen, Jo MacFarlane, AA McGill, Ross McGuinness, Noel Malcolm, John Marriott, Stephanie Merritt, Richard Middleton, Alex Mitchell, Fiona Mountford, Gerard O'Donovan, William Packer, Peter Paterson, Dr Richard Petty, Tom Phillips,

Nicholas Pioch, Diana Preston, Michael Prodger, Imogen Ridgway, Martin Rose, Brian Sewell, Miranda Seymour, Nicholas Shakespeare, Godfrey Smith, Charles Spencer, Chris Stewart, David Sweetman, Paul Vale, David Ward, Gary Warner, Amy Watkins, Robert Wernick, Robert Whymant, Nicholas Woodsworth.

Each of the above has written variously in the following Publications: *Art & Artists*, *L'Art Moderne*, *The Artist*, *Arts Review*, *L'Aurore*, *La Critique*, *Daily Mail*, *L'Écho de Paris*, *L'Écho Pontoisien*, *ES Magazine*, *Evening Standard*, *Le Figaro*, *Financial Times*, *Forum Républicain: Journal de l'Arrondissement d'Arles*, *Le Gaulois*, *Gil Blas*, *The Guardian*, *L'Illustration*, *The Independent*, *Independent on Sunday*, *International Herald Tribune*, *L'Intransigeant*, *Le Journal*, *Larousse*, *La Libre Parole*, *Live Magazine*, *The Mail on Sunday*, *Le Matin*, *Mercure de France*, *Metro Life*, *New York Times*, *The New Yorker*, *The Observer*, *Observer Magazine*, *Le Paris*, *Paris Illustré Paris Match*, *Perhinderion*, *Le Petit Parisien*, *Radio Times*, *Reader's Digest*, *La Revue Blanche*, *Seven*, *Le Siècle*, *Le Societé Anonyme*, *Le Soleil*, *Sunday Telegraph*, *Sunday Times*, *Sunday Times Culture*, *The Tatler*, *Le Temps*, *The Times*, *Times Playlist*, *TNT Magazine*, *La Vie Parisienne*, *L'Ymagier* and many others.

For general reading/listening, throwing light on, if not strictly relating to the life of Vincent, I would recommend *The Painter of Modern Life* (Charles Baudelaire, 1863), a significant paper that signalled a new movement in Art; *Belle Epoque: Paris in the Nineties* Raymond Rudorff (Hamish Hamilton, London 1972); *The Microbe Hunters* Paul De Kruif (Albatross Verlag GmbH, Hamburg

1932); *The Impressionists, The Bohemians* Dan Franck (Weidenfeld, London 2001); *Paris in Our Time: From Impressionism to the Present Day* text Pierre Courthion (Editions d'Art Albert Skira, Paris 1957; A. Zwemmer Ltd, London); *Essai sur le Duel* Le Comte de Chatauvillard; *Cézanne* Marcel Brion (The Wildenstein Foundation, Paris; Thames & Hudson, London 1974); *Satie the Bohemian: From Cabaret to Concert Hall* Steven Moore Whitely (OUP 1999); *Orsay Visitor's Guide* Françoise Bayle (Art Lys, Versailles 2002); *The Banquet Years: The Originas of the Avant Garde in France 1885 to World War I* (Alfred Jarry, Henri Rosseau, Erik Satie, Guillaume Apollinaire) Roger Shattuck (1955); *The Intimate Sex Lives of Famous People* Irving, Amy & Sylvia Wallace with David Wallechinsky (Hutchinson, London 1981; Arrow Books 1981); *Paris & its Environ*s Karl Baedecker (9th Revised ed. Leipzig 1888); *Larousse Gastronomique* Prosper Montagné and Dr Gottschalk (Librarie Larousse 1938; Hamlyn 1961); *Madame Bovary* (1857) & *L'Education Sentimentale* (1869) Gustave Flaubert; *Les Fleurs du Mal* Charles Baudelaire; *Bel Ami* Guy de Maupassant; *Germinal* Emile Zola; *À la Recherche du Temps Perdu: Du côté de chez Swann* (1913) Marcel Proust.

One should also offer some comment on the many films, stage, TV and radio productions on Vincent, Paul and their friends. Not all of these were specifically helpful in the historical time-span of my book, but their presence is felt. I was forced to miss the famous National Theatre production of *Vincent in Brixton*, based on incidents which I only mention in passing. But it seemed to me, when I caught up with an exemplary later production (by the Richmond Shakespeare Society) that along with the earlier Vincente Minnelli and Maurice Pialat feature films, it proved as near to one's own ideas of what Vincent was like, as any interpretation one can think of. My own favourite Vincent impersonators, apart from the once deemed 'definitive' Kirk Douglas, have been, oddly enough, on TV: John Simm in BBC's *The Yellow House* (2007) and Tony Curran, splendid, in an enjoyably surrealistic *Doctor Who* segment (2010) by Richard Curtis. If the real Vincent was not something like this, then the existing self-portraits and biographies must be wrong!

Several versions of Paul Gauguin's life (not as many as for Vincent) have proved worthwhile, including a 'to the manner born' turn by John Lynch (also in *The Yellow House*), and at least two intriguing biopics, *Wolf at the Door* (1987) and *Paradise Found* (2003) with a somewhat bizarrely cast Donald Sutherland in the former, his real life son Kiefer in the latter. There was also a play *Mrs Gauguin* (1984) – alas, at this time of writing I have still not seen nor read it, and this, too, may prove useful to others with a yen for taking the present game further. TV and radio documentaries enjoyed and consulted include those by Simon Schama, Tim Marlowe and, especially, Waldemar Januszczak. And one must not forget the late Mai Zetterling's well-praised 1969 *Omnibus* drama-doc, with Michael Gough as Vincent. Long un-revisited by me and, one imagines, most viewers, it lives in fond memory.

***

For those interested in similar interpretations of Vincent and Paul, herewith as near to a comprehensive list (in correct date order) as I've been able to conjure:

The Moon & Sixpence (Film) d. Albert Lewin w. George Sanders (Strickland), Herbert Marshall (Maugham). Elegant if unlikely view of Gauguin as a suave absconding English stockbroker. US 1942.

Paul Gauguin (Opera) by Federico Elizalde. 1943.

Gauguin (A Synthetic Life) (Opera) by Michael Smetainin & Alison Croggan.

Van Gogh (Film) d., ed. Alain Resnais short doc. France 1948.

The Moon & Sixpence (US TV) 30-min series segment w. Lee J. Cobb (Strickland), Romney Brent, Bramwell Fletcher. Somerset Maugham TV Theater. CBS 1950.

Paul Gauguin (Film) d. Folco Quillici. Short doc. Italy 1954.

Lust for Life (Film) d. Vincente Minnelli w. Kirk Douglas (Vincent), Anthony Quinn (Gauguin), James Donald (Theo). Respectful, gorgeous to look upon Hollywood in Europe biopic. US 1956.

The Moon & Sixpence (US TV) d. Robert Mulligan w. Laurence Olivier (Strickland). Geraldine Fitzgerald (Amy Strickland). NBC 1959.

Monitor: Van Gogh Cecil Day Lewis examines the life & work of Van Gogh. BBC TV 1962.

The Moon & Sixpence (UK/Can TV) d. Donald McWhinnie w. Charles Gray (Strickland), Barry Justice (Willie). BBC Play of the Month 1967.

Vincent the Dutchman d. Mai Zetterling, David

Hughes w. Michael Gough (Vincent/Narrator). BBC Omnibus. UK 1969.

Letters of Van Gogh (Opera) by Grigori Frid. Mono-Opera in 2 parts for Baritone & instruments. Op 69 1975.

Gauguin: the Savage [ex The Immortal Outcast/In Search of Eden/Gauguin etc] (TV) d. Fielder Cook w. David Carradine (Gauguin), Lynn Redgrave, Barrie Houghton, Flora Robson, Ian Richardson, Fiona Fullerton. 3-hour TV movie covering the high spots of Gauguin's life. US/France 1980.

The Savage: Paul Gauguin & His Construction of Paradise (TV) based on his book Noa Noa w. Leo McKern (Voice of Gauguin) BBC 1980; reptd BBC4 27 Sept 2010.

Vincent (Stage & TV) scr., d., pr. Leonard Nimoy. Based on the 1979 play Van Gogh by Phillip Stephens. Nimoy in one-man show as Theo Van Gogh, looking back on Vincent's life & struggling to compose his euology. Role was originally played in a university production by Stephens. Nimoy's video version was taped at the Guthrie Theatre, Minneapolis. A & E Network US 1981.

Self-Portrait by Van Gogh BBC History 27 Aug 1981.

In Search of ... Vincent Van Gogh (TV) Segment of ongoing series hosted by Leonard Nimoy. In this one, Nimoy discusses his researches in France & confers with other Vincent enthusiasts. US 1981.

Vincent (Opera) Einojuhani Rautavaara. Opera in 3 acts based on several events in Van Gogh's life 1981–2 [Some of the same themes were later used by the composer in his 6th Symphony Vincentiana (1992)].

Vincent Van Gogh: A Portrait in Two Parts (Video) scr., d. Jean Pierre Isabouts. Doc in '16 programmable chapters', weaving together the 5 main periods of Vincent's life. Critical comments by Leonard Nimoy, with Vincent's own thoughts, taken from his letters. US 1982.

Portrait in Two Parts Phillips International/North American Philips Corp (1983).

Mrs Gauguin (Play) by Helen Cooper d. Mike Bradwell w. Donald Sumpter (Gauguin), Rachel Bell (Mette). Almeida Theatre, London 4.06.84.

In a Brilliant Light: Van Gogh in Arles (Video) d. Gene Searchinger. The Metropolitan Museum of Art Video Collection. US 1984.

Vincent [Orig: Vincent: The Life & Death of Vincent Van Gogh] (Film) d. Paul Cox w. John Hurt (Voice of Vincent). Doc making exteisive use of Vincent's letters. Austral. 1987.

The Wolf at the Door (Film) d. Henning Carlsen w. Donald Sutherland (Gauguin). Mostly dealing with the artist's later life. France-Den 1987.

Van Gogh ou la Revanche Ambigüe [Van Gogh, the Double-Edged Triumph] (Film) d. Abraham Ségal. France 1989. 70 minute doc. examining the 'cult' & 'myth' of Vincent 100 years after his death. Covers the 1987 'Irises' auction, New York, plus the views of medical experts, citizens of Arles, Antonin Artaud, Johanna Van Gogh, Kirk Douglas & others 'obsessed' with the artist. Public Prize for Documentary Film at the Nyon Film Festival. (530v.)

In a Brilliant Light: Van Gogh in Arles (TV) d. Anna Benson Gyles w. Linus Roache (Vincent), Kevin

Wallace (Theo), Anna Cropper (Mother) BBC Omnibus 20.7. 1990.

Vincent & Theo (Film & TV) d. Robert Altman w. Tim Roth (Vincent), Paul Rhys (Theo), Vladimir Yordanoff (Gauguin) scr. Julian Mitchell. Intelligent low-key feature-length biography, later expanded to a 4-part mini-series. Fr/UK 1990.

The South Bank Show (TV) Melvyn Bragg presents views on Altman's Vincent & Theo LWT UK 1990.

Van Gogh: A Museum for Vincent (Film) d. Elias Marroquin. Brief entertaining look at Vincent's life and art. Vanguard Prods. US 1990.

Dreams [aka Akira Kurosawa's Dreams] (Dream 5: Crows) (Film) d. Akira Kurosawa w. Martin Scorsese (Vincent). Lovely surrealistic approach to Vincent's life and colour schemes. Scorsese, alas, is miscast. Japan/US 1990.

Vincent: Sun Painter in France (TV) d. Rob Brass w. Wick Ederveen (Vincent), Peter Bos (Theo) A Not Prod/TV6 short drama doc. Holland 1991.

Vincent and Me (Film) d. Michael Rubbo. Story of a young Canadian girl and small boy pal, visiting Amsterdam & Arles, in quest of her idol's magic. Most popular entry at that year's Chicago International Festival of Children's Films. Can/Fr 1991.

Van Gogh (Film) d. Maurice Pialat w. Jacques Dutronc (a non-lookalike Vincent), Alexandra London (Marguerite). Long, majestic, heavily fictionalised study of Vincent's last days in Auvers. 8 César awards, including Best Actor. The one undoubted masterpiece feature film on the artist. France 1991.

Vincentiana (Music) Symphony No. 6 in 3 movements. Einojuhani Rautavaara (1992).

Vincent & Theo scr. Julian Mitchell exec. pr. c. 1999 BBC History Channel.

Biography: Vincent Van Gogh (TV) 'an eerie tale: a portrait of the artist from starry nights to self destruction' History Channel UK 11 Jan 2001.

Beyond the Canvas – Nevermore (Radio) by Nicholas McInerny w. Anton Lesser (Gauguin), Inika Leigh Wright (Pau'ura). Investigation by Prof. John House into the painting of that name, by Gauguin on Tahiti, Afternoon Play R4 24 May 2001.

Clone High [aka Clone High USA]. Ep 1: Escape to Beer Mountain: Rope of Sand (TV) created by Phil Lord, Christopher Miller, Bill Lawrence. Animated series about a high school populated by clones of famous historical characters. Quoting Vincent (voiced by Andy Dick) on Teen Crisis Hotline: 'Sometimes I just turn the lights off in my room and cry'. Can/US 2 Nov 2002.

An Academy (Video Game) Nintendo DS game in which art teacher 'Vince' is modelled on Vincent.

Rolf on Art: Vincent Van Gogh (TV) Rolf Harris on Vincent's style, including some immortal quotes. Ser. Pr. Tina Fletcher. BBC1 18 Nov 2001.

Vincent in Brixton (Play) by Nicholas Wright d. Richard Eyre w. Jochum ten Haaf (Vincent), Clare Higgins (Ursula Loyer), Emily Blunt (Eugenie Loyer). Cottesloe Theatre, London 1 May 2002; Playhouse, Wyndham's Theatre 5 Aug 2002, July 2003.

Three Great Artists: Van Gogh pres. Tim Marlowe C5 11.9.02.

Vincent in Brixton (TV) Transm. with stage cast BBC4 20.3.03.

A Stranger on Earth (Play) Alexander Barnett (New York) Vincent, dreaming, in torment over his failure, is confronted by the people he knows. Theo brings him news of his first good review & sale of a painting. But the family mocks his paucity of income: one quarter of a franc for every day he's worked as a painter! [Barnett also made a Video version.]

The Eyes of Van Gogh (Film) d. Alexander Barnett dealing with Vincent's 12 months at the asylum in Saint-Rémy.

Sunflowers (TV) Tim Marlow, on 150th anniversary of Vincent's birth, considers how the Sunflowers were painted & follows Vincent's footsteps. Radio 4 FM 29.03.03.

Dear Brother (Radio) d., scr. Penny Gold w. Robert Glenister (Vincent), Jonathan Firth (Theo), Kenneth Cranham (Gauguin). Letters and memoirs as basis of Vincent's relationship with Theo. Afternoon Play BBC R4 2 Apr 2003.

The Highest Bidder (TV) story of Portrait of Dr Gachet & Vincent's relationship with him, leading up to the $82.5m (£50m) sale of said picture to a Japanese businessman in May 1990. BBC2 24.7.03.

Gauguin: The Full Story (TV) d., pres. Waldemar Januszczak. Rich, compelling, absolutely essential among great Artist documentaries. BBC2 2 Aug 2003 [Rept'd BBC4 27 Sept 2010.]

Vincent: the Full Story (TV) d. Mark James, pres. Waldemar Januszczak 3-part unmissable in-depth portrait. 16.5.04 to 30.5.04. C4.

Gauguin's 'Paradise' (Stage) star & dir. Fred Curshack.

Still ongoing: one-man multi-media portrait of the artist, based on Gauguin's writings. University of Texas, 2004.

Misadventures in Paradise Philip L. Zweig 2-part series based on Gauguin & Robert Louis Stevenson (Thor Heyerdahl later joined them as a trilogy). It was derived from Zweig's 3-month voyage in the South Pacific in 1969, when he (partially) followed in the footsteps of such pivotal figures as these.

Hula Girls, Imagining Paradise (Audiovisual) d. Trevor Graham, pr. Andrew Ogilvie, scr. Michael Sturma: Gauguin's Paradise narr. Jenny Armstrong. 2nd in 3-part online series, in which Gauguin discovers how the Tahitian paradise of legend has almost completely disappeared. Electric Pictures/ SBS [Australia, 2005].

Inventing Van Gogh (Stage) by Steven Dietz. In which a modern painter, conjecturing the existence of Vincent's mythical 'last self-portrait', is visited by Vincent, Paul and other 19th Century artists in his studio. Various US stock company and touring productions since 2005.

The Eyes of Van Gogh (TV) scr., d. Alexander Barnett w. A Barnett (Van Gogh), Roy Thinnes (Dr Peyron), Gordon Joseph Weiss (Theo), Diane Agostini (Kee Vos), Lee Godart (Paul Gauguin). Van Gogh Prods US 24 April 2005. Intelligent, at times hallucinatory study of Vincent, coming closer than some other filmmakers to what happened during his stay at the asylum in Saint-Rémy.

Family Guy [Ep 402: Fast Times at Buddy Cianci Jr High] (TV) d. Pete Michels, Peter Shaw. Animated series segment in which lead characters reference the 'ear-cutting episode' from Vincent's time at Arles. US 8 May 2005.

Bonjour, M Gauguin (Opera) Chamber op. by Fabrizio Carlone d. Anna Cianca, cond. Sandro Gallo w. Philippe Georges (Gauguin), Maria Soulis (Teura/ Narrator). Innovative, highly visual entertainment based on texts from Gauguin & his contemporaries. Sung in French. World premiere Teatro Fondamenta Nuove di Venezia 2006.

Simon Schama's Power of Art: Van Gogh (TV) written & pres. Simon Schama w. Andy Serkis (Vincent) BBC/US TV doc 24.11.06.

The Yellow House (TV) pr., d. Chris Durlacher w. John Simm (Vincent) John Lynch (Gauguin) scr. Simon Bent from Martin Gayford's book on subject, C4 18 March 2007.

Paradise Found (TVM 2003) Kiefer Sutherland, in his own father's footsteps, brings us Paul Gauguin in a different manifestation.

Composer of the Week: Erik Satie [5 one-hour segments] pr. Stephen Rajan, pres. Donald McCleod, readings Richard Elvin. BBC Cardiff R3 5–9 June 2008, reptd 9–13 Nov 2009.

Bartok & Van Gogh: Partners in Art (TV) pres., cond. David Robertson at the Barbican Theatre, London. Two audio visual concerts linking a pair of Béla Bartók's concert pieces with images from the work of Van Gogh BBC4 22 & 27 Feb 2009.

Death of Long Pig (Play) by Nigel Planer w. Sean Murray (Gauguin/ Stevenson). Contrasting twilight days of R. L. Stevenson and Paul Gauguin, 'condemned to life' in the South Seas. Finborough, London 12.7.09.

The Real Van Gogh (Radio) discussion on Saturday Review of The Artist & His Letters exhibition at the Royal Academy. BBC Radio 4 23 Jan 2010.

Tim Marlow on the Real Van Gogh (TV) Sky Arts 1 (HD1) on 14 Feb 2010.

Vincent Van Gogh – Painted with Words (TV) pres. Alan Yentob, adapt. Andrew Hutton & Alan Yentob d. Andrew Hutton w. Benedict Cumberbatch (Vincent), Jamie Parker (Theo), Aidan McArdle (Gauguin). BBC Scotland BBC4 5 April 2010.

A Good Read in which Bob Mills chooses The Moon & Sixpence. Pres. by Sue MacGregor. First of a new BBC Radio 4 series 1/4 June 2010.

Doctor Who: Vincent and the Doctor (TV) d. Jonny Campbell, scr. Richard Curtis w. Matt Smith (the Doctor), Karen Gillan (Amy), Tony Curran (Vincent). Fun all the way, as the good Doctor & his girl assistant confront Vincent's monsters, outside & in. Transm. 45-min single segment 5 June 2010.

An Education: Vincent Van Gogh (Play) by Jean Kempf. In which Dr John Newman, a local actor & school teacher, enacted this one-act play as Theo Van Gogh, using slides and lecture-style presentation. Utah. 24 June 2010.

Gauguin: the Right to Dare (Radio) pres. Louisa Buck, pr. Kate Bland R4 doc 28 Sept 2010.

Tim Marlow on ... Gauguin (TV) Sky Arts 2 (HD2) 16 Oct 2010.

Ego: The Strange & Wonderful World of Self-Portraits (TV) art critic Laura Cumming travels through more than five centuries of Western Art, to see how great artists, including Vincent, 'have transformed themselves into their own masterpieces.' BBC4 4 Nov 2010.

Vincent (Opera) 2-act opera, music Bernard Rands, libretto JD McClatchy. Christopher Burchett/David Adam (Van Gogh). World premiere University Open Theater Season, Musical Arts Center, Bloomington, Indiana, 8–9 April 2011. Using multi-scene narrative & electronic images of Vincent's art to offer 'a shifting panorama of his imagination & creativity.' [Some of the music was drawn from Rand's Tambourin suite, first performed in 1989 by Pierre Boulez and the Chicago Symphony Orchestra.]

The World's Most Expensive Paintings BBC2 Close examination of the ten top biggest sellers, including Portrait of Dr Gachet, their history & sales record.

The Impressionists (TV) 4-part series scr., d. Walerian Januszack, pr. Susan Doyden. Illuminating, in-depth history & critique of the well-known & lesser-known exemplars of what Januszack called 'The most exciting mutiiny in Art: the day everything changed.' BBC2 16 July 2011.

Loving Vincent (2017) UK/US/Poland Breakthru Prods-Trademark Films-Altitude Film; dirs Dorota Kaobala, Hugh Welchman w. voices of Robert Gulasczyc (Vincent), Jeremy Flynn (Dr Gachet), Saorise Ronan (Marguerite), Piotr Pamula (Paul Gauguin), Douglas Booth (Armand Roulin), John Sessions (Père Tanguy). Praised animated feature which conjured both the look and spirit of Vincent's work and last days. Produced at Three Mills Studio, London.

The Mystery of of the Missing Van Gogh: Six Sunflowers (2018), Dir. Giovanni Troilo. Sky Arts/

Ballandi Arts Co-Prod (Italy) 2018. Fascinating attempt at a digitally controlled reconstruction of Vincent's long since destroyed masterpiece. The orignal, bought for a Japanese museum, had been one of the seven 'Sunflower' paintings undertaken by Vincent during his time at Arles. It was burnt to ashes in a US firebomb attack on the Ashiya suburb during the same week as Hiroshima. Narr. James Cosmo.

At Eternity's Gate [aka Van Gogh – At Eternity's Gate] (2018) CBS Films/Riverstone Pictures/SPK Pictures. French-Swiss-Irish-US. Dir. Julian Schnabel, scr. Jean-Claude Carrière, Julian Schnabel, Louise Kugelberg w. Willem Dafoe (Vincent), Rupert Friend (Theo), Oscar Isaac (Gauguin), Mads Mikkelson (Priest), Mathieu Amalric (Dr Paul Gachet), Emmanuelle Seigner (Mdme Ginoux), Niels Arelstrup (Madman), Anne Consigny (Teacher), Amira Casar (Johanna Van Gogh). French & Engish language feature dealing with Vincent's last days at Arles and Auvers. With Oscar-nominated turn from Dafoe as Vincent – 'the tortured genius'. Includes the severed ear interlude (described rather than shown!) plus more psychological insight than most.

Van Gogh: An Exclusive View (2019) Sky UK Ltd pr. John Mullen, dir. Alison Grist. In advance of the Tate Britain's prestigious Vincent in Britain exhibition, Kate Bryan ably takes us through a young Van Gogh's three years in London and Ramsgate, while discussing his influences (John Constable, John Millais, Gustav Doré) and those notable British artists whom he, in turn, influenced (William

Nicholson, Francis Bacon etc). Some of their successors she here interviews.

The BBC Archive lists at least eighteen Vincent Van Gogh programmes transmitted between 1962–2009, like BBC History's David Piper visiting the Louvre to discuss Vincent's self-portraits in the context of his other works. And there have been others since.

Vincent has also been referenced and/or portrayed, albeit briefly, in numerous films and programmes which had no main connection with him, including *What's New, Pussycat* (1967) etc. To list them all is worth a book in itself. The Internet also cites at least ten Sherlock Holmes titles by authors other than Conan Doyle, which include Vincent as a character. And that's not to mention a dozen or so songs (apart from Don Maclean's) which plug or pay homage to Vincent. Indeed, at this time of writing, I note that some guy out there is already offering auditions to actors and singers for *Vincent Van Gogh: The Musical*…

One should also mention a number of unrealised film projects, including a 1936 Van Gogh biopic to star (a wildly miscast?) Charles Laughton. This was intended by Alexander Korda to follow the duo's *success d'estime* with *Rembrandt* (1936). Even more intriguing was *Noa Noa*, a Paul Gauguin film, to be based on the final screenplay of critic James Agee. It was planned by director David Bradley (1953), then Lionel Rogosin (1974). 'There's an intriguing parallel between Gauguin's life and my own,' Rogosin admitted, 'when we were both in our early thirties, we left our comfortable business careers to take up Art with a capital "A".'

Alas, this plan, too, failed to make it, as also the aforementioned documentary by the late right-wing journalist/

filmmaker Theo Van Gogh. This was *The Golden Brush*, based on Vincent, which vanished as a project with the director's tragic death on an Amsterdam street. This Theo Van Gogh, though, has proved hugely fascinating to US filmmakers, with at least three features so far released: *Interview* (d. Steve Buscemi), *Blind Date* (d. Stanley Tucci) & *Somewhere Tonight* (d. Michael Jiacomo 2011). [See *Variety* 18–24 July 2011 p. 19.]

On a more personal level, I would like to thank my friends and family, notably my sister and brother-in-law, Madeleine and Tony Clifford-Winters, for providing me with a number of examples of Gallic flavour at their fabulous pad in Southern France. Ditto my friends Judy Dalton and Neil Conway, ever hospitable in their holiday home on French soil. Also, my sister Elizabeth Campbell and husband Don, both pyschoanalysts, whose constant interest in the book's progress and their useful member-ship of The Royal Academy of Arts helped pave the way for a more thorough examination of Vincent's paintings and letters than normal time limits might allow.

I should also like to thank the Academy, itself, and the staff of its friendly Library and reading rooms, and the truly magnificent efforts in mounting that well-nigh overwhelming exhibition *of The Real Van Gogh: The Artist & His Letters*, in Jan–April 2010. Earlier Academy exhibitions – *Ingres to Matisse: Masterpieces of French Painting* (2001) and *From Russia: French & Russian Master Paintings 1870–1925* (2008) – also included several long-unseen Van Goghs. The same goes for the Tate Modern, where *Gauguin: Maker of Myth* (Sept 2010–Jan 2011) proved to be a visual and organisational triumph: a record-breaker before it even opened. Far from leaving them out, the permanent exhibitions in The Van Gogh

Museum in Amsterdam and the Orsay Museum in Paris, The National Gallery – plus *Manet to Picasso* (2006–7), *Cézanne in Britain* (2006–7), Impressionists in London & Inventing Impressionism (2015) – The Victoria & Albert, Wallace Collection, Hayward Gallery and The Courtauld Institute in London have meant for me many hours of happy visiting, from long before I even thought of writing this book.

That applies, too, to the extensive art book collections at Richmond Reference Library and the Central Reference Library, Leicester Square, to whose staffs, as also Dave and his helpful literary gang at my local Kew Library, I could never stop saying how grateful I am. Thanks, too, to Dr Alexandra Strachan, my friend and local GP, who helped correct some of the more outlandish medical conclusions I offered in earlier drafts of the story!

Enormous thanks to the judges of the Yeovil (Literary) Prize, 2008, whose strong Commendation of the early chapters of my book, when it was still a work in progress, gave me a measure of encouragement to continue to the end. As also Tanja Howarth (literary agent and loyal guardian of the Patricia Highsmith estate), whose comments on my original draft were invaluable.

Above all, I'd like to thank my wife Jane and daughter Annabel who have treated my long-time obsession with Vincent and his circle with a good humour and forbearance which I, perhaps, do not deserve, though the great Vincent and his fellow artists undeniably do.

Julian Fox – Kew, Surrey, June 2019